Praise for *Gratitude*

"*Gratitude* grabbed me and wouldn't let go; it is a huge, sprawling novel, yet beautifully precise. *Gratitude* brings new life to well-known history, but the lasting strength of this wonderful book is its people, in all their flaws and glories. It is a massive achievement."

—Roddy Doyle, Booker Prize–winning author of *Paddy Clark Ha Ha Ha*

"Harrowing and extraordinarily moving ... The characters are wonderfully vibrant."

—*National Post*

"*Gratitude* moved me as very, very few books do. And, as with any work of art, it taught me about the world in new and profound ways. Profound, in fact, is the operative adjective. Technically, of course, the book is beautifully made and beautifully written, yet craftsmanship only goes so far: a book must reach into my heart and head if it is to dazzle me. *Gratitude* deserves literary hoorays from all quarters."

—Tim O'Brien, National Book Award winner

"A major novel that spills over with humanity—by a master story-teller."

—Bruce Jay Friedman

"[A] splendid, page-turning novel ... Gratitude is as rich in its picturesque detail as it is in its spellbinding faith [in] man's ultimate humanity."

—*The Globe and Mail*

GRATITUDE

JOSEPH KERTES

PENGUIN
CANADA

PENGUIN CANADA

Published by the Penguin Group

Penguin Group (Canada), 90 Eglinton Avenue East, Suite 700, Toronto, Ontario, Canada M4P 2Y3
(a division of Pearson Canada Inc.)

Penguin Group (USA) Inc., 375 Hudson Street, New York, New York 10014, U.S.A.
Penguin Books Ltd, 80 Strand, London WC2R 0RL, England
Penguin Ireland, 25 St Stephen's Green, Dublin 2, Ireland (a division of Penguin Books Ltd)
Penguin Group (Australia), 250 Camberwell Road, Camberwell, Victoria 3124, Australia
(a division of Pearson Australia Group Pty Ltd)
Penguin Books India Pvt Ltd, 11 Community Centre, Panchsheel Park, New Delhi – 110 017, India
Penguin Group (NZ), 67 Apollo Drive, Rosedale, North Shore 0745, Auckland, New Zealand
(a division of Pearson New Zealand Ltd)
Penguin Books (South Africa) (Pty) Ltd, 24 Sturdee Avenue, Rosebank,
Johannesburg 2196, South Africa

Penguin Books Ltd, Registered Offices: 80 Strand, London WC2R 0RL, England

First published in a Viking Canada hardcover by Penguin Group (Canada),
a division of Pearson Canada Inc., 2008
Published in this edition, 2009

1 2 3 4 5 6 7 8 9 10 (WEB)

Copyright © Joseph Kertes, 2008

*Publisher's note: This book is a work of fiction. Names, characters, places and incidents either are the
product of the author's imagination or are used fictitiously, and any resemblance to actual persons
living or dead, events, or locales is entirely coincidental.*

Manufactured in Canada

Library and Archives Canada Cataloguing in Publication data
available upon request to the publisher.

ISBN: 978-0-14-305359-0

Visit the Penguin Group (Canada) website at **www.penguin.ca**

Special and corporate bulk purchase rates available; please see
www.penguin.ca/corporatesales or call 1-800-810-3104, ext. 477 or 474

*This book is dedicated
to the memory of
Raoul Wallenberg
and
Pal Hegedus,
to the memory of my parents, Hilda and Paul,
to my brothers, Bill and Peter,
and to my wife and daughters, Helen, Angela and Natalie,
with love.*

Above me, rushing time is rummaging through my poems
As I sink ever deeper into the ground.
All this I know,
But tell me:
Did my work survive?

—Miklos Radnoti (1909–1944)

GRATITUDE

One

LILI CROUCHED behind a wardrobe, dressed in a wedding gown. She was in her parents' bedroom and, despite her position, could still clearly see the dove-blue sky out of the window. It was the custom of her village that, when a girl turned sixteen, her mother would present her with a bridal dress she had made or worn herself. Helen had sewn this white dress out of a bolt of Egyptian cotton, adding some French lace her husband, David, had brought from Budapest.

A birthday cake was baking in the stone oven downstairs. Whipped vanilla cream sat heaped in a bowl by the window. It was to be folded over the warm yellow cake once it cooled a little.

The cake was just about done, but Lili couldn't leave her hiding place to check on it, because her mother had told her to stay put. And no one else was home. Helen, Lili's mother, had taken the four youngest kids out back beyond the town. David, her father, had left with her eldest brother, Ferenc, to show the new authorities the family's papers.

So Lili would wait behind the wardrobe—she couldn't say for how long. The big wardrobe had been made for Helen and David by Ervin Gottlieb, the town's ancient but skilled carpenter. It had been painted white to commemorate their wedding day, the same cream white as Lili's dress.

And now Lili felt a chill in the warm house. She did not know what her mother had been thinking. Wouldn't it have made more sense for her to go off with Tildy and Benjamin to the pond, where Helen had sent them, or with Helen and Mendi and Hanna to the woods? She could have helped them. What good was she in the house, squatting behind a wardrobe? Lili heard shuffling just outside the house, now, and thought it might be her father or her mother. Maybe someone had forgotten something. She considered stepping out, but decided not to until she heard a familiar voice. Instead, outside the window, what she heard was machine-gun fire, a scream—a woman's scream—then a German voice over a megaphone. She knew exactly what they were saying. She knew from her Yiddish. They were asking people to meet in the square in front of the synagogue. A Hungarian voice repeated the command.

"Everyone bring a small parcel of belongings," the German said, "and meet at the temple within thirty minutes of this order."

The Hungarian said, "Everyone out now. Now." People understood his Hungarian as well as their own Yiddish. Tolgy was a border town in the southeast, where people spoke Yiddish first, Hungarian second. It was a town of a thousand Jews, an enclave. Hungarian was the language of school.

Had the Hungarians joined ranks with the invading Germans? Lili's father had fought for the Hungarians in the Great War, had worn the uniform with pride.

Lili felt a spring in her legs, set to catapult her out of her hiding place, but she held her post. She smelled the cake in the oven. Certainly by now it was done. Warm and ready. She ran her hands over the soft lap of her dress, steadying herself.

And then someone slammed into the house, several men, as many as four, Lili thought, or even five. Lili heard a German voice, then the shout of a Hungarian. The soldiers stomped through the house, pulling at things, turning over chairs. They stormed upstairs. She held her breath as they worked their way through the children's bedrooms, pulling drawers to the floor.

Just as they banged out into the corridor, just as Lili expected them to rush into the room in which she crouched, breathless, they flew down the stairs instead. All but one. One stepped in. Lili could feel the net of his eyes falling over the room. The photographs of her grandparents, all four of them, above the bed. The dresser with the silver hairbrush and comb David had brought from Prague. The cedar blanket box. And then he ran after his comrades. Just like that. A moment later, they rushed out of the house.

Lili heard them bursting into Tzipi's place next door. She could hear the same crashes and slams. Far away, the popping of gunfire, muffled, like caps.

She could smell smoke, burning. Could it be? Could it? She would roast. She would stay behind her wardrobe and burn. She could smell it now, but there was sweetness at the edge of the smell. She would burn sweetly as cake. It was the cake.

Lili waited patiently for another half-hour, her ears open like cockleshells, waiting to hear the troops, the megaphones. She thought she heard the crack of distant gunfire again—machine-gun fire—and then a burning silence. Lili's heart beat against the prison of her ribs.

And then the telephone rang downstairs. Who could it possibly be? Was it her father? Was it Ferenc? Someone needing medical help? Someone hurting, wanting Lili's father to attend to them? The phone continued to ring for what seemed like several minutes, but Lili didn't answer, and then it stopped.

The cake burned gloriously now, its sunny sweetness melting into a lava flow in the thick chamber of the oven. None of these alarms could lure Lili out of her hiding place. Not the telephone, not the burning cake, not the soldiers who'd come and gone, who'd checked the Bandel house, then checked it off their list.

And not Dobo. Lili heard his voice, now. Dobo—his name was Artur Dobo, but everyone called him by his surname only, or sometimes even Captain Dobo. He was the town's crazy beggar, who got his meals at a different house each night, many nights at the

Bandels' house, where not only did Helen feed him, but David calmed him down with a sip of brandy and gave him a cot to settle down on. They would even have the Captain for the Sabbath, and he prayed with them. Each child who was able had to recite a passage by heart from the Torah, the older ones longer passages, and after that the Bandels prayed. Her father and brother also prayed each morning with their tefillin. Lili would sometimes watch the ritual, as each placed a small box containing a hand-written biblical passage on his arm, wound a leather strap around the arm and also around the head, where another small square box containing another biblical passage was placed against the forehead.

Lili had forgotten altogether about Captain Dobo until she heard his mad voice, suddenly, next door. Where had he been all this time? What hole had he crawled out of? He must have been standing now under the crabapple tree, which had bloomed then withered inexplicably very early that spring. Where Dobo had come from, and how he'd escaped the notice of the invaders, she couldn't even guess.

Dobo was determined to attract notice. "Hey!" he was yelling. "Hey! Hey! Hey!" Lili did not dare move at first. "Get back up there!" Dobo shouted. "What are you doing?"

It sounded for a moment as though Dobo were addressing Lili, standing below her window and calling out to her. She had to look— she had to peek at least. "What's going on!" he bellowed. "Get back up there!"

From where she crouched, Lili looked out of the corner of her window at the sky's blue insistence. She crept out far enough to peer into Tzipi's yard, where Dobo stood, hurling dry leaves up at the branches which had released them. "Hey! What are you doing!" he said. He threw armfuls of leaves up and then stood tall, his arms open to the heavens, pleading with the crabapple tree to hang on. "Hey!" His voice was dying down. "Hey." The call was melodic almost, like the song of an oversized bird. "What?" he asked the tree. He held out his arms. The geese in the pen behind him honked. A single dog barked from down the street.

Then shots rang out. Lili hadn't seen anyone approach. She darted back behind the wardrobe and covered her ears. But the shots sounded again. And then Lili heard men's laughter, the language that travels. Then still more laughter, right below her window. Minutes later, departing footsteps.

Lili spent the night behind the wardrobe. She heard German voices outside in the dark, then drunk Hungarian ones. But not a single Yiddish voice. For long hours, she feared someone would come tripping into her house again, help himself to some food, tumble on a bed. But night passed quietly into morning. Lili did not sleep. She waited dutifully for someone to come get her, tell her it was all right to come out, come and eat, rest. Where had everyone got to? Surely, the soldiers had not scoured the fields and woods far from the village. Surely, her brothers and sisters were staying put, waiting, like Lili, for the alien noises to be carried off over the Carpathian Mountains with the moon.

The images of the previous morning wheeled through her head. Her sister Tildy had wanted to try on the white dress in the worst way. Lili was the second oldest after Ferenc, who was seventeen, and then came the four younger ones, ranging in age from fourteen years to eight months.

The dress came wrapped in exotic frosted tissue paper, which itself felt as rich as cloth. Tucked inside the dress was a blue silk shawl to bring out Lili's eyes and complement her buttery hair. When Lili opened the precious package, her father had already been called away by the regional authorities under the new provisional government and asked to present papers verifying his Hungarian nationality and that of his family. Hungary was allied with Germany.

"It's a formality, for sure," David had said as he put on his shoes that morning. "How can it be anything more? I was an officer in the Hungarian army. The Germans will see the papers, and they'll send us on our way. The Germans live by papers and documents."

"And what about the Hungarians?" Helen asked. "If it's a formality, I can't understand why they would summon you."

"Because they want us to know who's in charge." David held up the papers. "We're Hungarian. That's all they're asking us to prove. They're asking everybody, I'm sure. They *have* to. It's probably in their rule book." He was grinning now as he spoke.

Ferenc insisted on going along. But the other children stayed home with their mother and cackled as Lili sashayed around the kitchen, wearing the shawl over her shoulders and holding the beautiful dress up over her faded beige one.

Lili's fourteen-year-old sister, Tildy, took a spin with the dress pinned to her front, the blue shawl gracing her head. She was batting her eyes like a temptress, letting the dress sail, then flow, over her younger brother Mendi's head.

The telephone rang. Its shrill novelty stopped everyone. The baby was the least startled. Of course, to her, everything was novel. Sometimes the Bandels stared at the telephone the way people looked at a radio, waiting for it to say something. The Bandels were one of only seven Tolgy households to own a telephone. Their phone number was 4. The one whose number was 1, of course, was the mayor. Number 2 was Rabbi Lichtman. Number 3 belonged to the Appels, Tolgy's most upstanding family, owners of the mill, the butcher shop and the small distillery just outside of town. The final three belonged to Colonel Sam Bilko, one-time officer in the Great War, now the town's police officer; the veterinarian, Samuel Katz; and the last one went to the temple itself, where people could stop (except on Sabbath) to call the other six numbers if they urgently needed to.

The call this morning came from this last phone. It was Frieda Weisz. Lili noticed the strained smile on her mother's face. Tildy stopped dancing with the dress. To amuse the children, Lili retrieved the dress and shawl, ran up to the girls' bedroom, pulled on the dress in a flash and returned to dance in the kitchen.

It was eerily quiet. Even the geese were still, as was Tzipi's mule next door. Helen listened with one ear to the phone, the other to the door, the window, the street. Several shots rang out, popping.

It sounded like the beginnings of a hailstorm. Lili turned toward the door, too.

"What's going on?" Helen asked into the phone. "Frieda, what's going on? Are you there?" Her mouth hung open as she waited, looked at the receiver. A flurry of voices outside excited the animals. She hung up. Lili embraced her mother, but her mother's body was stiff and unyielding. She was holding back panic.

"Mendi," Helen said calmly, "you head out to the almond trees and see how they're doing. Take a rest there. Tend to the trees. Don't come back until nightfall, even if you have to duck into the woods. I'll come after you with Hanna, but stay put, no matter what. Do you understand?" He nodded. His eyes were blue like his mother's, but his blond curls had already begun to darken.

"Tildy," Helen said. She spoke without hesitation. "Take your brother Benjamin out toward the pond and spend the day there."

"May we swim?" Benjamin asked.

"No, the water's too cold. But if you can gather berries, I'll bake a cake."

"They're not out yet," Tildy said. She pulled the rays of her hair back so that she could bind them behind. Her eyes were even lighter than Mendi's. She was a perfect child of the Carpathian sun and sky. Helen was relieved to note that she was also wearing green, like the pastures around the pond.

"So I'll take the baby with me, naturally," Helen said calmly, "and you stay, Lili."

"What?"

"Stay in the house and wait for your father and brother to get back. Everything will be fine. Go upstairs to our bedroom and wait behind the wardrobe, and don't come out until it's safe." Lili's mother picked up the baby and leaned closer to her eldest daughter as the others rushed about. They could hear people running outside, but oddly only the voices of children. "You wear that dress in the best of health," Helen said. "We'll be fine, don't worry." She looked her daughter directly in the eyes. "And you'll be fine. Don't be afraid." Helen caressed Lili's cheek. Then she followed the children out.

Lili waited through the day and another night behind the white wardrobe, waited for the muffled sound of gunfire in the distance to pass, for the bark of Hungarian and German soldiers to cease, the running feet to recede. Only once did Lili dart out to take a dress of her mother's from the wardrobe, then rush back to relieve herself in the soft and generous cotton folds. She even imagined the trouble she'd be in when her mother returned, but would have given anything now for the trouble. The telephone didn't ring again. The oven had consumed her cake and cooled. Her stomach gurgled and churned, but it, too, rested now.

Lili thought of Mrs. Wasserstein, her teacher for the past three years. She wondered whether Mrs. Wasserstein, with all her knowledge of battles and strategies and the outcomes of war, had managed to elude these latest invaders.

Lili recalled especially the discussion in school in the winter just past, about Pompeii, how captivated she'd become by it, how carried away by the photographs in a book that Mrs. Wasserstein had passed around the room. One was of a pregnant woman lying on her back, her knees up high against her chest as if she were about to give birth—the whole of her grey shape arrested, preserved in lava.

Another was that of Venus in marble, bending over to tie her sandal. Lili finally drifted off to sleep behind the wardrobe with the images in front of her, the warm rock flowing over her.

She awoke to the blue scent of stars, oblivious and comforted, unaware of where she was. It was not yet light, though she sensed the light was near, and to confirm the fact, their rooster, Erik, crowed on the white gatepost. Where had Erik been yesterday? Lost, too, no doubt. And who was there to wake up, now—his own brood, probably, sounding the alarm for his own kind, or were the chickens taken, too, for someone's pot along the way?

After two days, the only other sounds Lili could hear besides the crowing were the honking and gobbling of geese and the occasional bark of a dog in the distance. Hungry, no doubt. No one to feed them.

It was strange that no one had come back in two days, no one in her family, no one she could hear in the town. She could have imagined the worst, just from what she had learned in school. Invading armies sometimes levelled everything in their path, anything breathing. But she had never heard of everyone disappearing. Could this have been a new miracle of God, a miracle of cleansing, an act of retribution, like the Flood? Had any of them made it to the ark?

Lili thought of Ibi twenty doors down, the widow who had taken in Captain Dobo one evening for Sabbath dinner but threw him out in the rain when she discovered he had soiled her cot. She told him never to come back. Lili thought of Lajos Pentek, who cheated on his wife with Evi, the nymphomaniac, and, when he was found out, told everyone in a fit of rage at the temple after services that he wasn't the first to cheat and began to rhyme off names, even the names of innocent men. Lili remembered Evi's bottle-green eyeshadow—all the girls wanted to try some—but on this day, Evi cried black tears and left the town for good.

Was this why the Lord had turned "brimstone and fire" on her town, the way He had with Sodom and Gomorrah? There were certainly other examples of wickedness and depravity for God to choose from, even Lili's. When Helen's brooch went missing, the beautiful jewel made of turquoise, coral and white gold, which Helen had inherited from her own great grandmother, Lili said it was Tildy who'd misplaced it, although all of the older children had been playing with it, even Ferenc, who'd held it high in the sky and said he'd bury it in the field unless someone cleaned up his side of the room for him. But then it went missing. Helen had scolded Tildy when Lili told her and said she'd have to stay in her room for two days until it was found. It was only then that Lili went on a hunt for the jewel and discovered it under the white wardrobe she now hid behind.

Was this really Sodom and Gomorrah? There was much wickedness, now that Lili thought of it; the examples abounded. When Abraham pleaded with God to spare Sodom, God said He would do so if fifty righteous people could be found in the city. When fifty could not be named, He reduced the number to thirty, then twenty, then ten. The Lord's angels found only one, Lot, Abraham's own nephew, and his family. His daughter had been good, too. She gave bread to a beggar, and when the townspeople found out, they smeared her with honey and hanged her from the city wall until she was stung to death by bees. It was her screams that sounded the alarm for God to level the city.

Could it be that Tolgy was this bad? Could it be that it was worse even than other places? Could this be as big as that? Were they entering a new day of miracles? What was God thinking now? Whose screams reached his heavenly ears?

Lili remembered a passage she'd recited from Genesis. When people were united and spoke one language and began a tower in Babel to reach the Creator, why did He "confound the language of all the earth" and scatter his worshippers? Were we getting too close, Lili wondered, too perfect? And had this been part of the omniscient's design, to show us how imperfect we really could be?

Lili suddenly felt older, past needing a wedding dress, scared and excited, significant somehow, standing in the way of something, a force in history that had not yet swept her up. She felt for a giddy moment that she could face the Lord or the monsters of darkness, but she was afraid of the men who'd turned into monsters, because God was always great and the monsters always monsters, but these were men who had gone mad.

Lili's spirits crashed. She'd been the lark ascending and now she plummeted without a song. Could she be the last person standing in the gale of the oppressors? She could not resist the winds, she was sure. She could not stand up to history. She did not want her name recorded there, her form a curiosity to future students of volcanic eruptions.

Or was Lili's family all waiting for her? Was *she* the one whose fate *they* were talking about? *Did Lili stay behind the wardrobe? Did she make it? Was she captured and taken, while we are hidden and safe?* Were they all hidden? Gunfire would surely keep anyone at bay for an extra day or two. It had kept Lili at bay.

Lili stepped out from her hiding place into the bright morning room, stood at the foot of the warm bed, longed to sit for a moment on the blanket box to see the room from another vantage point, but she changed her mind. She crept toward the window and peered out of the lower corner as she had at Dobo. There was no one in the street, no one in the windows of the neighbouring houses. The geese honked some more. Lili crept out of the room, stepping over clothing strewn down the stairs, checking the bowl of cream in the kitchen, peeking into the cold oven, avoiding the scattered silverware and broken dishes.

She spied the outside world through the kitchen window, moved to the front door, then gently pulled open the door. She looked all around her as she stepped out, afraid of what she might see. She crept toward Tzipi's house, looked in the window and saw no one. There was an empty carpetbag on the table and a pair of rolled-up socks beside it. A lamp lay shattered on the floor and a single chair upended, but no other evidence of violence or life.

Out back, Lili saw dried blood spattered over the white fence. She gasped as she made out the huddled form of Captain Dobo, his body clumped at the foot of his tree like fallen fruit.

She could not bear to look too closely, so she dashed past Dobo toward the fields behind the town. Whatever hope she had left carried her toward the almond trees. When she got there, a cool breeze sailed through the grasses and stirred the canopy of leaves.

"Mendi?" Lili said weakly. "Hanna?" Her eyes darted after every sound coming from the grasses. Then she called out their names boldly.

She continued farther toward the pond and found herself shouting even before she got there. "Tildy! Benjamin! Tildy! Ma!" A squirrel skittered by and startled her.

There was no sign of human life anywhere—no sign that anyone had passed through here at all. At the edge of the pond, Lili gazed into the water, but she knew Tildy would never have allowed Benjamin in the water. Of all her brothers and sisters, Tildy was most like Lili. Tildy followed her everywhere, wanted to walk with her to school, share her friends, lie awake at night together talking about boys. Most importantly, as Lili had done, Tildy would have obeyed her mother to the letter by staying away from the cold water. Lili walked around the edge of the pond, examining the mud for footprints. She found none. She circled the whole pond, looking in every direction, reacting to every twig snapping in the bushes, every bird taking flight. The place seemed cheerful. "Tildy!" she called out. "Benjamin! Mendi! Ma! Hanna!"

She ran all the way from the pond to the Kleins' house at the edge of town. She slowed to a walk as she headed down the town's main street. Inside the Kleins' house, a lamp still burned in the daylight, but the place was empty. Lili checked in the door of the Mandels' poultry and egg store and found no one tending to the merchandise. Even Eva, who was *always* there with her hawk eyes when the doors were open, was missing. At the haberdashery, a hat still sat on the counter, its feathers combed back by the mountain breeze streaming in through the open window.

Lili wanted to say something, call out, but now she couldn't find her voice. She ran around the familiar houses. She could not find her cousin Eszty, or Jancsi, the neighbourhood bully. He had knocked over Ferenc once and even punched Lili when she tried to intervene. An iron sat poised in the front room of the Weisels' house, the freshly laundered white clothes piled beside it. In the Timors' place, she saw a newspaper open on the kitchen table, reading glasses anchoring it; a boiled egg sat perched in its cup, the spoon beside it on the wooden counter. She ran several blocks to the temple, and from a couple of blocks away she could smell the smoke. The temple had been half-consumed by flame and was still smouldering. Splashes of blood marked the square out front and even the trunk of the elm at the far side. Lili held her hands up over her face but peeked through the cage of her fingers. She stepped inside the synagogue, over embers. The walls, which her mother had helped paint with blue arabesques, were scorched black halfway up to the arched ceiling. The Torah had been pulled from its housing in the tabernacle, its blue velvet dressing cast to one side and burned, the Torah itself unfurled across the dais. Lili crouched down, careful not to soil her white dress, rolled the scrolls together again like a precious rug, but then left the Torah where it lay.

She walked around back to the graveyard, knowing she couldn't go in. The Bandels were from the tribe of the Cohens, descendants of Aaron, descendants of David, like the coming Messiah, like Jesus, and were therefore never allowed to enter the graveyard, even when a member of the family was being buried there. So Lili could not enter. She stood on tiptoe to see the stones of her grandmothers. Her grandfathers lay elsewhere. Helen's father went missing in action in the Great War, and David's father fell off a cliff as a young man when he lost his footing on a mountain path. David, the eldest of four, was only seven at the time. His father was never found.

Lili didn't know what message to send to her grandmothers. She felt puny and defenceless. She would have given anything to find someone to comfort her—Uncle Mark, her mother's brother; Mrs. Wasserstein, her teacher; her friends Hilda or Aurel; or even someone younger, someone whose hand she could hold. What was she to do now? She wanted her grandmothers to tell her. What could she possibly do? What would they tell her? Eat lunch? Go back to school?

Wash some linens? Play a record? Observe the Sabbath? Light candles? Pray? Who else was there to speak to here but God? Or had God, too, forgotten Lili in Tolgy? Was she speaking now to *no one*?

She turned away from the stones, looked around one last time and walked back to her house, hardly glancing at each door she passed. The buildings had turned cold for her and even frightening. She knew that they were empty or, worse, contained dead people—resisters—or dead soldiers.

Lili paused only for a cat who called out to her from behind a door. She released the animal into the daylight. The cat followed for an instant, but thought better of it and watched as Lili continued toward home.

When she arrived, Lili packed a satchel, took some of the money she found in her father's desk drawer, leaving the rest for her family should they return. Beside the bowl of vanilla cream on the window sill, Lili found her mother's wedding ring, which Helen had removed while she worked in the kitchen. She saw her father's name inscribed on the ring's inner surface. Lili fitted the ring on her index finger. She paused at the foot of the stairs, looked down at her simple, pretty white dress and wondered what she should change into—her green dress? The blue one, which brought out her eyes? She could leave her white dress for Tildy with a note. She took out paper and a pencil and wrote, "*Tildy, if you get back before I do, you can try on the dress*—" But Lili stopped herself. What if someone else got here before her family? Squatters. No, she would keep her white dress on. Her mother had made it.

She took some cheese, placed it in the satchel, then walked to the bakery, just a couple of doors down from the haberdashery.

One of the people Lili hoped might have escaped notice was Aurel Deutsch. When Lili was fourteen and Aurel twelve, Aurel had seemed to develop a crush on her. He was tall and strong for a young boy, likely from working in his parents' bakery and from sampling its wares, but Aurel puffed himself up even more when he saw Lili come in. He would have a small square of her favourite pastry, *flodni*, wrapped and waiting for her, compliments of the proprietor. *Flodni* was a three-storey pastry, with a layer of grated apple on top, poppyseed in the middle and sweet ground walnuts on the bottom. She never once had to pay for this delicious morsel and always ate it before she got home so she wouldn't have to explain or share. Even if she'd wanted to, how could Lili have hoped to share the little delicacy among eight Bandels?

Besides, Aurel wanted to see her eat it and would follow her out to the stoop, holding the bread she'd come for in the first place so that he could watch her enjoy the sweet. Lili felt his eyes on her, worried he'd get carried away. He watched her as though she were the sweet and he the taster. She found herself sometimes having to gobble her *flodni*, saying, "Please don't feel you have to do this for me. Please, it would be better if you didn't."

His answer was: "We should move to Budapest or Paris, you and I, and open a bakery, or a beautiful patisserie, and we could have you out front to draw in the patrons and me in the back up to my elbows in flour." He was covered in flour now as he spoke to her, a boy of twelve, rushing ahead of his age.

Lili sent Tildy in after that, but Tildy reported that Aurel didn't care for her. "He hardly notices me," Tildy said.

"Does he give you anything?" Lili asked.

"Like what?"

"Nothing, never mind."

And now at thirteen, Aurel was a giant beside his parents, powerful and grown up, his bar mitzvah under his belt.

But he was nowhere to be found at the bakery. Lili couldn't help herself. She glanced at the cake display in search of *flodni*, but found none. She selected a few buns, ate one hurriedly, placed a coin on the counter and ran out.

And where was her friend Hilda? Lili couldn't even fathom it, how anyone would have—*could* have—made off with her dearest friend.

Lili's father delivered Hilda as Lili, a one-month-old, cried in an adjoining bed. There had been no other way. Mrs. Blauman had showed up at the Bandels' door already "flooding the stoop," as David told it. Those waters were the elixir of life, he often said, where twenty digits sprouted out of hands and feet and where a warm and serene world made everything possible.

At school, Hilda often spoke to Lili about leaving Tolgy for the city and insisted Lili had to go with her. Even if Lili married and went away, Hilda would come with her and find someone to marry, too.

Lili approached Hilda's house with the greatest of dread. She didn't want to look in. She wanted to take away the faint hope that it was not empty. But she did. She walked in, called out Hilda's name, saw an envelope and glasses on the table as well as a blue hair ribbon, but then left.

Lili wanted to search one final place. When she was younger, ten at most, her mother used to take her to a field cut sharply by a precipice in the foothills of the Carpathian Mountains. It was a cool and even frightening place but the most beautiful Lili had ever seen. And it was the last place her mother might have tried to hide. In fact, in the two hours it took her to get there, the idea grew in Lili's mind that it was precisely where they'd gone, so she walked quickly and eagerly. She felt foolish in her wedding gown, but who was there to see her? Tildy had wanted desperately to try on the gown that morning, so now she could. Lili would meet her in the field with their mother, and Lili could swap clothes with her sister for the walk home.

Lili raced the last couple of hundred steps. She was warm in her white dress and could hardly wait to trade with her sister. But Tildy was not in the field. No one was. Lili headed toward the solitary tree, a big oak, standing in the middle of the open expanse. She and her family had enjoyed more than one picnic in the shade of this tree, and the whole of Tolgy once held its Purim celebration in this field.

She arrived at the oak and sat in its cool shade, careful not to soil her dress. She opened her satchel, broke off an end of a roll and ate without enthusiasm, hardly chewing, letting the bread soak in her mouth. A breeze blew up from behind her and carried the scent of grass and buds.

A whole town—how was it possible? A whole town, except for one person? She hiccupped as the bread made its way down her throat. She hiccupped again as she began to cry.

But then she felt rumbling in the earth beneath her, a sound like distant thunder, but deeper than thunder and bigger, as Vesuvius might have felt as it shook. Lili felt thrilled and scared at once. The storm rose and swelled behind her. Ahead was the cliff. A dusty wind flapped her wedding gown, and she gathered it up and clasped it to her. She was scared as she peered around the oak.

A stampede of horses was coming toward her. She'd been told stories her grandfather had passed down to her mother about the wild Carpathian horses that roamed these woods and fields, but she had never seen them. Her mother had said that they were nobler than all other horses and bigger and purer. Helen had seen them once, when she was younger even than Lili was now. She'd seen them make a run through the streets of Tolgy. They were as quick as lightning, a blur as they traversed the town, and they did not disturb a single post nor upend a buggy or a pail. They whipped into town, then out the other end, as if the gods had sent them to sound an alarm. Many of the citizens had heard that alarm and woke, but few saw them. Helen was one. She'd been standing on her own veranda. Her father was another. He was at the window. Lili's grandfather had said that they were like "the wild Olympians of our mountains."

And here they were now, bearing down on Lili in a cannonade of hooves and dust. Lili tried to climb the old oak but couldn't reach its branches. Still, she was safe behind the tree, surely. Surely, the horses wouldn't crash into the tree. And even if they did, the oak could withstand the blow. And they had to slow down soon. There was a cliff ahead.

They were not slowing. They were upon her, now, upon her and the oak, hundreds of them, led by a beautiful black queen. The horses fanned out to the very hems of the wide field. They ran as one huddled mass, a single body, with a gleaming black majesty at the front.

Lili couldn't stand to think what was coming. She wanted to cover her ears and close her eyes, but she did neither. Her back was to the horses, pressed hard against the tree. The queen flew by her, as did the brilliant black avalanche that followed. Lili couldn't breathe. The air was filled with dust and wood, a black rain beating down on her. Her eyes were stinging, but she kept them open.

And the horses didn't turn. The oiled beauties followed the queen straight off the cliff, ten at a time, or twenty, taking fatal flight. Each one soared for an instant, then plummeted—dashing itself on the rocks below. They could see where they were going, the ones in the front, and there was nothing to stop them. They ran as if the world had no end.

Lili watched in horror and amazement. She couldn't bear to look anymore. She turned her head to one side, and then she saw something else through the black rain. The last of the horses on the outer flanks could see what was coming, two of them, three. On the other side, another horse halted. When the earth stopped thundering, and the black rain ceased to fall, these four horses remained. They stood alone in the field, snorting and neighing.

The horse on the left was as black and brilliant as the queen had been. She joined the others on the opposite side, and the four seemed to gaze at the cliff edge before turning and heading back to the dark grove they'd come from.

Lili would not go to the edge to see the shattered bones and ripped flesh. She had to leave, now, not just her field, but her town. Just for now, until she could get her family back.

BY LATE MORNING, Lili had found her way by foot out of the mountains, through the outskirts of Tolgy and looked toward central
Hungary. She reached the small railway station at Golya, and she felt
relieved. There was no one there to buy a ticket from, but an idle train
stood at a platform with "Budapest" marked on its engine. The big
city was the only place to turn. Where else? She couldn't cross the
border into Romania. There would be someone in Budapest who
could help her find her family. So Lili climbed aboard, though it
might be some time before the train was to depart, and found a nearly
empty car where she could make herself comfortable. She took a seat,
and was instantly asleep.

She was rudely wakened by the slamming of a door, and realized
the train was almost full. How ridiculous she must have looked in her
wedding dress, its whiteness clouded over, and with her small satchel,
her mother's gold wedding band still on her finger. At least the dress
was simple and could pass for something else.

She didn't know how long she'd slept exactly, but the conductor
was upon her. He had white, curly hair and reminded her of an uncle
who lived in Prague. Lili offered him the remainder of her coins, and
he took them but laughed outright before handing them back to her.
She thought he'd put her off the train, remembered the Hungarian
authorities back home who'd joined the invading Germans. But the
man winked at her instead and carried on to check other people's
tickets.

Lili wanted to ask these passengers where they'd come from and
how their town was doing. She wanted to tell them about Tolgy but
feared what would become of her if she did. A large woman sat across
from her, a great burlap sack of bulbs of some kind on the floor at her
feet. They had an earthy smell. The woman wore a gold crucifix
pendant, and she noticed that Lili had noticed, but Lili looked out
the window right away.

Where were they taking people? Had they taken others in the same
way, and Lili's town was the last to know? Was *everyone*, finally, going

to have to move to this other place, like some kind of cosmic musical chairs? And was someone *else* moving to Tolgy?

Lili squeezed her satchel under her arm and closed her eyes. She slept again all the way to the city. And then there it was, outside her window, the imposing buildings coming into sight, the tall shadows, the throngs of people. She'd forgotten quite how impressive and immense the capital city was.

SHE STEPPED OFF the train and stood for a moment with her bag, watching the throngs of people walking this way and that, as if nothing else were going on in the world outside of this centre. She wandered down to the Danube to take in the air. The palatial parliament buildings rose like rounded and polished mountains. The bridges spanning the Danube, linking Buda to Pest, all differed in shape and colour, one iron and green, one grey and concrete, one black and ornate. They all carried buses and pedestrians back and forth going about their business.

Lili sat on a park bench and withdrew another of the rolls she'd taken from the bakery in Tolgy, this time with a bit of cheese. She felt safe at last amid the midday throngs doing their shopping and stopping for a meal or a sweet piece of cake.

Lili remembered the cake her mother had baked for her but sent the thought away. She was practical. She could not weigh herself down with fears of what might have become of her family. She recalled the shots cracking in the streets of Tolgy and smothered their sound, too. Here she was, sitting on a bench in Budapest. Early spring in Budapest and unseasonably warm. She gazed at the people around her. Cheerful, most of them—all of them, actually. Had no one heard? "They are clearing out the towns," she wanted to say but couldn't find her voice. She sat on her bench as though she hadn't a care in the world. Safe in Budapest. Springtime in Budapest.

Lili got to her feet and made her way to a vegetable stand. She selected a carrot and a parsnip, offered a pengo.

The woman sucked on her gold teeth as she examined the coin, front and back. Was it not enough? "Take the vegetables," the woman told Lili as she slipped the coin into her apron pocket. "It's all right. You take those. I'll take this."

Lili wandered the streets for hours, past the vast Kerepesi Cemetery—more like a gallery of sculptures and shrines than a graveyard. Again, she looked over the wall but didn't dare enter. Lili had heard that the country's famous people lay in state here: Hungary's first prime minister, Lajos Batthyany, and Ferenc Deak, the nineteenth-century statesman who brought Austria and Hungary together in his Grand Compromise, as Mrs. Wasserstein had described it. And there were poets there, too, she knew, like Attila Jozsef, who had taken his own life, and novelists like Kalman Mikszath. Stone upon stone, beautifully sculpted, glory upon glory, ending here.

She passed theatres graced by classical columns and passed the impressive, broad-shouldered buildings of the technical university, then made her way along a winding street toward the centre of the city. There were florists on the street and tailors, cafés and beauty salons.

Lili had been to Budapest once before, in 1938 when she was ten. She had come with her parents and Ferenc to visit an aging aunt. But she remembered only being struck by the lovely shop windows and the Goliath buildings, each of which, she was certain, could house the whole of her town under its roof.

She'd been to the cinema on that occasion. It was the Tivoli, the cheerful theatre with its small curtained-off boxes and carvings of angels and sirens in gold on its walls and above the proscenium. As the newsreel played, Lili had asked her mother what those curtained-off booths were. "Nothing," her mother had answered.

But Ferenc said they were for lovers, "So they can hug and smooch when it's a love story."

"Quiet, now," Helen had said.

But Lili and Ferenc were giggling, and as if on cue a couple did arrive, arm in arm, to occupy a *paholy*, as they were called. When they saw Ferenc and Lili watching, the woman released her boyfriend's arm, until he roughly pulled the curtain shut.

But after the grim newsreel about the depression, the lovers and the Bandels got *A Day at the Races*, with the Marx brothers and Margaret Dumont. The Marx brothers were David Bandel's favourites, and if the lovers had come to find privacy, they had come to the wrong place. David laughed them out of their booth.

In the vast Heroes' Square, featuring statues of Hungary's fiercest warriors, Lili heard what she thought was a concert. As she approached, she saw a Gypsy trio, a violin, mandolin and harmonica. With them was a fiery young girl who, oddly, sang a line here and there, but never a whole song. She was dressed in rustic reds and yellows, and she was bobbing like a flame, as if mesmerized, borne by the rhythm and sentiments. She bellowed out the words at everyone but looked at no one, not even Lili. In fact, her eyes were closed throughout. "*Turn your troubles into song,*" she was wailing. "*Come hear our music. Music makes you dumb.*" She dipped and spun. "*Turn colour into sound. Let your heart fill your ears, not the buzz of your greed. Music makes you stupid. Come hear it play.*"

Lili wanted to hold the girl still. When she looked closely at her, she realized the girl wasn't just mesmerized, not just in a trance; she was blind. She had dried-up eyes behind those lids, but her whole being bobbed and floated aboard these songs. She was more like a missionary than a beggar, more like the music's apologist, its philosopher. "*You can't leave footprints on the river, even if you try,*" she chanted. "*Hear the music play. Hear it, hear it. The music is a secret that leaves no trace.*" The trio then played a very sad song, a heart-wrenching song, about a lover gone away to sea. "*And you know it is true,*" the flaming girl sang, "*since we've never seen the sea but can feel the land.*" The song came out more like a hymn than a love song, and Lili found herself holding back tears.

People passed by as if the musicians were not there. Lili had never witnessed such a thing—people ignoring the lovely music as if they were strolling through a park and it was the birds that were singing. How could they not be drawn to it all, the girl possessed by the music, the wonder of it—reminding us that we're still here and it's a sunny day, and we're in love and the baby is coming and we're all going home to supper. Lili smiled brightly now at the group, and the lights of her charm came on. The men smiled back at her, and then, miraculously, the girl smiled, too. The players switched to a Gypsy dance. It sounded cheerful and exotic—Spanish, possibly, or farther even, African, Moroccan, Middle Eastern. Lili stood too long to watch these nice, sun-darkened men play here with their spinning blind girl, especially with people scattering to avoid them.

Had she landed on the moon? No, the moon was not far enough. Another galaxy? *People were being taken—whole towns full of people— and here the music played, and people ran to avoid it as if it were going to detonate.*

It was enough, too much. Lili curtseyed in her dress, and the three men bowed. It only then occurred to her she could give them a coin, and she tried, but the men wouldn't take it. Lili tried the girl, though she was still in her hypnotic state, no longer smiling, somewhere above the ground. And then the girl took the coin and clutched it hard in her hand, as if the hand were disembodied from the mesmerized girl. With more bowing and curtseying, Lili backed away.

Lili came eventually upon the famous synagogue on Dohany Street, an immense Moorish structure, with a multitude of towers rocketing toward heaven. Her skin bristled. She looked left and right and turned around, not wanting to show people what she was seeing, not wanting to be identified with it. When a woman and boy stopped beside her to see if something had happened, Lili fled.

On a corner leading toward Vorosmarty Square, she stumbled into Paris Yard. She felt again as though she'd stepped into another world, another century, stepped into a film. Arabesque arches welcomed her into the arcade and drew her toward beautiful wrought iron, like lace-work crocheted by some mythic grandmother working in the heart of an iron mountain. A handsome young man in a tan spring suit stood in the doorway of a bookshop, flipping through the pages of a book. He noticed Lili and smiled, but she clamped her silly dress to her sides and fled toward Vaci Street and all the way out to the grand cobble-stone square before Gerbeaud, a pretty patisserie bustling with busi-ness. She wished she could enter. People were eating pastries perched royally on Herend dishes. They dabbed their mouths with linen napkins, checked their makeup in mirrors.

Two women, one with a floppy black hat, hustled past Lili along the cobblestones. Lili felt a stabbing pain at her side, a pain so sharp she thought she would collapse. She ran, gasping, a limping run, now, as she made her way around another corner. An older gentleman with his wife on his arm stopped to point with his cane, but Lili continued on her way, found another small park—thank heaven for the small park—and dashed inside like a rabbit that had found its warren.

It was here, in a corner of the park, that she felt another stab of pain at her side, and she slumped to the ground, curled up and writhed in agony. She remembered for a moment even in her pain that she was now almost certainly adding green streaks to her grey-white dress, remembered even as the stabbing radiated over her abdomen that the humiliation of expiring here in this spot after her ordeal would be at least as sharp as the pain itself.

A shadow passed over Lili's racked face. She clutched her satchel, felt for the ring on her finger. She opened her eyes and thought she saw someone quite tall, asking her something.

Two

IN HIS SUNNY OFFICE overlooking Klauzal Square in Szeged, Istvan Beck was drilling a molar. He pumped the drill's motor vigorously by stepping down on a steel button beside his dentist's chair. He'd begun to wonder whether he could save the tooth at all.

Marta Foldi, his assistant, came in. "Dr. Beck," she said, "your friend Miklos Radnoti is on the phone. He says it's important." Istvan kept working on Ella Brunsvik's mouth. "It's important," Marta said again. "It's about your father."

"My father? What about my father?"

"Come," Marta said, indicating the phone.

Miklos Radnoti sounded out of breath on the phone, as if he'd been running. He was a calm man usually, a poet. Istvan had known him since his student days at the University of Szeged. They'd been in a philosophy class together and become fast friends. Miklos Radnoti had never known his mother. He was the twin that had survived, while the other one took his mother down with him. Radnoti had married Fifi Gyarmati, a Catholic woman who was charmed by his poetry and by his wit. He'd converted to Catholicism, but he'd still been taken away to a labour camp near the Ukraine to work with explosives.

What a time Radnoti had spent. These labour camps were not as bad as the concentration camps they'd heard rumours about, but the inmates were worked like slaves nevertheless. Many died. Others survived and came home. Heinrich Beck, Istvan's father, had used his influence as mayor of Szeged to persuade the authorities to get the poet out and back to Budapest. Radnoti had written to his friend Istvan to tell him that that experience made him appreciate life for the first time. Istvan still remembered some of the lines his friend had sent him:

> To forget would be best, but I have
> Never forgotten anything yet.
> Foam pours over the moon and the poison
> Draws a dark green line on the horizon.
> I roll myself a cigarette
> Slowly, carefully. I live.

Now Radnoti had returned to Szeged, briefly, to visit an ailing aunt. The poet told Istvan, "My aunt's housekeeper saw your father a few minutes ago at Mendelssohn Square. There's trouble, and you have to save yourself, Istvan. Get out, fast, save yourself."

Istvan was still picturing Mendelssohn Square, the bronze statue of the composer, the little park. "What are you talking about?" he began to say, but there was static on the line and then the phone went dead. Istvan tried to call his father's office, but couldn't get through.

Ella Brunsvik was now standing beside the dentist's chair with all the gear still in her mouth and the apron hanging from her neck. Istvan told Marta and Mrs. Brunsvik what Radnoti had said. "The Germans must be here," he said. "They're right here in Szeged." He rubbed his face and ran his fingers back through his hair.

Marta said, "We should leave right away, Istvan. I know where we can go."

"We can't avoid the Germans," he said, "even when we're allied with them. How can you invade an ally?"

The siren had begun to sound in the square below. Marta said, "Please, Istvan." She took both his hands and tugged as if he were a child. His eyes rested on hers. Never was there a more perfect specimen of a Jew than Marta, with her coal-black hair and eyes, yet she was Catholic. It must have been the Roman invasion, thought Istvan. Her devotion to him was striking, touching.

Istvan had felt close to Marta from the day he interviewed her. For her part, she looked after him as few assistants had, and while an electric current flowed between the two of them, they had always tried to keep their relationship professional.

Over the siren, Istvan could still hear the music in the outer room, coming from the Graetz console he himself had picked out with such care in Berlin—and at such expense. And now his patients—if they'd stayed—would have been treated to the *Enigma Variations* by Elgar.

He said to Marta, "I don't think Mrs. Brunsvik would appreciate my leaving such a gaping hole in her tooth."

Marta helped the woman by removing the apparatus from her mouth. "Don't be silly," the older woman said. "You've got to get out of here. It's not the same for you. If we had even a place on the floor for you, you could stay with us. But you have to hide, or the hole in your head will be bigger than the one in my tooth." She was taking off the apron herself. "Don't worry," Mrs. Brunsvik went on, "my husband, Lajos, will take care of my tooth with a pair of pliers. Now go. Please. Listen to your assistant."

She wanted to give Istvan a brooch for the work he'd done, but he said, "Don't be silly."

The old woman sighed before setting down her big purse on the dentist's chair to tuck the jewel in a side compartment. Istvan admired the chair as he waited. All the way from the Ritter Company of Rochester, New York. The latest in dentistry in this grand old building in Szeged: a newfangled air blower, a diamond-tipped drill, the largest supply of novocaine (thanks to a generous Greek supplier who'd brought it in from Britain), even a brass cuspidor into which Mrs. Brunsvik spat one last time before turning to leave.

OVER MARTA'S PROTESTS, Istvan insisted they go first to see what his father was up to. They drove together in Istvan's Citroën toward Mendelssohn Square. As they approached, they passed German tanks and Jeeps. "This is dangerous," Marta whispered. "Let me drive, and you lie low." They pulled over and switched seats with some difficulty, she climbing over him. She wore a soft perfume which reminded him of lily of the valley.

But there was not much driving for her to do. Teleki Street was blocked, as was Juhasz. The sirens still sounded. They parked the car and pushed through a crowd of several hundred onlookers. "What's going on?" Istvan asked a woman wearing a red-and-gold bonnet.

"It's the mayor," the woman said. "He's trying to prevent the soldiers from taking down the statue."

"Of *Mendelssohn*?" Istvan asked.

"If that's who he is," the woman said. "The statue in the park."

A man nearby wearing an ascot said that Mendelssohn was forbidden, "So they're pulling him down."

"And the mayor?" Marta said.

"He's trying to stop them. He's saying the composer stayed in town once, and his music is for everyone." Then the man added, "They're taking some Jews. They're rounding them up over on Kossuth."

Istvan froze for a moment. Marta looked hard at him, took his face in her hands. "Let's go," she said. "There's nothing you can do. Let's go back to the car. I'll hide you in the trunk."

"In the trunk? Marta, please, let me try to get to my father. I have to speak to him. Maybe I can get him to come with us." He resumed his push through the crowd.

"What can you say to him?" she yelled as she followed. "The sirens are blaring and Germans are everywhere. Are you going to *reason* with him? Are you *listening*?"

But they were close now. Istvan caught sight of his father. He was standing in front of the green Mendelssohn, his arms crossed. He was blocking soldiers, who'd wound a chain around the statue's shoulders and another around its neck.

Istvan wanted to call out, "Father," but Marta pulled hard on his arm.

Heinrich Beck could be heard shouting, "So this is the kind of regime you mean to have here, the most civilized of nations, the most noble of composers?"

Istvan watched as two soldiers turned to their commanding officer to receive instructions. His father stood firm. The commander signalled for a nearby tank, and it rolled up into the little park. The chain was removed from Mendelssohn's neck, and a small cheer went up. A pigeon cut the blue sky before drifting down and landing on Mendelssohn's three-cornered hat. Bird droppings had turned the composer's cravat and green shoulders white.

The soldiers climbed aboard the tank, fastened the chain to a lamppost, and made a loop at the end of it. No one budged, but people stopped talking. A couple of boys behind Istvan squealed. Istvan turned toward them. His stomach churned. Marta turned, too, and even though she was facing away from the square, she covered her eyes. The siren continued wailing. The wind furrowed into Istvan's back. The boys wore identical green-and-orange striped jerseys and woollen Parisian caps. Certainly, they were brothers, with the same brown hair and brown eyes, but they were at least two or three years apart. "Look at the Lord Mayor," the older one said. "They're winding the chain around his neck."

A minute later, Istvan could hear the tank grunt away. The onlookers gasped. Istvan couldn't look. He covered his eyes now, too. Marta gripped his other hand so hard the ends of his fingers tingled.

The older boy said, "Look, he's wriggling like a fish on a hook." Istvan felt faint. Marta pulled on his hand to lead him away, but he wouldn't move. Through the screen of his fingers, he could see the wonder and horror on the boys' faces.

The younger one pointed and said, "His tongue is out. He's sticking his tongue out."

It was then that Istvan turned. His father had stopped moving. He merely turned in the wind, toward Istvan, Marta and the boys, and then away.

The commander pointed again to the tank, and the crowd watched as the vehicle backed up, spun toward the hanging figure, then chugged over the curb and into the park, crunching through the flowerbeds, squashing the spring hyacinths, the rows of manicured boxwood, and rammed the statue, toppling the cheerful bronze in a single blow. The pigeon flapped off in a hurry.

The siren ceased to sound, though its wail still burned. Now the twittering and squawk of birds entered people's ears. Marta covered her mouth as she looked for the first time. Istvan took her hand and held on. Certainly this *was* the time to go.

But now she froze. He looked down, buried her face in his jacket, turned his back to the spectacle to watch the crowd watch his father. He could see the woman with the red-and-gold bonnet and noticed now that her gold teeth and scarlet cheeks matched the bonnet perfectly, as if she'd planned it that way. He couldn't spot the man with the ascot. He checked the boys again. They looked solemn now. Some people still covered their eyes, men as well as women. Istvan looked directly again at his father, stared as the crotch of his familiar charcoal suit pants darkened and the urine ran from the pant legs to his Oxfords and sprinkled the grass below. Even the Germans paused to inspect their handiwork. Though he was pained by it, Istvan wanted to memorize the sight. He stood in this place for his brother, Paul, and sister, Rozsi, too, and if Istvan lived and were ever to see his siblings again, he would have to tell them what he saw. He found himself already wondering whether he would conceal certain details from his sister. He imagined embracing her, smelling her hair, giving her something to calm her down. But how would it be possible to reach her or see her again?

Paul might have rushed forward to demand justice. It was altogether possible. He might have stood up for his father, the way his foolish father had stood to defend Mendelssohn—and not even Mendelssohn the man, or Mendelssohn the music, the achievement—but the likeness of the man, a Hungarian statue commemorating a visit. Symbolism. That's what it was. Paul might have thought twice, taken the fight higher. Istvan was glad his older brother was not there with him, just in case.

Marta and Istvan pushed back hard as they headed for the familiar black Citroën, the beloved car Istvan enjoyed showing off. They looked all around before she pulled open the trunk and he got in. "Hurry," he said before she closed the lid. He took a last look at the spring light before it went dark. In the cramped darkness, he could feel himself getting sick, and then, as the car jerked away, he had to turn his head as he emptied the contents of his stomach onto the floor of the trunk.

Three

THAT SAME AFTERNOON, Istvan's brother and sister met for coffee at the Gerbeaud Café in Vorosmarty Square. Paul had already had a difficult morning. He'd found out in the middle of a case—in the middle of a proceeding before the court—that his right to practise law had been revoked. He was on a break, sipping hot espresso when his private secretary, Viktor, came in to tell Paul the news. Paul was distracted by the case. He tried to brush off the silly man, but Viktor wouldn't leave. A letter had been brought to the court, and Viktor handed it to Paul.

The regent, Miklos Horthy, was quickly losing his authority. How could Hungary be allied with Germany and at the same time allow Jewish attorneys to plead before the courts?

"But my father—"

"I believe your father has lost his authority, too," Viktor said. The man's voice was quiet and respectful. He handed Paul the nearby phone.

Paul dialed the operator. He told the man his father's office number in Szeged. Heinrich Beck's secretary answered. Paul asked to speak to his father, and far too many minutes passed before Heinrich's secretary—or someone—hung up the phone at the other end. Szeged was three hours away by train. Paul, Rozsi and Istvan were all born and raised there, but when Paul set up his practice in Budapest, Rozsi came too to the exciting city to supervise his household.

When Paul asked the operator to try the number again, no one answered.

An hour later, Paul sat with Rozsi. He watched the café manager, Ervin Gaal, as he struggled to communicate with an elegantly dressed younger man with receding hair who had just entered. The manager seemed to be nodding at Paul.

Rozsi said, "Do I look presentable?" She was pinching her thick black curls to check for herself. Some said Rozsi reminded them of Vivien Leigh as Scarlett O'Hara in *Gone with the Wind*. Rozsi had the same rich hair, the same sparkling green-blue eyes which turned violet in a certain light. She also had a quality of helplessness, which, while annoying in some, was charming in her. It made people want to look after her, especially people like Paul. But she sometimes tired Paul out.

"Are you *listening* to me?" Rozsi asked.

"Yes and no," Paul said.

"Yes and no?"

"Yes I am. And no I'm not," he said.

"Well, thank you very much," she said and looked genuinely hurt.

"I'm sorry, Rozsi. You can understand I have other things on my mind today, can't you?"

Rozsi nodded and sighed. Paul watched his sister. Maybe she wasn't as certain of her beauty since their mother died. If she was, she didn't know how to wield it and often gave men the wrong impression. She unsnapped her small reticule, took out a patch box, removed a beauty spot and placed it at the left side of her lip. She then took out a slim mother-of-pearl case, pulled out a cigarette from behind its thin garter and leaned forward to accept a light from her brother.

She was wearing a cartwheel hat with a great brim, but now flung it down on the empty chair beside her. "Do I have hat ghost?" she asked.

"*What?*" Paul said.

"The *ghost* of the *hat* in my *hair*."

"I've lost my job," he repeated. "And I can't find Father. Have you heard from him this morning?"

"No, I haven't heard from him in days." She looked her brother in the eyes. "How will we live?" she asked. Rozsi looked mildly concerned. She bit her lower lip and then detected a bit of tobacco there. She gently hunted around for it with her tongue.

"Did you hear from Istvan?" Paul asked. "Did he call the house?" She shook her head. "Why?" she asked.

"I don't know. I'm just asking," he said. "Things are happening."

Paul gazed into the heart of the café. The long display cases in the centre of the room were overflowing with pastries that would sweeten Iago: marzipan goblins and chestnut purées crowned by whipped cream; strudel of all kinds—walnut, apple, cherry and poppyseed; hazelnut cream torte; vanilla cream cake; custard cake; Gundel *palacsinta* and milk chocolate cake with almond cream filling; Dobos torte; Linzer pastries; Napoleons; walnut crescents.

"Do you know what sets us apart from the animals, my darling sister?"

"What, my darling brother?" She aimed a stream of smoke at the chandelier.

"Dessert, that's what. Do you think a lion polishing off a zebra turns to his partner and says, 'That calls for a bit of Sachertorte'?"

Rozsi giggled and looked at the cases of cake. Kaiser Laszlo, Gerbeaud's popular monkey, screeched, grinned and yanked gleefully at the bars of his golden cage. The small monkey was dressed as a bellhop, complete with a pillbox hat. Rozsi was relieved to see that the Kaiser was as chipper as ever, chattering with the regulars of Gerbeaud, working on a crust of cake someone must have handed him through the bars. She thought she might say hello to the Kaiser, as she often did, but satisfied herself for the time being by staring at him until he met her gaze with his small, sharp eyes, like human eyes. A young girl, wearing a royal blue jacket-and-skirt ensemble, complemented by a blue derby hat, approached the cage and fed the Kaiser a marzipan monkey wearing a bellhop suit, fashioned after the original one.

"He's like a little cannibal," Rozsi said to Paul. "I wish I could speak to the Kaiser—learn his language and speak to him."

"As long as you don't make him learn yours. That's what we usually expect, isn't it? How many of us speak dog or cat?"

"You really are very silly, do you know that?" Rozsi said.

"Oh," he said. What would the mornings look like for him now, the long afternoons? "I don't know what I'm going to do with myself."

"You'll find something," Rozsi said and took her brother's hand. "We'll be all right. You can do almost anything you set your mind to, and I can help. I can take on more piano students. Father will help us. We'll figure something out." She patted his hand.

Ervin was coming toward Paul and Rozsi with the gentleman. "Paul, I'd like you to meet someone," Ervin said in German. He looked at Rozsi and kept up the German. "Excuse me, ma'am."

Paul got to his feet and Rozsi offered her hand, which the elegant stranger took warmly in his.

Ervin said, "This gentleman's from Sweden. I told him you speak English, so he wanted to say hello."

Ervin bowed and backed away. Paul then took the Swede's hand and introduced himself and his sister; his eyes never left the Swede's. The young man's eyes were dark, and searching. He was balding and had a slim but solid build. The bones in his hands were long and slender, yet his grip was firm. For a giddy moment it looked to Rozsi as though the two might embrace. Paul felt himself blush, felt his wit ebbing out of him.

"Please sit," he said in English.

The man offered Rozsi her hat and took the seat beside her. "Why are you called Paul? Isn't there a Hungarian version of that name?"

Paul found himself stumbling. "I—well—um—I studied at Cambridge. *Pal* didn't go over well there, so I guess I translated it." He paused. He pronounced it again. "Paul. I studied law," he added.

"I studied in Ann Arbor, Michigan. My grandfather sent me there to become an architect. He was an ambassador."

"And so you became an architect?" Paul asked.

"No, I work in financial services. I'm a banker. I'm here now only to visit someone I know, someone I met, but I'd like to come back in a more serious capacity sometime soon."

"Is banking not serious enough?" Paul said. Rozsi lit another cigarette and sipped her espresso. "You said your name was . . ."

"Raoul Wallenberg. I'm here to visit a friend, as I said. I was in South Africa and in Haifa. I—" Wallenberg stopped himself when he heard the shriek of Kaiser Laszlo. He turned around in his chair so he could see the monkey. "This place is extraordinary, this Gerbeaud. It's like the witch's candy house in Hansel and Gretel."

"Yes, the witch's house," Paul said. "Europe is burning, but here you can get its leaders fashioned out of marzipan. People can't find cornmeal or a horse shank for sausage. But in this place you can get anything you want."

"You Hungarians have been allied with the Germans," Wallenberg said, "so they've left you alone."

"They won't be leaving us alone much longer," Paul said. "Hungarians always complain that world history is what happens somewhere else. The world is coming to us now, so maybe the complaints will stop."

"Don't be too enthusiastic," Wallenberg said.

"Oh, I'm not being enthusiastic."

"Then don't be romantic."

There was something oddly familiar about Wallenberg's reproach, as if the two men were reuniting after an absence of some years. Yet there was something reassuring about his tone.

Paul looked outside the window as if to check for Germans, but instead he saw a young woman in a wilted white dress gazing in from the cobblestones. Wallenberg looked, too, as did Rozsi. The girl walked away quickly.

"I'm a Hungarian, and *I* haven't been allied with the Germans," Paul said. "I'm barely allied with my own country anymore. I can no longer practise law. As of this morning, I've been stripped of my rights. And yet here we sit," Paul said, holding up his hands, "in the witch's candy house." He smiled.

"Your legal wings have been clipped."

Paul shrugged.

"What will you do when they invade," Wallenberg asked, "throw cakes at them?"

"I don't know," Paul said. "Cakes and Jews, more likely."

Wallenberg smiled but didn't laugh. Rozsi did laugh good-naturedly, not sure whether she'd understood what the two men had said. Paul had tried to teach her some English, but she said she was full up.

"I'm afraid I have to go," Wallenberg said, getting to his feet and offering his hand again. "I'll look you up when I get back."

"Please do." Paul, too, rose. He took out a case and gave the visitor a card. "But why would you come back? You'll be safer staying in Sweden."

"Ah, safety," the Swede said, looking all around him.

"Why would you risk your neck?" Paul asked.

"It's just a neck. It holds up a head."

"*Really*, though. I don't understand. Why would you come back?"

"To help you throw pastries and Jews at the hating hordes. *May* I try to help you?"

Paul was stunned by the stranger's generosity and forthrightness. He said, "I've heard they can, and do, do terrible things to people— to Jews, Gypsies—whoever—homosexuals, communists."

"I've heard that too," Wallenberg said. "But they won't do anything to Swedes. Germans follow rules, even in butchery."

"But there aren't many Swedes here. Only Hungarians, Jews, Gypsies."

"So we'll convert some." He took a slim silver case with a tortoise-shell face out of his breast pocket, snapped it open and gave Paul a card too. He then offered his hand again. Rozsi said goodbye in

German but hardly looked up. Paul stayed on his feet until the visitor had gone.

Gerbeaud's pianist was playing Schubert. The Sonata in B-flat Major. Schubert was Paul's favourite composer. Little Schubert. Short-lived Schubert. Standing in the valley between Mount Ludwig and Mount Wolfgang. Little, perfect Schubert. His music gave Paul a feeling of fulfilment and sadness both, and always an undefined longing.

"What did he say?" Rozsi asked.

"Nothing, really."

"He said *something*."

"He said he was a banker."

"Is the trouble coming here?" she said.

"The trouble?" She made it sound like a dust storm. She'd paid no attention to world events outside their townhouse, outside this café. "Yes, the trouble's coming," he said.

"So what will we do, take another holiday in the Italian Alps until it passes?"

Even though the Hungarians had not participated in the war, they'd felt imprisoned by it. In times of trouble or tension, the Becks had taken flight to the French Riviera or to Majorca or to Santorini. How Rozsi had loved those trips. She remembered coming upon Michelangelo's *David* in Florence with her father and brothers, soon after her mother had died. "So there he is in marble," Paul had said at the time.

"Oh," she said, as she circled the sculpture.

She looked far too long. "He's too heavy," Istvan said.

"What?" She put her hand up to her mouth. She was blushing.

"He's too heavy. You can't take him home with you."

But now Europe was closing in on them. While Rozsi was not aware of daily events and tuned out when the subject of the war came up, she knew that her own question was not a serious one.

Still, she thought, surely all those nice people who ran those quaint lodges and chalets in the Swiss and Italian Alps, whose relatives made cuckoo clocks and glockenspiels and creamy chocolate and precision watches and music boxes that played the *whole* of Mozart's *Jupiter* Symphony, had not turned criminal, turned their white-capped green slopes into impenetrable fortresses.

A young man entered and came straight to Paul and Rozsi's table. He wore a tan herringbone spring suit—too cool for the weather yet, Rozsi thought, but he was handsome and confident. Though he wanted to speak to Paul, the young man kept staring at Rozsi. He seemed disarmed by her, unsure of how to greet her, even.

Paul rose and said, "Rozsi, this is my friend Zoltan Mak."

"The journalist?" she asked. She felt she wanted to stand, too, to get a closer look, but it would have been awkward.

"Yes," Zoltan answered for himself. She offered her hand and he took it. "Your brother has mentioned you sometimes—frequently, actually—even just a couple of days ago—and now, here we are. But he didn't say much more. I didn't know."

"What?"

He shrugged.

She said, "Your father is the famous—"

"Yes, photographer," he interrupted. "Or photojournalist, as they're called these days. He's the one who inspired me to go into journalism."

Paul had known Zoli, as he liked to be called, only for a little time. He'd known his father, Peter Mak, much longer. The elder Mak had covered some of Paul's better-known trials—better-known, sometimes, because of Peter Mak's attention to them and the respectful attention his stories attracted. Paul owed some of his reputation and fame to the Maks. Zoli got into the act now, too, and he and Paul became fast friends. They'd once had a heated discussion on how their friendship might affect Zoli's neutrality.

"Never fear," Zoli had said. "If it's between you and the story, the story comes first. Ice," Zoli said, pointing to his chest. "My words don't lie any more than a photograph would."

"Oh, even photographs lie. It depends on where the camera is pointed and where it isn't."

Zoli realized he was still holding Rozsi's hand. He blushed and let it go. He looked down at the table in front of her.

He turned to Paul. "I have something to tell you," he said, barely audibly.

"Sit down," Paul suggested. "We'll have coffee."

Zoli stayed on his feet. "I have to tell you alone. Please excuse us, ma'am—Rozsi."

"Go ahead," Rozsi said, and she stood. Zoli's blush deepened. Paul thought that a very warm species of ice beat away in the younger man's heart.

Zoli led Paul away to the door and then, unexpectedly, outside.

Their waitress, who'd been hovering, returned, and Rozsi ordered another espresso but nothing else. The woman replaced her pad and pencil inside the pocket of her white apron. She wore the same apron and black silk dress and white open-toed shoes as all the waitresses at Gerbeaud.

The café occupied the middle of an old cobblestone square as if it were sitting in the middle of another century, when the booming Austro-Hungarian Empire, presided over by the Habsburgs, looked west to Paris and north to Berlin and London for inspiration. The square was filled with strolling people, carrying parcels and flowers. For the first time, Rozsi noticed that the café's heavy green curtains were parted like those in a theatre, the bright light from outside slicing between them and casting dramatic shadows over the patrons' faces.

She felt awkward, felt a yearning she couldn't account for, a restlessness, having to do with spring, she thought at first, but maybe the times they lived in, or the friend of Paul's she'd just met. What would Paul do now? What would they all do? Too much was happening too quickly.

Outside, Zoli told Paul that he'd heard from Istvan's friend Miklos Radnoti. "I had a wire this morning. Radnoti's trying to get back here, but he says your father and brother may be in some kind of trouble."

"I tried to call my father," Paul said.

"The Germans have arrived in our country," Zoli said. "The invasion has begun."

Paul swallowed hard. "I'll have to get to them in Szeged."

"I don't think that's smart," Zoli said. "If they're in trouble, you can be of little help to them by yourself."

"We have quite a few friends in Szeged."

"Your friends are in trouble, too. You're better off lobbying from here."

"I'll start on it right away from my office." His gaze fell on Zoltan. Paul was a head taller than the younger man. "Zoli, please don't tell my sister anything, but do me the favour of taking her home."

"The favour?" Zoli asked. "You're doing me a favour, entrusting her to me. Does she—I mean, does she have anyone?"

Paul looked at his friend. "No, no one she likes."

"I'd be happy to—walk her home, I mean. Don't worry, please."

"I should say goodbye, so she won't be alarmed."

"Don't," Zoli said. "She'll ask you too many questions. I'll just tell her you were called away to your office on a legal matter. It'll be all right, I promise."

Paul thought of what Raoul Wallenberg had said. They could turn Hungarians into Swedes. He asked Zoli, "If papers were to be drawn up for people, could you take the photographs?"

"Quite easily. I have access to a studio. Just say when."

"I'll call you," Paul said. "Thank you for looking after my sister."

A FEW MINUTES LATER, Rozsi and Zoli were walking across the cobblestone square on their way to the Becks' townhouse. He watched the sunlight in her eyes. He asked if she minded stopping at his place first. "My father is developing a photograph, and I need to pick it up and take it to the paper for tomorrow's edition."

Rozsi said, "You go on ahead. Don't let me slow you down. I can make it home on my own." She felt uneasy about her brother's sudden departure and wanted to get home quickly.

"It's not urgent," Zoli said. "Your safety is more important."

She felt better right away and smiled. "Can you say what is going on, please, Zoli, and tell me why my brother had to rush off?"

"Not too much yet, not here, but your brother lost his formidable law practice today, and he has a lot to look after and clean up."

They hardly spoke again for several minutes. She was certainly reassured by the stranger's presence but felt anything but relaxed. They stared down at their feet as they walked. Finally, she said, "I'm worried about what is to become of us."

"To us Jews, you mean?"

"Yes, to us Jews, us Becks, us Hungarians."

He wanted to comfort her but didn't know how.

She thought he might be feeling a little unsteady himself. "May I take your arm?" she asked. She gripped him anxiously. He could feel the bird-like bones of her fingers. "Your face says it all," she said. She was looking directly at him. "It's a bad time to become attached."

"Attached?"

She took her hand back and blushed hotly.

"Please," he said, offering his arm again. "Please." She took it. "Maybe it's the best time to become attached."

They were both thinking the same thing. Why hadn't Paul introduced them earlier? When he dropped her off, he asked if he might see her again, and she said she'd like that.

PAUL WALKED QUICKLY toward Marko Street. He was now truly worried about his father and brother, but especially his father. He was so exposed. The last Jewish politician in the land to retain office. They were all gone, every last one of them: Kovacs in Works, Klein in Justice, Berkovics in External Affairs, and all the mayors, four of them, and councilmen. Except his father. And his father didn't even have his wife, Mathilde, Paul's mother, to comfort him. Cancer took her six years before this dark era began.

Paul found himself still struck by his encounter with the Swede. He recalled the penetrating eyes. Paul wondered why he had seemed so serious about the Hungarians. He couldn't shake the feeling of the Swede's presence.

As Paul strode through the small park on the corner, just over a block from his office, he was startled by a young couple dressed in dingy coats. The two sprang out of a nearby bush, wielding a hammer and an axe. In a minute, they stripped a park bench of its wooden seat, no doubt for firewood. Paul realized that the park had several seatless benches; their metal supports looked odd on their own, like modern sculptures, arranged in pairs here and there.

Paul heard what sounded like a woman grunting then stifling a shriek. He looked all around but couldn't see anyone. Another sound, more like a yelp. On the corner, between the lamppost and a great dark bush, Paul spotted a shoeless foot, moving as if it wanted to clasp something, then opening, trembling.

As he approached, he could see that the shoeless foot had its companion nearby, this one with a shoe. The missing shoe had been kicked beneath the bush.

Paul thought at first that the woman's attacker might still be nearby, but she was alone, in acute pain, and young, no more than a teenager, dressed in a fancy white dress.

"What's the matter?" Paul asked as calmly as he could. "How can I help you?"

"Oh," she said, writhing, and clenching her eyes shut.

"Who did this to you?"

"No—oh—please." She folded into herself. "It's my side." Paul could detect an accent, but only a faint one. It was tinged with Slavic and . . . what? German? Yiddish?

"I'll get help," Paul said. "It'll be all right, I promise you. I'll get help."

He rushed to the curb to wave down a passing car. It sped by him, followed by another car, and another one, nearly running him down. He leapt out into the road between the lanes of traffic and challenged the drivers directly, forcing them to swerve to avoid hitting him. Paul saw a cab a block away and flailed like a clown to get the driver's attention.

The Mercedes pulled over, and Paul ran to fetch the young girl. He lifted her up and carried her carefully. He laid her across the back seat of the cab.

Within a quarter of an hour, the girl was in a hospital. That night, Paul returned. The girl's appendix was floating in a bottle beside her. It was not until then that Paul learned her name, Lili, and found out what had happened to her, though she left out the part about the horses.

Lili was encouraged by the many questions Paul asked.

"My dress," she said. She was wearing a hospital gown.

"It's been sent out to be cleaned," Paul said. "Poor thing. I didn't know whether you were going to make it. I'm glad I got you here in time. My Uncle Robert did the surgery." Paul pointed to the bottle on the sill.

"Oh," she said. "He's a surgeon?"

"Yes, he's chief of surgery here, actually."

"Maybe my father knew him. My father would come to conferences here in Budapest."

"Maybe."

"Your name is Paul?" she asked.

Before he was able to answer, the doctor stepped in. "Yes, Paul, with a *u*," the doctor said. "He came back to us from England as Paul, and we don't know where the original young man got to."

"And this is my Uncle Robert," Paul said.

"Thank you for what you did," Lili said. She smiled for the first time.

"I'm sorry I had to leave you here this afternoon," Paul said. He stood looming over the bed. "I had to get to my office to make calls. I—"

"What sort of office?" she asked eagerly.

"I'm a lawyer. Or at least I *was*."

"My family's been taken," she began again. It might have been the remnants of the anaesthetic. She tried to sit up but winced. Robert eased her back down. "Near the southern border. In Tolgy. Do you know it?"

"I'm sorry, I don't," Paul said.

Paul looked at his uncle. He saw alarm in the older man's face and then felt it himself. How could it not reach them, Robert thought.

"Can you do something?" Lili asked. "Please." She tried to sit up again, but Robert kept a firm hand on her shoulder.

"I can petition," Paul said, "but I'm concerned about my brother in Szeged, too, I'm afraid, a dentist—that was another reason I had to make calls."

"And your father," Robert put in.

Paul sat on the corner of the bed. "Yes, my father." His voice hitched. "Uncle Robert," he began, "I can't get hold of anyone in Szeged. I tried all afternoon. My assistant, Viktor, sent a telegram. Zoli, a reporter friend, can't reach an acquaintance at the paper there."

"What's happened to them?" Robert said as he sat down opposite his nephew on Lili's bed. "The cancer has spread finally to Hungary. How could we have believed it wouldn't? Poor Heinrich. Poor Istvan. If this girl's family is any indication, I ..."

Lili was crying. Paul got to his feet and handed her his handkerchief. "I'll go to Szeged."

Robert stood too. "Why would you do such a thing?"

"They took everyone in my town," Lili said. "I was the only one left."

"It's not as simple in Szeged," Paul said. "And even more complicated here. I have to get to my family and help them out."

"Please, Paul. Don't be foolish. If anyone can do anything, Heinrich can."

"I don't know about his influence anymore," Paul said, "but I'll find out more before I go. I promise."

WHEN ZOLI GOT HOME, he was eager to tell his parents about the lovely girl he'd met. He couldn't stop thinking about Rozsi. He'd been seeing someone else, Margit Berg, until just months before, but Margit kept comparing him with other young men. She admired Laszlo Szent, an engineer friend they shared, who'd help draw up new designs to reinforce the Chain Bridge. She never missed an opportunity to tell Zoli how much she respected Szent, even as Zoli took her hand and strolled out on the bridge with her to admire the lights. Margit also insisted they catch every fencing match contested by another friend, Bela Festo, on his way to the Olympics. "Don't you wish you could do that?" she would say wistfully to Zoli. Afterward, over coffee, she'd giggle at every word Festo said, no matter how inane, and she winked at Zoli when she saw him staring. He called off the relationship, and he was surprised at how hard she took it. She cried bitterly. He wondered whether she'd be comparing her next date with him as she admired Zoli's pieces in the paper.

Zoli picked up his own paper sitting on the sideboard in the parlour and called in the direction of the darkroom. His father didn't answer. "Mother," he said, but then he became distracted by the paper and sat down. Zoli wondered why the article he and his father had produced on the ascendancy of the brutal Hungarian Arrow Cross had been moved from the front page. He flipped to the city pages but couldn't find the story there, either. He then realized that the house buzzed with silence. "Mother," he called out more insistently. "Father."

When he filed his very first story in the *Csillag*, he remembered he'd stayed up all night to finish it. The story was supposed to involve a shipment of beets to Austria, how Austria was taking less of Hungary's produce that season. But Zoli had filled it with high purpose, describing the train workers, who'd been underpaid for decades, and, even worse, the farmers, who'd have starved had they not had their own produce to consume. The story ended with a dissertation on the amorality of business and the dark forces of capitalism. Zoli also filed two photographs, which he'd carefully set up and composed: one of an empty railway platform and the other of an idle ox, standing in a farmer's field.

When he rushed the next day to the newspaper's offices and opened that day's edition to the page where his story should have appeared, he found instead the photograph of a simple moth and, under his byline, *his very first*, a composition he'd written for school as a boy of twelve. In it, an unwitting white moth took a trip with a pair of lovers on a sailboat way out to sea, riding along on the hatch and then the boom, even as the boat began to sink and the lovers, oblivious to the danger they were in, continued to gaze into each other's eyes. Believing the boat's sail to be her mother, the moth clung to the mast until the tip at last sank beneath the surface, and she was left to fend for herself. She couldn't smell the land, knew she couldn't reach it, so she circled the spot where her mother had gone down, *"whirling and fluttering, touching down once on the salt surface, but by doing so doubling the weight of her own legs, wheeling and now gliding to conserve energy, fluttering again to gain height and drifting back down to save the last bit of nectar burning within her belly, fuelling her wings, until at last she knows, she understands, the lesson having been simpler than she at first thought and, in knowing, lets out her last breath, becomes weightless on the surface, a scrap of tissue, swallowed by a gulp of sea."*

Zoli's father had urged him that morning to rediscover that boyish wonder, relearn the simplicity he was now trying to bury under grand thoughts.

Now, as Zoli searched for another story in the paper, he realized it wasn't there, either. And yet Zoli's family owned the *Csillag*. Zoli's mother, Adel, had inherited a profitable brickyard and used some of the proceeds to run two papers, the foremost being the *Csillag*. It was true they had appointed an editor, Odon Mihaly, and tried to give him free rein, but it was not like Mihaly to kill a story without notice, especially one from Peter Mak, Zoli's father. Had his father submitted the piece under his alias, Peter Vas? What difference would that have made? Where was Mihaly? Had someone spoken to him?

Peter Mak was one of the most celebrated journalists and photographers in the city, regardless of the fact that his family owned the *Csillag*. His feature stories were legendary. In one case, he exposed the royal Eszterhazy family to shame when it became apparent they had mistreated the thousands of serfs who worked their lands. Peter Mak had unearthed documents suggesting that the family had opposed and even suppressed legislation that would have given the serfs education and a modicum of freedom, at least brought them into the twentieth century. Hungary was one of the last European countries to cling to its serfs. The highest highs and lowest lows in terms of economic and social class coexisted in Hungary, and the nobility was often callous in its insistence on keeping things that way.

Many blamed the imperious Austrians. Zoli had witnessed some of the best debates between his father and Heinrich Beck on the union past and present with Austria. The men argued bitterly. Paul's aunt Klari and Zoli's mother, Adel, broke it up by bringing out a fragrant *arany galuska*, a pastry made with walnuts and apricot preserve. "We gave this dessert to the Viennese," Adel said, "and they gave us Sachertorte, a fair exchange. Look at the bright side, boys."

Zoli gazed around the quiet parlour. His father, travelling as Peter Vas, had taken a daring trip to Gyor the previous day. He'd received a tip from one of his underground sources that the Germans planned to evacuate a Jewish orphanage housing 320 children in the northwestern city, and Peter wanted to take photographs of the war crime. The purging operation turned out to be as mysterious as it was swift. Within an afternoon, the children were meant to disappear, as if the Pied Piper of Hamelin had lured them away, never to return.

The journalist had got quick shots of the children being stuffed into burlap sacks and loaded onto the back of a truck. He stood, helpless, and watched the wriggling sacks, until he felt something sharp from behind, a German brown shirt with a bayonet. The reporter furtively slid his Hasselblad under his arm, inside his jacket. He was experienced at concealing his camera.

"Enjoying the spectacle?" the soldier asked in German.

"I'm not sure. I'm here to adopt one of these boys," Mak said. "I'll take a couple if you can spare them."

"You can adopt one or two when they come back."

"That wasn't my understanding with the authorities."

"And who might they be?" the German asked. A Hungarian Arrow Cross guard approached, but the German held up his hand to stop the man.

Peter Mak could feel sheets of perspiration flowing under his jacket, especially where the camera hung, pressed against his ribs. The rivalry between the German and Hungarian was his ticket. "All right," he said. "I'll come back when the children do." And he backed away.

That night at dinner, when he recounted the story, Adel cried. She begged her husband not to risk his life the way he so often did.

Zoltan went to the foot of the stairs and called from there. A dog barked in the neighbour's yard. He took a peek out back and caught sight of his mother's foot in her spring sandal. He'd pulled open the window wide before he saw the spot of blood on the outer sill. And then he saw all of her. She was lying on her back on the terrace, looking quite at peace. Under one arm was tucked the strap of his father's famous Hasselblad, the camera itself resting languidly on her abdomen like a cat. From under her other breast, a great river of blood oozed out of the folds of her soft pink dress and onto the cobblestones of the terrace.

"Mother," Zoli shrieked. He stood up. Before he could think to use the door, he had leapt through the open window. He put his hand on the wound to stanch the flow, but he could see she was not breathing. Her pink lips were parted, and he could see the tip of her dry tongue, as if it had tried to escape.

The dog next door answered with a bark. Zoli tried the back door, but his mother's shoulder rested against it. He would have had to pull her away to open it.

Zoli got back in through the window and ran toward the dark-room, knocking over the piano bench and launching a sheaf of musical scores into the wind that followed him.

He found his father face down in a tray of developing chemicals. The picture he'd been developing was hanging above him from the line. It was an image of sacks in a truck, guarded by two German soldiers, with an Arrow Cross officer looking on. It was to go with the second instalment of their story about the rise of the Nyilas, as the Arrow Cross were known. The dim light was still on, and his father's arm was extended along the counter, his fingers spread wide, as if he were reaching for something that wasn't there. Was it the camera his mother had tried to rescue before making her escape? Had they drowned him first and shot her second?

Zoli stood for a moment, paralyzed. He was the Maks' only child. The authorities would come looking for him, too, now. He felt himself trembling—unable to swallow. He pushed himself to move.

He went out again to the back, out through the window, got to his knees and kissed his mother on her cold pink cheek. He gently pried the camera from her and took a good look at it. He even looked through the lens. The light refracted through his tears.

His father would have been saddened but perversely proud of this horrific scene. Peter had once told his son, "If you don't make your-self worthy of a bullet, you're not a journalist."

Zoli would have to take the camera now and keep it with him as he went underground.

Four

MARTA FOLDI HID Istvan Beck from the Nazis in the wine cellar of her cottage in Tower Town, near the outer boulevard of the city. The tiny, ancient house had belonged for generations to the Foldis. They could trace their lineage to a scullery maid and a stable hand who had worked in the castle of King Mathias in the fifteenth century. Marta's own brother, Ferenc, now lived in Chicago, answered to "Frank" and worked as a dentist, like Istvan. Marta and Ferenc's parents had died in a boating accident on the Tisza River when Marta was just fourteen and her brother seventeen. For generations, the cottages of Tower Town were inhabited by paprika growers and sausage makers. Marta's parents had been both.

The house, on Alma Street, was one of the least likely places to find a hidden Jew. The little building, divided now into two bedrooms, a tiny toilet and a small central room, which doubled as a kitchen and parlour, had two loose planks in its creaky floor leading to the cellar. Here, Marta's father, Jozsef, had stored some excellent vodka and several dozen dusty bottles of wine. Her mother, Maria, had kept her preserves, her pickled tomatoes and peppers, grown in the small, lush square of garden out back, together with some raspberry and apricot jam that her cousin had given her, on a shelf opposite her father's bottles. A ladder led down to the cellar, the walls and floor were crumbling stone, and when the planks came down shut, slits of light cut in from above and drew lines across the dark room.

Here, in this least likely place, Marta would hide Istvan, feed him and keep him strong. She hadn't given much thought to a plan or strategy before now, of course. Istvan had never even visited Marta at home, nor she him. But a line had been crossed—or rather they had been pushed over it—and now she was operating on instinct. Maybe this would all blow over. Surely it must. The Allies were at the gates.

At first Istvan felt protected, felt grateful to have a little time away from the world. He worried about Marta, the risk she was taking. As the hours became days, the challenge was to decide what to do to occupy his body and mind while Marta was away. Istvan measured his days by the rods of light coming through the floorboards, studying them as they travelled across his cell. As he lay on his back, he liked them crossing out his feet and crossing out his neck. He liked to shift himself from latitude to longitude to watch them divide his body straight up the middle, featuring his gonads on either side, lighting a highway between the telltale nose and penis that led him to this cell.

Who'd have thought? Must tell Marta when she gets back. Must tell Marta the line of destiny can be drawn between these two points.

Besides the movement of the lines of light, there was one other measure and one distraction from that measure: the clock and the cat, the latter called Smetana, after Marta's favourite composer. The clock ticked tirelessly. How ridiculous we are, Istvan thought, counting out eternity in bits of light and sound. Smetana scampered and slept, scratched and slept.

When the sun switched off, and the lamp above followed, right at curfew, Marta could creak down at last to join Istvan in the palpable darkness, to feel one of his points of destiny gain prominence over the other.

In this blindness, they felt safe at last, their dark union lifting them up the tunnel, out of the cottage, over the city. After, she would creak back up to get them their meal: beans, mostly, sometimes leeks, often cabbage or peppers, a treat of carrots occasionally, a potato between them, and once a week a tin of sardines. Istvan suspected Marta might have done better with her food coupons. He suspected she *did* do better and that Smetana got a sardine a day—the other tin to which Marta's rations entitled her. The authorities did not know she was feeding all of them. Two tins of protein were intended for her, not for all of them, not him, her, the cat and the clock. Then they brushed their teeth with salt, using a new shoe brush she'd managed to procure.

Oh, how sweet she was with her tins and her warmed potato and her fragrant visits. They whispered together for hours at a time, lying on his mat, holding hands beneath the prickly warm blanket. He fed off her news or at least the distorted versions of news she carried with her and what they could really make of them.

Within two months, the Germans took authority over the city, and within three months cleansed it of most of its Jews and Gypsies. There was a blackout on news. Listening to the BBC broadcasts earned you the death penalty, often carried out on the spot. So the news they got was from Anna Barta, who used to be the local florist but now issued food coupons, and Denes Cermak, who used to sell the papers but told the news now instead, whatever he could garner from Berlin, from Warsaw, from Prague and from the riot of rumour in the streets of Szeged and Budapest. It was this news that Marta brought home to Istvan.

It was news about the French underground and the coming fall of London. Hitler was in Africa. He would take Europe, followed by Russia. He would take on all comers, vanquish all enemies, and he would rule the planet. King Adolf of Austria! King Adolf of Arya! The Aryan Eagle spreads his fists into wings! *Aquila non capit muscas!* An eagle does not catch flies! Whoever of us is left—whatever vermin Jews and communists and Gypsies and homosexuals—can fly into the bush and buzz around the turds so generously dropped by the noble Aryan Eagle.

What is the issue, after all? Istvan wondered. What is it *really*? Is it that we cover our heads, warm a small patch of our offensive pates? Is it our music? Our dentistry? Our thoughts? Our mathematics? Our mimicry of you in dress and talk and appetite? Do you despise the softness of our gold, thinking it brass impregnable like good King Richard's? What exactly pings the chip that cracks the concord of your state? Is it that we flies make like eagles, aspire to be eagles, until, with battered impish little wings, we drone off to another dung heap—just as juicy, just as inviting? Is it that we never quite get that it is you who are King Richard, and we the antic, "grinning at his pomp"? You did a good job, now, a good job, finally: too much like you in walk and talk, we stand here caught in your midst, our wings atrophied, our grins gone. Let us say we're your competitors—even if we're not, but let us say we are. Don't competitors have the same aim, to score enough goals to win, not too many, not so many as to humiliate, but enough to win? Survive. Eat. Breathe.

May we look at your moon? May we borrow it one night to compose a ditty by its light? May we gaze at your stars? What constellation might you not be using tonight?

Could you lend us your caves, so that we can draw images of the passing animals? And then, in the bottom corner, where the feet are, can we leave the imprint of our hand—not to say, "I was here." Never that—that message is for you and you alone. But to say, "I was *also* here." I was also here, and now I've moved on. I was also here, and some day it might be all right for me to return.

For you, Emperor, our good Lord Franz-Josef, for you we'll conceal our past—we don't know where we came from anyway. For you, Lord, we'll take on good German names like yours: Klein if we're small, Gross if we're large, Roth if our hair is red, Beck if we bake a sweet cake, Tanz if we dance, Mondtanz if we dance by the light of the moon. For you, Herr Horthy, good Lord Regent, we'll take Hungarian names to blend with the scenery: Nagy if we're big, Kis if we're little, Halasi if we fish, Kertesz if we keep a garden, Ordog if

we're devilish. We'll put on a white shirt and white apron embroidered with folkland flowers and roll the strange sounds of the Huns
and Magyars and Turks off our tongues and make them all ours, eat
paprika and pork and horse, dance Gypsy and waltz—if only, in
return, Herr Adolf, Herr Nicholas, Herr Franz-Josef, if only you
promise not to point out our snouts, our bank accounts, our diplo-
mas, our afternoons with the violin. Promise us, and you'll stay our
lords forever—promise us, and we'll board airless cars with a bucket
for relief and travel to holiday destinations of your choosing and
devising.

When the rain fell, it fell like clocks clanging on the roof, and after
the clouds chugged past, the sun beamed out its long hour. Istvan
could smell the sun—could *hear* it—as the days grew longer. How
he'd always craved the warmth, loved feeling the summer opening up
its limbs to him. Istvan lived in chunks of air, cartons of his own dust
and follicles, and when he stood, it was to visit a new hemisphere
where exotic creatures flew and floated. He was a microscope, magni-
fying every jagged little black leg, extrapolating every eye and tail into
a resident, granting it citizenship by its persistence in the neighbourhood, the toy world, flecks of civilization colliding like epochs. Boxes
of darkness were piled in the corner, but sometimes their colours
could be unpacked, and they were wild and vivid: jewel green, wet
blue, fragrant red.

And Marta was his light-bearing creature. He sucked the street out of
her, the chlorophyll, the learning—let alone the love and nourishment.

Each day, Marta told Istvan as much as he could stand about the
dental office, Istvan's own practice, now occupied by a young dentist,
Dr. Janos Benes, whom the Reich had assigned to his office. Istvan
had fled the country, Marta had told them. The authorities confiscated Istvan's deeds and his belongings, emptying out the house he
shared with his father, piling up their household effects, together with
the effects of other evacuated Jews, in the synagogue on Jozsika Street.
Dr. Beck had said he was heading east through Russia, Marta told the

Germans—and she had no way of knowing—but she guessed he would not be back. He knew what was good for him. They made a mark in their black hardcover notebooks, followed by a scratched out sentence, and then snapped them shut. They looked at Marta, looked her in the eye, and, predictably, marched out. A day later a letter came to her at her little house on Alma Street, ordering her back to work in her old office under Herr Dr. Janos Benes.

Little had changed in the office. It was as if Dr. Benes had been away on vacation and had now returned to his gleaming dentist's chair and instruments he'd gathered from the Ritter Company of Rochester, New York, and Beethoven on his Graetz console specially selected in Berlin.

"Do you know about the cuckoo bird?" Istvan asked Marta one night.

"Yes."

"Why don't we call him Dr. Cuckoo?"

She suddenly found herself feeling defensive. "Did he have any more of a choice than you did or I did? It's the cuckoo's nature to occupy another's nest. It is not Dr. Benes's nature."

In fact, Herr Dr. Benes, as he was called, had no ill will, certainly none that was evident. He had been summoned from a village near Debrecen and assigned to Istvan's office just as surely as Marta had been ordered to return to it.

Days passed in this way, and the days became weeks and then months. Was it longer than that? He could have counted every second but had lost track. He listened to the ticking of the clock's heart and the beating of the cat's. Could he come out now, if only for an hour, to take in the sun? They could not take the chance. What if Frau Barta saw him, or Herr Newsman Cermak? Had Istvan not gone away, as reported, with the best of them, to hide his frozen carcass in Siberia? Wasn't that the story?

Oh, frigid Siberia! Thank the heavens for the books. During the day, when Marta was gone, Istvan would light an oil lamp or a candle in his lair when it could not be detected through the sunlit planks above. Autumn would come. He could see it ahead. What would happen in the long darkness when he was not able to light a lamp at all?

He had read *Anna Karenina* in Hungarian translation four times, though he wished he could have tried his hand at the original Russian. He had managed it once before, when his friend Miklos had lent him the book in university. But the Hungarian translation was a good one. It was done by that sad poet Attila Jozsef, the son of Szeged, who'd been expelled for disparaging his native land. He'd written bold lines, Istvan remembered.

I have no brother
I have no father
I have no god
And I have no country.
With pure heart, I'll burn and loot,
And if I have to, even shoot.

Attila had been branded a Marxist, an anarchist, a communist, but his translations of Tolstoy and Shakespeare could stand with the originals.

Marta had brought Istvan a weak translation of Victor Hugo, and to her amazement he'd stopped reading it the second time through. He told her that night, "Reading a bad translation is like listening to Beethoven played by a school band." He chuckled, but she didn't even smile. "I don't mean to complain," he told her. "I did read it once. More than once. It must be me. I'm sure it's me."

How could he complain to the woman who'd brought him sustenance, who'd provided the activities that would make the ceiling disappear?

Mrs. Anna Barta, bless her heart, had brought Marta a book published in German by a Czech writer, *Der Prozess*, "The Trial," released not long before and already forbidden, Mrs. Anna had said. In fact, she had transported it to Marta's house on Alma Street hidden in her ample brassiere and handed it to her, still warm from her breast. "Hide it, read it, then destroy it," the good woman had said. Istvan listened to her voice above his head one Sunday afternoon, happy to hear another human. She'd brought some Havarti cheese, too, good Anna, with the little Franz Kafka treasure, which had surfaced from the underground somewhere and needed to return whence it came: the trash heap, the ash heap, whatever was easiest.

A couple of weeks passed. Istvan devoured the new book six times, seven times. He was pierced through the heart by it, ready to make it his own suicide note as he boldly marched out of his den wearing it nailed to his chest in place of the cloth star issued to the Jews still standing, miraculously still resident, in Szeged, when the good Mrs. Barta came again on a Sunday to call on Marta. Smetana scratched on the planks above Istvan.

Had she destroyed the book? Mrs. Barta wanted to know. Had Marta read it and destroyed it as discussed?

She'd read it—yes—she'd read it, and—yes, no, she had destroyed it, of course.

Had she liked it? Smetana scratched. Marta's eyes darted about the little room. Istvan sat like a statue directly below them, fearing his eyes made noise as they shifted in their sockets. Yes, of course she liked it.

But nightmarish—she remembered what Istvan had said, though she'd hardly listened at the time—nightmarish. "Awful."

"I wouldn't know," the older woman said. "Who has time to read?"

Istvan wondered if good Anna had watched his father dangle in Mendelssohn Square, wondered if she'd made some sort of unconscious connection. He didn't know anymore what he was talking about, thinking about.

He thought again of Paul and Rozsi. Where had the remains of his family got to? Would the line end here? Rozsi had often talked about becoming a mother just like their own, like Mathilde. They had been inseparable, mother and daughter. Every boy who wandered into

Rozsi's sphere had to be assessed by their mother, the supreme judge and the wisest counsel on all such matters. She possessed radar—she knew before anyone else which boy would be wayward and which one loyal. On her own, Rozsi was bereft, needing Paul, needing him, Istvan. He longed to introduce Marta to his brother and sister.

That evening down below, a warm evening in June, Marta sounded more cheerful than usual, almost careless, wanting to leave the planks up for a little air just a few minutes more, risking both their lives, the slits of light inadequate for their food and love. Blindness inadequate.

When they were finished, sitting naked on the warm blanket in the cool cellar, she said she wished they could throw aside the planks above them forever, but of course they didn't. Then she said that Dr. Benes had been nice to her, given her more food lately because his patients had little else with which to pay him. Istvan had noticed: sausage twice that week, a half-dozen eggs, three tins of herring (who knows how many for the cat?), crusty German rye.

"Why not before?" Istvan asked. He was gnawing on a parsnip. He had grown to love them raw. "Why hasn't he given us food before?"

"He has. You know he has—as far back as early April. Don't you remember? The peppers in April? The radishes in May?"

"Yes, I remember."

Her skin felt coarse in the darkness. Gooseflesh. She heard him crunch on the parsnip.

"Is he in love with you?"

She pulled away from him. "Of course he's not in love with me."

"He doesn't know you have someone else. You're not married."

"*He* has someone else. He has a wife and two daughters. *I* have someone hidden in the cellar."

"And you would die in an instant if they found out," he said. "You'd be shot in the head where you stood." He exhaled. "I'm sorry. I'm very sorry. It's difficult being the invisible man."

"It's just as difficult being the visible woman." She fumbled around beside her among the food things she had placed out of harm's way and, in the darkness, put a book into his hand. "It's Alexandre Dumas's *The Three Musketeers* in the original French. A cousin of Dr. Benes had it. I asked to borrow it, and Janos visited his cousin on Sunday. I had it with me all day, and I was bursting to tell you I did."

"You are precious," he said, grinning. "Janos, is it now? You call him Janos?"

Marta went silent, then she left. The next morning, he heard her shuffling about as she got herself ready. She usually knocked three times gently with her heel to say goodbye, but this time she spoke only to Smetana before departing.

Istvan had waited all night to open the Dumas, but when morning came and he could light his lamp, he didn't. He had badly wanted to gallop off with the musketeers. He had once fled Budapest for Paris for his own silly adventure, but now, instead of Athos, Porthos or Aramis, he had become Edmond Dantès, the Count of Monte Cristo—no, even better, *even worse*: Kafka's Joseph K. It was a life-and-death adventure, after all, but not as he'd imagined it, not along the paths of glory. The paths of glory were illuminated by celestial beams, not thin filaments cut through floorboards.

The Three Musketeers. Istvan laughed out loud and startled the cat— startled himself. Dumas in the original French. Tolstoy in Hungarian, Kafka in German, as written by the Czech author himself. Heavens above!

That night Marta was agitated when she arrived home. He could hear her banging about, not tiptoeing and shuffling as usual. Smetana meowed, and Marta, usually so protective, let him out of the house. "Go," she told him, "go," and he went.

An hour later, she came down to him. She was not wearing her night things, nothing comfortable or loose, and he got the message. She brought a cabbage roll—what next!—a rich, beefy cabbage roll and, as he ate alone (she had not brought one for herself), she said loudly, carelessly, "They came by today unannounced as usual. They searched the office, then cross-examined Dr. Benes. They wanted to know about me. They didn't ask me, just him. Did she live alone? Did she have a lover? Where was her original Jew boss? What did she do with her nights? Had she read one Franz Kafka, or did she listen to Mendelssohn?"

"What did he say?" Istvan asked.

"He said nothing. What could he say? He *knows* nothing. He told them that he really didn't know anything and minded his own business. I'm like that, too. People keep mostly to themselves. They trust no one. The Jews are being transported away from here somewhere— Poland, they're saying, Oswiecim—Auschwitz, they're calling it. The temple on Jozsika is filled with their belongings. That's where your own books are, I suspect, with everything else from your father's house." She looked down. "When Janos asked me this morning if I'd started the Dumas, I simply smiled, and that was the end of it."

Istvan gulped down hard. "Then what?" he asked.

"Then he left it alone."

"No, I meant the visitors, the SS."

"Then nothing. Then the bastards turned and walked out." Marta's voice was agitated. "Europe's gone mad. What happens when the world is mad?"

He took her hand and squeezed it. The hand was limp, lifeless. It did not correspond with her voice.

"Another letter came from your Aunt Klari," she said.

"No wonder they're suspicious. They must be watching everything. Klari must still be hoping we're here somewhere and the letter will find us." Istvan looked across the dark at Marta, measuring her shape with his eyes. "I have to go," he said. "I have to locate Radnoti. He's a Catholic now. He'll get word out to my family. Then these visits will stop."

Istvan could feel Marta glaring back at him in the dark. The two of them were like bats. "Are you mad, Istvan?" she said. "You want to leave this perfect hideout—perfect for all of us—and risk whatever future we may have just to get word out? Your uncle and aunt are smart, and so are your brother and sister, from what I've heard about them. After a while they'll stop writing."

Istvan thought of his family. He was surprised especially that Paul had not managed something. Paul was the capable brother, but it was not so much that Paul *could* do things—Istvan *could* too. It was that Paul *would* when others wouldn't. Istvan didn't know if he'd stand in the storm the way his brother would, but how hard it must be, how absolute the Aryan Eagle's hold, if Paul had not managed to free his only brother.

"We're at greater risk this way," Istvan said to Marta. "And who's *all* of us? Do you mean you, me and Dr. Benes?"

"No, actually." She went silent, then said, "I meant you, me and Smetana."

"Well, Smetana we can risk," he said and chuckled.

She neither responded nor laughed with him. "It's been tough in this dark hole for you," she finally said, "but my freedom is as much a prison as yours, only bigger."

"I'm sorry," he said to Marta, and then she left him without saying good night.

The next evening it turned dark while Istvan read *The Three Musketeers*. He felt his own helplessness battering at his chest as he waited for Marta, his one ear cocked always for Marta, but she did not return home.

Five

PAUL BECK COULD NOT REACH his father or brother in Szeged, nor could he learn anything of what might have befallen them. The news services had gone silent, and Paul could not even find reliable sources, like his friend Zoltan Mak. Where had he got to, all of a sudden? Rozsi seemed as worried about the young man she'd just met as she was about their own family. She called the *Csillag* and asked where Zoli had got to and learned he had not been in for a couple of days.

The authorities couldn't be trusted. They had deprived him of his career and rights and could no longer be depended upon for answers, let alone help. But Paul clung to hope. He thought often of Wallenberg, how confident the man had seemed. He decided to visit the Swedish embassy on the other side of the river in Buda. He took a taxi to Minerva Street on Gellert Hill and asked the driver to wait. He climbed the stairs toward the three gold crowns of Sweden, which graced the arched white entrance.

Above the building on the northeast slope of the hill stood the bronze statue of Saint Gellert flanked by Grecian columns. Paul paused to take a look in the evening light. Gellert had brought Christianity to Hungary from Venice in the eleventh century at the behest of Hungary's King Stephen, but when Stephen died, some Hungarians, who still preferred their pagan gods to the solitary one, stuffed Gellert into a spiked barrel and rolled him down the hill into the Danube.

The embassy was still open, but a couple of secretaries and assistants were leaving just as Paul walked in. He made his way along the pink marble floor toward the receptionist's desk. It was a good minute before the woman looked up at Paul.

"I'd like to see the ambassador, if I may," Paul said in German.

"The ambassador is not here," the woman said. She spoke German, too, but not comfortably. She had dark features and looked more like a Gypsy than a Swede. In fact, Paul looked more like a Swede than she did, with her red curly hair and dark green eyes.

Paul asked in Hungarian, "Is the chargé here, then?" She didn't respond, so he added, "I'm a lawyer. My father is the mayor of Szeged. Is he here, the chargé?"

She nodded yes, but said in an accented Hungarian, "He's busy at the moment. If you take a seat, I'll tell him you're here to see him."

The woman looked familiar to Paul somehow. She reminded him of someone from his youth. The woman went into an inner office but soon returned, and now it seemed she recognized something about Paul, too. She looked too long at him before turning away. He kept staring.

Paul had once met a young Gypsy woman who'd haunted his dreams for years. Ruth, she was called. She'd had the same green eyes. Exactly. When Paul was fourteen and his brother not yet twelve, their uncle Bela, Aunt Etel's husband, whom they were visiting in the big city, one summer evening made off with the boys to a place on Aldas Street out in Rozsadomb. It was a dingy building he took them to, at the end of a narrow lane. Paul asked where they were going, and Bela told him, "Never mind," as he paid the cab driver and then winked at him. Bela pushed the boys in through an unpromising door to a colourful entranceway. There was a girl just inside, not much older than Paul, with stark green eyes, like beads of olive oil on a white dish. She wore a feathery head scarf, a pearl necklace and a revealing black silky top held up by thin straps. She drew on a cigarette, let its smoke stream up through her hair and wreathe the colourful scarf. A small silver crucifix, suspended from the pearls, rode the valley between her breasts.

"Welcome to the Gypsy palace of love, boys." Both boys looked around again, as if they'd missed something. "How many girls this evening, gentlemen?" she asked. The cigarette bobbed on the girl's red lips. She pronounced the Hungarian words too fully, the words lush and robust, like her outfit. She pulled up Istvan's chin with a finger as if she were twice his age.

"Give us just two juicy ones, this evening, my dear," Uncle Bela said. "I'll just have a dancer out here, maybe. My dinner isn't agreeing with me." He patted his stomach. Istvan looked at Paul with frantic twelve-year-old eyes. Paul tried to look cooler, ever the older brother. He patted Istvan on the shoulder. There was no escape.

"And make them as lovely as you've got," Bela said.

"All we got is lovely."

"Lovely like you?" Istvan blurted out, not knowing what he was asking.

Uncle Bela laughed hard, sat down behind the boys, slapped Paul's bottom and lit a cigar, still laughing as he coughed.

"Yes, like me," the girl said, "but I will go with this one," indicating Paul, "the stick with the gorgeous red hair." She stood and ran her fingers through it, tugging. Paul pulled back. "I'll get you Maria," she said to Istvan. "Younger." Then she turned to Paul and took his hand. "I'm Ruth."

Bela laughed again. "Give them whatever they need."

Paul was soon alone with Ruth in a curtainy boudoir, a room from straight out of *One Thousand and One Arabian Nights*. He forced a cool stare as Ruth removed her blouse and red-and-green striped skirt. When she was down to her underwear, with reptilian green frills at the thighs and the sides of her breasts, Paul was breathless. She slithered onto the bed and opened herself up. Paul could see the small, plump divide behind the panties and the creamy abdomen above. He tried to drop to his knees on the bed but missed altogether and ended up on the floor, peering over the mattress. Ruth giggled and turned on her side toward him, awaiting another antic. Paul pulled himself up to a worn armchair by the bed which was so soft, he sank deeply into it such that his knees loomed above his hips, giving him the aspect of a grasshopper, a nice snack for a reptile.

When the girl noticed Paul's arousal, she cackled and caused Paul to wag his knees open and closed as if he had to pee.

Paul tried to laugh with the girl, but the laugh erupted from his throat like a cough. He couldn't think what to say. He told Ruth, "I have some dreams for us, all of us."

"What kinds of dreams?"

"For all of us. For the human race."

She was still on her side, propped on an elbow. "That's strange," she said, clutching at her pearls and crucifix. "Why do you have dreams for me? Just dream for yourself."

"That's not it. That's not what I mean." Paul had been reading Voltaire and Jean Jacques Rousseau and the poet Sandor Petofi, memorizing verses to impress his friends. He was on the verge of reciting a stanza.

But she spoke first. "Oh no, you want to fix me." She sat up abruptly. "You're one of those."

"No, I'm not," he said, and it was true. He did not want to reform her. On the contrary, he wanted her to corrupt him. He didn't want to hold a single thing back, yet he was letting loose in just the wrong way. Paul said, "You are just so right for me, but not just now. You are better than right for me. You make me feel as if I could take us to a place like Byzantium in its golden days."

"Where is that?" she asked. She was looking less amused.

"It's—I'm not—it's not anywhere anymore. It's like Jerusalem. I want to take you to a new Jerusalem, Ruth. I am baring my soul to you, my nakedness speaking to your nakedness."

"I want your *actual* nakedness," she said. She looked at Paul's hair. "You got a thick red bush down there, too, or haven't you begun sprouting yet?' She giggled as she sat up, took Paul's hands and pulled him by her side on the bed. She flung herself back. Paul was terribly aroused now and kissed her deeply. Her lively tongue snaked its way into his mouth. Her waxy red lips greased his mouth and chin. She placed his hand on one of her plump breasts, beneath the loosened brassiere. Her eyes were closed. He separated himself from her. His hand was memorizing her breast for future reference, and he was overcome with excitement and suddenly embarrassed himself—he could feel it. He could feel his hot cheeks, and she felt them, too. He pulled away from her and lay on his back. She hovered over him, sensing what had happened, sparing him by not laughing anymore.

"I can do it. I feel I can," he said.

"What do you feel you can do?" She was serious, not mocking.

"You know."

"What?" she asked.

He didn't know how to say it. "I feel I can stand on my head."

She brightened up considerably and she sat up and clapped her hands. "Show me."

Paul bounded out of bed, shoved the armchair aside and reversed himself, unfurling his frame into a headstand in a single move. He had got a nine out of ten for the procedure in gymnastics, losing a point for excessive reddening of his face.

Ruth laughed again. Then she pointed and her laughing continued. "You're all wet down in front. You've spilled all your long, thin children into your pants."

Paul collapsed and climbed back into the chair, folding up, locking his elbows into his knees and staring into the shadows at his crotch.

Ruth scuttled on the bed toward him. "What is Jerusalem?" she asked softly. The crucifix swung now in the heaving valley of her breasts, bare now, pert and perfect.

"It's where Jesus walked," he said. He was breathless nearly. "It's where he died."

"Why would I want to go there? I like it here." She pulled Paul by the hands onto the bed again and encouraged him to stretch out. She then ran her hand down his abdomen and paused as she kissed him tenderly. She looked into his eyes. "You think. That's what you do. People who are good at thinking think. What else would they do?" She was staring at his red locks now, running her fingers through them. "I don't want to think. I want to be with you just now. Why aren't you wild like your hair?"

"I'm sorry," he said. "I can't tonight. I'm so sorry." He was a little in love with her, would have run off with her through the back door if she'd asked him.

"It's all right." She kissed Paul on the cheek. "I like you." She gripped his hair again and tugged. "I get the feeling that, if I pulled hard, cords of this stuff would come out of that long body of yours. Like you're a bell tower." She laughed a throaty laugh and sat up to get a cigarette. She applied her sultry red lipstick flawlessly without a mirror and hung the cigarette from the fresh paste on her lips. Paul sat up to light it, taking her tarnished silver lighter from her. It was monogrammed "MM."

"I thought your name was Ruth," he said.

"It is. Someone left that here. A gentleman—Miksa somebody—I can't remember. He left it for me, on purpose, I think, to light my cigarettes with and think of him when I do."

Paul felt tears welling up in his eyes.

Ruth saw and ran her fingers through his hair again, gently this time. She blew smoke to the side, away from him. "When I was a little girl, I used to think that the thing that stood out about a person came from something inside." She patted her own white abdomen. "I used to think a big tubby man would have a balloon maker inside of him, waiting to float him away somewhere."

"Like Jerusalem?"

"Like that, maybe. I used to think a very hairy uncle of mine—hair all over his body—big tufts of it—and down his neck—you couldn't even tell where his head ended and his neck started—and it went all the way down his back—I used to think about this Uncle Sebastian that he had a weaver living inside him."

"I must have the same," Paul said, holding onto his own hair now.

She laughed. "Yes, tall boy, you must have that, too, but maybe only up in your head, since you're hairless everywhere else." He was smiling. "And his wife," she went on, "my uncle's wife had purple eyes and purple makeup she spread over her eyelids—I used to believe she had a mulberry bush growing inside."

"And what do you have inside?" Paul asked, poking at her abdomen and gulping. She blushed for the first time and didn't giggle. She stubbed out her cigarette, kissed him warmly on the lips, a moist, tobacco-waxy kiss, and then pulled him to his feet. He helped her on with her gown, and she stood and stared at him for a moment.

Out front afterward, Paul learned that his kid brother had acted like someone about to sire a new race. He had managed every exercise known to the bedroom in just the couple of hours allotted to him. He'd climaxed six times. A second girl had to be brought in to lend a hand. Ruth told their uncle, "Tall boy is on the house. No charge for Jerusalem." Both Istvan and Bela looked at Paul. Had she meant he was so good she'd fallen for him, or had she meant he was a flop? Paul remained mute for a week. His uncle Robert had to be called in to examine his throat and ears.

That was Paul's Big Night. His first and last.

This woman in the Swedish embassy, who tried not to look at Paul, had Ruth's green eyes, but she had Ruth's youth, too, and Paul had met Ruth years before.

"Is the chargé really here?" Paul finally said. His voice bounced off the marble floor and walls.

"Yes, he's here."

"I need to speak to him."

"I told him," the young woman said, but she didn't sound annoyed. She added, "I'll be leaving in a few minutes."

"I won't," Paul said. "Not until I've spoken to someone."

"All right," she said and stood again. "I'll go see."

"Please say it's important."

She wanted to say, "I will," but her Hungarian was not perfect, and instead she said, "I have," then went away again through the white door behind them.

Paul waited far too long this time. He felt under suspicion, disrespected. Was this his new lot? Was he to be among the dispossessed? His blood clanged against his neck. Soon he would have his right to vote revoked, too, and his property confiscated. Here he sat, in a Swedish chair in the heart of Budapest, for no good reason. He was not a lawyer anymore, not a complete Hungarian, not even a man, as Ruth's youthful incarnation reminded him. All that time he'd spent becoming what he'd become, all that strain, that single-mindedness, neglecting even romance to avoid distraction. Many thought him the best in the whole country at casting doubt on evidence, a genius at calling into question what at first seemed self-evident. He could send the first autumn cloud over a summer sun, and then, subtly, the second and third, until the whole courtroom believed the sky was overcast. Truth was grey with intermittent sun, small sudden bursts of it.

What was he now? Was he the outlaw, awaiting his own day in court? And who would defend him, use the hidden dry-ice machine and launch the first cloud? And what would be his defence? That he looked and acted like other humans, looked like a tall man, had curled russet hair like a red-headed man, but shorter hair than a red-headed woman, unless indeed she had shortish hair, had the same green eyes as either, and the same red blood, the slouch of the tall, a similar chuckle (though it is true his squeaked idiosyncratically on occasion), the same frown, but a whiter white—the white of the eye, eyes used to acting in self-defence.

Yes, he was dispossessed. Yet in the dust of this very place, this Sweden on Minerva Street, on Gellert Hill, in Buda and in Pest—in the dust of this place blew the molecules of his forebears. These indiscriminate particles as they commingled were more advanced, more civilized than the integrated whole they'd fallen from. Was there a better defence?

Paul had to challenge someone to act. They wouldn't do so of their own accord. Though he didn't know for sure what he wanted, he wanted *someone* to share his concern. A young girl had stumbled into Budapest after everyone had been taken from her town. Surely, someone could be stirred by such a revelation. It was true Hungary had gone about its business for five long years while much of Europe burned. Germany's Jews had been evacuated; France's; Poland's; Czechoslovakia's; Greece's. It was true Paul was a slow learner. But the steel roulette ball had finally settled in its slot.

He couldn't wait any longer. He stood and turned, adjusted his suit and shirt cuffs. A Swedish guard wearing a white cap and gloves appeared by the door the receptionist had passed through, but Paul merely smiled at him. Elegant as he was and mannerly, Paul hardly looked the part of the assassin, so he simply went on smiling, opened the guarded door gently and stepped in.

The young woman, the receptionist, was nowhere to be seen inside. Was there a back door? Had the man sitting at the imposing cherry-wood desk conspired with her to keep Paul out?

The man stood and offered his hand. "I'm Tomas Holmstrom," he said in German.

Paul shook the man's hand and told him his name before taking a seat opposite him.

"Ah, yes," the man said. "The distinguished lawyer."

"Now a distinguished outlaw," Paul said and smiled. But then he jumped right in before explaining. "I met a man a couple of days ago at Gerbeaud, a Swede, Raoul Wallenberg."

"Oh, yes," Tomas Holmstrom said. "I know him. He stopped by here, too. He comes from a well-to-do Swedish family. He seemed concerned about the government the Germans are about to set up in Budapest, maybe as soon as tomorrow. Wallenberg asked our Mr. Anger quite a few questions."

Paul found himself staring at a formidable letter opener on the desk. It stood like a dagger sheathed in a black onyx pedestal, with an ornate ivory handle carved with writhing jackals and a lion at its crown.

"It's from the Belgian Congo," Holmstrom said. "A gift for the ambassador. On his visit there."

"Nice," Paul said. He rubbed his hands together.

Then the Swede said, "You said you met Raoul Wallenberg in town."

"Yes, I did. Mr. Wallenberg mentioned that your government might be willing to convert Hungarians into Swedes if their lives were in danger."

"What sorts of Hungarians?"

"Jewish ones."

Holmstrom sat back. "I don't know if that will be necessary or possible."

"It will certainly be necessary, but I'm here to ask about your willingness to help. Mr. Wallenberg's idea is ingenious. The Germans obey rules. They'll leave Swedes alone."

"Who knows?" Holmstrom said. "It seems to me more fanciful an idea than ingenious. Who knows if the Germans would fall for such fakery?"

"Yes, who knows? What I'm asking is whether you think it's worth a try."

It occurred to Paul just then that he might walk out of this building empty-handed. He realized how easily he might hate this man across from him. The era of civility in Hungary had come to an end. Paul could convert his fear and anger into strategic disobedience, or he could go underground and become a killer, at least as long as his own life lasted. He found his hands trembling and gripped the arms of the chair.

Paul moved quickly. Holmstrom flinched. Paul reached into his vest pocket and withdrew a small photograph of himself. He'd removed it surgically with a razor from his own Hungarian documents. He handed it to Holmstrom. "I'd like to be your first Swedish convert," he said and took a deep breath.

The two men both looked again at the dagger, and for the first time Paul wondered whether it might be put to use.

"I know you're an accomplished man, Mr. Beck, but I do not have the authority to grant you Swedish citizenship."

"Oh, you have the authority. What I'm asking is, are you willing to do it?"

Holmstrom thought for far too long. He glanced at the dagger, then took a walk around the spacious office, over the silk Persian carpet behind the desk.

"There will be no real Hungarian authority in power soon, as you yourself said, Mr. Holmstrom. If you're here to make yourselves helpful in any way, this way would be marvellous. And the idea came from one of your own prominent citizens."

"I'd have to speak to the ambassador," Holmstrom said.

"My father and brother have gone silent. They may be dead, but they may not. I'm not asking you to rescue them. I'm asking you to give me the means to do so. I'll go to Szeged myself."

"Then you'll be passing battalions of Germans coming this way."

"Yes, but I'll be passing them as a Swede. And I speak their language, as do you."

"We'll be implicated," Holmstrom said. "This embassy will be implicated very quickly."

Paul got to his feet, and Holmstrom paused on his own side of the desk. "If I'm caught," Paul said, "I'll say I stole the papers, which you and I are going to forge tonight. If you don't issue them to me, I'll forge them myself, one way or another. But this way I'm less likely to be caught because the forgery will be more convincing."

"So you're giving me no choice."

"Do I have a choice in what is going on in *my* country, *my* home, *my* office, *my* courtroom?"

"What I'm going to do," Holmstrom said, "is leave the building right now and not return until tomorrow. You do whatever it is you have to do. I'll tell the guard to leave you alone. I've never seen or met you."

Holmstrom's eyes fell on the cabinets to one side, and Paul understood. After he watched the man go, Paul got quickly to work.

When he left, he took extra blank papers and an embosser, marked by Sweden's three crowns.

BY THE TIME Paul got home, he felt like a beggar and a thief. Rozsi was giving a piano lesson when he walked into the parlour, so Paul took a seat and waited until it was over. He heard nothing. He could not have said, on pain of death, whether the young pianist had played Chopin or just scales. The boy of no more than ten then embraced Rozsi.

Rozsi asked if Paul had eaten and told him that Magda had made a nice meatloaf for them, but Paul shook his head. He could see that the table had been set for the two of them, so he sat nevertheless at his place in the dining room and poured some brandy into a snifter.

"I did what you asked me to," Rozsi said. "I called that friend of yours at the paper who knows Zoli, and he said that Zoli was staying with him. He said something terrible has happened, so I took the liberty of inviting Zoli over right away. I hope he comes."

Paul didn't react. He just took a breathy sip of his brandy and set the glass down. He said, "Getting your hair right and smelling delicious won't be the point from here on in. We won't need to create a drama for ourselves. Life will supply plenty for us."

"What are you talking about now?" Rozsi said. "I don't create drama. Oh—" she added, but didn't go on.

He merely looked at her.

"Please don't be cruel," she said. "You can leave that to others now." She looked as if she was getting set to cry and pulled extra hard on a curl.

"You're right," Paul said. "I'm sorry. You're right and I'm wrong." He stood up. His look had softened and she stood to accept his embrace.

Just then, Zoli walked in behind them, startling them. "How did you get in?" Rozsi said. Despite her question, she was relieved to see him.

"I'm so sorry. The back door was open, and I didn't want to be seen at the front. I don't want you implicated. I've been stealing around like a cat lately." Zoli was wearing a North German seaman's cap pulled low over his eyes, but he now removed it.

Rozsi took a fresh snifter from the sideboard. "Why don't you want to be seen?" She poured Zoli some brandy. "And why would we be implicated in anything?"

Zoli accepted the brandy and followed Paul out to the front room. "Please," he said and took the liberty of closing the curtains on the tall bay windows before sitting. Rozsi switched on the lamp beside him, and he looked around the impressive room. He glanced at the old portraits of distinguished Beck forebears. One of them looked out from the picture's deep frame as though he were regarding the room from a casement window.

"What's going on?" Paul asked.

Zoli told them about his parents. Rozsi gasped.

"I'm so sorry," Paul said.

"Yes," Zoli said. He took a swallow of brandy. He tried to speak again but couldn't for a couple of minutes. He got to his feet. He looked as if he were going to excuse himself. Rozsi stood, too, and hugged him lightly, gently. He could smell her hair.

Then he said, "Please, sit down. I'm afraid I have bad news for you, too." He stayed on his feet, set his glass down. "Your father has met the same fate."

"What?" Rozsi said.

"He was hanged in Szeged. By the Germans."

Rozsi began to sob, and Paul took her into his arms. Zoli explained what had happened. "I heard it from my editor at the paper. We're not going to run a story until we have instructions from the authorities."

"The *authorities*," Paul said. He released his sister, who continued crying.

"Yes, the new authorities."

"Oh, my Lord help us," Rozsi said.

"What about our brother?" Paul asked. He'd gone to the window to peek out, to check whether an invasion had begun.

"I contacted a friend of a friend in Szeged, another newspaperman. Your brother appears to have gone into hiding."

"In Szeged?" Rozsi asked, turning to look at Zoli.

"All I know is that he hasn't left the country, but I also know he has not been killed and he has not yet been deported."

"Not *yet*," Paul said, turning on Zoli. "How reliable is your source?"

"He's reliable. It's better that no one knows where your Istvan is. He's safer that way."

Rozsi fell back in her chair. "Oh, Father. Oh, my father, my father. Oh, my dear father." She was sobbing. She waved off her brother, who had moved to comfort her.

"I have to go to Szeged," Paul said. "I have to do something."

"Don't go to Szeged," Zoli said. "What could you do there?"

Paul reached into his jacket pocket and showed Zoli his papers. "I'll go as a Swede," he told him.

Zoli looked at the papers, and Rozsi wiped away tears to look too. There seemed almost no time for grief. Urgency blew it away. Zoli said, "You'll go as a Swede to search for your Hungarian Jewish brother?"

"Please, Paul," Rozsi said. "Let's think things through."

She went to get the brandy and poured out some more for the men. She took a sip of her brother's before passing it over. "Let's go talk to Aunt Klari and Uncle Robert," she said. "We have to work this out together. We have to tell Uncle Robert his brother is dead." She put her hands to her face and sobbed again. "Oh, my God, our father is dead, Paul." She ran to her brother and looked up into his dark face.

Paul said, "I have to go. I can't just stand by."

"And what will you do?" Rozsi asked. "Please, Paul, we've lost our father and possibly our brother. We may be all that's left. It's too much, all of a sudden. Please, we have to stick together."

"I can get Istvan out," Paul said. "I can talk to someone, persuade someone."

"Out to *where?*" she asked. "Are we safe?"

"Forgive me, Paul," Zoli said, "but these are not civilized people and this is not the Cambridge Debating Society you're visiting. Even if you prevail in an argument with someone, they'll shoot you before you finish making your case. My parents were murdered because my father took good pictures and told revealing stories for the newspaper."

"I'm not going with Hungarian papers."

"Oh, please, Paul." Rozsi gripped her brother's shoulders. "Please. It doesn't matter what you are. If you go as a Hungarian, some German will arrest you. If you go as a German even, a crazed Arrow Cross militiaman will assassinate you. It's not good to be anything. What you'll *be* is annoying, and if you're a Swede, you'll be an annoying Swede."

Zoli said, "It doesn't take very much provocation to be eliminated these days. The laws are meaningless."

"But we *have* to be annoying," Paul said. "Don't you think the fun will come here to Budapest, too?"

"I beg you," Rozsi said. "Let's see Uncle Robert and Aunt Klari before we do a thing."

Paul looked down at his feet and then up at the curtained windows. Paul knew that his sister and Zoli were right. His father was dead. If he hunted for his brother, he would be exposing him to great danger, uncovering him when the Nazis couldn't. Istvan was better off hidden, and presumed gone or dead, than on the run and risking capture. "All right," Paul said.

"Promise me," Rozsi said.

"All *right*, I said."

Six

WHEN ROBERT TELEPHONED AHEAD to say he was bringing home a girl to stay for a while, his son, Simon, thought he'd meant a *girl*, not a young woman. He'd got himself ready to play the big brother, the happy host who might take her out to see *Snow White*. When she walked through his door in her newly laundered wedding dress, he couldn't take his eyes off her. She was blond and her eyes were blue as a mood. She was so fair she could pass for an Aryan, but an unsullied one, one who hadn't heard the edicts from on high. And she had a wide warm smile that did not suit the story she came with.

And Lili noticed him, too, even before she took in the surround-ings, saw his black surprised eyes, his black shiny hair. Klari, his mother, said, "Simon, you haven't asked Lili in."

He chuckled and coughed before saying, "I'm so rude. Forgive me."

Lili blushed. She felt like an intruder, felt unworthy of this kindness.

Klari said, "Let me ask Vera to get us coffee." Klari gestured again to Lili to come in. "Look at you, dear," she added. "We'll have to get you a couple of things to wear."

"Please excuse me. I need a few minutes," Robert said, as he pushed through to his study to set his briefcase down.

When he got there, Robert slumped heavily in his chair. The story of the young girl out in the hall whose appendix he'd removed shook him profoundly. A colleague had told Robert that morning that the borders were under siege. How was it possible? He had heard the news from across Europe, of course, but the reality had somehow not visited him any more than it had his country. It was one thing to have his Simon barred from university. Hungarian Jews had experienced such periods of constraint before. There was a time when they couldn't legally hold property. But generally they endured those times and even prospered. Then the girl had come from Tolgy. Before her, Klari's sister Hermina and her husband, Ede, had been taken, kidnapped it seemed, the crime unsolved. One neighbour said she'd seen German soldiers. But how could it be? Hungary was allied with Germany. How could it possibly be? Robert had studied in Berlin, had written a medical textbook in German, which was studied by students in Germany. The copies of the book would make a magnificent bonfire now. They were entering a new age of darkness. The Germans had been the light bearers. The Hungarians had followed them into the light, and now they were following them back into the darkness.

Robert dialed the operator for Szeged. He couldn't get through to his brother Heinrich's office. He dialed Istvan's office. No one was there. How could Heinrich have been so naïve, a Jewish mayor in a country allied with Hitler? They were all surprised by the coming of the Nazis—Robert was surprised—but Robert did not hold political office. Where are you now, my brother? Are you standing guard over the city hall, or better still the temple? You foolish bastard. Are you crossing your arms on the steps in defiance, your public office your shield, your adoring citizens your armour? Let's see how the good citizens of Szeged stand up to the enemy on your behalf. Their approval is love, isn't it, my brother, the populace finally in love with the big Jew, the Lord Mayor, Lord Jew? Let me make it easy for you, invading hordes. Let the Jew mayor make a symbol of himself and stand on the steps of the temple, the beloved mayor, so you can make a public display of humiliating him. Being huge and powerful is not what brings the love, dearest brother. Quite the contrary. Oh, dear brother. It will be hard without you, a thick line of memory ending in this way.

Robert had no need for a cause. He wanted to make people well when they were ill, and he wanted to see them happy again, or at least comfortable. Robert was a maintenance man. He was not interested in the world's creation, except insofar as it required his maintenance work. He was not interested in the world's destruction, either, except insofar as it disrupted his work. He was not a philosopher and didn't aspire to greatness. But sometimes Robert knew—he knew today— that his aims were not enough. In these circumstances, maybe even simple ambitions had to be abandoned, and the exalted called in to defend what was right and restore order and dignity.

And then what? What if there were none left among the exalted? What then? Could the maintenance people step in? Could he, Robert? If he had to, would he?

Oh, my dear Heinrich, my dear brother, abandon your post, and come to us here. Come stand guard over our house, if it makes you happy. Come to where the Jews still roam, for today at least, for the time being. May we enjoy harmony and good cheer together again sometime. Klari and I can still make it all right for you, even if your Mathilde is no longer by your side.

Robert drew the curtains and lay his head in his hands on his desk. He was hoping to dream of his only brother, held his image from an earlier time in front of him. He wanted to find a solution to their plight submerged in an ocean of sleep, but that's not what came. It rained instead, under the surface, rained air, the bars of it drilling into the muck at the bottom—lightning striking like a god with a deep, reedy throat—striking a capsized tram which had drifted to the bottom, smashing its windows, releasing a murder of crows, fifty of them—one hundred—sloshing upward in full flight toward the wobbling stars, until they collided with an invisible wall, each crow dissolving as its beak clanged against the plate— Robert could see it now himself, read names there, inscribed on the transparent wall, in alphabetical order—*K*, he could make out—was it *Klari*?—or the shape of a chromosome—wondered now frantically if he himself could cross, rise past the plate toward the surface, opening his mouth toward the drilling air, lightning striking again—a great bomb of lightning—would it part the waters the way it had parted the Red Sea?

Klari was saying to Lili, "I was sorry to hear about your family, you poor dear. My sister was taken," she added. "Hermina and her husband, Ede, were taken two years ago from their home on Andrassy. Kidnapped." Klari looked ready to cry. "We haven't heard from her since. We have no idea where she got to, or whether they're even alive." And now she was crying. "What's happening to all of us? What's happened to Europe?"

"Europe should be paved over," said Simon abruptly. "It's a failed experiment."

Klari sniffed and said, "Europe produced *Faust* and *Hamlet* and *The Marriage of Figaro*, the Parthenon, *The Merry Widow*, the Sistine Chapel." Lili could tell they'd had this discussion before. Klari took a breath here and wiped her nose and eyes with her handkerchief.

Lili thought of Pompeii, what Vesuvius had done to everything.

"Europe should be turned into a parking lot," Simon said again. "We should start from scratch. We don't get along—or hasn't anyone noticed?"

Lili wanted to say, "How will that help us? My family is somewhere they shouldn't be. I need to find them and get them back home." But she kept her thoughts to herself.

Klari put her arm around the young woman and said it for her. "Let's get this young woman's family out first."

"Of course," he said. "That was insensitive of me. Please forgive me. It is Europa, the old witch, who offends me, that's all."

"But we are European," Lili said. "What good does it do to scorn Europa?"

"It makes us feel better, that's all," Simon said. He felt utterly foolish now. "You, Lili, are definitely a *good* European, whereas I . . . I don't know."

"You are a silly one," Klari said, "a young man trying to show off with his cleverness at an inappropriate time, and failing at that." Simon dropped his hands to his sides. "Oh, look at us here," Klari said. They'd moved toward the living room but were still standing outside. "This unfortunate girl has had surgery, and we haven't even invited her to sit down yet."

Lili turned toward Klari. "How can I be called unfortunate when I am the one who landed here for whatever reason, by whoever's grace?" Lili blushed. She was surprised by her own forwardness.

Klari said, "This girl will put us all to shame before long. I'm so glad Paul found you."

She watched her son trying, in his clumsy way, to impress Lili, saw him gawking at her. She couldn't blame him. It was easy to see how he might be attracted to her warmth and charm.

Was chance any better, Klari sometimes wondered, than planning and deliberation? She and Robert had had an arranged marriage, as had her sister Mathilde and Robert's brother, Heinrich. It was a deliberate bringing together of two families. Their fathers had put the deal together and came home with the news. The young people didn't meet until just before their wedding.

The two couples married in her parents' grand summer house in Kiskunhalas, and her father, Maximillian, and her mother, Juliana, were as happy as they would have been had it all come of a happy accident.

Yet the arrangement was successful, certainly more so than many a match arrived at by lovers. Still, there was something alluring about chance, something romantic, electrifying. It would have been nice to have been attracted to someone by accident, as happened sometimes on a stroll or in a shop or café.

Klari had to learn to love her Robert, but she was successful at it, as was he, she believed—as were Heinrich and his unfortunate

Mathilde. It was simply the order of their lives together that was reversed. As far as she could tell, they grew from friend to darling and were now finding their way back to friend again, while her son and Lili might start out as darlings and end up friends. One thing for sure: she and Robert were very attached, indeed inseparable. She would wish no less for her son.

WHAT FIRST CAUGHT LILI'S EYE in the living room was its centre-piece: a lacquered cream grand piano, like an albino alligator with its great jaws open. Did Simon play? Lili wondered.

Portraits in oils adorned the blushing peach walls. One was clearly of a young Klari sitting calmly the way Mona Lisa must have sat, with the beginning of a smile. How Lili had admired the image of the da Vinci portrait when her father one day brought home the book about the Louvre. In her portrait, Klari seemed serene and confident, sitting darkly in the middle of the bright wall.

"What do you do?" Lili asked Simon. She didn't want to sit in a chair that might have been Dr. or Mrs. Beck's customary place, or even Simon's, so she took a seat on an ottoman.

"You'll never guess." She smiled and shook her head. His voice was quiet now, barely audible. "I'm a tool and die maker," he said. "I was going to go to university like my father and my cousins. I wanted to become a lawyer, like Paul, but they closed the universities to us, so my father hustled me off to get a trade. Being a tool and die maker is not so bad. I might even be useful in the war effort. Who wants to be a lawyer anyway in a place where the laws are meaningless?"

"Yes, who wants to?" Lili squirmed slightly in her chair. She didn't know what to say. She felt stunned, felt pinned to a board. She felt guilty, unnatural, admiring art and talking about university when, not two hours away, whole populations were being snatched and—and what? She felt she'd been transported to another time, felt she was sitting in a pretty room about to be preserved forever by a river of hot lava, right in the middle of her chat with this sweet young man.

For his part, Simon felt he was struggling hopelessly. He'd lost much of his confidence in recent years, was early to believe the world was going down, possibly because it was his generation that had been stopped short, his peers who either had to go to war now, if they were purebred Hungarians, or were barred at the Jewish *Gymnazium* from further advancement. He'd tried to follow in his father's footsteps, had always admired his cousins, particularly Paul, eighteen years his senior—why had Simon's parents waited so long to have children when the difference in age was so crucial? But they couldn't have been blamed—how could they have seen what was coming? What then were all the swimming ribbons for? Why had he memorized Homer in Greek and Ovid and Petofi, and aspired some day to owning a summer home a tenth the size of his grandfather's? Why did meeting a girl mean he would have to take her off somewhere to a cave to avoid a hail of bullets? Or was it better, if they survived—half a millennium of achievement destroyed, the family's money and possessions all gone—to start again from the ground, or *beneath* the ground, even, proving your own mettle, not relying on history, the tall shadows of success to dwarf you? However it came out, Simon's was the generation caught out and bereft. Their lives were defined for them as surely as this lovely Lili's was, and she was even younger and more vulnerable. Was it possible, though, that all of this would be gone? Simon wondered. Could it happen, after all these centuries?

Lili looked at another wall, another striking painting. "It's called *Yard with Trees*," Simon told her. It featured a country house, lush greenery and, mysteriously, two faceless children in the foreground.

"Do you like the picture?" Simon asked, unsure of how to speak to this girl.

"Yes, very much."

"It's by a painter named Sandor Ziffer," he said. "He was a patient of my father's. I remember he came to the clinic one day when I was quite young, saying he'd been experiencing terrible pains in his abdomen. He said he wouldn't be able to pay his bill, but could my father please help him. My father hesitated but then said, 'It depends on how good an artist you are.' Ziffer looked stricken, not the effect my father had wanted—or not for long, at least. 'Of course I'll help,' my father told the man, 'regardless.' I inherited my way with the bad joke from my father, as you can see. Anyway, it turned out the guy had a twisted bowel, and my father was able to take care of it. A week later the man presented my father with this painting."

"It's very gloomy and mysterious," Lili said, "but lovely."

"Do you like this place?" Simon asked.

Lili said, "Oh, yes, I do," and she smiled warmly.

Lili wanted to say something more. She wanted to impress Simon with something. She wanted to tell him she saw wild horses fly off a cliff to their deaths, except for four of them. Four of them that veered off. But who would believe her? What if she was the only person in the world to have seen such a thing? She was not sure, now, that she believed it herself, believed she ever saw it, as she sat in this room with its cream-coloured grand piano.

Why had she been spared? Surely, she must have got away for a reason. If she'd been taken on the march with her family and every-one else in their town, and her appendix had flared up as it had here in Budapest, would someone have helped her, one of the authorities, the invaders, the kidnappers? Or would she have been shot to death with her father as he tried to help—and her mother and siblings as they tried to shield him as he helped. The offending appendix would have put everyone at risk, a Jewish organ standing out in a population of Aryan ones, the dark organ. The Jewish appendix.

She heard a telephone ring. Lili thought it might have come from the hall or maybe the kitchen. She said, "Oh, you have a telephone."

"A telephone?" Simon said. "Didn't you have a telephone?" He asked the question as if to say, "Do you *know* what a telephone is?" And both reddened again.

"Yes, we had a telephone in Tolgy," she said, "but most other people didn't. Our phone number was 4."

"4?"

She nodded.

"Whose number was 1?"

"The mayor's."

"Whose was 2?—Don't tell me—the mayor's brother?"

She smiled again as she sat on the edge of her ottoman. She thought of the phone back home, how it had rung while she was hiding behind the wardrobe. Who had it been? Where had that caller gone?

Simon wondered about this girl's town. His mother's father, Maximillian, was the first to have a telephone in Kiskunhalas, at his summer house. No one understood the point at first, since there was no one to call. Simon pictured the beautiful grounds, the peacocks roaming freely, the swans in the pond. His grandfather had an unforgettable meerschaum pipe. It had a bowl with the face of Poseidon carved into it and was longer than his arm. It had to rest on a stand. His *kulcsar*, or key man, had to come in to light it for him, when he sat in the atrium. When Simon or other grandchildren were around, they got to do the honours. Over the years, Simon watched Poseidon's face darken with the smoke and flame, until he looked like a Moor. He asked the key man how dark the bowl would get, and the key man shrugged his shoulders. "Pretty dark, I think." Simon followed him around sometimes, studying his ring of keys: keys for the outer doors, of course, and the inner ones, too, the bedrooms and main floor rooms, keys for the wine cellar, keys for the gates, keys for the cabinets, keys for the piano, the boxes of silverware, and a small key even for the silver sugar box. The servants were not to steal the sugar cubes. Not even the grandchildren were allowed.

Lili was almost writhing now in the Becks' living room. She was not making the impression she wanted to make on these lovely people who'd taken her in. She felt weak, light-headed. She tried to concentrate on an unusual table beside her.

It was Klari who saved her, arriving followed by Vera, the house-keeper, who was carrying a tray laden with espresso and biscuits. "Do you like it?" Klari asked, indicating the table.

At first Lili thought she meant the Becks' home and nodded as enthusiastically as before. Then she saw Klari was referring to the table. Its top was raspberry-coloured marble, supported by an impressive cast-iron pedestal, built to withstand the ages. "Do you like the painting on the surface?" Klari asked. "It's by Edvard Munch."

Vera set down the tray on a side table. Lili stood to help, but everybody urged her to sit again. She crossed her arms and then sat. She realized that Klari was trying to distract her and reassure her, Simon too. They were all trying to please her, and she them, in the way that only strangers do.

Simon positioned himself on the end of the nearest divan, so he could admire Lili. "Yes," Lili said, "the table is quite lovely. It's—" she wanted to say *alluring* but could think only of the Yiddish word and didn't want to use it. Hungarian Jews who did not live on the border didn't speak Yiddish and in fact frowned on it. It smacked of the lower classes.

The setting in the painting was a dark blue churchyard cemetery at dusk. A crow sat on one of the gravestones, or was it a small imp, or a dark angel? Yet the picture seemed strangely hopeful and uplifting. Lili thought for no good reason of her field of wild horses and the cliff. "I like it very much," she said again.

"Do you know how we acquired it?" Klari asked. Lili watched as Klari reached across to a lamp table, took a silver cigarette case, pulled a cigarette from inside and lit it with a monogrammed silver lighter.

"I can't imagine," Lili responded. "It's so beautiful. Who'd have thought—a painting on a tabletop?" The place was not only rich with art, but the paintings all came with stories.

"You know how it ended up here, don't you, Vera?" Klari asked. Vera nodded. Klari looked at her son. "Simonkam?"

He rolled his eyes. "Of course you do, dear," she said.

"I want to know," Lili said.

Vera gave each person a little cup of espresso and offered lumps of sugar and a biscuit. Klari settled back into a plush peach chair as smoke, thick as silk stockings, streamed upward from her mouth to her nostrils. She said, "My father owned quite a bit of land and had some good buildings here in Budapest, too. But he had one unusual practice. He didn't care for the lovely cafés, like Gundel and Gerbeaud and New York, but preferred the Japan, which was a legendary bohemian hangout. He loved the talk there, the flavour of the place. It was frequented by poets and artists and philosophers. Some French artists passed through there—famous ones now: Claude Monet, Pissarro, a frail Austrian named Egon Schiele, a Spaniard living in Paris, Pablo Picasso, and Edvard Munch, who was a Norwegian, actually. Anyway, at the time many of these artists weren't exactly well off, so one—I think the first was Matisse, if I'm not mistaken—painted his tabletop in payment for his meals. The owner laughed off the matter until a second artist offered to do the same. It soon became a tradition after that. Even if you were able to settle your account, the owner offered a week of free meals in exchange for table art. I myself remember—because I begged my father to take me there just as often as he would and could—seeing a beautiful tabletop done by our own Bela Ivanyi-Grunwald, the Naturalist, a luscious landscape which seemed to beckon like the pastries that often sat on the table's top. When *all* the tabletops were done, guests of the café, unfortunately, did not prize what they themselves had created, and cigarettes would roll off the tray onto the table and burn little ditches into the work, or coffee cups left permanent rings, some of them—some of them deliberately—Picasso *deliberately* set his cup down on the wet surface he had just painted, and the ring remained in the work.

"The place became so legendary that you'd go into the café and ask to sit at the Matisse or the Mondrian, or even wait for it if you had to. And you hoped to meet someone exciting, because anyone who was anyone in the arts or the world of ideas passed through the smoky chamber to sample the café's strudel or chestnut *palacsinta*. My father went for his conversations with poets—arguments, more like. He heard about the state of the world, about the rich *owning* the world and not sharing. These were the first conversations, really, about communism, before the authorities cracked down on such people. My father was of two minds about these matters, because he felt all the liveliness of the world emanated from such rare places as the Japan, but he had done very well himself and enjoyed the good life, as did we all, we children.

"After a time, the famous tabletops could no longer take the abuse without permanent damage, some beyond recognition, so the owner had round plates of glass cut to fit them. And then one day the owner of the Japan died, right on the job, hunched with chest pain right over the top of his Bela Ivanyi-Grunwald. His sons did not want to carry on the legacy of the establishment and sold off the building and its furnishings. When it came to the tables, the sons auctioned them off. My father tried to get several and, of course, did manage to get his favourite, the Munch. He couldn't get any others. Another one he especially wanted was a table with musical bars painted on its top by Maurice Ravel, the French composer. They were notes to his symphonic rendering of Modest Mussorgsky's *Pictures at an Exhibition*. Do you know the piece? It's lovely. Very mighty." Lili shook her head, and Klari said, "Maybe we can listen to it sometime on the phonograph, when we get past this trouble."

Lili took "this trouble" to mean the German invasion, the abductions, the war. She blushed again and put her hands to her cheeks. She felt terribly tired, all of a sudden.

"The table gives me comfort," Klari said wistfully.

"It does?"

"Very much. I love that it said something to my father and that the artist meant something by it. Though they never met, their medium was the table at the Japan Café. And now they're both gone. The artist died just this past January—I saw it on the newsreels at the cinema—and my father died five years ago. Yet here it is, still speaking to us, having a word with everyone it encounters. And some day, when we ourselves have taken flight, it will speak to yet another little gathering over coffee and cakes—your children possibly. It will always bring forward another time—what was precious about it—and what's precious remains."

Klari broke off speaking with her hand on her heart, and when she saw that Lili was crying, she cried too. The women stood up together and hugged.

"Who was on the phone earlier?" Simon asked, but he had to wait through the hug to find out.

"It was your cousin Paul," his mother finally said. "He and Rozsi want to come by. They need to talk to us about something important."

"I wonder what," said Simon.

"I don't know."

"Well, it can't be good news."

Vera came to ask about dinner, and Klari excused herself and followed her back into the kitchen.

Lili said, "I don't want to take up your whole day."

"My whole *day*," Simon said.

"I don't know how long I can stay. It would be too much—"

"What would?" Simon felt he wanted to sit beside her but didn't want to seem too forward. "You're doing us a favour. We'll be helping each other. My parents wouldn't hear of your leaving. Nor would I. Please."

A knock came at the door. Robert emerged from his study, looking groggy and puzzled. "It's Paul and Rozsi," said Simon.

"Thank goodness," his father said. Simon and Lili followed Robert to the front, where Klari, too, had just arrived.

They quickly lost their moment's respite. Even before Robert had managed to close the door behind his nephew and niece, Rozsi burst out with the news about Heinrich. "Oh, Aunt Klari, Uncle Robert, Father's dead."

Klari froze. The blood seemed to drain from her face. Lili thought the older woman would faint. But Robert stepped in to hold her, then her niece, her nephew and her son. The whole family stood this way, in a kind of huddle, swaying slightly.

Simon saw that Lili was standing alone, but it was Klari who broke away from the group. She took Lili by the hand. "Come on," she said, sniffling. The two women immediately set to turning the place into a house of mourning. Rozsi felt she couldn't, felt she needed to stay with her brother and followed the men into the living room and sat on the piano bench. She stared blankly at the piano as the men poured brandy. Rozsi played a single high note.

"No music," Robert snapped. So she closed the lid on the keys.

He'd said no music, but Robert immediately regretted his own edict. He couldn't imagine anything that would have given them more comfort. Why was it they could not have music in the hours after a death? Maybe it was the pleasure they were not to indulge in, the beauty. Unless it was the beauty that most resembled death, the kind of beauty that beckons us, like death, to a place of peace, away from pain and old age and memory. That kind of music might have been all right.

Lili followed Klari into her bedroom, where Klari immediately set to rummaging through her closet. She found a black dress that she held up to the light. It had a silk carnation in the lapel, and Klari pulled it off and threw the flower onto the floor of her ample closet. She then strained to tear the lapel on the left, the one that was to go over her heart. She dug deeper and found another dress and held it up too. "Is this navy or black?" she asked Lili as she took another look at Lili's white dress.

"It's black," Lili said.

"Isn't it charcoal?"

"It's night black."

"Night or late evening?" asked Klari, but she was already tearing at the collar of this dress, too, and she grunted as she did so. "It will be a little big," Klari said, "but it will have to do." She held it up against Lili. She then raised her index finger. "But don't—and I mean *don't ever*—think of this dress as a memorial to your own family. It is for Robert's brother, my brother-in-law, and for him alone. No one else is dead," she said with a rasp.

She took out a shirt for Robert and tore the smallest tear at the collar. "For a brother," she said again.

Lili was putting on the dress. Klari watched and said, "It's very bosomy." Then she hugged the young woman. "Never mind," she whispered. "It will be this once and once alone. May you never grow into this dress." And she spat dryly into the air behind Lili. "To ward off evil spirits," Klari said.

"I know," Lili said. "My mother used to spit a lot. She didn't want us to be too beautiful."

"I see she didn't get her wish," Klari said, cupping Lili's face in her hands. "Lili, please ask Vera if we have any eggs to add to the dinner. They need to be boiled." As Lili turned, Klari added, "And ask her to get out some tea towels to cover the mirrors and a big linen bath towel for the hall mirror."

As Lili was about to go, Klari said, "Shall we sit in low chairs or on the floor?"

Before Lili could answer, Klari said, "Never mind. God will understand about my knees."

The sight of the Becks' kitchen made Lili think she'd stepped into yet another world, like Alice in Wonderland. "Oh," she said, as Vera took a pot from the oven.

"Yes, oh," Vera said. "It's the Alhambra. Mr. and Mrs. visited Granada back in the twenties with that poor Lord Heinrich and his wife, Mathilde, the parents of the two out there. Dr. Robert wanted a taste of the place and kept talking about it, so he called in a Viennese designer, Mr. Albrecht Kuhn," Vera spat out the words, "so he could give him a kitchen like one of the rooms of the Moorish kings of Granada. 'I know I can't have a citadel or a palace,'

Robert told the fellow, 'but let me at least behave like the *Bourgeois Gentilhomme* when the fancy strikes me.' That was exactly what he called it. The Mrs. rehearsed it with me so I could impress my friends." And Vera showed off the French again. "*Le Bourgeois Gentilhomme.*"

Vera turned toward her casserole. "I have to tell you," she said, "people didn't go in much for design back then."

"Do they now?" Lili wanted to know.

"Not much even now. So Mr. Kuhn and Dr. Robert were happy to lead the way." Vera showed off the room's features with sweeping hand gestures, like a magician. "They got this mosaic floor with the medallion pattern." Vera closed her eyes. "It is warmed by the memory of the Hall of the Two Sisters, Dr. Robert kept saying. And out that back window looking onto the courtyard you could easily expect to see the Fountain of the Lions, though that might have been going too far. The fellow made the cabinets out of a lacquered white walnut—I've never seen anyone do that to good walnut. They were made to look like Moorish entranceways with crystal windows cut out with the arches at the corners and the horseshoe arches like the Alhambra's southern and western walls."

"It sounds as if you've been there yourself," Lili said.

Vera poked Lili in the chest. "Well, that's because I did what you did when I first saw the finished result. Only I squealed. I said, 'Look, I'm standing in an Eastern palace. Which of my girlfriends gets to go to exotic places like me? Look, I'm standing in a great room of a palace!'

"The Dr. and Mrs. Robert felt embarrassed. 'It's really just a kitchen,' Dr. Robert said to me.

"'Ha!' I said. 'It's more than a kitchen now. But you brought it here to me. I get to work in the Alhambra all day long.'" Vera stood too closely to Lili, as if they were conspiring. She was speaking of the room as if it were her own.

"And do you know what they did for me, the Mr. and Mrs.?" Lili shook her head. "The next Christmas, the Christmas of 1929,

Dr. Robert and Mrs. Klari presented me with two return train tickets to Granada, *and* vouchers for a week's stay in a beautiful hotel. So I got to go to Spain with my mother, the first time out of the country for both of us."

And now Lili was impressed. She appreciated the distraction. The room was exotic, to be sure, but not overbearing. It was cheerful and inviting. But Lili was not entirely comfortable in this big and generous place. She didn't feel right having this conversation. She felt guilty marvelling at the kitchen, just as she had felt a pang of guilt admiring the family portraits and the tabletop by Edvard Munch while her family was bound for . . . what? Not Spain. Not Granada.

Lili said, "We need some eggs boiled and we need some cloths to cover the mirrors."

"Ah, yes, I remember. Like when Mrs. Mathilde went." She sighed.

They heard someone coming toward the kitchen. "Well," Vera said, "you're safe here in the Alhambra, young miss."

"*Safe?*" Klari said as she joined them.

"Yes, ma'am. You're safe with me, safe in the city. It's too big a place. We're all mixed up here. *I'm* not Jewish."

Klari said, "Safe with you?" She collapsed blackly into a kitchen chair. It hit her again—the full impact of what was happening: the abduction of Hermina and Ede—the murder of Heinrich—and what about Istvan?—where was he?—did anyone know?—had he been murdered?—and even the family of this girl who had come to stay with them in her wedding dress—what had happened to them? Klari's grief was oceanic.

Simon arrived in the kitchen to get Lili and his mother. "Come, ladies, sit with us. Rozsi doesn't look too good." He read the despair on his mother's face, so he crouched down to repeat the request, gently.

She looked at her son and caressed his cheek. "Yes, I'll come. Come, Lili."

Vera said, "I'm sorry, ma'am. I meant no offence."

Klari stood. "No, of course you didn't."

When her father died, it was as if the whole country mourned. The casket, loaded into a plain carriage, utterly without ornament, was drawn by white Arabian horses as Klari's mother, Juliana, walked in front like a dowager queen. Her five daughters and five sons-in-law walked behind her, trailed by her eight grandchildren. The carriage was followed by Regent Horthy himself and members of the cabinet, and a thousand of Maximillian's workers marched behind. Most stopped at the gates of Budapest's Orthodox cemetery. It was not like the Kerepesi Cemetery, with its monuments and sculptures, nor like the grand synagogue on Dohany Street. Modesty and simplicity ruled here. How unlike every other thing in Maximillian's life.

Lili and Simon escorted Klari into the living room, where the conversation was taking a turn.

Paul said, "What are we going to do?"

"Do?" Robert asked.

"Yes, *do*. We can't stand by."

"So far Great Britain, France, Russia and the United States have not been able to vanquish Hitler, but *we* will?"

"Please, Robertkam," Klari said before sitting.

Paul stood to approach his uncle. "You can't fight them, of course not: you have to undermine them instead."

Robert stood up, too, and brushed an imaginary crumb from his shirt. "You're just like your father," he said. "Heinrich didn't need to be strung up. What a waste—what a goddamn waste." He pointed a finger at Paul. "You're just like him. You always were—somehow bigger than events—needing to get in the way of them."

Simon blushed. He took a seat on an ottoman beside Lili.

"Please, Uncle Robert," Rozsi said. "Let's not."

"*Trust* me," Paul said. He gave his uncle a wintry look. "If you need to, you can criticize my actions, but let me act first." Paul didn't want to argue. He knew that if he wanted to win an argument, he would win. That was what he did for a living: win arguments. But his uncle glared at him as if he were staring down his own brother.

Klari said, "To think we were planning to have a concert here tonight. That was how the day started."

"A *concert?*" Lili asked.

Simon blushed again. He whispered, "Mother plays piano, and Tibor Novak, the violinist, was going to come over tonight to play a duet with her, but once Father called to say he was bringing you home, Mother cancelled the concert. She didn't think it would suit the occasion."

Klari didn't want to add to what her son had said. She looked at the piano, with its gaping mouth. Rozsi still sat on its bench.

Lili reached over to take Klari's hand, but they didn't speak. Klari looked into the young woman's sapphire eyes. Lili was old before her time.

And even when they moved to the dining room, the feelings that had been building did not abate, but little more was said. They ate dinner quietly, as if it were a last supper. They looked solemnly at the burning candles as they ate their sweet dumplings covered with walnuts and plum preserve.

Paul, in particular, held himself back. He wondered whether he would have stood in front of Mendelssohn's statue, as his uncle had implied. He might have stood in front of Mendelssohn himself, but not his likeness. Defending symbols didn't pay. The country was full of fallen statues, prized by one horde, despised by the next. And even when symbols were resurrected, they would fall again. And so it went.

Paul didn't want the role of protector or saint. Saints were bores. Luckily, there were no Jewish saints, and if Jews were ever to get into the beatification business, they would have to make saints of the non-Jews who stepped in to help. It was hardly heroic to defend your own kind. Seeing over the heads of your own tribe was the mark of a saint.

Paul said finally that he wanted to take the young people out "on a matter of business."

"What do you mean?" Robert said.

Klari said, "It's too risky."

"No, I know where to go. I need to get everyone's picture taken, starting with Simon, Lili and Rozsi, and then I'd like to take you, Aunt Klari and Uncle Robert, tomorrow night."

Robert said, "This young girl has just had surgery. It's just not safe."

"It's not safe even if she hasn't had surgery," his wife put in.

"I need to make them safe. I have a photographer friend, and we have some papers to turn us into Swedes."

"Zoli?" Rozsi asked excitedly.

"Yes, Zoli. We have a meeting planned at a photography studio. We need to get this paperwork done before it's too late."

PAUL TOOK THE YOUNG PEOPLE by taxi to the Danube, just by the Chain Bridge, where Zoli was to meet them. A breeze blew off the river, and Simon took his cousin Rozsi under one arm and Lili under the other to warm them. The lights were strung out along the bridge like a necklace. Paul was on the lookout for Zoli. He said, "We're early, quite early. And Zoli might have been delayed. He had something he needed to do first, some arrangements he had to make."

Another gust brought with it a spray off the river. Then it began to drizzle. There was a boathouse just a few steps away, and they headed toward it. Lili looked back at the bridge, at the wet light. Simon said he knew the boathouse's owner. "His name is Erno Halasz. He lets me take the boat out whenever I want. Father treated his wife for an abdominal complaint of some kind. Let's go in there for a bit. It'll be warmer."

When they stepped in, a boy sprang out at them like a startled cat.

"What are you doing here?" the boy shouted. Even in the dim light, the visitors could see the whites of the boy's eyes. He was no older than thirteen or fourteen and looked half-crazed, his hair matted down, the cuffs of his shirt frayed, the sole of one shoe separating from the upper so that it looked like a gaping mouth. Simon thought of Charlie Chaplin. Lili remembered the blind Gypsy girl and her trio. She remembered her saying, "Music makes you stupid." This boy was dark, like the men.

"We're the owner's friends," Simon said. "Mr. Halasz, the man who hires out his boat from here, do you know him?"

Rozsi said, "Let's leave. Zoli will miss us if we're hidden in here."

Paul said, "It's all right. He'll figure out that we came in from the rain. It's the only shelter close to the bridge."

The boy stepped back further into the darkness of the boathouse. Simon wanted to follow, but Lili held him back. Rozsi didn't want to touch anything or lean on anything. She kept checking her hands and rubbing them together, until Paul called her Lady Macbeth.

They listened to the little slapping sounds of the boat bobbing on the water. "I know the owner, too," the boy said. "He lets me stay on the *Petofi* all the time."

"What's that?" asked Lili.

The boy lit a match, illuminating the brass letters on the bow of a boat. "The *Petofi*," he repeated. The boat was named after the great Romantic poet, Sandor Petofi, one of the leaders of the Hungarian Revolution of 1848 against Habsburg rule. The name sent Paul back to the days when Istvan and he and the poet Miklos Radnoti, Istvan's friend, used to debate the merits of Petofi's work. Radnoti was a modernist down to the Bloomsday cards he sent to friends—he must have been the first Hungarian to have read *Ulysses*—but he admitted that Petofi had "qualities."

"Oh, he had qualities," Paul said. "He was the country's greatest asset, and he acted on his principles." They were having coffee at The Rose in Szeged. "'You cannot forbid the flower,' Petofi told his countrymen. 'Let's fight to the death for freedom.' And death took him quickly," Paul added dramatically. "He was only twenty-six years old."

Radnoti said, "He was about as good a poet as he was a soldier."

"He inspired the nation," Paul said, pounding his fist on the table, rattling the dishes. "He led the country to freedom."

"That explains it," Istvan said.

"It is true, he may not have succeeded, but he tried his best. It was the example he set that counted. Not everyone has done well here, but you two have it very bad," Paul said. "Don't forget to finish your chestnut purée, boys," and he huffed off.

For a moment in the boathouse, while the match was lit, the intruders glimpsed a cloth bag on the floor of the boat. A grey shirt-sleeve hung out of the bag's opening, and beside the bag lay a violin.

"Did you come to live on the boat, too?" asked the boy.

"What?" Rozsi said.

"No, of course not," Simon said too sharply. He glanced at Lili and his voice softened. "We've just come in out of the rain."

"Why don't you sit down, then?" the boy said. He ran to get a burlap sack and laid it out on the wooden floor for Lili. It didn't look clean enough, so Simon threw it back to the boy and spread his jacket down in its place. Again he looked at Lili to see if he'd done the right thing.

Paul was about to do the same for his sister, but she said no, she was all right. Paul wanted to keep his sister company, so he stayed standing, too. Leaning his back against the wall, the boy slid down to the floor. Simon joined Lili and the boy on the floor, but made it down only as far as his knees. Paul was as tall as a tree, his head lost in the shadows of the ceiling, beside the figures seated on the floor. They could hear the pattering of the rain on the roof.

A moment later, another match burst out of the darkness as the boy lit a cigarette and offered the pack to his guests.

Paul shook his head. Rozsi said, "I have my own, thank you."

Simon looked at Lili and then took one. His face glowed amber as he drew in the first puff. Simon coughed and said it had gone down the wrong way. He took another drag and coughed again.

"What's your name?" Lili asked.

"Zindelo."

"You mean Zindel?" Lili asked. "It's Jewish. Zindel. 'Son,' it means."

"Zindelo is what my mother called me."

Lili asked, "Where is she, and your father?"

"I don't know." He took a long, crackling puff of his cigarette. "I haven't seen them for a couple of years. I play violin in the squares. That's how I get by." The boy said this cheerfully, and he smiled. "It's the only thing I got from my mother: music—oh, and begging, two things—oh, and my name, Zindelo. Son. Big deal." And the boy laughed a big, throaty laugh, like someone older.

"Your name's all right," Lili told him. "I like it."

"Well, I guess it's better than 'daughter' or 'monkey.'" Zindelo let out another smoky laugh. The boat bobbed and slapped at the water. Simon threw his cigarette into the dark water and listened to it sizzle.

Paul was impressed by the boy's charm. Clearly, charm was not restricted to the upper classes, not to the Hungarians nor the Jews, any more than any quality, any more than birth or death. It dawned on Paul, standing with his arms crossed in this dark little shelter with the rain sounding on the roof, with his uncomfortable sister by his side, this young couple already in love in a single evening and this charming Gypsy boy, that they might not make it out alive. It was not a profound truth, nor a brilliant observation, but it struck with the force of original thought. Paul remembered the day with Istvan out on Lake Balaton, an August day at their grandfather's house. Istvan went under the water and didn't come back up. Little Rozsi screamed from the strand that she could see only Paul's head out there—"It's just *your* head," she screamed again. Paul put his hand on the back of his wet head as if to confirm what she'd said. A cold calm flowed down through his veins just then, Paul recalled, and he dipped under the surface the way a loon does, saw nothing all the way to the bottom, his eyes blazing open and scouring the rocks, greenery and sand. Then up again for a draft of air and down for even longer, until he felt a searing cramp on his left side, like a stroke. It coursed down his long, thin frame from shoulder to ankle, and it was in that very moment that he learned he would not live forever. He could see himself being lowered into a narrow bed in the earth, could see the end of things, the utter absence of things, the cool earth neutral against his numb skin. He knew in that airless moment that it would happen in a finite number of days, not infinite—finite. When Paul came up for air again, Istvan was screaming with Rozsi, both of them on the shore, and their father, grandfather and grandmother were pushing their way toward him like motorized swimmers. Death comes to all of us equally, whether we are cooked in oil or boiled in mother's milk—death, the democrat—dimming all the animal sounds in this little hut, quieting this small, new alliance.

How vulnerable Paul felt after a single day of bad news. How much more could they endure—*all* of their family, *all* of their friends, *all* of them going down—or *up*, swinging from a lamppost like his father, a short clownish leap toward heaven, leaping after his wife, their mother, the day you feel your neck go numb, the day the cops and robbers are true, the day the bullet is true, the day the bullet breaks your *true* skin—you—the clipped advocate, ready to stand in the path of crazed hordes, knowing they need to devour you for their fuel, and for the first time you feel just a little afraid.

"My mother could read the stars," Zindelo said. He pointed to the ceiling. "The stars spoke directly to her, like a telegraph."

Lili was smiling. Zindelo said, "Do you know what my mother said?" Lili and Simon shook their heads. "Our sun is someone else's star to wish on, someone living in another galaxy."

"And someone who is not yet born," Simon said. "I mean the sun may have extinguished itself by the time the light reaches someone else far away. It takes that long for the light to travel."

They were looking at him intently, and Simon shrank into himself, not meaning to be giving a lesson. "I didn't know that," Lili said. "It's very interesting."

Rozsi said, "Why don't I go check for Zoli?"

"I'll go," Paul said.

"But I want to go," she said, already at the door.

"I have some *kolbasz*," Zindelo said. "Do you people want some *kolbasz*?" He was pointing somewhere at the boat. Lili and Simon shook their heads. "It's nice and spicy. Horse."

"*Horse?*" Simon asked.

"No, thank you," Lili said. "We just ate."

Rozsi felt a twinge of sympathy. "No, thank you, Zindelo." And she went out.

"Do you people beg?" the boy asked, then broke out laughing again in answer to his own question. "Are you related?"

Simon looked at Lili. She was blushing. "You two don't look alike," Zindelo said. "I was just asking."

Zindelo's dark eyes saddened in the dim glow of the single light bulb hanging down from above their heads. He looked like a miniature man rather than a boy.

"Why don't you play something on your violin?" Simon asked. "I'll pay you." He reached into his pocket for some coins.

"I don't want you to pay me," the boy said solemnly. "You're my guests here."

Lili said, "We can't have violin music today. Your uncle just passed away."

"Of course we can," Paul said. "These are not regular times."

His sister came back in just then with Zoli. He looked wet and slightly alarmed, though he didn't say why.

"We're having some music," Paul said.

"Oh," Rozsi said. She took Zoli's hand. "That's all right." Now she looked at the floor to check its suitability for sitting, and Zoli made the decision easy by spreading out his jacket. He had his camera with him, wrapped in a linen cloth.

Zindelo fetched his violin, the floorboards creaking where he stepped. As he came back, he held the instrument up to his ear and plucked the strings. "Would you have some kind of cloth with you by any chance?" Zindelo asked.

Simon reached into his pocket and pulled out a white handkerchief.

Zindelo seemed to be examining the handkerchief. "It's clean," Simon said, rolling his eyes.

"I wasn't looking at that. I was looking at the letters." The handkerchief was monogrammed. "These are nice letters," Zindelo said.

The visitors realized the boy couldn't read. "Yes, 'SB,'" Simon said.

"Oh, 'SB.' Fancy." He rubbed the handkerchief against his cheek and smelled it. Then he wiped the violin as if it were a small child's body, folded the handkerchief and placed it on his shoulder against his neck. He set the violin under his chin and, like a sigh, drew the bow along the strings, the instrument humming dolefully in response.

Zindelo played "Brahms's Lullaby" and then, his face brightening, his own rendition of "The Blue Danube"—"My own lullaby," he said, laughing over the melody. He started with a single sustained note to draw in his audience, the note clear as sunlight beaming through the string. "The Danube rocks me to sleep like a mother," he said.

He played for what seemed like an hour—Haydn, Sarasate, Irving Berlin—melodies Paul and the two couples recognized right away, songs the people would call out for in the squares around the city, tunes anyone could hum, helped along by the jingling of coins tossed into Zindelo's upturned hat. The greatest miracle was that he could pull such sad old sounds out of the instrument with a child's fingers. The boathouse was transformed into a dance hall and then concert hall and then saloon with the notes the young Gypsy drew out of his instrument. So the visitors had their concert after all. Simon took Lili's hand and looked at his cousin Rozsi with Zoli. Lili squeezed his hand back. A warm current ran through him.

Zindelo finished with the famous waltz from *The Merry Widow*, and Simon whispered to Lili that it was his mother Klari's favourite tune. "She hums it all the time but never plays it on the piano, for some reason."

Lili shrugged and smiled. She tried to think what her mother's favourite song was. There was a Czech song she sang to them—Helen's own mother, Lili's grandmother, was from Prague. It was about chocolate and cherries. And there was a Yiddish song that got her up on her feet, dancing and clapping, "*Chiribim, Chiribom,*" about the rabbi who finally took a wife.

When Zindelo was finished, Simon insisted on giving the boy the coins he'd originally offered, but Zindelo held up his hand. "Please," he said, "not this time," and he bowed.

"Take half," said Simon.

Zindelo looked him in the eye and accepted the smaller fee. Simon bowed, too, as he backed out.

Paul was the last to leave. He told Zindelo, "You should go. You won't be safe here."

Zindelo said, "I'm never safe anywhere. I'm used to it."

"You might have more trouble than usual. Come see me. I have an office. I can get papers for you."

Zindelo held up his hand. "Come see me in the square," he said, "and I'll play something for you."

Paul tipped his hat and he bowed, too. He watched the boy as he climbed into the boat to retire his violin. When Zindelo had his back turned, Paul took a gold coin from his vest pocket and placed it on the wooden floor by the door before slipping out.

Seven

ISTVAN'S BODY had begun to turn on him. He was sure he had developed a bladder infection, because he had crawled to his pail in the corner to urinate a dozen times in a single morning, only to find the passage too tight and painful to emit anything but a few drops. He wished he could tell whether the drops were tinged with blood, but he would have to drag his bucket out of the corner into the dim bars of light, and he could not bear to keep company with his toilet. That same night, his left eye developed an uncontrollable twitch, which spread eventually to the other eye. Then in the darkness, both sockets became sphincters, straining to eject their occupants. He was not without knowledge in medical matters, and when his straining detonated blinding flashes of pain in his skull, Istvan speculated about an aneurysm and awaited the call to judgment.

Where had Marta got to? Had she decided to make off with Dr. Cuckoo? Was the good doctor not infinitely preferable, after all, to Istvan? Was the sanctimonious doling out to Marta of the food he earned in place of wages not a ploy to make her smile while he spread her legs? What better game could there be, in the middle of this madness? Was there such a thing as morality left? Why should there be? Did Dr. Cuckoo know about Istvan? How could he blame the poor sod even if he did? Did it not make the game all the more wickedly delicious? What more successful devil was there than the one dressed as an angel?

But what about Marta? What about his raven-woman? Would she have abandoned him without at least leaving him provisions to prolong his foolish hope for a few days, stoke up his insanity? Never mind him, what about the silly cat? Clawing overhead, clawing at the floorboards, whining, scratching. Adorable little vampire. Who would devour whom in the coming days and sip dispassionately on the tepid blood?

Istvan thought frequently about Miklos Radnoti. He'd often sifted through his friend's verse as he sat waiting for the world to settle down.

You see, now fear often fingers your heart,
and at times the world seems only distant news;
the old trees guard your childhood for you,
the memories turning ever more ancient.

Do the trees still stand guard over our childhood, my Miklos, my dear poet, or have they been deported too, their lush branches stripped and piled in the temple on Jozsika Street? And where are you, poor soul, poor songbird? Did you find cover for yourself?

Poor Rozsi, poor Paul. What fate awaited them? Was Istvan not better off in his den than they were? But surely they saw the writing on the wall—on the *sky*—if they cared to look. It was worse to believe yourself safe, as did his Budapest kin. Poor Aunt Klari, still thinking about him, her nephew Istvan, and not herself. Dark days lie ahead, dear sister of my mother. Get yourself to higher ground.

Morning came. Blessed morning. And it was quiet overhead but bright. No oil left for his lamp. Istvan could at least light the candle. He would treat himself to a little light, a small repast for his eyes. Should he read in the light, visit another country with the musketeers? Spend the light on reading rather than seeing? Was there a single particle of dust he'd not turned over and studied? What was there new to see? Where was Smetana? No hungry scampering above. No hungry floorboards. Was it over for Smetana?

Istvan thought he heard someone tapping at the door. He held his breath. In the darkness, all his senses rushed to his ears and huddled there. Nothing. Then, *bang! bang!* Now he heard the cat move after all. Could the visitor hear the cat? *Bang!* Possibly not. This tight, thick little cabin had withstood the centuries. Who was calling? Surely someone friendly. The first taps said it all. Istvan sat still as a portrait.

The knocking stopped, but the hammering in Istvan's chest persisted. The cat was silent again. The world was silent. Istvan could hear the velvet thud in his ears. Where had the caller gone?

The house waited. Istvan felt ready to expire. He *wanted* to expire, take a couple of days off from—what? He felt the first shiver of death course through him. Oh, God, if people weren't faced with death, what would become of their faith? But You knew that all along—didn't You—You Clever Little Omniscient? Otherwise, why would You have planted the Tree in the Garden? It was all part of the Grand Design. Fall and we shall Love You. Fall and we shall Worship You. Fall and we shall bring Burnt Offerings. What's a Little Creation Party without Burnt Offerings? They were too easy for You, weren't they, All-Knowing One? No sport in that. All part of the Plan. The honeymoon with Your creatures was over. They'd become dull. The Creation was a Bore. A Grand Bore, albeit—Spectacular in Spots—Thunder and Lightning, the Thunder and Lightning Polka—but it was Nothing beside the Floods, the Vermin, the Seas Opening, the Angel of Death passing through. Ah, the Angel of Death. Then what? Someone in a Whale. Someone on a Ladder. Someone in a Lion's Den. Something in Leopard. Something in Herringbone. And then: Oh, my God. The Pièce de Résistance: The Crucifixion. How Delicious. Let's hear it for The Father, The Son and The Holy Ghost. The Crucifixion. The Resurrection. The Salvation for All. Does It get any better than That? Oh, yes, oh, yes, the Honeymoon is over. And now we have the Marriage. Succulent Fruit. Fruit Verboten.

Oh, Forget Forgiving Them, Dear Lord God, Creator of the Universe. *Baruch Ata Adonai*. Forgive *Me*, Please, Dear Lord. You know Me. I have arguments with Myself and almost always Lose.

I have waited for you, oh, Paul, oh, my brother. Where have you got to? Have you no armies to send to me from Budapest? Can you not sway the courts to pass new laws, make outlaws of the invaders, not the invaded? Oh, what a coward am I—what a rogue and peasant slave. *I* have forsaken my Father, my brother, my sister, my mother's grave. Oh, my father's grave. Did anyone think to give you a proper burial after they let you down from the lamppost, you dear foolish man, standing up for—what? For the triumph of German education and culture, for Mendelssohn, for music, for sweetness and light, for reason, for sanity? Did they at least give you a place to lie, out of the way of traffic and buzzards, where peace resides, and civility?

How I loved my brother and my sister—worshipped Paul—who else could defend the most powerful Jew, the most powerful Manfred Weiss, against the powerful Hungarians who wanted to share his lands and wealth, wanted a small piece of the Big Jew's dominion, and Paul defended him and won against the state, as only Paul could, and then Paul persuaded Monsieur Weiss, as only Paul could, to hand over some of what they were asking for. Weiss's Hero, the People's Hero, Our Hero, Our Paul. Even he could not unclench this cellar and liberate his lowly dental brother, shrinking each day, dissolving into a Jew.

Is it a symptom of the disease that we transfer our shortcomings to remote bystanders, hold them responsible for what ails us, find a locus outside of ourselves for our demons, fail to recognize that it's neither their shortcomings nor ours that have altered grand social and economic forces which have darkened this century—any more than it's their short-comings or ours that fan a typhoon or crack the earth? It's not personal, in short, not individual, not idiosyncratic to groups, not racial.

To whom does the land belong? To whom does Hungary belong? To the invading Tartars or Huns or Magyars or Turks? After World War I, it was sliced up at all its borders and the slices handed to its neighbours, Czechoslovakia, Ukraine, Romania, a good portion of it, and now our friend and ally Hitler has given the lands back in a gesture of magnanimity, before himself finally drawing Germany's borders around the continent and around the planet and, God willing, around the solar system and the universe.

Imagine that moment—imagine the first glimmer of its possibility. Imagine the moment when the light of possibility gurgles out of the darkness of your nightmare, like the moment just before you hear your own neck snap and, while you can no longer breathe in air, you breathe in calm, your ears buzzing, your eyes bubbling over with remembered sight. You still feel your fears, faintly, but can spy the light burning through them. Yes, France can be yours, *and* Italy, *and* Poland, *and* Czechoslovakia, *and* Hungary, and, yes, your tormentors will be defanged, your hook-nosed Jews who deny you your genius, your beggar Gypsies who beckon at your hoary door, your Homo-Ss— can it be, Adolf, that you once desired a protrusion, not a recess, a rump, not a front, a m—, not a w—? Imagine. A moment as powerful as the splitting of the atom. A moment in which all other selves fuel the conflagration of the single self, the Only Self.

And your tormentors will be stilled forever, the nightmares washed over with celestial light—oh, come to me, Jesus, come, Sweet Jew Jesus, and throw your good dry kindling onto the pyre, with you still nailed to it. Fan the flame with your heavenly Jew wind to confound hell and outwit Lucifer. You are our King now, the Jewblood boiling out of your nail holes into the flame, the blue Aryan rain soothing, feeding the rivulets of your resurrection.

SUDDENLY SOMETHING SLAMMED above Istvan. The cat cawed like a crow. And it began. A record. The cat had set off the gramophone! The last record Istvan had asked Marta to play. Still on the turntable. Friedrich Flotow's *Martha*, of course. Why not drama to accompany death? The opera was in English as befitted the words of Thomas Moore. Lady Harriet Durham singing "The Last Rose of Summer" from Act II. Now here was the voice, sweet as heaven, sweet as Mother. He wished he could know all the English, strained to recall the Hungarian lyrics. But the music was enough. The music told him what he needed to know.

'Tis the last rose of summer, left blooming alone;
All her lovely companions are faded and gone;
No flow'r of her kindred, no rosebud is nigh,
To reflect back her blushes, to give sigh for sigh.

I'll not leave thee, thou lone one, to pine on the stem;
Since the lovely are sleeping, go sleep thou with them.
Thus kindly I scatter thy leaves o'er the bed,
Where thy mates of the garden lie scentless and dead.

So soon may I follow, when friendships decay,
And from love's shining circle the gems drop away!
When true hearts lie wither'd, and fond ones are flown,
Oh! who would inhabit this bleak world alone?

Now he knew—even a sleeping bird has a song waiting within its breast. Istvan reached through the floorboards for the beautiful voice, reached for the verse, and sobbed. It was the first time. It came now from the great gulch within him, wrenching him. The tight little house shuddered from roof to root. Act II whirled on at seventy-eight rotations per minute, but Istvan could no longer grasp it nor even hear it. Where was his lovely Marta? What bleak world would he re-enter—*could* he re-enter—alone? Was she dead now and gone forever? Had they tortured her, then killed her? Had she suffered long? For what? For *him*—for Istvan? Oh, misguided, misspent beauty—how could he have allowed it—his raven rosebud dashed by this German summer? Oh, please do not suffer—lie sleeping—lie dead.

Istvan rose in his dark cellar. He boldly mounted the creaky ladder for the first time in two months, slapped open the boards above and emerged into the afternoon house. The scrawny cat's paw was still jammed in the controls of the gramophone. Istvan approached calmly, switched off the power and liberated Smetana, who looked meekly up at his champion and emitted a vowel. The cat rubbed itself against his hand. Istvan stroked the bony creature and glanced up above the console to behold himself in the mirror, withered as the cat, his cheekbones pushing their way through the skin, his shirt dingy, grey and rumpled, its glorious old white ghost fled.

The sky grumbled with rain, which pattered now on the sturdy roof. Istvan stepped intrepidly to the window and looked out onto the day—the sky's laundry line hung out with grey. And right by his hand on the kitchen's wooden counter was the tin of sardines.

His hands trembled as he found the opener and summoned his strength to cut the tin's silver lid. The cat dropped down to the floor and whirled around Istvan's ankles like a furry snake. The cat choreographed Istvan's life now, whatever life remained in his spindly bones. Istvan's days danced around him where he stood. Let all the linens and cakes and goblets, let all the newspapers and arguments, let the surf of the fields and lakeland pontoons of his youth rejoice and dance around this tin! No silver was ever so dear as the supple, silver-coated flesh of these four small fish in their silver coffin. *Baruch Ata Adonai.*

Into Smetana's grey, polished dish on the floor, Istvan placed two of the fish, slid to the floor beside the cat and ate his share, morsel by morsel.

Eight

PAUL LAY AWAKE all night. What had bored into his mind like a worm was the fact that he didn't know where his father was buried, that a green place had been waiting for Heinrich beside Mathilde and that now there would be no locus for their grief, his and Rozsi's and Istvan's, if his brother made it, if any of them made it, no place to stand and remember a family together. Was the good mayor left to hang until the buzzards got to him, a pocked and dangling warning to the citizens of Szeged? Was he carted away with the rest of the breed on wagons, a pile of one-time Hungarians with which to build a Jewish fire? Was he granted a state funeral, as befitted his station? Or would his mother lie alone?

Paul remembered how enthusiastic his mother had been when Heinrich was first elected. Paul was fifteen, Istvan not yet thirteen and Rozsi barely four. Heinrich had fought a fierce battle with a gentleman farmer, Janos Horvath, who had spoken of Hungary's roots and of protecting the nation against what Horvath had called "external and internal enemies." Heinrich Beck had won handily, and that night he had gathered his three children around him. Mathilde looked on from a settee nearby and took Rozsi in her lap. The two had lost some of their lustre over the course of a long day and looked very tired.

But not Heinrich. "Look at us," he beamed. "Look at you. We Becks have been in Hungary for half a millennium, probably after we were expelled in the Inquisition, or maybe not. Maybe we came from the north somewhere—who knows?" Heinrich's beard was already turning white, and as he spoke, he pulled the end of it into a point. "It hardly matters is my point. Look no further back beyond Hungary for our forebears. This country has given us more than life. I've been *elected* mayor, *selected* by the people, by Hungarians, all of us. It's better than becoming king, believe me. If you are in line for the throne, it's because of some arbitrary royal lineage. Whether you like it or not, and whether the people like it or not, you most surely will be king, and they will have to suffer through your reign, for better or worse.

"Szeged is our Jerusalem. Even better, it's where a majority *selects* a Jew to lead them. Here is the land where Jewish women bake strudel, where Jewish men bank in forints and Jewish children recite Petofi. Here's the place where we can build architectural masterpieces to rival St. Peter's Basilica—look at our temple in the centre of this city—look at the monument to our health and achievement, the monument to Judaism—and yet we can relax our hold on the old faith, as it relaxes its hold on us. You are the rightful heirs of this place. Never forget it."

Even the little green rectangle of Hungary Heinrich had arranged for himself would now stay vacant, Paul thought bitterly. It was a sentimental concern, not a religious one—far from it, as his father had intimated. Paul was a proponent of the Neolog movement, the reform faction which led Jewry away from its Orthodox, and even Conservative, leanings, the ones which admonished Jews for driving a car on the Sabbath, or tearing paper, or lighting an oven, or smoking or shaving their heads—the women, at least—only to cover them with fashionable wigs, to satisfy God but fool dumb humanity. Or turning on a light. Or eating pork. Paul had wondered, as a child, what would happen if a pig ate a human. Would it be rebuked by the rest of piggery?

Was Sabbath meant to be a chore? Paul wondered. Live six days, spend the seventh showing contrition and gratitude? And if you are not naturally contrite or grateful, whom do you think you're kidding? Do you think the Lord can't see through the ruse?

And now the trains had begun to take away the undesirables on the Reich's list—Hungary's own trains, transporting Hungary's citizens against their will to where Lili's family awaited them, if the Bandels were still alert enough to wait—if the Bandels were alive. Was it conceivable that the list of undesirables could broaden and a whole country be emptied out—a vacant country for the taking, like the vacant town Lili left behind? They'd begun in Szeged and Debrecen and Miskolc and Komarom. How many had they already taken? How many would they succeed in taking?

Paul knew himself well enough to know that he was a poor candidate for a restricted life. He couldn't remain for long the struggling man being jostled by the superior and the immortal. It was not vanity that made him feel this way, but the injustice, the unfairness—he, the advocate, unable to have his day in court to talk about the rightness of things, to put his faith in Justice with her blindfold—not sniffing out the impure, the striving Jew, the uncombed Gypsy, the homosexual on his way to the thermal baths.

A moment later, Paul thought he could hear them again, his sister and Zoli, the velvet banging, the gasps and sighs, down the hall in her room, the spectre of law removed for them, the restraints of civility, of the right and wrong time for things. What right time could there be when one hears of one's father's execution or comes upon one's murdered parents? Anything was possible now.

Rozsi had moved from Szeged to Budapest ostensibly to look after her big brother, but the truth was she wanted to live in the exciting capital and felt safer in Paul's company than in anyone else's. He had always been her guide. He taught her the difference between what was right and what was legal, a difference that was especially important now. Once, when Rozsi was young, a housefly flew in through an open window, and she called for her brother Paul to please come in to kill it.

He found it resting on her blue curtain. "Why should I kill it?" he'd asked.

"Because I hate it."

"Is that a good enough reason to end its life?"

She thought about it and said, "Because it might harm me."

"*Might?*" he'd said.

"Because it's *trespassing* in our *house.*"

"Oh, trespassing," was Paul's reply. "But the fly does not know property law. It might not even know national law or civil law. It could have flown in from Paraguay, for all we know. Laws are lines we draw for ourselves. They can't involve the rest of nature."

Rozsi groaned in frustration. "Well, we're *bigger* than it is." She ran at the insect like a mad warrior, and it flew out of her room into the corridor.

"Yes, but it's faster than you."

Later, when she started dating a young lawyer in Paul's office, Aron Borbely, she confessed to her brother that she found the man boring and wanted to see someone else, Elek Beker, a piano teacher like her. Paul's response was that she had to tell Aron first.

"But what if it doesn't work out with Elek, either?"

"You shouldn't deceive Aron. That's all I'm saying. And don't deceive Elek, should you ever feel the need."

She didn't question her feelings for Zoli, that was for sure. What little time and commitment Paul had given to love. As a boy, he had known Ruth a little, briefly, passionately but prematurely. His fancy and fantasy had fed on her into his adulthood.

But the memory he revisited even more often was the one of Zsuzsi. He had met her ten years before, in Komarom, a town near the Czech border. He was visiting his aunt Hermina and uncle Ede's summer home, their sunny white palace, alight with glass on every side. He'd been reading there, relaxing, sleeping too much after his biggest case of 1934, when Paul was just thirty-one. It was a national case, involving Manfred Weiss, the country's first and best-known billionaire, and a Jew. His empire was encroaching on Eszterhazy land, royal land, with Hungarian blood flowing through its brown roots, and the nation wanted him stopped, but Paul saw no good reason. Was it for the greater good that Manfred Weiss be stopped, merely because he was bumping up against Hungarian royals?

What disease had Paul, the advocate, come upon? Was the disease differentness, or was it blindness to sameness? That was the argument Paul wished to make in court in defence of Manfred Weiss, even though the argument could have been made against either side, since his Mr. Weiss thought no more highly of his adversaries than they did of him.

So Paul had to find a neutral beneficiary both could tolerate. Both sides believed they were specially selected by history and the forces of evolution and by the creator himself to inherit the world.

Leave the disputed land to nature, then. Let the disputing families see that true nobility is expressed in largesse. Let Hungarians see the generosity of both noble families. Manfred Weiss could live with that. His client could be made to live with that as could the Esterhazys. Let the Hungarian people enjoy the land. The judge agreed, and Manfred Weiss left the court beaming and shaking hands.

Now, victorious, Paul was unwinding in the summer home of his uncle and aunt. And today he was visiting Komarom's famous stonework museum in the Igmandi Fortress.

He was studying an ancient Roman carving of the young Mercury, probably, standing on tiptoe on the back of his dog—Mercury looked ready to take flight—when Paul first heard her voice. "Why do you suppose he's standing on his dog?" And he guffawed like a schoolboy before he could even take her in.

She was tall and elegant, her collar like a calla lily, the white flower offering itself up. She wore a brilliant cream silk dress that was almost too elegant for an afternoon at a museum. He said, "I guess standing on your dog places you closer to the sky."

"Not much," she said and giggled herself. He could feel himself suddenly, urgently, wanting to taste her lipstick. Then she ran her fingers, light as feathers, over the soft marble back of the carved Mercury, barely touching the mythic figure, possibly not at all. Paul felt his ears burning, big as conches.

Paul and Zsuzsi Rosenthal exchanged names only as they were departing. He said he knew some Rosenthals in Budapest: Leopold, the lawyer. "No connection," she said, and she waved, looked down at her feet and slipped away. That was the whole of their encounter.

And when Paul told his devilish Aunt Hermina about it, she said no more than "Oh," but then he heard her speaking on the telephone to her sister Klari in Budapest, and the following morning Klari arrived to take in the country air and to ask about flightless Mercury.

"I don't know how long he's been like that," Paul mused. "Two thousand years, possibly, and he will never fly. He's like the lovers on Keats's Grecian urn. '*Never, never canst thou kiss, though winning near the goal,*'" he said in English. How pretentious I am, he thought, but the feeling was nevertheless real and pure. "For millennia they have been about to kiss," he said, "waiting for it, hoping for it, their warm marble hearts alight, but they never quite make it."

"Hmm," Hermina said, and Klari smiled. Ede headed back to Budapest to perform an operation, and the ladies and Paul saw him off, Paul helping his uncle with his bag.

And just then Zsuzsi walked up the path. "Oh," Paul said. "How . . ." and he turned to look at his aunts, hovering by the door.

"Oh," Zsuzsi said too. "Nice to see you again." Neither was expecting the other—Hermina had called Zsuzsi simply to invite her for a meal—and now Zsuzsi, too, looked at Hermina and Klari.

In Hermina's billowy parlour, after a lunch of pheasant with summer squash and bell peppers, followed by cool cherry soup, Zsuzsi was to play piano and he was to accompany her on cello. Schubert. Well of course Schubert. Paul could still picture Zsuzsi, still taste her image, as she sat poised, her pink fingers resting on the ivory keys of that silly creamy grand piano, exactly the same as her sister's in Budapest, both of them bought on the same day, from the same instrument maker, in Vienna. And so they played Schubert. The composer was to be the translator of their feelings—and just in the nick of time—for in the past hour Paul had found himself stumbling over every subject that arose. He found himself trying to impress Zsuzsi but frightening her instead. Anyone would have run from him. He would have run from himself.

Klari had said over lunch that Komarom was paradise on Earth. Through the wide-open windows, you could hear birds chirping outside and smell the lush greenery, so he could certainly see why she would say it.

But Paul couldn't hold his tongue. He found himself saying, "Paradise for everyone, or paradise for the four of us and Uncle Edward and whoever else we condescend to invite?"

"Why are you being rude, Palikam?" Hermina said. "All my sister meant was it felt good to be alive today, nothing more."

The comment prompted Zsuzsi to ask, "Are you a socialist, Mr. Beck?" She was holding a spoon of creamy pink cherry soup to her lips.

"No," Hermina said on behalf of her nephew. "He's showing off. He wants to let you know how clever he is."

Paul blushed. "I'm not a socialist, not an -*ist* of any kind. I just want to do some good things, as I'm sure you do."

She was still holding up the spoon in front of her. "Does this soup not have cream in it?" she asked. "We've just had pheasant—meat, I mean, followed by milk."

"Oh," Paul said, looking at his own spoon. He filled it, drained it again, licked it clean.

Zsuzsi gently put down her spoon. Zsuzsi's pale slim face gleamed in the light reflected off the silver. Her eyes were brown, almost black, yet they shone as if they gave off light rather than took it in.

"You're still a Jew, aren't you, Mr. Beck?"

Klari said, "Yes, a Jewish child, sometimes."

Paul uncrossed his arms. "Thank you, Aunt Klari. I am a Jew, Miss Rosenthal, but not *just* a Jew."

"Is that what you think I am?"

"It's the last thing I think you are."

"Meaning what?" she asked.

He blushed again.

She said, "When your Jewish resolve weakens, aren't you falling prey to the people who dislike us?"

"Oh, I wouldn't say my *Jewish* resolve has weakened. My resolve is not determined by the degree of my observance but by the degree of my sympathy."

"But if I feel very much sympathy, it is nourished by our particular history."

"My Judaism has informed my sympathy, but my Jewishness is not diminished by my sympathy for other people and causes, the repressed and exploited Hungarians, for instance."

"We are not guilty of creating the hardships endured by Hungarian peasants."

"But we're *also* guilty. We don't help, most of us."

"Oh, here we go," Klari said. She brushed a crumb from her forest green dress.

Zsuzsi said, "My parents invite a beggar to our dinner table every single night, and he sleeps under our roof and under a warm blanket, and in the morning eats a hot breakfast."

"Of course he does," Paul said, "and of course your family does these things. I didn't mean to make you defensive."

"What I'm saying is that being religious doesn't make us less sympathetic to the misfortunes of others, I assure you."

"Maybe not, but it draws a circle around you and makes you less tolerant of others, of differentness."

"You're doing the very thing you're criticizing, assuming things about people you don't know personally. *I'm* not less tolerant of anybody."

"Then why would you define yourself so rigidly?"

Hermina glanced at her sister and rolled her eyes. What had they done?

Zsuzsi was now as red in the face as the blushing Paul. "We are not responsible for what ails the world and shouldn't be held responsible."

"You couldn't be more right, Zsuzsi—Miss Rosenthal. But the sick thinking of the rest of the world doesn't indemnify us, any more than it indemnifies anyone else who contributes to the misery of humanity."

"You are blaming victims."

He had taken his silver napkin ring in his hand and was gripping it so hard it was bending. His aunts looked on, helpless.

"I am not blaming victims, per se. I would never. I am a Jew, too. My ancestors have been victims, too, but being victims does not necessarily make us right, either. Victimization and rightness aren't always connected, nor are history and the present."

"They're not mutually exclusive either."

"No, they're not."

"What a speech," Hermina said, "and over summer soup no one is having."

Zsuzsi looked as if she was getting ready to stand. "Be a Neolog, by all means, Mr. Beck, be a reformer, but don't be an anti-Semite."

"Why do you insist on defining me?" Paul asked. "I'm—I'm—"

"I guess we've done that to each other, shown our prejudice."

Zsuzsi laid her thin white hands on the table on either side of her bowl of cherry soup, getting set to push herself to her feet.

"Please," Klari said, "don't leave. Stay a bit. You and Paul can play a duet. That way you won't talk."

Paul said, "You can experience my cello. I sound like a cat with a bad stomach."

"You're not that bad," Klari said. "You're tolerable." Paul took this as a reference to his character as well as his cello playing.

Zsuzsi didn't get up. Paul looked at his mischievous aunts, whose experiment had gone so badly. How could he be angry, really, when they had taken aim at his own heart—and with such dazzling accuracy? Paul wanted somehow to hold on to Zsuzsi's image. He knew as he studied it that it would hang in his mind for months to come like a portrait in a gallery, the lights going down on it, the lights coming up, the eyes waiting serenely to see who was visiting today.

Neither young person wanted to leave things as they were. Their ears buzzed. The air coming in through the window smelled green.

The housekeeper came in to clear away the dishes, and Paul's aunts helped out. Paul and Zsuzsi, still stinging from their chat, watched as the others fussed. Paul believed he was the most obnoxious suitor who ever lived and hoped this young woman had a great capacity for forgiveness and tolerance.

Later, in the parlour, as he rode his cello, he gazed at his musical partner sitting before the keys of the cream piano. They played sad little Schubert together, whose beauty that afternoon was as sad as could be. Paul couldn't help but smile. The smile caught on with his aunts as they digested their lunch in their soft chairs. But no such sentiment travelled to Zsuzsi. After a time, she began to play hard, as if she were playing Beethoven, as if she wanted to push her way through the piano to get to the other side. Even though she imposed her own mood on the piece, Paul could tell she was a much better player than he was.

Later, at the door, Zsuzsi said, "Is this what you do, Mr. Beck— attack your guests and then play bad music together?"

Hermina said, "He also stands on his head," but Klari dragged her sister off again to the parlour.

"I'm sorry," Paul said. "I couldn't be sorrier." And then he asked, "May I walk you home?"

"It's all right," she said. "It's not far, and I like walking alone sometimes. I have a big family."

"Oh," he said.

They stepped outside. She turned toward him as if she were about to change her mind.

"We're going to Philadelphia," she said.

"Philadelphia?"

The word hung in the air between them like exotic fruit.

"What's in Philadelphia?" He felt like a perfect ass, as if he'd been responsible for her wanting to leave the country. Their faces shone red again in the sunshine.

"My father has a brother there, but it's not what's in Philadelphia so much as what's here, what's been happening. Hungary's changing. Europe's changing."

It was 1934. Her family had more foresight than most.

And then she said, "Your aunt tells me you speak English."

It sounded unmistakably like an invitation. He saw the whole of his future determined by what he said in reply, as surely as the Rosenthals' future might be determined by their decision to leave Hungary behind.

She was looking away from him, over her shoulder at the walk ahead. He said, "My work is here. I have a lot I want to do."

"If you can visit sometime, we would be happy to have you."

Did she mean here, in Komarom? Could she have meant Philadelphia? She couldn't have been more candid and yet more ambiguous. He would revisit this conversation a thousand times to guess at her intention.

And on this sleepless night, ten years later, in his bed in Budapest, he was convinced she had just been asking him over for tea, perhaps to prove to him how wrong he'd been about the good people who lived in her house. What hurt was that he'd appeared to lose an argument rather than a chance at love, and he'd been conducting the argument only to give him the chance at love. He wished he had not spoken at all. He would have fared better as a deaf-mute. Zsuzsi became the measure for him of all things comely and sympathetic in a woman, this elegant white calla lily, now turned away from him to the light. He'd often thought of writing to her in Philadelphia, possibly even a letter in English. He did write a card a few years later to say he'd looked in again on Mercury and found the fleet-footed messenger of the gods still earthbound and standing on his poor dog. But he didn't mail the card. How corny and how transparent, he thought at the time, as he stared at the sealed envelope, wanting to ask his aunt for the Rosenthals' address in America, fearing she would write to Zsuzsi herself instead if he waited too long.

Yet he could not dam up the river of hormones raging within him.

"Come away with me," he now said to the darkness.

"Where?"

"Come away with me nowhere—*anywhere*."

"What do you mean?"

"I mean nowhere. Zerowhere. I'm not going anywhere and I want you to come with me."

"I can't."

How easy Zoli and Rozsi made it seem, down the hall, and even young Lili and Simon, across town. What an utter ass he was, what an ass.

PAUL GAVE UP, finally, by dawn and got himself ready to go out. He set off to his office to send out some letters to clients whose cases were now being managed by other lawyers. He was still providing advice on the side, and the new lawyers were glad to have it and pay for it. Lately, though, he felt his movements were being watched. He had twice, in the past few days, seen the same cream-coloured Alfa Romeo outside his townhouse, and now here it was again, across the street from his office building. They could have tried to be more subtle, or maybe that was the point. He had, after all, been the son of a prominent Jewish mayor, and was a prominent lawyer himself. Was it his inquiries about Istvan that interested the men in the Alfa Romeo? Had they followed Zoli? He knew, now, that Istvan had not been taken away and was not listed among the dead of Szeged. Paul just didn't know where his brother was, and maybe that was best. If he didn't know, probably no one did.

Paul walked across the pink marble floor toward the elevator. His assistant, Viktor, passed him going the other way. Why was he leaving so early? "I'll be back soon," Viktor said.

"Did you get out the papers for the Meszaros case?"

"Yes, they're all on your desk. After you've looked them over, your stand-in, Mr. Kedves, will come by himself to chat and take the notes." Viktor looked anxious.

"You'll be back?" Paul asked.

"Of course," the shorter man said, but then he hurried to the door.

Paul continued toward the elevator. It was a grand old Elisha Otis with a walnut-panelled car and polished brass door, operated with pride by Hermann Nagy. He wore white gloves and a maroon tunic with brass buttons to complement his vehicle. The outfit was crowned by a military cap featuring a bold silver double-headed eagle of the Austro-Hungarian Empire. Hermann bid Paul good morning as he approached.

Hermann pulled closed the metal gate, then looked straight ahead as he swung the brass lever to lift the car. He had his back to Paul. "There are some men waiting for you in your office," he said.

"What men?" Paul asked.

Hermann shrugged. "They were speaking German."

"German?"

Hermann didn't say anything more.

Paul felt the blood beating at his neck. "Where was Viktor going?"

Hermann shrugged again. How glorious to be riding up and down all day in his carefree wooden box. If the men were German, was Paul not walking into the enemy's lair? Was Hermann taking him to his deportation or arrest? The man piloted the elevator as though he were the captain of a spaceship, with a confident gloved hand on the brilliant lever, taking his rider to the moon and beyond. Did he truly not foresee the danger that might be awaiting Paul, or, worse, not mind either way? Was he not paid enough to mind? Paul felt like ripping the double-headed eagle from the man's cap and ramming it down his throat.

But if they were Germans, and Germans had been shadowing him, why had they not arrested him already? Why the charade?

German wasn't the language Paul heard when he walked through the door to his office. It was Swedish. Raoul Wallenberg stood to offer Paul his hand.

"You're back," Paul said. He let out a big breath.

"Not yet, not officially. I hope I'll be back by the beginning of July, officially," Wallenberg said. "Paul, I'm happy to introduce Per Anger." The man was tall, like Paul, and had a warm hand and kind eyes. "He is the second-in-command at the embassy after Carl Danielsson, the ambassador, and I hope to become Mr. Anger's deputy."

"And I hope to become yours," Paul said.

The Swedes laughed. Wallenberg said, "Mr. Anger's German isn't great, and his Hungarian and English are worse."

Anger said in broken Hungarian, "If I forget my Swedish, I'll be a deaf-mute."

Paul chuckled as he gestured to the gentlemen to sit down.

"It's good to see you again," Wallenberg said.

Paul thought the Swede had aged in the short months since they'd met at Gerbeaud. Paul must have aged, too. The world had aged.

Paul was happy to be speaking Churchill's English. He said, "You've lost more hair."

"You've gained some," Wallenberg said.

Paul ran a hand through his thicket of curls. He needed a haircut.

"You said you were going to come back, and you did," Paul said, still amazed at the visitors in the room.

"I needed to. I can be more useful here. I heard from Mr. Anger that the transports have begun. We can't stop them, but we can impede them."

"I'm very pleased," Paul said. "I thought our one meeting at Gerbeaud was—"

"Forgive me for quoting the New Testament to you," Wallenberg said, "but our Luke once said, 'From those to whom much is given, much will be required.' So, I—"

Per Anger leaned forward to interrupt. "We can issue Swedish papers," he said in Swedish, before switching, for Paul's sake, to German. "Raoul is suggesting we issue official, colourful Swedish papers with our state seal and photographs. If the Germans round up Jews here in Budapest, as they have elsewhere, we'll meet them at the stations and present the papers. We'll ask the Germans to release people who match up with these fake papers we issue."

"And I can help you," Paul said. "I'm a Swede already," and he showed the men his new papers.

They burst out laughing, and Paul joined them. Then Wallenberg said, "What other talents do you have?"

"I can stand on my head."

They laughed again, and Wallenberg translated for Per Anger, but the diplomat had understood. Much had changed since Gerbeaud. The atmosphere felt different. There was a tension in the room.

"How did you know where to find me today?"

"I didn't. Your assistant said you'd be in, but I've had my driver look for you."

"Ah, the Alfa Romeo."

Wallenberg nodded. He noticed the lamp on Paul's desk. It had been a gift from his mother when Paul opened his office. It had come from the Tiffany Company of New York. It featured brilliantly coloured dragonflies, pointed downward, like a winged bombs.

"I was sorry to hear about your father," Wallenberg said. "I never knew my own father—he died before I was born—but I suspect it would be worse to love a father and lose him, and in such a disgraceful way."

"Thank you."

"We do want your help," Wallenberg said. "Your network is probably extensive."

Paul shrugged modestly. Wallenberg looked at Anger. "It's not
enough just to issue papers. We'll have to find safe houses around the
city and raise the Swedish flag over them so that we can put the new
Swedes out of harm's way. We'll annex places. Mr. Anger says the Dutch
are game, and the Danish, the Spanish, possibly even the Italians. Ha,
I wonder if Mussolini is still in charge of things!"

"I have a photographer," Paul said. "A good one. He's eager to help.
He's a young man named Zoltan Mak."

"His parents were murdered, too," Anger said in German.

Paul was impressed by what the two men knew. Imagine doing
what the two Swedes were proposing. Who did such things?
Angels, possibly, but angels were invulnerable. They were better
than angels. Paul knew he was doing good work, but it was for his
own people. Wallenberg had come back to Hungary, to someone
else's cause, to someone else's misery, to stand in front of the most
formidable army in the world, and with what? Papers. Common
sense. Law. Civility.

And hope. Because that was the key. Hold papers up to barbarians,
and what did they do with them? But the Germans believed themselves to be civilized. Hold papers up to them, and they'd know how
to read them. They were educated. They had produced Goethe and
Beethoven.

Paul stared at the two Swedes. Wallenberg had chosen to return
and was determined to do some good work here. What drove the
man? What possessed him? Do we open the doors of our homes to
shelter the Jews fleeing their own houses? Do we, what's more,
venture out on a stormy night to look for people to whom we could
give shelter? It took a special species of person, one for whom enjoying life was not enough—success was not enough.

Mr. Kedves came by to get the notes Paul was to give him, but Paul
didn't invite him to stay. He said they could talk later.

Then the diplomats and Paul got out maps. Per Anger had brought a topographical map of the city with him. They spent the morning planning their moves, anticipating the moves of the invaders. Paul told the Swedes more than they knew about the Hungarian Arrow Cross. They would not be quite as predictable as the Germans, and while their aim was similar, the Arrow Cross would want to be in charge. "Insecurity is a fact of life," Wallenberg said.

Paul kept an ear open for Viktor, but Viktor didn't come back to work.

Nine

ISTVAN FELT as if he'd had a feast. So did Smetana. The two sat glowing together on the floor, digesting their sardines. Then Istvan said, "Time for some Dvorak, my boy."

He dug out *Rusalka* and selected his favourite aria, "Mesicku na nebi hlubokem." He sat back down with Smetana, who stepped lightly into his lap and purred. Istvan closed his eyes and let the song fill his ears as full as the little meal had filled his stomach. The thorny cat made himself at home in the tangle of Istvan's legs, and Istvan held his little neck. Istvan's raw, crude voice rose to meet the singer's. "Sing your song to the moon, my sweet Rusalka, sweet, plump angel. Beg the shining oaf for your lover's return." Istvan's eyes were closed; his head swayed bonelessly; his fingers gripped the scrawny, purring neck. "It's all your fault, isn't it, my feline friend, my Smetana, with your Fatherland? Yes, it is. Switch off your purring motor, Bedrich; switch off your sentiment, my small companion."

Are there ancient sounds, too, which we confuse with modern ones, sounds that drift down to us like the ancient light of the stars, some of them long gone? Time is really our only captor, isn't it, Smetana? In the ice age before us and the ice age after, there is no trace of us. Time has no dominion over us. It has a beginning and an end only in a flat world. We don't exist in this time any more than the dead or the yet unborn live in it. We are mere *examples* of the original design, nothing more—I, a dentist, a Hungarian, resident of Szeged, brother of Paul and Rozsi, now orphans, all of us, the lover of a Catholic girl, caged on this day in who I am in a house where, at one time, peppers were ground into sweet paprika—you, a scrawny grey cat, named after a Czech composer of the nationalist period, domesticated, beyond hunting for your meals, sharing sardines with the human example of humanity beside you. We are not individuals. We mock individuality, and we reprise the themes of intolerance and love. And then we join the dead, Smetana, with the leaves fluttering down on us and then the snow, leaving behind us, some of us, sometimes, other examples of the next epoch ambling about until they, too, join us. Let us charge forward to the end of the flat Earth, some of it in night, some in day, some summer, some winter, all at once, like a sphere. Spheres have no perspective, young Smetana. They are examples of balls. They join the hunks and colours of the universe, examples of red, examples of rock. It's not the colours that pass on, merely the individuals sporting them. Creations outlive their creators.

Marta, the ancient light of extinguished stars shine down on our present love. It is our Marta we love—isn't it, you and I—don't we—little instance of cat? We yearn for her and her alone, no other example, no other time or season, just Marta. I, time's minister, need a single moment more with her, before we are out of time.

Miklos, my friend, my poet—Radnoti—help me with these feelings:

For a long time only the burned wind spins
Above the houses at home.
Walls lie on their backs,
Plum trees are broken,
And the angry night is thick with fear.
If only I could believe that,

If the things of value are not inside me yet,
I could have a home to go back to.

If only I could hear again the quiet hum
Of bees on the veranda, the jar of preserved plums
Cooling with the summer, the gardens half asleep,
Voluptuous fruit lolling on branches dipping deep,
And she before the hedgerow standing with sunbleached hair,
The lazy morning scrawling vague shadows on the air . . .
Why not? The moon is full, her circle entire.
Don't leave me, friend—shout out—I am still standing.

Istvan had begun to grip the cat's neck too tightly, had not heard the squeak, felt the motor turn off before he gasped and let go. The cat looked meekly up at Istvan but stayed in his lap. Do the old trees guard your childhood, too, young Smetana? Look at us. We sit here like beautiful still lifes, the two of us, awaiting our Marta. Memory sits like a still life, safe and quiet.

We once had lead soldiers, Paul and I, when we were young. Our Uncle Bela surprised us with two regiments of soldiers, one in brilliant gold and white and the other in red and blue. Paul's were cavalry, mine were infantry. My brother had an impressive clay mountain from which his general and mounted men could look down on my green field of fighters, not well disguised, on account of the red. It took hours to set them all up. They occupied the whole of the floor of our playroom. Little Rozsi was upset about it, so we let two of her smallest dolls join the men on the floor. One of the dolls had Shirley Temple curls, like Rozsi, and the doll even got to sit on one of Paul's lead horses, but in the back, out of harm's way, looking like a curly giant on a horse.

When we were done, making certain with a straight edge that our men formed perfect lines, which Rozsi's dolls could admire, we both stood up finally like the Colossus Brothers of Rhodes and looked down on our work. The soldiers were sparkling, exquisite—fierce in what they were capable of—but we didn't want to get them dirty. We didn't want to see them piled like scrap metal in the middle of our green field, not that day, so we looked at them for some time more, let them stare one another down, and then turned off the lights on them and quietly exited the room, taking Rozsi with us, whispering to her that they needed some rest now.

The light was receding on the little cottage in Szeged, but Marta was not home. Istvan took Smetana down to the cellar with him, replaced the planks above them, and they waited.

Ten

ROZSI WAS TO MEET ZOLTAN promptly at 6 P.M. in their favourite spot off Andrassy Street, in the Epreskert, the Strawberry Gardens, though of course it was already past strawberry season, and it had turned suddenly cold this late spring night. The Epreskert was located a stone's throw from the State Puppet Theatre and the Academy of Fine Arts, sprawling out in its Neo-Renaissance splendour.

Meeting at all was becoming problematic, but at least Rozsi and Zoli did not wear cloth Stars of David. They carried their Swedish papers everywhere. It was in the Strawberry Gardens, especially, that they liked to take in the fragrant breeze and speak their hearts. Rozsi had insisted on meeting Zoltan at their favourite bench, even though the bench had been—how had he put it?—deboned or pitted or shelled, she couldn't remember which. She would have wanted to meet at that spot even if the bench had been removed altogether; if a building had been erected in their favourite gardens, she would have arranged to meet in the room where their bench had stood.

How selfish she felt. How could she want just one thing, day and night, how could she care only that she saw her Zoli? Would *not* wanting to see him make things right? Would starving herself of him make her virtuous? Should she abstain until she went to her grave? She wished, in fact, she could take flight with him—land on top of the Matterhorn and wait until all the smoke beneath them cleared. Avalanches fell downward—that much she knew. They should have headed for the Alps when they were able and not come back. Rozsi would have traded all of Hungary for Zoli—all of Europe—as long as there was a single peak they could alight on together unharmed.

She would happily have answered for it all later. She had been placed in a difficult time and situation. Surely, allowances could be made when the time came to answer. How simple the choices were, ironically, in extreme times: survive or perish, do this job or none, be with Zoli or no one.

Rozsi's father had once set her up with a young man, Lorant Cukor, treasurer of Szeged, who was elegant, if a little too stocky. He was ravenous for her, thought Heinrich was arranging their marriage, the way it had been for Heinrich and Mathilde and for his own parents. Wherever they went, Rozsi felt Lorant was ready to drop to one knee in front of her and present her with a ring as he wetly kissed her hands with altogether too much saliva and innumerable sucking sounds, as if he were going at a plate of chicken wings. Much as she would have liked to please her father, and much as she appreciated Lorant's parents, who'd held a lavish dinner and dance party in her honour in their white chateau in Szeged, she couldn't go through with the arrangement. Her friends were already picking out a gown for her and a tiara decorated with subtle pink pearls, but she called them off.

For his part, Zoli was on a mission. His parents' death compelled him to do a job he believed no one else would do now, the job his father alone had been willing to do. His Hasselblad was his primary companion, and it took him away to document things Rozsi barely wanted to hear about, let alone witness what he witnessed. And it was the camera that often came between them.

Today, Zoli was meeting with Gyula Halasz, a Hungarian photographer who'd made himself famous in Paris as Brassaï. It was Paul who'd told Zoli that Brassaï was briefly returning home. "I've seen his work. He's very special," Paul said, then sipped his drink. They were at Paul and Rozsi's townhouse, polishing off what Paul had said was "the last bottle of brandy in the city." "Brassaï's work has begun to appear now in American magazines," Paul said. "I came across Halasz in *Harper's Bazaar*. The naïfs of the New World want to know what Decadent Old Bitch Europe looks like, and Brassaï gives it to them. I met him once, way back when."

"I've seen some plates of his work," Zoli said. "A friend of my father's had a portfolio of Halasz's photographs—*Brassaï's*, excuse me. His 'Lovers in a Café' is masterful."

Rozsi couldn't understand how someone could be so captivated by a photographer. He was not a painter, not a musical composer. "How can a photograph be *masterful*?" she asked. "The work is all practically done for you by a machine."

"Hardly," Zoltan responded. He was sitting at the edge of a plush scarlet armchair, rolling his brandy glass between the tips of his fingers. "Photography is about vision; it's never about a single moment but all such moments, if I can put it that way. The photographer composes with his eye the way a painter does." Zoltan set his glass on the table beside him. "I know it sounds pretentious, but Brassaï's photographs have illuminated not just a street corner or the shadowy room of a brothel. They have illuminated the whole world." Zoli sounded to Rozsi like someone in love. "He caught the world of overheard conversations," Zoli went on, "the world of spyglass intimacy. How else can I put it?" Zoltan was tensely rubbing his hands together now. "Brassaï had his own secrets within the dark chamber of his camera. He unearthed my own secrets, Paul's—*yours*, possibly."

Rozsi was blushing, as if Zoli were telling Paul one of *their* secrets. "So this is what it's all about. This is what you want to do for a living, turn your camera into a spyglass; you want to follow lonely, unsuspecting fools as they step into brothels or pee in a bush?"

"You know that's not what I'm doing." He looked truly hurt. "I am not interested in recording people's secrets." He couldn't look directly at her now. He regarded Paul instead. "Our time has eliminated the need for miniaturists. I am not interested in shooting weddings, or landscapes, nor will I record sittings." Zoltan gestured to the walls around him. They were covered with photographs and paintings of Heinrich and Mathilde's families. One portrait done in oils featured a family matriarch, some hundred and fifty years before, sitting erect in what looked like a throne, her purple dress resplendent, honey light pouring in from one side. Another canvas captured figures at a seaside who could easily have inspired Georges Seurat. A photograph in soft focus in a gilded frame showed Heinrich and Mathilde at the Taj Mahal with Klari and Robert, happy and carefree, if a little warm (as suggested by the fans the women held, caught in mid-flutter). Another gilded frame could barely contain the imposing figure of an army commander sporting a tall hat with a taller feather, not long before marching off somewhere—possibly to his doom? Grandest of all was a photograph, in an ornate cherry frame, of Heinrich as a young boy, gazing out of the heavy frame as if out of a casement window at the world below. He was adorned with a Victorian dress like a delicate young girl, his mother no doubt looking on with delight over the photographer's shoulder.

Zoltan said to Rozsi, "I want to chronicle our time. There's important work to be done. I want to bear witness. It's not a *profession* I'm looking for now. It's not about finding security."

Rozsi knew she had misjudged him, and he was striking back. She had begun to cry, quietly, while her brother stood up tall. "You're an inspiration to me, Zoli," he said.

Zoli suddenly got to his feet, too, and said he had to go. "Thanks for the good brandy."

He was half a block away when Rozsi caught up with him and grasped him to her.

"Please forgive me," she said.

"It wasn't you," he said, though they both knew it was. "I had to get out of that staring gallery," he said.

"Those are my ancestors."

"Maybe I'm no good for you."

She continued to hold on to Zoltan's hands. "Please don't say that. It's nothing personal. I'm just jealous of your mechanical girlfriend, the one with the spyglass eye."

Now he broke free of her. "Oh, it's entirely personal," he said. "If I'd been a junior solicitor in your brother's firm, I wonder what you would have thought."

"If you'd been junior solicitor in my brother's firm, you'd be out of work now. It's not your being a photographer that disturbs me. It's that you've put yourself in the line of fire for some pictures." Rozsi drew him close again and pressed her face against his chest. She could hear his heart beat.

He said, "It's important to me."

"If it's important to you, then it's important to me."

He turned her face toward the lamplight and looked into her lakeland eyes. Zoltan reached into his jacket pocket. The jacket was charcoal grey, but in the light it looked brown. "I want to marry you," he said, "if it's possible." He pressed a small black velvet pouch into her hands. Rozsi could feel the contours of the ring inside. "It was my mother's. I want you to have it." And he turned and ran off, leaving her standing there.

Rozsi rushed the little treasure inside her house and up to her room, clutching it in her fist. She sat on her bed beneath the canopy with its green fringe highlighted by drops of red silk rosebuds. Her heart beat frantically. She could feel something hard and square nestled with the ring inside the black pouch. It was a card, a note, muscularly folded a dozen times into a little square fortress of paper. The ring fell out and rolled against the white, curved Florentine leg of her settee. Rozsi rushed to retrieve it, then sat again on the bed.

It was a ruby ring set in a garland of gold filament leaves. Rozsi slipped it on her finger. It fit perfectly. It electrified her. She might just as well have stolen Zoltan himself into her room for the night, might as well, from that moment on, have been setting up house. The ruby radiated on her finger, warming the room.

She turned to the tightly folded note and opened it like a Japanese paper puzzle. The note had been written too carefully—boyishly—in thick blue ink with the Waterman fountain pen he told her he'd taken from his father's study. Her eyes fell on the words:

Dearest Rozsi,

I want to outwait this bad time, and then marry you, if you'll have me. This ring was my mother's. May its ruby heart stand up to your stout Beck heart. Please take it and accept it.

Zoltan
I love

He'd forgotten to finish the note. *I love*. Like someone opening his arms to love. Rozsi heard a door opening in the hall and slipped the note and the ring under her pillow. She darted over to her white settee and perched herself on the end of it, stiffening her back, making herself obvious. She waited a good long minute, took out the pins in her hair, then returned to her bed, took her treasures from their hiding place, put the ring on her ring finger, opened the note and gazed at her favourite words. *I love*

ZOLI WAS NOW a half-hour late for Rozsi in the Strawberry Gardens. She was frantic by the time he did come. "What *kept* you?" she said. "Do you know what I've been thinking, what I tried *not* to imagine in the past half-hour?"

"I'm so sorry," he said. He saw that she was wearing his mother's ruby ring.

"Where have you *been*? I thought you were seeing that photographer, Gyula Brassaï?"

"Just Brassaï," he said. "I saw him, but then I heard they were taking Jews to the new ghetto, out behind the Dohany Street synagogue. I wanted to see the wall going up there, get some shots of it."

"Oh, those poor people. We could be behind that wall before long. Are there whole families—children—*everyone?*"

Zoltan nodded.

"Did Brassaï encourage you to do this—take pictures, I mean?"

"On the contrary. Brassaï saw some of my work, and . . ."

"And what?"

"And he urged me to get out and save myself, 'live to fight another day' sort of thing." Zoltan was looking down at the grass. "But I had to get the pictures."

"You *had* to."

"Yes."

"Were the Germans there, and the Nyilas?"

"Yes, both, but so was the Swede, Wallenberg, and so was your brother."

"*Paul?*"

Zoli nodded. "It's hard to understand what's going on," he said, "hard to feel secure in the hands of our prime minister or regent. Hitler knows Horthy is not his pal. He thinks even less of Miklos Kallay. He's not enamoured of either, because their secret is out. Kallay is well-known for his two-step: two to the left, two to the right, as the situation requires. He's very adept at it, bless his heart. Horthy doesn't want Hungary fighting alongside Germany. But it's true he's had to release Kallay from his post to appease the Reich. He's had to appoint Dome Sztojay prime minister, and as you know he's a pal of Ferenc Szalasi, the fascist. I saw them there today, Szalasi's Arrow Cross goons, at the ghetto wall. They hate the Germans probably as much as they hate us, because they want to be boss, the thugs—bastards."

Rozsi took Zoli's hand. "What will happen," she asked, "if Hungarians are drawn into the Russian campaign alongside the Germans? We'll be crushed."

Zoli said, "It's very tricky. It's more difficult to be Hitler's enemy than his friend. As his friend, at least you know where you stand— *never* as his enemy. And we're the pawns in the middle, waiting for the bullet in our heads. And we have no friends. There aren't that many of us in this country, and yet we're the professors, doctors and judges and at least one photographer. You need look no further than our circle. We're terribly exposed. We've been called the Magyar Israel. So we'll take the fall for failing our own nation. You can't look out only for yourself when European Jews are disappearing all around us. You can't be seeking land and knighthood from your leaders when a quarter of your own nation or more is hungry. Here we are, building baroque palaces and opera houses and banks while children in villages a few kilometres from the capital haven't got shoes to wear to school."

"You can't be finding reasons to justify people's hatred of us," Rozsi said. "We are not to blame for all that."

"No, but we're fat scapegoats, we Hungarian Jews, easy targets for a madman with a cannon."

Rozsi said, "It's hard to believe that what happens to the unfortunate of this country is of concern to Hitler."

"No, it's of no concern to that prick, but it is of concern to *them*, to the unfortunate themselves, and when they have their day, they will not be kind to us, many of them. How long could this country's feudal system survive? We've turned farmers into paupers. Do you remember the journalist Gyorgy Olah? He called them the 'three million beggars.'"

"How sad, in a country so rich," Rozsi said. "And then the rumours start that we're to blame. How terribly sad, for *everyone*."

"Yes," Zoli said, taking her face in his hands. "But saddest of all, rumours are truer than truth, because people *want* to believe them."

A cool breeze blew up, and she put her arms around Zoli again. "I just got engaged. Most of the people I love are falling all around me. Zolikam, I need you—do you understand that?" It was the one thing she had to hope for, look forward to. She didn't want to stand alone—*couldn't*—she knew that.

"I need you, too," he said.

"Then please don't go everywhere that there's trouble. I won't get another wink of sleep until this war's over."

"I'll do my best," he said. They had to leave the Strawberry Gardens now, before curfew.

Eleven

BEFORE LONG, there was almost no food left in Budapest. The supply lines seemed to dry up. As money became worthless, farmers were hoarding food for themselves and their families. The trains had been taken over by the military and were being used to deport Jews. The Becks had gone from eating cakes and marzipan squares, veal shank and sauerkraut, and drinking brandy and teas, to scrounging for sacks of beans or rice in outposts around the city and hoping that Robert's patients who needed to come in from outlying hamlets would bring him food, prepared or not. But Robert's patients avoided him as much as they could. They assumed he might not be there when they came back to have him check on their recovery after surgery. And he was losing cases to other physicians, who quietly took them without a word to Robert.

Simon went out with Lili to scrounge for food, but he'd been stopped twice, once by a squad of Germans, who looked over his Swedish papers, then at him, then back at the papers, while hardly glancing at Lili's documents; and once by the Nyilas, who didn't care about his papers and took him to the outskirts of the city, broke his nose and two of his ribs and threw him in a dump. He managed to make it home on foot by night, to the relief of his horrified parents and Lili, who had sat by the window, waiting and crying, and holding Klari's hand when the older woman joined her.

Robert bandaged his son's side and his nose, and with Klari and Lili's help gently put him to bed. Lili sat by his side through the night, experiencing for the first time since she'd left Tolgy what it would feel like to lose someone close. Simon's eyes were closed, but he put his warm hand out from under the duvet to hold hers. She cried again and kissed his knuckles.

From that day on, Lili went out on her own, insisting that the Becks stay put. She found all kinds of food. She brought home dandelion leaves, which her hosts had never eaten. She found tins of Spanish anchovies, a crate of them, for which she traded an ice-blue satin dress Klari had given Lili for the purpose of bartering. And she took a trip to a farmer's field with another girl she met, a Catholic girl, Maria Nap, and together they harvested a sack of potatoes.

The scarcest commodity was meat. Chicken or goose had become a delicacy. One night, Klari said she was so hungry for meat she would eat a bat if it flew through her window. She'd clamp it into a pot and get it cooking before it had even calmed down. She said she'd eat a crow, if she had to, as soon as she had torn off its feathers. Robert said he felt like a wolf, and would *eat* a wolf, if it happened his way, even if he'd be branded a cannibal for his efforts.

Lili saw the desire in their eyes. They had never known hunger. Neither had she. Lili imagined if she had stayed in Tolgy, or could return to it, she'd find plenty to eat. She wondered what they were feeding her family, if her mother's milk had dried up for little Hanna, if the baby was still enjoying the sensations of the world. Lili didn't mind the world's disintegration, in itself. She could hunt for food. She didn't care about buildings, bridges, temples and cafés. She remembered the tales of Babel and Sodom and Gomorrah. It was only a matter of time before most civilizations were razed in favour of new and cleaner ones, until they too became tarnished. Lili didn't need buildings. She could manage in a cave. But the thought of losing people—*her* people—*anyone's* people—was abhorrent to her. And to what end? Knock down a building to show how mighty you are, but why would you have to make it impossible for a baby to drink her mother's milk?

Sometimes, before sleeping, Lili imagined talking with her mother. She imagined sitting with her, once Helen had put Hanna down, and telling her how she was getting on, what had happened since the last time they'd seen each other, how she'd lost her appendix, how she'd travelled in the wedding dress Helen had made, how these nice people had taken her in without question, insisting that she stay, be a member of their family until hers returned. What would her mother do when that day came? Would she present the Becks with something, her thanks at the very least, invite them for a country holiday, thank God for the goodness of strangers, thank God for the good that these bad times brought out in people?

Lili tried to imagine the man who had caused all this to happen to her and to everyone she knew. The conditions had to be right, for sure, for such a man to succeed, but it also took a certain kind of daring, like madness, surely, like Captain Dobo throwing the leaves back up to the branches that had dropped them. A certain kind of daring in dark times, so that everyone behind you said *yes*, this will surely set us free, and they all took flight behind you without once checking your wings.

Hitler was so powerful, he had turned the dial on every personality within his range, so that cheerful people turned melancholy, mad people turned criminal, melancholy people became suicidal, courageous people turned heroic, charming people became irritable and dark—all so that the maddest hatter at the front could turn himself into something mythic.

Lili saw this change in herself, saw her own optimism flicker, and she saw it in Simon. When she'd first known him, she'd thought he looked a little hungry around the eyes, but now he looked ravenous, like a stray dog. And once, he found her sitting alone in the corridor beside the hall table with its silver eagle carrying a clock in its beak, flanked by silver griffin candlesticks. She was wiping her nose and eyes. He asked what was wrong, and she said she thought she might be getting a cold. He said, "If I hold you a little, you might feel a little less rheumy."

Still, people were not fundamentally changed, not changed at the core. Klari and Robert, for instance, happily stood in as her parents, treating her with as much love and respect as they did their son. She felt herself clinging to the Becks every bit as much as they clung to her.

Lili even got to learn the tallest of the family tales. One evening, after eating a good plate of salami and beets, which a colleague of Robert's had given him, Lili asked about Klari's younger days and about some of the people in Klari's family.

Klari said, "Let's start with my cousin Sandor, who's one of my favourites." Klari took Lili into the parlour and brought out a bundle of letters and photographs tied with a red ribbon. Simon, who, after his beating, had two black eyes to go with his swollen, broken nose, sat with his favourite women.

"Who are those from?" Lili asked excitedly.

"They're from Sandor Korda—*Alexander* Korda, the film producer," Simon said.

Klari looked annoyed, as if her son had spoiled a surprise.

He said, "Mother was a little in love with Alexander—with *Sanyi*, as she used to call him."

"Oh, be quiet," Klari said, and swatted at her son. "And don't be impertinent."

"I'm sorry. I don't mean to be," he said, and appeared to fold up his limbs where he sat.

Simon seemed extra sensitive these days, and Klari saw it right away. "Go ahead, tell Lili more, then," she said.

He sat up straighter. "They're cousins, all of them—my mother, Aunt Hermina, Aunt Mathilde and Alexander Korda. My mother's father, Maximillian, and Alexander Korda's mother were brother and sister, except they all had an unfortunate falling out." Simon looked directly at Lili. She couldn't fathom what she was hearing. The movies were so otherworldly to her, so magical. She hadn't thought that anyone made them.

"Alexander Korda founded London Films," Simon went on. "He was really the father of the British film industry. He's still there, and he still writes to Mother."

Klari blushed. "He does sometimes."

"Yes, but *only* to her," Simon put in. "He seems to hold the rest of the family responsible for what happened."

"What happened?" Lili asked.

"He practically came to blows with our father—that's what happened," Klari said, "and then Father disowned him. They disowned each other, I guess." The room lit up with the sun again, brightening Klari's auburn hair.

"Maximillian's sister, Ernesztina, married beneath her station. She settled down with a handsome but wayward sort by the name of Kellner. They had three sons, and when the eldest was thirteen, their father died. As time went on, Ernesztina, Alexander's mother, asked her brother Maximillian in Budapest to please set her son up in some kind of profession.

"Alexander Korda, or Sandor Kellner, as he was then known, came to Budapest at his Uncle Maximillian's behest. My father established an office for Sandor right next to Odon Grunwald so that his nephew could study law with the best of them. It was not easy for my father to extend such a hand. When others in his family faltered, he let them fall—that's how he was. When his brother Gyorgy gambled away his inheritance, night after night, over a backgammon board, he came to his elder brother for help. Maximillian would not meet with him at first. He'd barely come down to say hello to Gyorgy. He would not visit Gyorgy when his brother took a fall and broke his ankle. He would not respond to any of the notes Gyorgy sent him. He wouldn't even open them. Finally, an appeal on behalf of their brother by Ernesztina, the only sibling for whom Maximillian had a soft spot, weakened Maximillian's resistance. He arranged to meet Gyorgy at the Japan Café, an establishment Gyorgy also cherished for its bohemian character.

"When Gyorgy got there first, the proprietor hugged him and offered him his favourite table. 'No, Max's table tonight, please, Attila,' Uncle Gyorgy told him. 'The dark Munch.'

"They both laughed just as Maximillian walked in. Attila snapped to attention. 'May I get you something, a drink, some fresh cherry strudel?' Attila asked him even before he sat down with Gyorgy.

"My father wanted only *palinka*. Then he told Gyorgy it was time for him to leave Budapest because nobody would trust him here even if he did succeed in slaying his demons.

"Gyorgy asked my father, 'Why do you hate me?'

"My father told Gyorgy he didn't hate him, but they'd both started out of the same gate. Uncle Gyorgy was wounded. 'So is that what this is?' he asked. 'Some kind of race? Some kind of competition? I didn't even notice the starting gate until you came charging out of it.'

"My father was exasperated. He implored Gyorgy to take whatever he had left and start a new life in France or England or Austria. But Gyorgy had nothing left, so my father offered him enough money to make a start elsewhere but not enough to return. He wanted Gyorgy to earn his way back.

"My uncle asked my father, 'Take me in with you, Max. Take me into your business.'

"'You're joking, surely,' Father said. 'I don't want you near my business, let alone in it. If you don't want this money, I'll take it back with me. I don't part with it willingly, because I don't trust you, Gyorgy. I don't know what you'll do with it.'

"I can imagine how Gyorgy felt. He must have looked my father up and down for a good while before he took the money and stormed off.

"And now, years later, came his other sibling's request, Ernesztina's appeal, this time on behalf of her eldest son, Sanyi. It was easy to see why the young man who came to Budapest was thought to be wayward. His mentor at the law firm, Odon Grunwald, made some effort to get Sandor to appreciate the law. Instead of hearing him out, though, the young man made Grunwald listen to him as he prattled on about *The Birth of a Nation* or about the pratfalls of Fatty Arbuckle. Grunwald certainly would not have played along if he hadn't been asked by Maximillian Korda himself and, oddly, if he hadn't found the young man so captivating.

"Sandor stayed for a short time at our house on Kaldy Street, off Andrassy. When he first approached the house, he asked if he was being taken to temple, so grand was the walkway leading to the entrance. 'Goodness!' he said, looking at the frieze above the door and colonnades holding up the roof. 'Is there an Ark of the Covenant inside?'

"My father didn't answer but spoke only to Lajos, his aide. 'Take his things upstairs to the green room, the guest room.' Then he turned to his nephew. 'You have time to dress for dinner if you like,' he told Sanyi.

"At dinner, Sandor cast a spell over us Korda girls, Hermina, Anna, Etel, Mathilde and me, and even over our mother.

"Oh, where are they now?" Klari said, interrupting herself. "Where is Hermina? Where is Anna, and Etel—and their boys, Bela, Janos— poor frail Janos—"

"Mother, please," Simon said, and Klari looked up at the young couple.

"I'm sorry," she said, "but these times—you know . . ."

Lili nodded sympathetically. Klari went on. "Sanyi was tall and awkward, but his dark brown eyes gleamed with cheer. The boys and Father seemed less moved. Sandor asked us over dinner, 'Have you read Karl May?' When no one answered, he said, 'What about Jules Verne? Are you familiar with *Around the World in Eighty Days*?' I said

I had read it. 'How about *Twenty Thousand Leagues Under the Sea*?' He said if he were being tested he thought he could describe every single detail of Captain Nemo's quarters on the *Nautilus*.

"'Unfortunately, there is no test for such a thing,' my father said. We all glared at him, even my mother. 'Is that what you want to do, Sanyi?' Father asked. 'You want to travel in a balloon or crawl along the floor of the sea?'

"'Not at all. I'm afraid I'm not quite heroic enough for that. But I love the stories about people who do want to do those things. I'd love to capture such adventures myself, if I could.'

"'*Capture* them?' my mother asked good-naturedly.

"'Yes.' He leaned forward. 'Imagine capturing such a thing, such an adventure, on film, so the whole world can join in.'

"Sanyi did not last long at our house. He preferred living with a poor cousin called Miksa, from his father's side of the family. Miksa was a poet who supported himself as a *hordar*, a porter."

As Lili tried to imagine what it must have been like to have such a man, this young man from another planet, traipsing around Klari's living room, the room they sat in brightened, as if the light of heaven were shining through the window.

Simon looked restless. He said, "Is that when Sandor started courting you, Mother?"

"You really are a troublemaker, my dear son, my only son."

"You should have had another one," said Simon, "to balance me off."

Klari said, "Sanyi didn't *court* me. I wouldn't describe it as courting."

"How would you describe it, then, Mother?"

Lili thought Simon looked especially tough with his black eyes and broken nose. He looked like a warrior.

"Wouldn't he skip out in the middle of the afternoon at the law office and come get you to take you to the movies?" Simon went on.

Klari giggled as she remembered. "Yes, we went to the very first moving picture house in Hungary, and guess where it was? In the New York Café, that's where. They started it at the New York because the coffee grinder was a big brute of a man who could crank the projector the whole way through a film. It took some strength. It was before I met Robert, needless to say. I spent a great deal of time with my cousin Sanyi."

Lili shifted uncomfortably in her seat as she watched Simon, felt his restlessness, his discomfort, perhaps, at hearing about his mother's earliest infatuation.

"I must confess," Klari went on, as she checked a wave of red hair at her temple, "Sanyi was a silly boy, really, but a strikingly handsome and smart one. And a dreamer—my Lord, what a dreamer he was! Aunt Ernesztina had three sons—Sanyi was the eldest."

"And the handsomest," Simon put in.

This time it was Lili who said, "Troublemaker."

"Yes," said Klari, awkwardly. "He was the handsomest. Anyway, you should have seen the nice office Father had renovated for Sanyi, against his own better judgment, in his building on Vaci Street. He would do things for his sister that he would never have done for his brother."

"Why don't you talk about when he came calling on you?" said Simon, and he walked to the gramophone. He winced as he bent down and put his hand on his ribs.

He selected Beethoven's Seventh Symphony and pulled it from its sleeve. A moment later, the composer's insistent music filled the room. Klari turned an invisible knob in the air, and Simon obeyed, turning the spirited symphony down somewhat.

"The trouble was that Sanyi was not interested in the law," Klari said, "and hardly ever visited Mr. Odon Grunwald. He would slip away to watch movies.

"I still clearly remember that man in there, cranking that projector. How ridiculous. How ridiculous and wonderful at the same time." Klari chuckled. "What an experience! What magic, really!

"Sandor loved that place, loved the moving pictures he saw, loved the very aroma of the place. And he used to tell me that he wanted to make pictures like that. They were pictures, he was sure, that could move people the way he had been moved.

"When more theatres were built, like the beautiful Tivoli in the seventh district—"

"I've been there!" Lili shouted and clapped her hands together. "We saw the Marx brothers there. It was wonderful."

Simon put his arm around Lili. Klari said, "Sanyi loved it, too. He would steal away from his dreary office, come take me out of school and spirit us over to the Tivoli, or later the Octagon, where we would sit in a *paholy* so as not to be spotted."

"I've seen those," Lili said, "the private boxes around the sides of the theatre and in the mezzanine. They were intended for lovers."

Robert put his head in to say, "When you put on Beethoven, you have to listen only to him. Beethoven is not background music." But then he saw the bundle in his wife's lap. "Oh, the letters and pictures," he said, and went away.

The parlour fell silent, except for Beethoven. Klari closed her eyes to listen. After a time, she said to Simon and Lili, "Do you ever wonder, as you listen to a beautiful piece of music, the kind that goes straight to your heart—do you wonder, is it all right for me to love this melody in this way, or did the composer not intend it for my ears? In other words, am I *welcome* here? Or conversely, if Wagner, say, disapproved of us Jews, is it all right for my heart to go on this voyage at all, or must I hold it back?"

Klari looked down at her feet. It was another minute before she resumed her story. "Of course, we were not lovers, Sandor and I. Cousins sometimes were, but we were not. At the theatre, Sanyi would clasp my hand in his as if we were getting set for a ride on a Ferris wheel. The lights would dim, the piano player would start to play, the great curtains would be drawn open as if upon the panoramic windows of a palace, but instead of looking outside, we'd gaze upon another world altogether, the world of an Alaskan in *The Spoilers*, the world of a penniless little hobo in *The Tramp* with

Charlie Chaplin. Sanyi loved them all, and so did I—Mack Sennett with his Keystone Cops, the chilling *Birth of a Nation*, made by a man named D.W. Griffith, then Cecil B. DeMille and Erich von Stroheim, that lovely Mary Pickford . . ."

Her voice trailed off here as Beethoven's lilting allegretto began, rhythmic and imploring. Klari said, "Oh, now listen to this impossibly beautiful music." Klari closed her eyes and placed her right hand over her heart.

They all listened, but then Lili asked, "How old were you and Sandor then, Miss Klari?"

"I was eighteen or nineteen, and Sanyi was a year younger—too young, really, to apprentice to a lawyer."

"But not too young to fall in love," Simon said.

"No, not too young, but he was more interested in the love on the screen, the adventure, the safe adventure, I suppose, the safe love—the unreal love, that's what it was—than he was in me or anyone else. Little did I know at the time that he was apprenticing to the film directors, not to Odon Grunwald with his hefty law books, poor man. He tried so hard."

Klari sighed, but then she smiled. "Things went quite badly between Father and our cousin after a time. Young love was too frivolous for our father."

To Lili, it felt as though they were talking about the love stories in films, not in real life. They paused to listen to the Beethoven. Simon wished they could go out to the movies themselves, sit in a *paholy* and drink coffee. How did that world slip away? He listened to the Beethoven again. He said, "My cousin Paul loves to quote that American poet, Emily Dickinson. She wrote, 'Some cannot sing, but the orchard is full of birds, and we can all listen.'"

"That's lovely," Lili said.

"He's referring to himself, dear," Klari said to Lili. "Just don't ask him to sing."

Lili giggled, and he laughed, too.

Klari got to her feet. "I think we've had enough of these ancient recollections. We'll continue another time."

"I haven't had enough," Lili said. "I want to know what happened."

"Show her one of the photographs," Simon said.

Klari looked down at the bundle of letters and photographs in her lap. She gingerly untied the knot in the ribbon and pulled a photograph from the bundle. She passed the picture to Lili. It was of an elegantly dressed man and woman, the man in a light suit and a white Panama hat, the woman in a wide-brimmed sun hat, laughing up toward heaven. The man was throwing some bits of bread to pigeons by a fountain. The pigeons were everywhere.

"That's Sandor and—guess who," she said.

"You look so much younger, but lovely as ever," Lili said.

"We were in Siena—Sandor, my mother, my sisters and I. By the fountain in the square—Il Campo, they call it—where the horses run. They have a race there, in this ancient piazza."

"What a nice couple you were," Lili added, "happy and carefree."

"Thank you, but we were hardly a couple, as I've said."

"Ha," said Simon.

"Don't you be smart," his mother said.

"What went wrong?" Lili asked Klari. "You were saying things went very wrong between him and your father."

"Sandor had violent arguments with our father," Klari said. She huffed out a breath with some force, as if she were expelling smoke.

Klari said, "When word got back to Father that his nephew had been spotted at the New York Café or the Orpheum, he began to speak of him as an ungrateful lout. And whenever he found out I had been with Sanyi, he punished me terribly. I was to stay in my room, without music, without walks, without family meals, for a week or longer at a time. And he banned me from the picture palaces for a year.

"Sandor seemed unperturbed. He would show up at our house anyway. It was a big place, and he'd stayed with us, so he knew where to hide out. He'd sneak me out of my room and steal me away for the last show of the evening."

"Didn't anyone catch you?"

"No, because everyone was in on our little racket. My sisters enjoyed Sandor's company, and he was generous with it. There was plenty of wit and charm to go around. Even the servants thought he was sweet and were eager for him to regale them with tales of Jules Verne or Victor Hugo. The trick was that our parents' room was at the back of the house, half a city block away from ours, so it was easy enough. But our father's wrath would become the least of our problems."

"What happened?" Lili asked.

"We snuck out to the movies late one evening, Sandor and I. My sisters knew we were going, as always. In the end, everyone knew, even our mother. Juliana loved him as much as the rest of us.

"Sanyi and I sat in our usual spot at the Tivoli. Sanyi even had wine and flowers brought to our seats—he really was silly. I don't remember what film we saw that evening. If my life depended on it, I couldn't tell you. All I remember was the news. That was in the day when serious people went to the movies to watch newsreels, to get a better sense of what was happening in the world. On this particular night, there was news of a crackdown on communists in Budapest . . ." she hesitated ". . . and even pictures of young men who had been hanged, friends of Sanyi's, people he used to meet up with at the New York and the Japan—artists, bohemians, people just like Sanyi.

"We left the cinema numbed. Sanyi said his days in Hungary had come to an end. It was time to start life over in a more sensible place."

"Was he a communist?" Lili asked.

"Hardly, but his artistic friends were, some of them. Miksa was, the cousin he was staying with, the poet. But Sanyi was anything but. He was more like our father than either of them liked to admit. He had a fire in his soul, but he seemed to have command of that fire, if that's possible, and command of the people around him, much like Father.

Much like my nephew Paul. He even looked like Paul. He was tall and dashing.

"That same night, the night of the newsreel, we were caught again by Father as Sanyi tried to sneak me back into my house. Hermina, bless her heart, tried to stop our father, but he cursed Sanyi from the door."

Klari stood now to act out the role. "'How dare you defy me in this way?' he said." Klari used a deep voice. "'It's not just your life you're wasting, here, but my daughter's, your mother's. How dare you disobey me so flagrantly and senselessly? I want you away from here. I want you to pack your things in the law office and clear out. I want nothing to do with you. You are a disgrace to the family name.'"

Klari paused dramatically. Then she said, "Sandor looked at our father and said calmly, 'A disgrace? A disgrace to the family name? In what way could I possibly be a disgrace? The only disgrace to be brought upon the family will be the disgrace of hypocrisy and blindness. Uncle Maximillian, I will not take your kindness for granted anymore.' Our father turned his back on Sanyi, and he never saw him again, nor heard from him directly.

"And he did bring plenty of honour to the name," Klari said. "In Britain, he became known as Alexander Korda."

Simon said, "And he wrote only to Mother, never to the rest of the family." Klari hung her head. "Show her a letter, Mother. Show Lili the one about one of the films."

"Did he come back?" Lili asked.

"Once or twice. Mostly, he stayed in England and helped found the British film industry, as we like to brag, although we had little to do with his achievement except to drive him away. Suddenly, it was his name we were seeing up there on the screen for some of the big pictures: *The Private Life of Henry VIII*, *The Four Feathers*, *The Scarlet Pimpernel*. Sandor was even knighted by the king recently, with that silly name he'd picked out. Sir Alexander Korda, he became. I could barely contain my excitement every time we went to the movies, Robert and I, because it was like a postcard from abroad with moving snapshots thrown in, and yet I must confess it was never again as exciting to go to the picture palaces as it had been with Sandor."

"Why?" Lili asked.

"Because I was going with someone in love."

"With you?"

"No, with movies." She looked Lili directly in the eye. "He had a kind of glow about him, like someone already in the movies, someone born to it." She sighed. "I'll never forget those evenings. Impossible days. It's not at all what Simon says. It's a good thing our love was never realized. Reality wouldn't have been good for it."

Klari coughed and got to her feet.

"Do you have that letter he wrote to you from America?" her son asked.

"Was he in America?" Lili said.

"Oh, yes, he tried to make a go of it there, too, and in Berlin at first, and Vienna. But he went to the United States at the outbreak of the war. He wrote from there."

Klari found the letter with the American postmark and handed it to Lili.

Beverly Hills Carrington Hotel
Beverly Hills, California
August 16, 1943

My dear Klari,

Did you manage to get out again in these dark and depressed times to catch that old movie of mine called *The Man Who Could Work Miracles?* I can't remember if you saw it the first time around. It's a slightly corny affair based on a story by that clever H.G. Wells, about a man named George Fotheringay, played by Roland Young. He's a clerk who finds he has the power to change anything in the world simply by command. The power naturally goes to his head—why should he be any different from the rest of us?—and he wants ultimately to stop the Earth's rotation. I won't tell you how it turns out in case you haven't caught it.

But I will say that, as I saw it again on this side of the Atlantic, I kept remembering the afternoon seven or eight years ago when I was sitting with my director, Lothar Mendes, and my editor, and we were cutting the film in a mad hurry to get it ready for its release, and we were looking at take after take of Roland Young saying something inconsequential, but he had trouble spitting it out—getting the one bit right. Mendes had made him do it over and over. As I watched, and we selected the right take to attach to the previous scene, I realized that the magic had almost evaporated for me, that cutting this movie was like cutting up the miracles themselves. It took me back to the days when we used to sit in our *paholy*, you and I—do you remember, Klarikam, our booth at the Octagon? Or even better—do you remember the coffee grinder cum projector cranker at the New York Café? Good God! What magic he cranked out of those first transparent moving pictures. Do you recall, *galambom*?

Forgive me for getting carried away, but I find myself doing that more often in these stormy times, looking day after day for the sky to clear, searching my memory for the sunny days. They were hardly carefree but they seem so now. Everything was ahead of us, wasn't it, Klarikam?

I also remember one thing you said to me, on one of the last days we spent together, when you knew your father and I were going to come to blows. You said, "Be kind." That was all, and it has remained with me since. I always have to remind myself in this nasty place, this nasty world, just to be kind because when I am I feel better. It's all so simple, isn't it?

Please pass on my love to your family, whichever members you choose to share my love with. I leave that judgment with you. Be well, and as I said last time, get out of Europe. It's time.

With much affection,
Sir Sanyi

"So, there you have it," Klari said. "I'm sure now you've had your fill." She was looking down, folding up the letter again, preparing to tie up the bundle with the red ribbon. Lili thought Klari might cry.

That night, as Lili helped Simon into bed, she said, "Your mother was so smitten."

"How about you and me?" Simon asked. "Do we have a chance at smittenhood?"

She took his hand again. "No, something more meaningful," she said but then blushed right away.

They kissed softly, Lili conscious of his sore nose.

THIS DAY, Lili was on the hunt for meat. She walked quickly and with her head down, but she tried not to look conspicuous. She was to meet her friend Maria at the Madar Café, where Maria was a waitress. Lili had run into her in a park one day. As Maria was feeding the pigeons, Lili took a risk and told her about herself, and Maria sobbed and hugged Lili hard. That afternoon, Maria arranged to get Lili a good-sized Emmenthal cheese and some crusty bread to take home. Still, Lili avoided calling upon Maria too often; she didn't want to get the kind young woman into trouble. On this occasion, though, Maria had insisted. She said she had something for Lili.

Lili walked the twenty blocks without incident, but right outside the Madar stood a German officer, a lieutenant. Lili was about to turn sharply to the right and head down Szemzo Street—as casual as could be, as if she didn't have a care—but the officer stopped her. Her heart lurched.

She felt for her papers in the front pocket of her blue skirt. She wore a blue blouse, too, with a white collar. The German didn't seem to care about papers. "Where are you going?" he asked in German, speaking slowly and quietly.

"I was coming here to meet my friend Maria." Lili was able to answer in German, but she had to watch she didn't accidentally throw in a Yiddish word.

"Oh, Maria," he said, as if he knew her. "My name is Horst Immel."

"We're going to her uncle's church," she blurted out. "He's the priest there. Father Ambrus. It's the little Church of St. Margaret, over on—"

"Why don't I walk you there?" he interrupted.

"Because I'm supposed to go with Maria, as I said."

"All right, with Maria, then."

Horst Immel took off his cap and rubbed his forehead with his sleeve. He was quite tall, and blond, though not as blond as Lili. The sun was at her back, and he closed one eye to block it out. He seemed gentle and trustworthy, but three months before Lili had believed most people were that way. Could he have already completed one campaign and now been reassigned to another? Had he been promoted to lieutenant because of the good work he'd done as a sergeant back in Tolgy? Could he have been one of her family's captors? She wanted to ask him, What have you Germans done with my family? With my friend Hilda? If you want to do something nice, ask your friends, please, what became of them. Ask your colleagues for me, your compatriots. Yes, I am one of *them*. Lili had to cross her arms to muffle the drumming of her heart.

Suddenly, Maria was beside them on the sidewalk, still wearing her apron. She had seen them outside. "Lili," she said, a little breathless.

"Oh, Lili?" the officer said.

"Are you ready to go?" Lili asked Maria.

Maria said she'd just be a second and ran back into the café to shed her apron and get her purse. The coffee shop was a modest one, but clean and cheerful. It was a favourite of soldiers, mostly German ones. They were able to get a good schnitzel and wurst there, and the best Pilsner in town. The owner often bragged that he drove all the way into the country to get the supplies he needed, and they were all fresh.

"I want to walk with you," the German said to Lili. "There are some dangerous elements around these days who might not treat you as kindly as you'd like."

Lili tried not to look astonished. He still had an eye closed to the sun—the other eye this time—as he looked at her.

Maria was back. "Come on, then," she said. She wanted to get the walk over with. Her German was not as good as Lili's, but no one would ever suspect Maria of anything. She had the look of the ancient Hungarian tribes, thick black hair, slightly oriental brown eyes, with a good strong thickness about her body.

"Where do you live?" Horst asked Lili.

"Over on Jokai Street," she said.

He shrugged his shoulders.

"She and her family attend our church," Maria said. "Are you a Catholic, Lieutenant?"

"No, I'm Lutheran."

"Oh, we have some of those in Hungary, too, though most are Catholic—the Christians, I mean."

Lili saw that Maria was looking the other way, as if at a store window. She knew her friend was blushing. She was anxious and talking far too much.

"I grew up on a farm," Lili said, "in the southeast." She wanted to see if there was anything suspicious about his look, but how could there be? He was invading Budapest now. Horst smiled at her as they walked. His teeth were very white. He took long strides, so the women had to walk quickly. "Geese and chickens, mostly," Lili added.

"My family is in Dusseldorf," he said. For the first time, Lili realized that he might have someone waiting for him, too, a mother, a sister, a girlfriend—all the men in their lives scattered—and that Horst might never be back. "Is your family here with you now, in Budapest?" he asked. "On Jokai Street, is it?"

"No, I'm staying with an uncle and aunt here, just for a little while."

"She has a fiancé too," Maria said. "She's engaged."

"Oh," he said, sounding genuinely disappointed. They slowed down slightly, as the lieutenant saw that the women were almost out of breath.

What dangerous elements did the German have in mind, Lili wondered, from which he could protect them? Was he not the one out of place on these streets? What was he expecting? Wild dogs? Wild Hungarians—psychotic ones, turned Nyilas? What would happen then? Would they duel it out for the privilege of protecting the honour of these two fine girls?

The streets were surprisingly quiet. They felt, for a shiver, like the streets of Tolgy. Lili and her sister Tildy, not too many years before, used to think that the windows of empty houses were eyes that had been blinded as a result of staring one another down for too long. Her friend Hilda said no, they were not blind, but saw everything, and could report it at will to "the authorities," whoever they were.

On the corner was a barbershop where, short weeks before, Simon and his father used to go for a haircut. The place was now dark, the owner and his family having been taken to the walled ghetto behind the temple on Dohany Street. Lili felt ashamed as they passed the shop, felt like a betrayer, or a bad actress playing a betrayer alongside her German guard.

They made it to the church without incident. Lili wondered anxiously what might happen next, but Horst merely saluted casually and said he hoped to see Maria and Lili at the Madar Café again sometime. Lili could picture him dressed as a gentleman back in Dusseldorf, someone who tipped his hat as he came and went. And then he was gone. Lili actually paused on the steps to watch him go before following her friend into the little church.

Father Ambrus greeted both girls warmly if a little solemnly. Candles burned behind him. They stood in a bed of sand. Maria had apparently told her uncle Lili's story. He handed Lili some fresh wafers, wrapped in a tea cloth. "These are for your Budapest family, and you, of course," he said. "Have one now, if you like. They're very nice."

"They're the flesh of Christ," Maria said, and she laughed out loud. No one joined her. "I mean at Mass on Sunday," she said quietly, "when people take communion."

Lili felt like an intruder. Father Ambrus asked the girls to sit and wait. Lili didn't know what for, but she and Maria made themselves comfortable at the back of the little church. Lili set the package of wafers down gently on her lap. She didn't want to damage them.

Lili had never been to a church before, but she felt utterly safe. What better place to be concealed? Someone off to the side began playing the organ. Lili searched the shadows.

"That's my uncle," Maria whispered. "He plays Bach. It gets him into moods." Maria tapped her temple. "It stirs the spirits."

Lili looked at her friend.

"The music, I mean, the Bach."

Lili listened some more and soon understood why. The music fluttered like a bird flying up to the belfry, searching for a door out of which to soar even higher. A porcelain Jesus looked down from his cross at the altar, his expression serene despite his circumstance. Lili was carried away by what she saw and heard, almost forgetting the package in her lap.

Maria said, "Everyone is afraid." Lili looked straight at her friend. "We *are*," she said. "Nobody knows what's coming. The Germans are here now. They're shovelling people around. Russians might come, or, my fiancé says, even Americans, possibly, or Japanese—who knows? And we're hungry, too. Not me, necessarily, because I have the café, but some of my family, and Patrik's family—my fiancé."

"I didn't know."

"He's coming for us now. He's taking us somewhere."

"He is?"

"Yes, don't worry. It'll be all right."

The music stopped, and a minute later Father Ambrus came to tell the girls that Patrik was out back. Maria said, "He's brought a carriage, pulled by a horse." Then she said again, "It'll be all right."

The priest nodded as he helped the young women into the carriage. Patrik looked rustic, though of course he couldn't have been. He was a big man with broad shoulders and straw-coloured hair. Lili sat in the back, guarding her wafers. Maria sat with her fiancé in front, and between the couple lay a formidable bayonet. Behind them were burlap sacks; one of them looked to be full of potatoes.

"Where are we going?" Lili asked.

"Patrik is a zookeeper," Maria said. "You'll see."

"We're going to the *zoo*?" Lili had been to the zoo only once in her life, and that was the small one in Szeged. What a thing to propose on such a day, with the worries they had.

"The zoo's closed," Patrik said, without turning his head, "but we can get in."

They clopped through the city at a reasonable pace. After a time they turned a corner and saw a long line of people, each wearing the yellow Star of David sewn to their jackets or coats. They looked like families, most of them; they included the old and the young, and the line extended from one end of the avenue all the way to the other. They were being marshalled by Germans. Lili felt her stomach convulse, felt herself gag. She'd heard from Paul and others about these processions, but this was the first she'd witnessed.

Patrik pulled up on the reins—"Whoa"—and turned the horse around to take another route. The bayonet clattered to the floor, and Maria retrieved it. She turned to look at Lili, who clung to her wafers. Lili wanted to ask to be let off, but Patrik turned and said, "We'll be there before too long, and you'll feel calmer."

It was another hour before they arrived at the zoo, but the summer trees gave the travellers shade, and the rhythmic clopping of the horse's hooves on the stone calmed Lili down the way the church music had.

The gates of the Budapest Zoo were closed, and as Patrik leapt down and unlocked them, Lili admired the ironwork: figures of animals of all kinds, in pairs, merrily prancing toward the apex of the gate, where Noah, his welcoming arms open, awaited them in his ark.

Maria took the reins to drive the carriage through, and Patrik locked the cheerful gates behind them. Lili caught a country whiff of manure as they entered, and she thought again of Tolgy—Erik, the rooster, and the geese and horses.

Patrik took over the reins again, and bent into the task of steering the carriage down the lanes of the zoo. Maria glanced over her shoulder at Lili and smiled. Lili heard the exotic shriek of birds she couldn't recognize. They passed an expansive pen marked "Ostrich (*Struthio camelus*)," but Lili couldn't spot an ostrich anywhere. She'd never seen one and would have liked to.

Around the corner, a lone giraffe in a forested enclosure stood and chewed the leaves of a tall tree. Lili said, "Can we get down?"

"No," Patrik said too abruptly. "It's better if you stay in the carriage. We won't stay long."

They passed the primates: the "Ring-Tailed Lemur (*Lemur catta*)," a scrawny and curious-looking animal that had the most lively striped tail; the "Chimpanzee (*Pan troglodytes*)," but he or she, too, was hiding out somewhere, like the ostrich; and grandest of all, the "Eastern Lowlands Gorilla (*Gorilla beringei*)." The great beast was lying on its side, facing away from the visitors. It looked utterly still and silent.

"Is he all right?" Lili said. She wanted to stand up in the carriage as they passed. Patrik didn't answer. Lili thought her little brother Mendi would have been thrilled to be here. She wondered what the chances were that she could ever come back here with him. Lili's eyes stayed on the ape. She asked again, "Is he all right?"

Maria tugged on Patrik's sleeve. "I don't think so," he said.

"Is he *dead*?"

Patrik shrugged his shoulders. "It's a hard time for them, like us," he said. "It's a hard time for all of us."

Even before they turned the corner ahead of them, Lili could hear shrill, mocking laughter. She saw an expanse of sand and rock, a few trees, clumps of grass. She soon found the sign: "Brown Hyena (*Hyaena brunnea*)." She wished she could write down the names for Mendi.

Two hyenas were at the gate of their enclosure. Patrik dismounted. They were ready to jump on the fence when they saw him. They laughed and barked at Patrik. He placed his hand flat on the gate so they could smell him. One of the hyenas loped off, but the other one stayed. He looked like a large unkempt dog of some kind and seemed to like Patrik the way a dog might. Patrik pulled a key out of one pocket and a scrap of gristle out of the other. He let the hyena get a whiff of it, then reached back into the carriage for the bayonet.

He turned to the girls and raised his finger to his lips. "Don't spook him," he whispered. Maria turned to Lili and shielded her eyes as if from the sun.

Patrik entered the pen. Lili wanted to ask what was happening but stayed silent as instructed. Maria kept her gaze on Lili, one hand still shielding her eyes from the sight in the pen. With her other hand, she clutched Lili's, much too hard. Lili was still protecting the wafers. She turned toward the animal just as Patrik slashed the hyena's throat. The strong animal slumped to the dirt. The blood splatted out as far as the wheels of the carriage. Now Lili did feel she'd be sick. Maria loosened her grip. "It'll be all right," she whispered to Lili. The hyena that had run off now cackled from a distance at its fallen friend.

"She's a good one," Patrik said. He had blood all up his jacket and on one side of his face. "Meaty." He raised the bayonet again and brought it down with the force of a guillotine, slicing deep into the hindquarters. "She's a good forty-five—fifty kilos. We'll each have a hunk. You too, Lili." The hyena's friend came a step closer and cackled again, then turned and ran off into a clump of bush. "Maria, toss me those sacks, three of them."

Maria jumped down. She patted the grey horse on its cheek. "He's a Lipizzaner," Maria said. "Klaus. He's from Vienna."

Lili calmed down as she looked at Klaus. The horse threw his head back a couple of times and neighed. Lili said to Patrik and Maria, "I'll help you if you want me to."

Patrik said, "No, we can manage." He worked the bayonet now like an expert butcher. The animal was chopped into front, middle and back. "I'll give you the front," Patrik said to Lili. "The head will make a good soup—the brain is good. The rest will make a hearty stew. And you can have some of the potatoes in the back there." Patrik worked up quite a sweat as he hacked away at the animal. "I'll bring an axe next time," he said, grunting.

They heard a roar some distance away. "The cats," Patrik said, as he wiped his forehead with his bloody sleeve. "That's a panther. A beauty." He smirked. "Another time."

Lili smelled the iron of the blood. It filled the air. Maria and Patrik grunted as they hauled the sodden sacks back to the carriage and hoisted them into the back. Lili ran her hand over the wafers covered in the tea cloth.

Patrik steered Klaus expertly all the way back into the city's core and to the Becks' house on Jokai Street. Simon had evidently been looking out for her; he was outside by the curb in an instant. Lili saw Patrik taking in Simon's black eyes and broken nose. Maria was transferring some potatoes into a smaller sack. "I can help you up with these," Patrik said to Lili.

At the door, Simon asked, "Can we pay you?"

"No, some other time, maybe," Patrik said.

He handed the bloody sack to Simon, who took it against his white shirt and winced as it met his ribcage.

"Thank you so much," said Lili. She kissed Maria, avoiding a drop of blood on her friend's cheek.

Maria winked and departed with the burly Patrik.

Simon grunted and asked, "What's in the sack?"

"Mine?" Lili asked. "Potatoes."

"No, this one."

"Hyena."

Simon almost dropped the sack, but grunted again as he heaved it higher and headed quickly for the Alhambra. "I hope we have the laughing end," he said.

"Yes, with potatoes."

Twelve

ROZSI WAS TO MEET ZOLI at the place he thought was safest: the boathouse where they had found Zindelo, the Gypsy violinist. It was their new rendezvous. The Strawberry Gardens had become too risky. Zoli had seen a young woman and her father being beaten there by the Arrow Cross. He had managed to get a single photograph of the incident.

Rozsi arrived early, looked in and called Zindelo's name, but there was no response. The boat was there, the *Petofi*, and Rozsi searched it to be sure. She saw the wooden scroll of Zindelo's violin peeking out of the bag he kept it in. Where would he go without his violin? She shivered and felt cold. The rain had started again, just like the last time she was in this hut, and everything felt damp.

The boat bumped against its mooring, and Rozsi jumped. She was skittish these days wherever she went and nervous even around their house. Though Paul was spending more time at home than he used to, she was anxious when he left her alone, even though she had her Swedish papers at the ready. He was out always with the Swede, Raoul Wallenberg. They were trying to set up "safe houses," as they kept calling them, because the Jews they were saving from the transports had no place to go. Many of their homes had been confiscated and were now occupied.

Zoli was rarely late, but this morning he was. He said he'd be there by nine, and now it was almost a quarter after. What could have happened? Zoli and his camera. It was worse than a weapon. It was a weapon you might as well turn on yourself. And she had told him so. Was this to be the new pattern? He'd be late, she'd worry; he'd arrive, she'd plead; he'd calm her down, and then he'd be late again.

Rozsi woke each day wondering how this could have happened to her beloved Budapest. All of her thoughts centred on the perpetrator, this Adolf Hitler she had rarely considered until he sent that other Adolf—Eichmann—to torment Hungarians. What was it about her land that was so offensive that they wanted to topple the lovely theatres and cafés and bridges? What did Adolf Number One think, each night, before he drifted off to sleep with his Eva Braun—that everything was right with the world as he bulldozed its buildings on one front and evacuated certain of its citizens on another? How could he appreciate it all in a single head? Did he think, Now I've wrecked Poland, and that was a very fine *Jagerschnitzel*, my darling, as he patted his tummy? It didn't make sense, even to Rozsi, who rarely tried to make sense of such things. Did he surround himself with adjective-makers who called him Great and Glorious, Magnificent and Brave, Brilliant and Powerful, Blessed and Noble, Eloquent and Tough?

And why did her Zoli feel he had to capture the man's far-fetched deeds on celluloid? What would we want to remember it for? Rozsi didn't want to be part of an exhibit about their lives. She wanted to continue her life.

That was what Zoli told her he was doing: fighting for the lives they had. She looked at her ruby ring. She wondered now where Istvan had got to. She felt she could show him her ring and the note that ended with "*I love*." He was more in his gut, like her, and could have understood why she'd fallen for Zoli. She'd shown Paul the ring, and he said it was nice, but he seemed to be examining the gem itself, holding it up to the light, rather than considering its implications. Was Istvan long gone now? Was he listed among Adolf's daily tallies? We've moved this many now, like so many head of cattle. We like to level buildings and move residents, then settle down to *Jagerschnitzel*. Rozsi felt closer to Istvan than she did to her eldest brother. Rozsi had come to Budapest because she needed to, for her own sanity—she didn't want to be the first lady of Szeged after her mother had died, didn't want to entertain her father's windy friends. Besides, Paul had needed someone to look after and to keep him company.

The minutes passed. Rozsi would have asked Lili to come with her, but Lili was on a scavenger hunt, as always. Lili, the miracle worker; Lili, the *wunderkind*. Rozsi was so tired of being the overlooked *kind*, the forgotten *kind*, the *kind vergessen*. A tall new tree had moved into the woods to stand among the others—Paul, Istvan, the spectre of her father, the spectre of her mother, and now that Lili—all of them overshadowing her, blocking out the sun. Lili was so extraordinary that, when Rozsi had said her house was drafty in the evenings and she was always cold, Lili had broken into someone's abandoned place and stolen a good lambswool coat for her, even though Rozsi had a perfectly nice lined suede coat. Two other coats and several dresses they had traded for meals. Rozsi should have worn one of the coats today, even though it was summer.

Rozsi was close to her uncle and aunt. If part of the reason she moved to Budapest was to be with Paul, then another part was to be near her Aunt Klari. She reminded Rozsi of her mother—looked like her, reacted to things in a similar way. Mathilde would have taken to Zoli right away, as Klari had. Rozsi often talked with Klari about Zoli's dangerous work with his camera, and Klari told her, "You wouldn't have it any other way, Rozsikam. His ambition and integrity are what make him who he is, but he's more than a romantic figure in your life. His passion excites you, too—doesn't it—and his integrity?"

ZOLTAN MAK HAD INTENDED to be on time for Rozsi, but he'd been delayed, first by Paul, who'd needed extra pictures done that morning, and then again by an incident on the Liberty Bridge.

Zoltan had been held up for some time. He'd been shadowing a small group he had come upon on the Street of the Martyrs, four Arrow Cross officers of the Hungarian special police. They'd taken a Jewish man and a young boy, a one-time journalist Zoli recognized and his son, and hustled them—dragged the hysterical boy—all the way to the Liberty Bridge. The Arrow Cross tied father and son together with rope thick enough to secure stallions. They slapped the boy to shut him up. When the father protested, they slapped him, too. Zoli watched as the boy whimpered. One of the guards had a machine gun, another a rifle. They wore leather gloves. Zoli stood close by, but managed to keep in the shadows behind a stone brace. He snapped his seventh photo, and an eighth.

The one who seemed to be the leader said, "We have a little game we like to play." As he spoke, he stepped right up to the man and boy, tied back to back. Now he spoke only to the boy. "There's a rhyme you must remember from when you were a toddler." From the tone of his voice, you'd have thought he was a kind uncle, a gentle guardian. He said, "Even Jewboys learned the national rhymes, didn't you?"

The boy continued to whimper.

"Am I wrong? *Didn't* you?" The officer's mouth came within an inch of the boy's ear. They were standing by the railing of the bridge, pressed against it. Zoli took a photograph.

"Yes, we did," the father said.

"Well, then," said the officer, adopting the avuncular tone again. "Let's repeat the rhyme, shall we?"

Now a couple hurried across the bridge toward the men. They were rushing to get out of the rain, which had just begun to pock the Danube. The man held on to his fedora, the woman to her plastic rain bonnet. They slowed as they passed the small clutch of people. Zoli heard the man ask what was going on. He took a photograph: *A man with his wife on a rainy bridge, his hand held out in inquiry*. Then a shot rang out, launching the fedora skyward, then all the way down to the river. Another photo: *Flying fedora, blurring against a wet sky*. The man was dead even before his body buckled to the bridge. Snap: *The woman wails*. Snap: *She drops to her knees over her fallen husband*. Snap: *She takes a bullet to the back of the neck*.

Iron drops of rain fell now. The father stood in horror as he watched the Nyilas officers. Zoli hid behind his camera. Snap: *They fling the woman first, then the man after her, into the darkening river*. "Your hat went that way!" one of the junior officers yelled, pointing into the water.

Now there could be little doubt as to what was coming. The father pleaded for the life of his son. "Just the boy at least," he was saying. "Please."

Zoli couldn't think what to do. He gazed into the lens at the scene before him, a small black and white square cut out of a nightmare. His heart no longer beat, it seemed, but gushed within him, sending hot currents to his cheeks and extremities. What was he to do? What could he do? He could rush at the men to stop them, or rather delay them, for that's all he could accomplish, surely. He could aim his camera well and click as often as his film would allow him. He could hold absolutely still so that he could live to tell the tale someday. Or he could flee and never look back, never think back—just take nothing and vanish.

Zoli felt ready to vomit. He could not move. He must not vomit. He raised the camera yet again to his eye. Was it light enough still to get a picture? He heard the boy's voice cut the rain with the childhood song, cut it as sharply as cut crystal.

Brightly coloured moocow,
Without ears or tail, cow.

We are going to live where
We can get our milk there.

Boci boci tarka,
Se fule, se farka.
Oda megyunk lakni
Ahol tejet kapni.

A pistol rose, as did a lens. A shot punctuated the song. Shot: *The boy begins again as his father's head bobs forward lifelessly, then backward against the top of his son's head.*

Brightly coloured moocow,
Without ears or tail, cow.

Snap: *They lift the dead man onto the railing, still tied to his singing son.*

We are going to live where
We can get our milk there.

The one with the machine gun said, "The trout need a song."

"And the carp," his comrade added, the one with the rifle. Snap: *He butts the two into the blueblack river, the singing boy secured to his dead father.*

By the time Zoli made it to the boathouse, he found Rozsi sobbing. She was sitting on the floor. He drew her to her feet and sobbed with her. He didn't have to say a thing; his eyes showed their horror. She felt the bulge of the infernal camera beneath his wet jacket.

"I'm sorry," he said.

"Where were you?"

"I can't say."

"What pictures did you take?"

"I can't say. I never want you to see what I just saw."

She looked up at the horror still registered in his eyes and shud-dered. "We've got to leave this place," she said. She held his face in her hands. "We've got to leave Hungary."

"I won't," he replied. He spoke calmly now. "I can't."

"Then we'll never get away from here," she said. She pressed her face against his chest, expecting to hear a caged bird flapping wildly. But she heard nothing.

He raised a steadying, even warm, hand to the back of her neck. "I can't. I need to take pictures."

She pulled back from him. Her fingertips were cold and numb. "Do you know what's going on? They'll kill you!"

"Do I know what's going on? Yes, I do. They can kill me, but the photographs will be secure—I'll make sure of it."

"What are you, insane?"

"Possibly. I have a job to do, a cause."

"What *cause*?" she cried, then hit his chest. "We have no cause. Survival, that's our cause. We cannot afford other causes. You sound like my fool brother. What possible cause? Do you know who these Germans are? Do you want to take pictures of the world gone mad?"

"No, I'd rather take pictures of picnics and swans, but the world has gone mad, as you say, and I want people to remember just how mad. It's the only thing I can contribute."

"But why can't you just let people's memory glue things back together? Destruction is destruction wherever it happens. Who's ever going to say it was pretty, even without pictures?"

"Please," he said.

She cried some more and he held her. After a time, he asked, "Where's Zindelo?"

"Who knows?" she screamed. "Probably shot or transported or drowned. Who knows these days? *I* am going mad," she said. "Do you understand that? *I* am part of this, too. Aren't you? Can you look into your lens and think you're invulnerable? There's a person connected to that eye—a soul—*my* soul—*our* soul."

Her voice lost its force. They swayed together like the boat. The rain beat down hard now on the little roof, so the couple stayed put, waiting for it to pass. Rozsi asked, "Do you think we can go to the Strawberry Gardens, just for a bit?"

"No, not today," Zoli said. "It's not safe."

"Why won't you tell me where you stay?"

"I'll show you sometime."

"Show me today."

"All right. Tonight."

ZOLI SOMETIMES STAYED at Rozsi and Paul's townhouse, but most often he went somewhere else. When he did show up at the Becks' home, Zoli always tried to bring food. Once, when Klari's family was visiting, he arrived with a pan of roast potatoes, still hot from the oven. He'd persuaded his old friend, the owner of Lekvar, to hand it over just as he was going to serve it. The restaurant had been his favourite bohemian haunt until just months before, when it became too dangerous to visit regularly. Zoli set the pan down before them in the kitchen and made a grand gesture with his hands, like a magician, inviting everyone to partake.

Robert nodded his appreciation as the frenzy began around the pan, but Zoli took Rozsi aside. "Look what else I have for you," he whispered dramatically as he pulled a kilo of smoked ham from inside his coat.

"Goodness," she said, gasping, covering her mouth with both hands. "Just what I need." She giggled.

He withheld the ham, concealed it again in his coat.

"I didn't mean anything," she said. "I'm so sorry. This has all been a bit too trying for me, that's all."

He didn't answer but stood stiffly in front of her.

"I know you've been through a lot, too, even more, but I'm no good at this," she said. He started to turn away from her, but she stopped him, clutched his shoulders and aimed his gaze at her. "I don't know how to do this," she went on. "I'm not very good at starving or not having freshly laundered clothes and linens. I feel like a Gypsy."

He shrugged out of her clutches and stepped back. "You're not starving yet, and you're not a Gypsy."

"Well, if I were, I'd be happier. I'd know that I was indoors, at least. It would be home for a time, and then something else would be home." She was crying now. "I need roots. I'm not a rootless type. I'm not saying I'm special—quite the contrary. I'm not daring. I'm not adventurous, except in my choice of men."

"And you're adventurous with me because of what I have chosen to do?"

"No, I guess it's because I've chosen love over some other, tidier arrangement."

They embraced, and she could feel the great ham hidden inside his coat. She laughed out loud.

ZOLTAN WAS EAGER to get his lab to develop his film of the journalist and his boy on the bridge. He took Rozsi to a building that had already been cleared out by the Nazis, its residents deported by train. Zoltan had moved into the boiler room, which was next to a basement meat locker that served the kosher butcher on the ground floor, now gone. Few remnants of the meat remained, only scrapings in steel canisters. The day the Germans came, Zoli hid in this locker behind an empty *schmaltz* vat and narrowly eluded notice. When the Germans returned, Zoli was in the next room, inside the cold furnace. He worried as much about his camera equipment being discovered as he did about himself. He had heard gunfire upstairs on this second raid and wished he could somehow have captured it on film.

The building now seemed to Zoltan safer than most, safer than Rozsi's own place, so he brought her there with less reluctance than he pretended to have. The only dangerous part was getting there. Zoli had strung together a clever route through a park overgrown with willows, followed by a stockyard, a cemetery, railway tracks, over which one night deportees were carried past him as he hid in some scrub brush, and a back alley where the week before he'd found a wheelbarrow full of ears of corn, their owner and destination unclear. He'd also found a rabbit, or one had found him, a plump one, and followed him home one night. Through a clever swing of a wooden gate, Zoli had managed to bash the creature dead. He skinned it and roasted it beneath an open window in his meat locker. He worried that the scent of the roasting flesh would give him away, but he'd tried stoves in apartments upstairs and found, of course, they were without gas. So he cooked it over a little fire downstairs, staying on the lookout throughout the process. Whenever he sensed danger, he fled to his alley or cemetery until he was certain he could return. And everywhere he went, Zoli carried his camera like a weapon of defence.

On this night, as he stole with his Rozsi back to his lair, he wanted to pause in the cemetery, aim his long lens over the headstones at a convoy of army trucks parked on the street. A man and woman lay across each other before them on the cobblestones as if they were huddling to conceal the wine-dark pool beneath them. But Rozsi pulled him along, whispering, "Are you insane? Do you want to join those two on the street?"

"Do you still not understand what I'm trying to do?" he said.

"*Come with me*," she whispered again, hoarsely, but emphatically.

He was not insane, but he allowed himself to be led. He was strangely excited, creeping in the shadows within sight of the invaders and the fallen lovers. He yanked Rozsi behind a stone angel, pushed her up against the marble and kissed her, despite her struggles, languished in her anxious, humid breath. He felt she found him most exciting when he was bold, felt her push him away only momentarily before she pulled him to her. He felt her shudder against the cold stone. They were panting as they stopped themselves and continued on their way, scuttling from shadow to shadow.

They made it back to his basement quickly. He was so excited, he didn't know what to do first. He asked her to sit while he prepared a nice place for them. "Where is your developing lab?" was the first thing she asked.

He pointed to a door at the corner. "It's really just a big closet."

On an earlier foray through the building, Zoli had scrounged a small round table from an apartment upstairs as well as an embroidered linen tablecloth. He took dishes from the same home, two whole place settings of amber Herend porcelain, plus silver cutlery he was surprised had remained, a candelabra, a flat pan, a pot, a kettle, some tea and—impossibly—a small box of sugar cubes he'd found in a drawer. He'd hauled down a mattress from the fourth floor, clean sheets and pillows, even a plush chair—an assemblage as incriminating if discovered as he himself would be, standing before it.

Zoli now added candles to the tableau, and Rozsi smiled broadly and clapped her hands. They drank tea with sugar by candlelight, and he surprised her more by withdrawing a small amber bottle of *palinka* from beneath the tablecloth to top up their tea. He made her giggle as he poured the plum brandy. "Where on Earth did you manage to get that?" she asked.

"From one of the flats upstairs. I moved a small metal chimney panel in the kitchen for no good reason except that I was curious, and I found the bottle there. The poor bastard must have been hiding it from his wife."

"Or she from him," said Rozsi. "I wonder where they are now."

"I wonder," he echoed. "I wonder if she or he hopes to find that bottle again when they get back."

They stared at each other. She looked sad, unwilling now to drink her tea with *palinka*. "Let that be the worst of their problems," Zoltan said, and he raised his glass in a toast. She followed him, and they clinked.

"I'm afraid," she said, setting down the cup. "Look where we're sitting. Look what's become of us. I don't know what's going to happen tomorrow or the day after that. Your life scares me."

"We've been fortunate until now," Zoltan said. "The war passed us by for five years, and we went on practically as if it weren't happening. But it's here now. It's caught up with us. The Russians will come for us one of these days, though, so we can't despair. They'll come free us, and the mighty Germans will have to retreat. They can't hold off the whole world forever."

"They have enough might yet to clear us out," she said. "Paul told me they're throwing everything they have left at us."

They drank silently for several more minutes before Zoltan rose to lead Rozsi toward his makeshift bed. She seemed reluctant, but he urged her on and she succumbed without much resistance.

They'd begun to kiss again with abandon when they heard a noise, and she jumped. "It's nothing," Zoltan whispered into her mouth.

She pulled away. "It's something—*someone*. I heard."

"It's an animal, a mouse, most likely."

"Or a rat?" she asked. She sat up in his bed.

Then they heard something heavier, running feet, in the alley above the window on the far side of the room, the window Zoltan opened when he cooked. A gun went off. There was some scuffling, the sound of a woman's voice, a yelp, the slamming of a door. Was it in his building? Were they in Zoltan's building now?

"Oh, my God, Zolikam, they've found us."

"Who has?" He was clutching her.

"They're not *friends*," she said. "That's for sure."

"They may be Hungarians. They may be like us. They may be Resistance fighters. I'll find out," he said, and he took his camera as if to defend both of them with it.

"Zoli, please."

"It'll be all right."

"I'm going with you."

He would have said no, but they heard another door slam. The intruders were in his building for sure. Zoltan was on his feet, staring at the ceiling, waiting. "The roof," he said, quietly. "We'll be safer on the roof than in the street."

"Let's go back to my place, please," she said. She was crying.

"We will, but it's not safe just yet. We'll be safer on the roof than the street or here." He pulled her gently forward, extinguished the candles. "I know the apartments we can stop at on the way if we have to."

Zoltan took Rozsi by the hand, slung his camera over the other shoulder, and they took the stone steps one at a time, barely breathing. On the railing between the second and third floor, Zoltan's hand swiped across something wet, but it was too dark to tell what. He smelled his fingers, thought he could smell blood. "What is it?" she asked.

"I don't know," he said. But he did know that someone had come this way ahead of them and he contemplated turning around. The trouble was that the shots had come from just outside the building. They were better off inside somewhere. He knew the building as well as anyone by now.

Halfway up the next flight, they discovered a damp rag, and Rozsi knew it was blood. She stifled a squeal. "It's all right. They're running away themselves," Zoli said. They could hear whoever it was up ahead, heard a door. "It's the door upstairs to the roof."

"Let's turn around, then," Rozsi said, pulling on his arm.

"I think we'll be all right. I have an instinct for these things. I've been out in the jungle longer than you have."

"I don't want to be in the jungle. Let's go home, please."

"We can't go out just yet, *trust* me."

"It's not about trusting you or not. You would risk your life for a photograph."

"I wouldn't risk yours, though," he whispered.

Rozsi allowed herself to be led to the same door they'd heard the others go through. They paused and listened. Rozsi could hear the thrumming of her own heart. They heard agitated whispering on the other side, a man and a woman. They were Hungarian, for sure, as Zoltan had guessed, but spoke haltingly. The man grunted and whispered something inaudible.

Rozsi pulled hard on Zoli's hand. He squeezed hers reassuringly in response, but in the calm coming through his hand, there was an alloy of fear and excitement in his eyes. And then he did the most surprising thing of all: he opened the door and said, "We're friends."

The woman asked, "Who are you?"

Zoli gestured for Rozsi to stay behind, but she wouldn't let go of his hand. "We won't harm you," Zoli said. "We're unarmed. We can help you."

And then he opened the door wide to reveal a soldier on his knees on the gravel rooftop, bleeding from the shoulder. His rifle lay at his side. He didn't reach for it. Rozsi gasped as her Zoli stepped boldly out.

Zoli had seen right away that the two people were as afraid as he and Rozsi were, that all four of them were caught in a circumstance not of their choosing. They were not SS, not Nyilas, not Russians, and consequently not a threat, probably.

But the man said something, took up his rifle and struggled to his feet. He was asking if Zoli and Rozsi lived in the building. Had they been overlooked? That's what Zoli thought he was saying. Zoli said, "I know you're not fighting with the Hungarian army, officially. It's all right. We're unarmed. We're not your enemies." Zoltan held up his camera, nothing more, and that was when the man raised his rifle. Rozsi thought her life was at an end.

Shots rang out from somewhere—another roof—and the man fell forward to the gravel. The woman gasped. "No," she was saying, "oh, please, no." She embraced the fallen man from behind. "Please, Bernat. Why did you have to stand up now? We can still get you help."

Zoltan and Rozsi had hit the gravel, too, and he covered her body, but then lifted his camera and aimed at the couple. He snapped a picture. Now it was Rozsi pleading. "Zolikam, please, don't, not now, show respect. Our heads will come off, too, in a minute." Rozsi's heart heaved against the shoals of her ribs. She could barely breathe.

Zoli refrained from taking more pictures. "There's not enough light anyway," he said. A raving summer wind blew across the gravel of the roof. The Hungarian woman was sobbing quietly against her man's back. The clear sky arced sweetly above their heads, the stars dressing up the moon.

The unfortunate woman was sitting up now and rummaging through a small reticule. "Keep down," Zoli whispered to her. "It's better to keep down." He was certain they were all in danger, was sure the shooters from the other roof would ferret them out before long, that he and Rozsi and the woman should crawl on their bellies off the roof and hurry down through safe apartments until they could get out.

The woman ignored him. She'd withdrawn lipstick and a compact. She was sitting up boldly, powdering her face. "Listen, please," Rozsi said softly. And then they watched as she applied red lipstick expertly to her lips, puckering as she did, then tightening her lips into a grin as she gazed into her little mirror.

When she was done, the woman reached under her companion. At first it was difficult to see or even imagine what she was doing. She took some pains to pry the rifle out from under the dead man. She set her reticule on the gravel and got up on her knees.

"No," they said, both of them, and then they shook their heads. Then Rozsi pressed her face into the gravel and covered the back of her head with her hands.

Zoltan told the woman, "Get down. They might not be gone yet. Please get down."

But she didn't get down. Instead, she rose to her feet, aimed the weapon out into the darkness at the roof from where she thought the bullets had come at them. And then she fired.

From quite another roof, to the south, a spray of bright bullets flew at her, and she glanced down before falling beside her man.

Zoltan and Rozsi didn't move. Rozsi was still covering her head. She hadn't watched. When she did look, she thought she saw the woman's back lifting, but it was more likely her tan jacket billowing in the wind. Even the slightest movement was magnified.

They lay where they were for several more minutes, listening through the darkness for their enemies. Who were they? Germans? Nyilas? Would Zoli and Rozsi be shot because they were with the renegade soldier and his woman?

"We have to go, Rozsikam," Zoli whispered. "We have to try to find our way back to safety, but we can't get up. We'll crawl back through the door and make our way out to the street. I know a dark stretch of the alley out back."

"I can't move," she said. "I'm scared. Let's stay just another minute."

"They might be on the move by now," he said. "We can't really wait."

She rolled over on her back under his warmth. "Will there ever be any going back?" she asked. She was crying but managed to keep her voice down. She craned her neck to see the dead couple one last time. "What's going to happen next?" she asked. She was pleading with him. "Where did we take this bad turn? What happened here? Will there ever be any going back?" He held her a little longer. She felt as safe with him as she possibly could, safe as she had with her brother Paul.

Rozsi looked into the starry sky glittering indifferently above the bleeding couple. She was reminded that each of these sparkling suns might easily have had a globe in its orbit with life and ideas on it, with a raving maniac able to spawn a roof full of fighters raining deadly fire, a pile of dead lovers here, live lovers there, still willing to give rise to new life and new ideas. How vain they all were, the moon included, preening with its stolen light.

Rozsi and Zoli made it all the way back to within two blocks of her house when they saw the flames lighting up the night sky. "Oh, no," she said. "Paul." She starting running.

"Wait," Zoli shouted. "You don't know who's there, waiting."

"I have to know about my brother. Oh, my God."

They ran the rest of the way together. As she ran, Rozsi was taking stock: her mother, her father, Istvan and now—? She saw the house first, saw the fire helping itself to her own bedroom, the damask curtains going up. Her eyes darted around the sidewalk. The residents on either side stood and watched. One neighbour, Mr. Lukacs, came up beside her and said, "Rozsi, your brother is in the cab." He pointed to a dark car at the corner.

When they saw each other, Paul leapt out of the car at his sister. They squeezed each other hard and rocked together. They looked as though they were dancing by the light of their burning house. "I won't ask you any questions," he said, as he held her head and tugged at her hair. "I don't care."

"I was with Zoli."

Now Zoli was beside them. "I'm so happy," he said to Paul. "You're all that we had."

Rozsi and Paul both looked at him and welcomed him into their huddle. Rozsi said, "You are all I have left, you men. Oh, and this." She reached into her pocket and got out her Swedish identification and her note from Zoli, which ended in "*I love*," and which she carried with her. "And this." She wiggled her ring finger, so they could both see the ruby.

Even as the moment was upon her, Rozsi knew there would never be another one like it. She folded her other hand over the ruby.

Thirteen

MARTA STUMBLED into the house after dark. Istvan had taken the cat down to the cellar for a rare visit, and the two were keeping each other warm. Smetana was fast asleep, but he jumped when Marta entered, leaving painful scratches on Istvan's comforting arm.

For a second, Istvan thought his time was up. The authorities had arrived, but then he heard Marta's voice, calling his name. Smetana complained loudly, as if he'd been holding it all in. Istvan groped around for the cat, but Smetana found him and rubbed himself up against his ankles, soft as a feather duster. Istvan picked up the cat, climbed the wooden ladder and threw aside the planks.

Marta was crying, her face swollen, shiny, the right eye black, her lower lip cut and bulging. "I was desperately worried about you," Istvan said. He released the cat and rushed to her. "What happened to you, Marta? Who did this to you?"

She looked at him strangely, did not respond to his embrace. "What are you doing out of the cellar?" she said, pushing at his chest but still trying to keep her voice down. "Are you mad? You'll be seen. And all this trouble and evasion will be for nothing! Stupid fool!" She pounded his chest until he toppled backward, scattering the cat into a corner.

"Your Dr. Cuckoo is dead," she yelled. "That's right. Dr. Janos Benes is gone. They suspected him of a link to you because the mayor's assistant dropped by to leave you the last of your father's effects. His house has been taken over by the Germans. They didn't know where else to take what was left of his belongings."

Istvan didn't dare answer. He felt utterly responsible for what had happened and for Marta's state. But what could he have done? Would the pill have gone down any better if Istvan had appreciated Dr. Benes more? Maybe.

He *was* responsible for all of it. He should never have let her hide him, risk her life and the lives of others. He had the right to risk only a single life. He thought of other people like him, successfully hidden, possibly with children. What a burden they'd all suddenly become, the bane of the world. The scapegoat as bane. How clever the evil design was, the forethought of it. How delicious to watch the dark fruit ripen.

"I'm so sorry," he said. "I couldn't be sorrier. I don't know what to say." And then he found something. "My Marta." He noticed now, as they moved further into the light, how hurt she was. The sight was frightening. One eye was scarlet with stormy swelling around it, her sable hair was wild, her skirt torn, the white collar of her black blouse hanging by a thread.

"My Marta." He tried gently to kiss her eyelid, but she winced and backed off. He still held her softly. Smetana purred and encircled their ankles.

"Please tell me what happened."

"Not here. Downstairs."

"But let me help clean you up first." He swept her hair away from her forehead where some of it had stuck. "What did they do to you?"

A sob rose in her body like a current. He kissed her cheek and neck and ear. He took her by the hand and tried to move her to the little bathroom.

"You'll tell me in the cellar."

"I can't make it to the cellar," she said. "I can't climb down tonight. My legs."

She was limping. He inspected her legs and found the knee and upper thigh of one leg bruised. "I will fix you up as well as I can, you will tell me what happened, I'll go back down to the cellar, and you'll get a good sleep in your bed."

He was fighting back the rage. He needed to be the nurse now and she the patient. Marta was here and alive.

They took off her clothes, and he washed her gingerly with a linen cloth as she stood in the tub. Her skin bristled with gooseflesh. She looked as if a bear had mauled her. Istvan got some clean towels and patted dry her wounds.

It was then, once the faucet had been turned off, that she began to tell him what had happened. "They killed Dr. Benes. They took us to some kind of stone meat room and hanged him from a hook." A scene of horror filled Istvan's head. He couldn't ask her to tell him more. He took her into his arms again and she trembled against him.

He led her by the hand to her room, lit a candle and helped her on with a flannel nightgown. He got her into her bed, covered her up to the chin and lay beside her, careful not to disturb the bed. Smetana leapt up, rubbed his soft ribs against Istvan's arm, the one the cat had scratched earlier, and poked through the blanket at Marta's feet, as if he were tenderizing her. Finally he curled up there to sleep. Istvan tried to stay as calm as the cat.

"I was afraid I would never see you again," Istvan said. He held back tears himself, now, flowing behind his eyes, as he stared out at the candle.

She spoke quietly. "They saw that I knew something—looked for a glint of something in my eyes—and they saw—they're like blood-hounds—they saw that I must have known something and that Dr. Benes must have known, too. When I saw that they saw, I said I'd wondered where you'd got to myself, following your father's hanging. Would anyone stay in a place where the authorities had hanged his father? I asked them, 'Is there something else I should know?' 'Just this,' they said. 'Problem Number One: Istvan Beck is a Jew. Problem

Number Two: An awful lot of food flows through this office on its way to—where?' They looked at Dr. Benes, waiting for an answer. And then they turned on me." She pointed to her black eye. Istvan wanted to kiss her there, but couldn't find a spot, so he kissed her on the forehead. She flinched. "They told Dr. Benes, 'Maybe you don't follow instructions so well, either. You're turning out to be a disappointment to us.' And then they hoisted him up onto that meathook and stepped aside to watch me as I watched him. They hanged him up just to test me." A frightening sound came from Marta's throat as she paused. "The life fluttered out of his eyes. There was not a note of vengeance in them, no war, not even irony. And yet . . . They watched to see if I would flinch, if I was upset, until finally I said, 'What are you waiting for? What are you hoping to find? What kind of experiment is this? Most people are going to be disturbed by such a demonstration—aren't *you*? I'd be disturbed if you did this to a plant, let alone a human being.' And that was when they began to beat me." She paused. "That was when they raped me. Two of them did it. It didn't take them long." She was whimpering, and Istvan tried to hold her. She looked up at the ceiling. Her eyes were filled with horror. He gently took her hand. "They thought they had destroyed me. But they were the ones who were scared. How could they not be? How could you do such things and not know somewhere in your heart that this is madness?"

Istvan lay back and looked at the dark ceiling. "Does everyone have such a place in his heart?" he asked.

She raised a hand to her mouth and sobbed into it, waited to catch her breath. "Everyone has a place," she said. "However small the place, it's where the memory lives. Don't you think so? Doesn't everyone have at least one memory of a grandmother taking them into her lap and counting their fingers with them, or their mother stopping them before they pulled the wings off a butterfly?"

"Maybe not everyone," Istvan said. "Maybe only those who have known tenderness."

She looked at him in the candlelight. He placed his hand on her heart. "You have a place like that," he said, "and it has filled your whole chest, this whole house. I'm so relieved and grateful and glad you are back with me, my Marta. For weeks now, especially the last few days, I didn't know if I could hang on—if I could *try* even—if I *wanted* to hang on. But now I feel I can."

"Much as I love you," she responded, "I know it is the circumstances talking, the time we live in—that much I know."

"Then you haven't learned enough. You haven't learned who I am, just as I hadn't until now. It's the terrible circumstances that have put us here, yes. But they've helped me to find out who you are. How could I have otherwise?" He managed to get his arm around her, and they rocked together so gently that the flame of the candle did not waver. And then she fell asleep.

He blew out the candle and went downstairs again to his cellar and replaced the planks above him. He was shaken by what he'd seen and heard. He wished he could do something for Marta. He felt closer to her than ever, certain now that he could spend his life with her. They had never known love with abandon, love among the larks, only furtive love, yet it was as pure as any love could be.

It was hours before he managed to get some sleep, and then minutes, it seemed, before someone banged hard on the door. "Frau Foldi," Istvan heard them shouting, and they banged again.

Istvan didn't know what to do. He had to wait it through. Any other course of action was suicide, for both of them. Above him, he heard the cat jump down and then he heard Marta make her way to the door.

The men spoke German. "Get dressed, get a few things. You're coming with us."

"Where?"

"Get dressed," the man said again.

Within two minutes she was gone.

Fourteen

ON A BALMY SUMMER DAY, Robert Beck left work early because he had no surgery and only one patient to look in on. Most often lately, Robert officially assisted in the surgery others conducted, though once the patient was under, he was frequently asked to take the lead. He decided to walk home and left his jacket at Sacred Heart. It dawned on him, halfway home, that his Swedish papers were in the jacket and he contemplated turning around. Moving about without papers these days was punishable sometimes by deportation, sometimes by execution on the spot. Paul had told his uncle about a whole family, including children and grandparents, who'd been shot merely because one of them couldn't produce the required papers in the allotted time of one minute.

But Robert had told his assistant he'd be back by the end of the day to check in on things, so he persuaded himself he'd be all right until then.

He went straight home to Jokai Street. What he found was an empty apartment. The breakfast dishes were still on the table and the meal only half-eaten. He could see no disturbance whatever in the rooms, though some of Klari's clothes were left out on the bed, and a pair of tan open-toed summer shoes lay on the floor, the ones she liked to wear on warm days. It was unlike her not to leave a note, at least.

Similarly, there was little evidence to be found of his son's or Lili's whereabouts. Had they been called away somewhere?

He was relieved to find Vera outside, but she didn't want to speak to him. When he asked if she knew anything, she merely shook her head, but he could see she was distressed. "Are you all right?" he asked, placing a gentle hand on her shoulder. The question set off the woman's tears. "Do you know what has happened to my family," he asked, "where they've gone?"

"They've cleared out half the building," Vera said. "They took Mrs. Beck and young Mr. Beck and that nice girl of his."

Robert tried to steady his voice, but it quavered as he said, "Do you know who took them, exactly, and where?"

Vera held a red-checked handkerchief up to her nose and spoke into it. "They were taken to the railway station, to Nyugati Station. Germans took them."

"Are you sure it was Nyugati?"

She nodded and took a deep breath through the handkerchief. Robert laid a comforting hand on her shoulder again, but she shrugged free of it. She took a step back. The friendly woman had turned cold. Did she have him confused with the authorities? Had she hustled his family along in the courtyard before they were herded away? He understood she was afraid. He understood she was alone and could have been banished herself or shot for harbouring or even colluding with "cosmopolitans," but as she turned her back to him after all these years, venom flashed through him. He forgot for a second that he was a physician. He wanted just then to snuff her out as she stood on the cobblestones with the privilege of her culture.

She was just scared. Fear was enough. Why should she be braver than he'd been?

He asked her, "Did they not have their papers?"

Vera nodded yes, but she still wouldn't face Robert. "Vera, I don't want to play guessing games. Did my family not show their Swedish papers?"

Finally, she turned toward him. She was crying. "Yes, sir, they showed their papers," she said. "Mrs. Beck even said, 'We're Swedish.' But the officer said, 'Not today.'"

"And that was a German officer?"

Vera shook her head.

"What was he?"

"He was one of us."

"*Us?*"

"He was a Hungarian."

Now Robert turned from her, ran upstairs and dialed Paul at the Swedish embassy. He told his nephew what had happened. Paul asked what station they had been taken to.

"Nyugati. I'll meet you there."

"No, don't meet me there."

"It's not safe where I am, either."

"So go back to the hospital."

"I can't," Robert said. "My family—"

"Uncle Robert, don't go to the station."

Robert was nodding but he said nothing. He found he was shaking. "I have to go," he said. "Please, Paul, I—"

"Uncle Robert, do you have your papers? Do the others?"

"I don't know. I—"

Suddenly Paul was speaking slowly, as if to a child. "Because if you don't, I'll have to find Zoli. He'll have the negatives."

"I don't know," Robert said. "Mine are at the hospital. I'm a fool."

"Of course you're not a fool, Uncle Robert, but please go back to the hospital. I'll get new papers made for all of you, just in case." Paul knew his uncle would not do what he told him. He was restless, like his brother, like him, Paul, and he followed his own mind.

Robert hung up the receiver. He ran outside and stopped again. He was alone. Suddenly, the place as familiar as air had turned noxious. He couldn't see Vera anywhere now. He was panting, bracing himself against the cold brick of his building. He looked up at his own windows, at the stone balcony wrapped warmly around the corner like Buddha's arms.

How Robert loved this place, this building, this city, felt steady here. He knew others didn't feel the same way, didn't agree. Simon hadn't had the same chances. The country had taken a turn. But how easy just to write off a home, he thought. Without another thought the young are ready to bury the Motherland, which sheltered us, suckled us, fattened us, educated us, enriched us, sang to us from its concert halls. Why be so hasty? Are other places better? Are people superior in other lands? Do we have to tear down the institutions founded on industry, good sense and good will, even if bad will preceded their establishment, or prevails today? Bad will comes and goes here. Bad will comes and goes everywhere. Let's outwait the bad, let good sense prevail.

They may take us away today, but we can outlast them. Our diminished numbers will rise again. It is called *flux*; it is called *mood*; it is called *the temper of our times*. And all moods change, all tempers subside. History is patient. Nature is patient. She has seen it all, and she'll see it all again. Let's wait patiently by her side.

Tear down the palaces, storm the Bastille. Off with their heads. I have seen marble generals awaiting new heads, and palaces can make very nice schools and museums. Let it all come around again. It *will* all come around. But spare the Motherland, my son. See it for what it has been and can become, not just for what it is in a bad hour. Our ties to this country can withstand single assaults, regardless of how deplorable. Great Britain introduced slavery, and the United States adopted it freely and enthusiastically. Stalin's Soviet Union watched as millions of his Ukrainians died of starvation in the Holodomor, the Grand Famine, because their own wheat had been taken from their fields, their own bread from their tables. Yet these are the countries now taking on Hitler.

Hungary is as good a place as any, better than most. Can you blame an apricot tree or a lake for being situated here, for standing within the boundaries we've drawn around them, for bearing the names we've given them: *fa, to; Baum, See; arbre, lac; tree, lake?* Take what we have—eat the fruit, swim in the lake—it *is* our lake you're swimming in, where your cousins swam, where your grandparents had a summer home—it *is* our fruit you're eating, rolled with *our* walnuts in a *palacsinta* and served up at *our* Gerbeaud with cream and espresso.

Robert struggled to the corner of Jokai Street and rushed a half-block up, then the same half-block back. He couldn't get a cab to Nyugati Station, but he managed to get aboard the subway on Andrassy, and then he took a bus.

He couldn't think through what he was doing. He just kept remembering his own parents and the world he grew up in, how they'd urged him toward success. He thought of his brother, Heinrich, who'd pushed Robert into medical research and surgery. He had told Robert he was far too brilliant just to sit in an office and prescribe headache pills. And Robert had believed him and had taken his advice. Yet it was not in his nature to dazzle the world. His brother would have done what Robert was now doing. Heinrich would have been surprised and proud to see Robert jumping in this way.

When Robert disembarked, he could not recognize his beloved Nyugati Station. What awaited him were not passenger cars but cargo cars, windowless and unadorned. And they were not passengers assembled there but a frightened herd being pushed by soldiers up ramps and through the railway-car doors. Robert felt he couldn't breathe as he hunted for his family. "Klari," he was thinking, "Klari." And the sound rose to his lips. "Klari," he said, and the people around him could hear.

And then he saw the blond head of hair bobbing on the dark sea. It was Lili's head, surely, not far away, in front of Car 17. "Lili," he said, and then shouted. "Lili!"

She turned to see him, raised a hand to her mouth, got Simon's attention, then Klari's. Klari cried out when she saw her husband. Why had he come? What was the matter with him? Was he insane? Had he been dragged along, too? She was shaking her head, using her hand to shoo him away. *Get away. Get away.*

He began pushing to get through. He didn't know what he was going to do, but he felt he had to be here with Klari. No one knew what to make of him, but they let him pass. No one was pressing to get ahead. Of the hundreds of people assembled on the platform, everyone was waiting to be told to get aboard. Robert could smell fear around him, like perfume turning bad. He could see it in people's eyes. He knew the look from his patients.

In a moment, he was by his wife's side. "You're a fool," she whispered to him. "Where do you think we're going?" she asked. He gripped her hand. The fool, she kept thinking, but she felt a little better now, despite herself. "Look at these trains," she said, whispering.

"Why don't you shut the hell up?" a small woman beside them said too loudly. "Give me some room here. Don't crowd me."

"Shh," Klari told her.

"Just shut the hell up, especially you lot," she said, pointing to Klari and Robert.

Simon said, "What's it to you?"

"I'm sick of you, all of you. Just shut the hell up."

Robert said, surprisingly gently, "Keep your voice down, or you won't be going much farther. I don't think our captors care for trouble-makers."

She shot him a murderous look. The woman then shoved aside another woman and her child in order to stand farther away.

"Father, where do you think they're taking us?" Simon asked.

"I'm not sure."

Robert began looking for Paul and this Mr. Wallenberg he'd heard so much about. He hoped their captors would be slow in boarding them all.

He looked at Lili, and she shrugged. She'd been thinking all morning about her parents, about Tildy, Ferenc, Mendi, Benjamin and her baby sister, Hanna. Were they up ahead, waiting for her? Lili felt unaccountably relieved. She'd managed to dodge these trains until now, but she should have known it was only a matter of time. Her real identity beneath her Nordic hair was bound to reveal itself. So she understood her fate, understood the verdict meted out to her today within the new and perverse justice of the world. Finally, she would see her family again, one way or another.

Klari was thinking the same thing. She, too, would be listed now among the deported, as her sisters and their families had been before her. Her sisters could be up ahead somewhere, with Lili's family. Was it possible they had met and got acquainted, Lili's family and hers? What were the chances?

"*Achtung*," a soldier said as he pushed through. Another soldier holding a sack followed him. "*Gold. Silver*," the first one said, and the second held open the burlap bag as people surrendered their valuables. "*Geld. Silber. Schmuck. Armbanduhren. Taschenuhren.*" Robert disengaged his pocket watch, his son his wristwatch. Klari gazed down at her wedding band as she slipped it from her finger. It was loose, looser than ever before. Lili parted with her mother's wedding ring, her father's name, David, inscribed inside the band. A third soldier then hustled people onto the dark train. He used his rifle butt for emphasis. Through the open door, they could see into the car. Only a pail, their toilet, awaited them in a corner.

A man beside them was protecting a small leather bag as he boarded. "Careful," he said.

"What do you have in the bag?" Simon asked.

"A record." Several of his neighbours looked at him. "My favourite record. *Orpheus and Eurydice*. Gluck. Edit Lager performs."

"You brought your favourite record with you on this trip?" Robert asked. They were aboard now, being shoved deeper into the car, into the darkness.

"Yes, what would you bring? I had five minutes to put things into a bag. What did you pack?"

"Nothing."

"Well, I have more than you." He was a small man, and he was being squashed between Robert and an equally large woman.

Someone behind them said, "Where do you plan to play it? Here on the train or up ahead at our holiday destination?"

Robert strained to look out at the yard to see if he could spot Paul. What could possibly have delayed him? Robert took his wife's small leather bag and held it himself, and Simon followed his father's lead, putting Lili's bag over his shoulder with his own.

Simon had believed things would turn, and soon. He'd been thinking he had to do something, take some action, and now he was captive to events. How foolish and vain he felt. He hadn't been to work lately, because of his injuries, but this very morning, before the men came, he had been eating an apricot and holding forth about the glories of the Hungarian fruit, orange, sweet and juicy, the best fruit for preserves on the planet. He had also been telling Lili, not three hours before at their table at home, that he thought he might make use of his unexpected expertise as a tool and die maker. He'd been reading about clever devices. He told Lili about Mary Anderson, an American woman, who, on a snowy day in New York, had observed that the driver of a trolley car was struggling to see through his windshield. He ended up having to stick his head right out into the elements. Mary Anderson went home that night and sketched a device, to be operated by hand from within a vehicle, to clear the windshield of snow and rain. "Hence, the windshield wiper was born," Simon had said to Lili and clapped his hands. "How would we drive today without windshield wipers? Unthinkable." It was just then the authorities came, ending any further chances for him to impress Lili. His enthusiasms suddenly seemed foolish.

And now here they stood at the gates of hell, Simon thought, with Satan's best gatekeepers. How vain—how idiotic he felt. He needed to wipe his nose and realized he hadn't brought a handkerchief.

As Robert looked one last time out of the cramped car for his nephew, he remembered the jacket he'd left at Sacred Heart. Were they heading into the cold? Or would they stay long enough for it to turn cold? No one so far had come back from wherever they'd been taken. Not one person he'd known about. What would happen? Would his jacket hang from the back of his chair for a month? Would someone hang it up for him in the closet? Would his assistant try it on after a time, find the papers in the pocket, toss them out, find the jacket didn't fit, give it away? What would Vera do with their things? Was she Queen of the Alhambra now? Would her mother move to Jokai Street? Would Vera try on Klari's shoes, the navy ones she liked so much? Would she sell the silver eagle with the clock in its beak, or had she coveted the bird too much to part with it? Would she have her own tea party for the first time in her life, the poor thing, and invite the housekeepers from all of the abandoned homes? And was that what they'd be called, if the Becks and the others did not return: abandoned homes? Abandoned homes for sale. Abandoned homes: cheap but nice. What a foul organ the brain was. It couldn't be turned off any more than the heart could. Robert had watched it pump its scarlet food to the far corners of the body, marvelled at its ingenuity. But each waited for the other, the heart and the brain. The two went down together. The moment they found the light, they found darkness.

Klari was thinking about her parents. Their lands were gone, now, sunk into another time. There were beautiful lush fields and farms where her parents had had their summer house, where Klari and her sisters had so many carefree hours in the warm Hungarian summers.

Klari's mind returned to the train station where she stood. Her father had often met these cargo trains to sign the transit papers required whenever his goods were being sent off to Austria, Switzerland and France. And here they were now, Maximillian's descendants, being herded onto the same cars, headed—where?— toward Buchenwald, Auschwitz and Treblinka, destinations whose meaning was not entirely clear. The men on the platform wearing the uniforms of the Third Reich knew, certainly, probably. Or the others: the small, eager army of Hungarian sympathizers. Or maybe even they didn't know.

The Becks found it warmer in the car than outside. The soldiers, German and Hungarian alike, were trying to cram still more people in before sliding the door closed, seeing if a young woman could not be shoved into the space beside Klari, or a child into the spot below her elbow. But Klari's bag on the floor was getting in the way, so she shoved it with her foot behind her.

The train's whistle soon blew, and the doors were finally slammed and the journey begun. The engine steamed along out of the city, pulling the rickety cars. If this was the beginning, Klari thought, who knew what indignities lay ahead? It was dark, and she was glad not to have to see her husband's face, or her son's or Lili's. She was anxious that their fear would exacerbate hers. She wanted to isolate her dread, drive it deeper somewhere where it couldn't overwhelm her. She took her husband's hand, felt the uncertainty there, heard the woman who'd asked them to shut up announce that she had to go to the toilet, and soon the people around the woman could smell the reason and tried to make way to let her pass. It was difficult to get out of someone's way. She said it over and over. "I have to get to the toilet—*move!*" She scared people. Even in the midst of this terror, they feared her special breed of hysteria.

The girl at Klari's elbow whimpered, and Lili got down to her knees to comfort her, but then the girl's mother appeared. She said, "It's all right. It'll all be fine, I promise." The girl said, "Why are we travelling like this? Where are the other trains?" "Don't worry," Lili said. "It's an adventure in the dark."

Klari closed her eyes. She allowed her mind to roam outward again, out of the train. It landed in a place she'd almost forgotten. Years before, early in their life together, Robert had taken her to a city on the Aegean in Turkey, called Kusadasi. Robert loved the luxuriant carpets they made there, painstakingly by hand, the little silk knots rich with the scarlet colours derived from the mulberry and other fruits.

It was May, and they were young and still childless. They travelled to the ancient town of Ephesus, a marble city inside Kusadasi, a city that must have been founded by the Greeks some twenty-five hundred years before and been conquered by the Romans and by others until the Turks grabbed it during the Ottoman Empire. The Turks snatched Hungary, too, along with other countries during the same grand, grasping enterprise.

Robert and Klari found a lovely tour guide named Geneviève, she still remembered, a French woman who spoke German—a language Klari and Robert had both learned at school—and Geneviève took them by taxi to Ephesus, the ancient marble city, a white city that had been excavated since the beginning of the century. When they arrived, they were both drawn to the remains of a marble library, the Celsus Library, built by the Romans. Klari could vividly picture those columns again. At the entrance stood several arresting statues: she recalled the one of Sophia and another of Arete, wisdom and virtue—what better attributes were there to set before a library? And then along the marble walk between the library and the gates leading in were several other headless statues. Robert ran his hand along the smooth neck of one of them. "They are headless," Geneviève told them, "because the few talented sculptors of the day capable of accomplishing such brilliant pieces took quite long to create each figure, and each depicted a great commander or noble. But so many commanders and nobles came and went over the life of the city that the sculptors found it easier simply to replace just the head of each statue with the new man's likeness. Why worry about the body?" Klari ran her palm over the same spot her husband had. She looked at Geneviève, who kept freshening her poppy red lipstick. She matched the landscape, Klari remembered thinking. Red poppies nodded everywhere in the green grass and guarded the fallen marble apexes, columns and marble limbs. "So each statue had a weakness at the neck," Geneviève continued, "where the head was removed to be replaced with the new one. Over time, they broke at those points of weakness, leaving the figures headless."

"I wonder what they did with the discarded heads," Robert said. Somewhere buried, there's a warehouse of undesirable stone heads," he said, smiling broadly.

Outside the gates of Ephesus, a woman sat on a child's wooden chair crocheting tablecloths with hands as skilled as those of the ancient sculptors. Klari held Robert back, and Geneviève smiled and waited, too. Behind the miniature chair which could barely contain her, the poor old woman had spread tablecloths all over the ancient rocks, ready to sell them to people just like Klari who happened by or came expressly to marvel at Ephesus. "Look at me," she seemed to be saying. "Marvel at me, too, just for a moment, please." It was a breezy day, a beautiful spring day, and the woman, after draping her tablecloths over the great boulders, had weighed them down at the corners with small stones. Klari wanted to buy one, and Geneviève easily negotiated a price for her. It was a great, white, medallion spread—abandoned now in their dining room on Jokai Street—the centre medallion mimicking the brilliant carpet on the floor beneath it, which the young couple also purchased on that same day and arranged to have shipped home.

When they'd departed that day from Ephesus, Klari glanced back one last time at the ruins of the marble city and, before it, that old woman with the tablecloths spread out over the ancient dry rocks as if she were setting a table for the gods.

Had Robert noticed the tablecloth and carpet this very morning, Klari wondered, taken one last look around before leaving their place to the Germans or other Hungarians? She'd had no time. She wished she'd had another minute. Does one tidy up for invaders? Had Robert picked up the breakfast dishes? Of course he hadn't. He'd seen what was there and come straight here, her sweet fool. He'd been spared by chance but had leapt after them into hell.

She wondered what the others around her were thinking. They weren't speaking much, surprisingly, yet she could taste their fear, smell it—it was palpable. She felt foolishly, selfishly relieved to have Robert by her side.

Simon suddenly piped up. He said he'd barely had time to start breakfast this morning, let alone finish it. "Who knows where our next meal will come from, if there *is* a next meal." He said it tragically, like an ancient Greek chorister, and he said it with a finality that infected Lili. She believed him utterly—he always had such a convincing way of speaking—so she began mentally to say goodbye to the world. She felt an Arctic wolfishness had come over Simon, something that drew him inward upon himself, especially when he was hungry. She'd seen it overtake him frequently lately, as supplies stopped flowing freely to Budapest. She wondered, here on the train, whether he would soon lose his capacity for kindness.

The train ride to the border took hours, and they were long hours, each like a morning or afternoon itself. The air was thick with the stench of worry. People in Car 17 lost their propriety and removed their tops, even bottoms. Some stumbled all around in search of the pail in the corner to evacuate their bladders and bowels, but the pail was really more a token than anything else, because people missed most of the time anyway in the crowded darkness, and the pail filled quickly before sloshing and splashing its contents on the people standing closest to it. In the end, people emptied themselves where they stood. "It doesn't take long to become what they already think we are," Robert said aloud. "We'll become beasts."

The little girl said something in response, something anxious that no one could hear, and her mother comforted her again. "Please," the woman said to Robert. And Robert apologized. Klari found herself envying the woman. It was better to have someone to comfort, because some of the comfort came back to you, preoccupied you in the right way. The children on board, though, imbibed their anxiety from the darkness and the air, from the stench, the huddled uncertainty. It was very basic, Klari thought. Robert was right. All of life's dignity, painfully built up pebble by pebble with tiny accomplishments, could be stomped flat by a single, ingenious act of degradation.

We're like insects, like beetles, an infestation of beetles, dark and shining, crushed together in a dark box, hoping to be released into a green field. How oppressive, Robert thought, to be cast so absolutely in the shadow world of this car. How cleverly the arrangement establishes the order of this world. There is the sun, the absolute ruler. There is the moon, which reflects the sun's glorious light. And then there are the shadows, devoid of light and glory. There is only one sun—the Sun King, Louis XIV—*Louis le Grand*—*Le Roi Soleil*. He was the state—*L'État, c'est Moi*. One King, One Sun. But there can be many shadows, millions, *trillions*. So keep those shadows away from the glass. Keep them away from the lens. It can only be a shadow who one day peeks through the telescope to discover that there are a trillion suns out there just as radiant as ours.

Klari turned her mind to poor young Simon and Lili. They had their whole lives ahead of them. If Klari could lie down and die for them, she would. What use would Klari be if they didn't go on? What use was she except as a reminder of the grim past?

No, they had to go on, her Simon and Lili—had to prevail. If Lili had been orphaned once in her own home town, and orphaned again in her adopted home, the burden would be heavy on the few left standing to survive and prevail, to fill her town and the emptied towns behind them with reminders of their ghostly inhabitants, reminders of their looks, their determination, their love of cake and living. What a burden it would be, too, poor things, and how presumptuous to think that Klari and Robert could have stood in, even temporarily, for the girl's fallen parents. Or were they fallen? Were they labouring up ahead instead, awaiting their emancipation as Klari had already begun to?

Klari's son put his familiar hand on her shoulder, and the hand was dry. She kissed the knuckles. With his other hand, Simon held onto the back of Lili's neck. Klari could sense what he was doing, sense his mind racing.

Simon knew these railcars. As a child, when he and his cousins would visit their grandparents in their country house out in Kiskunhalas, they would climb into these cargo cars at night in the rail yard to talk about girls and to smoke. The cars were easy to open, from inside as well as outside. If he and Lili could get some men to help him force the door from the inside, Simon thought, they could all jump and make a run for it. But what would happen then, if the Nazis caught them? Would they shoot them instantly? If they got away, would they shoot everyone else on board? Lili wouldn't let him do it. She would think of Simon's parents and know they couldn't make the jump. She'd think of Robert and Klari, and she'd want to hang on to them.

Klari found her husband's hand again in the darkness. He pressed his face into her neck, taking in her fragrance, blotting out the stench of the car. But she was no flower that day, she knew, not anymore. No dignity. No flower. Just the memory of poppies.

PAUL SEARCHED the Swedish embassy frantically for Zoli, but couldn't find him. An office had been established in the building to manufacture false Swedish *schutz-passes*, and a dozen Jews turned Swedes helped to create the documents there. Zoli was the primary photographer, but when he was out, an older man, Lajos, seemed to know what he was doing. When the subject was not available to be photographed, Lajos was also adept at removing existing photos with a razor blade from older documents and attaching them convincingly to new ones. Zoli, of course, could not be reached by phone, so when he wasn't at hand, there was no fast way to find him. A couple of times, when Zoli showed up with his Hasselblad too late, Paul had to tell him a train had already departed, carrying people they might have saved. Paul saw the horrified look in Zoli's eyes and said, "But there's no time to despair. Other lives are waiting."

Zoli helped for the rest of the day and the next without a rest, and Paul was sorry he had to be the one to tell Zoli.

On this occasion, Lajos spent an hour searching for the duplicate papers for Paul's family and for Lili but couldn't find them. "It's too late," Lajos kept saying, as he shuffled through the files. "No matter what, it's too late. The train is gone."

Incredibly, Zoli arrived just then and told Paul that whatever duplicates they had were kept in the basement. The three men rushed down and found the papers in a hurry.

"It's too late," Paul said. "But I have to do something."

"*What?*" Zoli said.

"*Something.*" Paul took the papers and ran out of the room.

He interrupted a meeting Wallenberg was having with Per Anger and a couple of other Jews, who, like Paul, were helping with the campaign. Wallenberg took Paul into an anteroom. "Raoul, I need to borrow the embassy's Alfa Romeo. It's more convincing."

"Of course," Wallenberg said. "Convincing to whom?"

"The authorities."

"I can't go with you," Wallenberg said. "We have another transport to visit in a couple of hours."

"I'll go alone." Paul was making up the plan as he stood there.

"And?"

"And I'll try to stop a train that has already departed."

"The one that wasn't scheduled, the surprise one this morning?"

"Yes, that one."

"Paul—"

"Please," Paul said.

Wallenberg got the keys and handed them over without another word. Paul's hand was shaking as he took them. "I'll be back," Paul said.

Paul raced toward Miskolc and, beyond it, the northeast border. It was a bright, warm day. Only once in a half-hour did the shoulders of a cloud obscure the sun. *What was he doing?* Was he really going to pull this off? Decisions had to be taken so quickly these days. Hesitation, equivocation and doubt brought death. Hamlet's flaw brought about the prince's own death and the death of others, innocent others. Paul wondered if he would be driving back this way in the hours to come, or if this was a one-way excursion. Exit ghost.

If Paul could not argue the law, did he have any business enforcing it? And what law? Moral law? Divine law? He took a peek again at the sunny heavens. He had already lost too many family members, and too many others were missing, in trains ahead of this one. His father gone now, he felt cheated, felt he'd been deprived even of the time to mourn, hold photographs in his hand and weigh what had been lost. One photograph in particular he'd been meaning to dig up featured the whole family when they were all young: on New Year's Day, 1920. Mathilde and Heinrich had arranged a costume party, and Paul, Istvan and Rozsi were dressed as the Three Musketeers, Istvan's favourite figures. In the picture, Istvan was staring straight into the camera, the honourable warrior holding his sword up flat against his heart. Mathilde and Heinrich had always blocked Paul's view of mortality, and now he could see it clearly.

As he drove, a bird took flight behind Paul's ribs.

He considered Zsuzsi. His Philadelphia Zsuzsi. Had she found someone else in the city of brotherly love? Did she and Mr. Philadelphia worry, now, as they sunned themselves on a porch and read the papers, about what had happened to her homeland, about how far the enemy had penetrated, how capable her people were to resist, how able *he*— Paul—was to survive? Did she look up from the paper once to wonder that, glance at her man and wonder? Did she look up once from her soft-boiled egg, which had been blessed by the American Rabbinical Society? Did she dress like a calla lily on this day, or was it too warm a morning in the northeastern United States of America? Did Mercury stand on his dog still, waiting to fly?

It wasn't morning at all but night—wasn't it?—night becoming morning in the northeastern United States, and Zsuzsi fast asleep still.

Paul knew the train would wait in Miskolc. He knew he had a little time to catch up to it and even overtake it at this speed. He knew they would take on whomever else they had smoked out, as well as other resisters, criminals. He raced to the train station to see, and, lucky him, he had calculated correctly. But Miskolc was too busy a place to stage a drama, too many variables. No, he had to do it out of town. He raced ahead, thought he might be sick, tasted something bitter rise from his gut.

Far out of town—as close to the frontier, in fact, as one could possibly get—Paul Beck parked the Alfa Romeo across the train tracks. It gleamed in the sun. Its little Swedish flag flapped from the radio antenna, the reclining yellow cross against a blue background. It reassured Paul a little, as it reassured Eric the Holy. Even the Swedes had once had a crusade and, at the moment when his confidence flickered, Eric had looked up and seen a yellow cross against the blue sky, urging him onward.

Paul stood on the tracks in front of the car and crossed his arms. He could feel in his breast pocket the papers he'd forged for his relatives. He wore a white Panama hat and a camel hair cape, as befitted the driver of an Alfa Romeo limousine. It was his own outfit, but he didn't wear it often. He looked himself over in the mirror when he did, as he'd done that morning. He wondered whether it looked like a costume of some kind. From not too great a distance, he could have passed for Jay Gatsby.

Paul heard rumbling, felt it through his feet and up his legs, his blood shivering through his veins, the bird's beak stabbing out from between his ribs. From where he stood, he could not tell if the train was slowing, but the Czech border was not far behind him, so the engineer would know that he had to slow down soon, would be on the lookout. The train came booming toward him. Paul's heart roared. Some finches and at least one cardinal that had perched on a nearby line flapped off toward the distant poplars. The wind from the train whipped up the leaves in the nearby fields and parted the grass by the tracks, like the Red Sea. Paul held onto his hat.

And now it was in close view, hurtling toward him. His breath caught. There was too much air to breathe. He heard the welcome screech. The locomotive could have crushed him like an insect, could have crushed the car behind him, but it clutched the rails, lurched, shot sparks and stopped in front of him. He could almost have reached out to touch it.

Three German officers of the Einsatzkommando were upon him in an instant. Paul held up his own forged papers and declared in German that he was a Swedish diplomat, and then he offered the other papers. "You are deporting Swedish nationals," he said, "and I demand their release."

Paul appeared impatient, annoyed even.

The commanding officer looked through the cut of his eye at the tall man in the cape and took the papers, studied each of the four photographs, read out the names: "Simon Beck, Klari Beck, Robert Beck, Lili Beck." The officer's eyes, Paul noticed, were surprisingly soft and brown, like the eyes of a deer, yet what lurked behind them was a deer hunter.

"Get them," he said to the soldier on his right. "The Becks. Four of them."

The officers, followed by Paul, walked down the line of closed cars, unlatching and throwing open each of the doors. The sun fell like a searchlight on the captives in each car. "Beck," the officer shouted, and again, "Beck." The people in the cars did not know whether it was good to be a Beck or not, whether the Becks were being singled out for release or for slaughter. The odds were not good.

As each sliding door was slammed shut, the soldiers, followed by Paul, moved to the next, and the same routine was enacted. "Beck," and again, "Beck. Simon, Klari, Robert, Lili."

In each car the people looked at one another, waiting for someone to croak out, "Here." When no one did, they waited for the officers' next move. The next move was to clamp the captives back into the security of darkness and the warmth of one another's huddled bodies.

Car 17 was in the middle. The door flew open. The same frightened looks as the light fell upon the Jews. A child called out from the
back. Paul's gaze ranged across the faces. And then his eyes met his
Uncle Robert's. Paul caught his Aunt Klari's eyes. He could tell his
aunt and uncle wanted to smile, but they didn't, they mustn't. He saw
his cousin Simon next. Simon seemed to be having the hardest time
restraining his youthful glee at seeing Paul. And Lili, not a Beck at all,
but a Beck for the purposes of this day, Simon's wife.

The officers ordered the Becks out. *"Achtung! Raus!"* Paul helped
his Aunt Klari down, and Simon helped Lili. When the Becks stood
on the gravel beside the train, the officer studied their faces and
photos. He looked extra long at Lili, her golden hair, her blue eyes. He
handed back the photos to Paul.

"What about their valuables?" Paul asked in German.

Klari Beck flinched, and one of the Germans saw. He glanced at
the others. His eyes were periwinkle blue, but he all but closed them
as he squinted in the sun.

"Did you take their jewellery?" Paul asked again. As the wind
picked up, his auburn curls rustled and whipped against the brim of
the Panama. In the midst of this madness, Klari thought her nephew
could use a haircut and was conscious she was thinking it just then.
She felt faint. She had to resist falling over. "Watches? Rings?
Bracelets? Necklaces?" Paul said.

The commanding officer removed his cap and ran his fingers
through his light brown hair. He rolled his deer eyes. He half-turned
toward the caboose. He said nothing, but merely pointed until one of
his soldiers ran to fetch a burlap bag.

When he returned, Paul and his relatives could hear the bag
jangling. Paul said to his family, again in German, "Find your
things."

The locomotive's engine rumbled, the cars stood windowless and
shut, their human cargo waiting to hear a sound, waiting to proceed.
Robert sifted through the jewels quickly until he found his watch, a

gold Omega. He slipped it into his vest pocket. He handed the bag to his wife, but Klari passed it immediately to Lili.

Paul intercepted. "What about your wedding ring?" Paul asked again in German, taking the bag and handing it back to his aunt. Either the Becks were Swedes and had been wrongly taken and then robbed, or they were not. They couldn't be *somewhat* Swedish. "Were you wearing a necklace? A brooch?" he asked.

Klari trembled as she tried on one ring after another. She found her emerald pin, the one Robert had bought for her in India on their twentieth wedding anniversary. She tried on two more rings, but they didn't fit, and she wasn't wearing her reading glasses to check each name engraved on the inner surface. She looked pleadingly at her nephew before passing the bag to Lili.

This time Paul let her. Lili had put her mother's ring in the bag, but there was no time to read inscriptions—imagine—and as Paul held the bag for her, she reached in and tried on several rings without looking. She quickly found one that fit perfectly and took her hands out. She pulled the ring from her finger, held it up and said, "*Mein.*" She glimpsed the inscription: "*Ivan. 13 Aprilis 1935.*" Whose ring could this be? Who was Ivan's wife? Lili took a look at the train. She slipped the ring on again and clasped her hands together. She smiled. She wore a look of satisfaction, though she felt a thief herself now, the way the Germans were.

Simon pushed out a breath. He claimed he had nothing and shrugged. Paul handed the bag back to the commanding officer. "*Danke,*" he said and steered the Becks toward his car. The Alfa Romeo, more yellow now in the sun than cream, had an absurdly long snout, longer than the cabin and trunk combined. The officers watched them, waited until they got in before boarding the train again.

Paul reversed the car off the tracks and crunched over the gravel. No one dared speak until he had found the road back to Budapest. Paul ground his teeth. He looked in the rearview mirror and saw his Aunt Klari, sitting between Simon and Lili, looking straight ahead, her hand on her heart. He could feel his right knee trembling, the leg he'd need for the gas pedal just as soon as they made it out to the open road.

Paul finally said to his uncle, "So you came to the train after all."

Robert felt humbled, ashamed. "I'm sorry. I don't know what to say." He felt like Lazarus, looking at his saviour behind the wheel. What could he say? What could anyone say?

Paul took his family to an old Dutch insurance company at Number 2, Ulloi Street, in Budapest. "It's been annexed by the Swedish embassy," he told them, as they pulled up.

They looked at the plain grey four-storey building. "What are we doing here?" Klari asked.

"This is your new home for the time being."

"We're staying here?" Lili asked, smiling. The place looked like a fortress. She put a warm hand on Klari's shoulder. "We'll be safe," Lili said. "It will be fine. We'll make it a home."

"I have a surprise for you inside," Paul added.

"Oh," Klari said, placing a hand on her heart. "I don't know how many surprises a girl can take in a single day. I'll never forget today. Never."

"Wait," Paul said. He had his hand on the car door handle, but didn't move. Two off-duty German soldiers walked by the car and looked but did not linger. When the soldiers had turned a corner, Paul opened his door and hustled his relatives out of the car. The grey building flew the blue Swedish flag with its reclining yellow cross.

As they stepped inside, Klari asked her nephew, "Do you live here, too?"

"I do sometimes, but I move about. I have work to do."

They stood in a marble hall with banks of offices on either side and took in a cool deep breath. "Well, I enjoyed our little country excursion," Robert said. "Did you, my dears?"

Simon said, "Quite," and the new Swedish men laughed the grim laugh of victors. They felt they'd pulled off a great heist of some kind—or at least Paul had—the heist of their lives.

Paul sighed. "This way," he said, and he led them to an office on the far side. Inside the door was the surprise. Rozsi was now living there, too.

Rozsi squealed when she saw her uncle and aunt and rushed at them.

"What a miracle," Klari said, as she kissed her niece. She told Rozsi what Paul had done.

Rozsi finished greeting the new arrivals, and then she embraced her brother. She whispered, "I didn't know you had this in you." He shrugged his shoulders. "Have you seen Zoli today?"

He pulled away and looked into his sister's eyes. "I saw Zoli," Paul whispered back. "We wouldn't have been able to pull this off if Zoli hadn't shown up at the embassy."

Rozsi beamed.

"It will all be fine," Paul said. "Let's all just survive—and bring Istvan home to us, too."

Rozsi still clung to Paul. "I found a gramophone here," she whispered. "Could you get me a Gershwin record? One of his suites—or that rhapsody?"

"Rozsi, my dear," he said, "Gershwin is forbidden. Jazz is forbidden, as you know. Jewish composers are forbidden."

Rozsi held on. "I love him. I love Gershwin. He's such a delight."

"I love him, too," Paul said. "All he wanted to do was write hits, but instead he wrote masterpieces."

Robert joined his niece and nephew. "And what about Beethoven," he said, "now that we're putting in orders? I guess he's allowed. Imagine the land that produced Beethoven and Hegel and Schiller—*Alle Menschen werden Brüder*—packing cultivated people into airless railway cars with a bucket in the corner. Who'd have thought? Until now, I didn't know Beethoven belonged only to them. And we are without our Gershwin—without our Hungary. We reside now in Sweden," he said, raising his hands and turning to indicate their surroundings.

Klari, Robert, Lili and Simon took a closer look at their new residence. Cots had already been set out around the spacious office. There were pillows and sheets for each cot, and there were several lamps. A sizeable washroom was a few steps down the hall—no bath or shower, but ample sinks, certainly, and two toilets. Food was an issue, and cooking was not possible. There were tins of beans that Paul had found and several precious tins of herring. Paul and Zoli would try to get some clothing out of the Becks' own closets, if they could.

Paul looked at his watch. "I have to go," he announced. "I'm meeting Raoul Wallenberg in an hour."

The new arrivals mobbed him. His Aunt Klari reached up and took Paul's face in her warm hands. "You dear boy." Her caramel eyes were swimming with tears. "You are our saviour," she said.

"Saviours are tedious, Auntie. I'm not that good."

She smiled. "Will you be all right on your own?"

"Well, you know me. I'm part dog, part man. I'm my own best friend."

Rozsi joined the mass huddled around Paul. She remembered the huddle at her Uncle Robert and Aunt Klari's place when she and her brother had come with the news that their father was dead. For a moment, they swayed together as they had then. Then they released Paul, and he was gone.

Fifteen

Szeged – June 8, 1944

MARTA FOLDI WAS DEPORTED to Auschwitz-Birkenau for no reason other than that she had a whiff of transgression about her. Marta made a stop of a week in Theresienstadt, a camp carved out of an old fortress town in Bohemia, and a showplace for naïve visiting dignitaries concerned about what the Germans were up to. At Theresienstadt, Marta heard a concert played by inmates and led by a Jew who had been famous as the conductor of the Prague Philharmonic Orchestra, Jan Perecek. It dawned on Marta, as she listened, not as a guest but as an usher at the event, that she had not been to a concert in several years, and here was one being brought to her in her prison. It was quite a lively concert, too, of Bavarian oompah music, as if the assembled listeners were getting set to break into dance and hoist tankards of beer.

Toward the end of the concert, a well-dressed gentleman in his fifties leaned into the aisle and beckoned Marta over. He told her, "You are beautiful for a Hebrew woman." Marta smiled. She was about to tell him the truth when she realized the remark was intended as a compliment: She had risen to beauty even out of the dross of Jewry. In any case, she couldn't prove she was not a Hebrew even if she'd wanted to. How did a woman prove it? She'd ask Abraham, she decided, the next time she saw him.

And then, short days later, she was on her way somewhere else. She didn't know where, because no one told her, and she was not asked to purchase a ticket for the trip. She was being treated to the ride. But was this even a train she was on, windowless and airless, Marta crushed against fifty others? Was it a train travelling across the land, or was it an elevator car, plunging to the centre of the Earth where the hot devil awaited them?

And Auschwitz was different. It represented Germany at its murderous best, humanity at its murderous best. At Auschwitz, a tired looking SS officer decided Marta would join the line of people to be murdered later rather than immediately. She was issued a number, to be worn not only on the striped jacket she was given but also on the skin of her left forearm: "181818," a quaint number, she decided, to wear on her flesh to the grave. The striped uniform also bore an insignia next to the number: there were green triangles for criminals, red ones for political prisoners, and red and yellow Stars of David for Jews. Marta was awarded a red triangle, which both surprised her and distinguished her from the baser Jews and Gypsies.

She was shaved up top and below. She felt her rich raven hair sliding down her naked back and rump with a feathery lightness. A woman behind her with an unfortunate single bushy eyebrow hooding her eyes had that shaved off, too. The four barbers laughed. They were giving the woman fashion and style help she should be grateful for. And then they hosed the women down and de-liced them.

They were in Birkenau, an extension of Auschwitz originally built for Russian prisoners that had a complete railway-station façade, but no real railway station, as if it were a movie set.

The guards placed Marta in a *lager* with two hundred other women, two to a bed. Some of the women had just arrived there and some had been there for months and even years. These were the ones who gave Marta hope, though they'd rob her in an instant or trick her out of a crust of bread. They gave her hope because they'd miraculously survived here for several years, and they were Jews, most of them, horrifyingly skeletal and weak, but still alive, still going, still working and talking and eating whatever scraps could be boiled in a pot and ladled out. These women, these senior veterans, Marta began to admire. The most prominent of them was a woman named Libuse—after the princess, she told everyone, who led the West Slavic tribe and envisioned Prague, the woman who settled the rumblings in her tribe by taking a ploughman as consort and whose dynasty lasted for four centuries. "Except of course the original Libuse was not a Jewess," Libuse said. "A detail. And she was not from the city of Brno. My parents must have been a little touched." She pointed to her temple. "They must have been a little too settled in the Czechoslovak nation, too complacent. It went to their heads." She tapped her temple again. "Hence, the Great Libuse, the Great *Princess* Libuse." This tall woman spoke German, and the first night she silenced Marta's many questions, about when they got to shower and what work they had to do and where the men had got to, by giving Marta simple advice: "Shut up and have a dreamy night."

And that first night, Marta lay down gingerly on her straw bunk beside a Polish woman who would not speak to her. They lay back to back until the woman thought Marta was asleep, and then the woman shifted for a moment before turning over to face her outright. Marta could feel the woman's breath. She thought she could sense the woman sniffing her, felt her spidery hand brush against her hip, then her shoulder, relishing Marta's luxuriant flesh. Marta was fresh meat, still warm enough with life for a feast. Now the woman's fingers were worming over the slope of Marta's shoulder. Marta's skin crawled. It was like lying with a corpse in a coffin, the corpse hungry to suck her warm blood. And then the fingers tweaked the nub of Marta's pronounced nipple, and Marta flinched. The woman hurriedly turned over again to face the other way, moved as far away as she could get on the narrow bunk, her bony shoulder blades bumping up against Marta. In another minute, the woman was asleep.

They were neighbours in a cemetery, not lying in bunks at all but in graves. Each day, some of the women disappeared and were replaced with new recruits. Marta shared her bed with the Polish woman one more night and then, unaccountably, never again. Had she been transferred to another *lager* or transformed into gas? The stench of the incinerator was thick and relentless. It was Libuse who kept Marta going, barking out remarks in German across the darkness that most of the women could understand and most ignored, but some were reassured by them, by the gall of them. Marta was reassured.

The third night, as Marta was beginning to believe the Polish woman would not return and that the authorities had forgotten to replace her, a smaller, rabbit-like woman joined her, quivering, in bed, also a Polish Jew, also silent like her predecessor. This one didn't want her body even to drift into contact with Marta's, let alone to fondle her, even though *some* closeness helped warm up the bed.

An Italian Jew cursed as she tried to settle, and her fierce Greek bunkmate answered in Ladino. A Ukrainian woman asked in Yiddish what the hell kind of language the woman was speaking, and Marta heard the woman spit. The woman was new, evidently. She spoke too boldly and confidently and naïvely. She asked in Yiddish, a language Marta understood, because it derived from German, where they were holding their belongings. Several people laughed out their answer: "Canada."

She laughed, too—she didn't know why—and asked, "What is Canada?"

"It is the land of abundance," Libuse said.

"*Kanada*," someone repeated in Ladino, and then said something else, and laughter erupted again in a small corner of the *lager*.

The Ukrainian woman said she'd brought an emerald brooch her grandmother had received as a little girl from the Tsarina Katarina. The comment caused another round of laughter. The woman was a comedian without knowing it.

Finally, Libuse said calmly, "The brooch from the Tsarina is now in Canada, the land of abundance. It's a warehouse here in the camp filled with all the confiscated valuables. They're sorted, assessed and then sent to Berlin for 'redistribution' or to Switzerland for cash for the German war effort."

Marta remembered the temple in Szeged, piled to the ceiling with confiscated effects. She wondered if some of it ended up here, in Canada.

Someone said something sadly in Yiddish, then someone else spoke in a language Marta couldn't identify, Serbian, possibly, because the words had a Slavic ring.

One of the first things that had impressed Marta in the *lager* was the many different languages floating in the darkness. So many languages, but the tone of the voices was universal—angry, plaintive, scared. One understood hesitancy or longing in any language. The *lager* was a little League of Nations, except that it was not united in the pursuit of harmony and peace, but united in anguish, united in the transmogrification of the group into another species, rodent or insect, but ineffectual rodents—toothless ones—and sterile insects.

Marta's thoughts drifted to home again, to Szeged, and to Istvan, whom she'd left without saying goodbye. Where must he think they've taken her? Did he think her dead? Did he shed a tear as he considered her fate? What was going through his smart stubborn head as the meagre supplies dwindled to nothing, his cramped, dark world closed in altogether, the cat now silent, now dead, provided four, maybe five, additional meals for its enslaved master? Could he hang on for Marta? How long would it be? Could *she* hang on for *him*?

She remembered the little garden out back—the tomatoes and peppers—always the peppers. Could Istvan get to the last of these, quietly, in the dark of night? And the angelica, which sprang out from among the tomatoes every second year, the great balls of green blossom reaching up toward heaven. He could see these plants and feel encouraged, could sit down among them and get lost.

At roll call the following morning, the SS officer in charge, a muscular woman named Ute Schlink, asked "241," the last three digits in a frail woman's identification number, whether she was planning to accept the breakfast of bread about to be offered to her. The Hungarian woman looked down at the mud she was standing in and didn't answer, or not audibly. Schlink struck her across the head with her gloved hand, and the woman dropped to one knee, but then stood again quickly and remarkably, pulling her knee out of the mud with a squelch. "You declined dinner last night as well, I was told. Can you tell me why?" The woman didn't answer, so the officer asked for an interpreter as she removed her truncheon from its sheath in her belt. Marta stepped forward. Schlink put the question to the woman again, and Marta translated.

The woman looked at Marta and then at the SS officer. She said, barely audibly, in Hungarian, "Last night and today are Yom Kippur, when we fast."

Marta turned to the officer and haltingly translated, almost as quietly as the woman had spoken. "It was Yom Kippur," Marta said. But she said to the woman, "It's not Yom Kippur. Even I know that much. Yom Kippur is in the fall."

"Quiet," the officer said to Marta.

The German circled the woman and asked her to remove her clothes, which she did without hesitation. She stood in the damp air without a gram of fat to insulate her bones. They looked to Marta like bones pressing to break out of their prison of flesh. Marta wished she could help the woman, say something to the officer to make it easier, but her mind raced. Why hadn't the woman accepted the food, even if she hadn't planned on eating it, so she could give it to someone else? Was that a sin? Was it a sin even under these circumstances? Could an inmate commit a sin at Auschwitz? The officer said, "241, if you don't eat, you will no longer be much use to the work effort." She circled the woman again and touched her bony rump with the truncheon. "I cannot eat today," the woman said, "but only today." Marta translated.

The guard said, "What if I decide you will not eat tomorrow? What if I decide that tomorrow is Yom Kippur and, in your case, the next day, too?" Schlink said it like a German, naturally: "Yom Kippah," she called it.

And suddenly it made sense to Marta: you didn't have the right to eat much here, but you didn't have the right to starve yourself, either, because that would have put you in control of your own demise.

The woman simply shook her head, but only just perceptibly. Schlink thwacked her across the skull with her truncheon this time, the hollow clang as it struck bone resounding around the yard. The woman fell to the same muddy knee again but didn't rise.

Then came a voice from behind them, in German, "Maybe the fare doesn't agree with her." It was tall Libuse, Princess Libuse.

Schlink rushed at her like a mad dog and thwacked her, too, the same way, but Libuse stood firm, a dark welt of blood forming immediately beneath the skin at the base of her skull. Then the officer rushed back at 241 and clubbed the kneeling woman yet again, again with the truncheon against the skull. The woman fell face down in the mud. The others from the *lager* watched, waiting for her to pull her face out to take a breath, but she didn't. She looked like a mythic white creature emerging from the mud rather than sunken into it.

Marta imagined for the first time what 241 must have looked like filled out and with a rich head of hair, as auburn as her eyebrows. Did she take this trip with her family, and was she the final one to go, erasing their auburn line with a single last assertion that on this day, the day she imagined was Yom Kippur, she would not eat or take food to share with others, because it was the day of atonement?

And then came the selection—an impromptu selection this morning—a little rushed and without the usual fanfare of handing out cards with names and numbers on them. In the exercise, those who were to be left working, standing, sitting, lying down, rising up, eating and evacuating their bowels and bladders were to be separated from those who would no longer be performing these functions because they were to be gassed and incinerated.

With the help of her attendant guards and the *kapo*, the Jewish inmate selected to rule each *lager*, the one who was bloodless, Schlink took her customary march up and down the line of prisoners, pointing with her truncheon at those to be excused from life and calling out numbers, "141, 775, 416, 225," the *kapo* marking them down on a chart, signalling with her head for each prisoner to step out of the line. About twenty were selected that morning from the group of two hundred, the same number in each of the *lagers* down the line throughout Birkenau and Auschwitz. One of the women selected was the Ukrainian whose emerald brooch had ended up in "Canada." She didn't seem sure what had happened to her. Perhaps she clung to the hope she was being relocated again, which is what she'd originally been told, that possibly she'd see her husband and son. The selection of this woman was peculiar, if only because she was a recent arrival and hadn't lost enough weight or colour to suggest she couldn't carry on in work detail. She seemed calm as her lips moved rapidly in prayer. Some of the other women selected cried out but then covered their mouths, worried about stepping out of line even now. Others looked on as blankly as they had when 241 hit the mud. They looked as though thoughts no longer moved behind their eyes.

Marta could hear an orchestra playing in the distance, the notes riding on the foggy air toward them, and she knew what was coming—she'd heard, and she knew the drill: the executions up against a wall of the uncooperative and the "criminal," the ones, for instance, who'd managed to trade a contraband British cigarette for an extra half bowl of soup. The ceremony was marked by a round of shots, puncturing the notes, followed by another round, the music— marching tunes, mostly—making the occasion festive.

Schlink worked her way back to Libuse, and the two attendant guards raised their rifles, expecting to lead the woman off for execution, but uncharacteristically Schlink said, "You will spend seventy-two hours in confinement block, and you will not eat or drink. Yom Kippah." Libuse's life was to be spared so Schlink could affirm her cleverness and reassert her authority, even without a truncheon, authority that had faltered in the hands of 241.

The officer then strolled over to gaze at Marta. She smiled at her eerily, as if the two were acquaintances meeting in a park. Marta shuddered. Schlink's dark blond hair under her cap was tied in braids wound tightly around the sides of her head like rope, as if she were getting set to string herself up by the top of the head. Schlink said, "I understand you worked in a dental office, 818. You will not join the others for work detail. You will help out in the infirmary."

Marta nodded. She felt the eyes of everyone upon her. She was a medical assistant all of a sudden. Rarely did anyone in the camp rise out of the dross of shorn prisoners in dingy uniforms. No one had a past or future. No one had been a florist, a professor of chemistry, a chambermaid. Curiosity faded rapidly when starvation and filth attended upon the women hourly and daily. Marta had learned a short, sharp lesson. She learned not to be amazed, not even surprised. Anything that was possible here was probable and even likely to come about.

Marta found herself feeling buoyant, grateful even. The sun still went on shining. And then she saw a pigeon land on a small flat stone in the mud, a white-grey stone the colour of 241's skin. And another landed beside the first, crowding the other bird on the little platform. Here were animals who could fly over an electrified barbed-wire fence, and they flew *into* Auschwitz? But why not? They awaited scraps of food here as they did each day in the town, as they did in Oswiecim, in the square in front of the church. How were they to know that everyone who stood in the mud before them today awaited the same scraps, that the birds themselves were scraps if the inmates could snatch one without being seen? What a treat were these pigeons to the condemned and the not-yet-condemned: they reminded the assembled women of the miracle of flight; they reminded them of the statues in their own cities and of the fountains and squares, of a time when the birds seemed to live for their amusement. Marta thought of Mendelssohn Square, the pigeons, Istvan's father, the horrible scene that was routine here.

Now, for the first time, they felt humbled by the pigeons as the grey birds sat on their royal rock and cooed. Here, nothing belonged to the many women stripped of their citizenship, not the sky, not the air, not the earth, not the cramped wooden shoes that kept their feet from sinking into the earth. The women who were to be exterminated this day were to pass their belongings to women who were yet to be exterminated, new arrivals. Everything belonged to the authorities, from the wooden shoes to the sky. Everything was for the authorities to lend to you and for you to receive. In that sense, the authorities displaced God. They could say when Yom Kippur was to occur and when Christmas came, if they so chose. It was a tidy ecosystem and hierarchy: Germans, pigeons, inmates to die later, inmates to die today.

The pigeons flew off when Schlink dismissed the women. They flew toward the sounds of the orchestra and firing squad to see if they might have better luck there.

MARTA SPENT HER DAYS in a building along whose sides stood a row of cedars of Lebanon. They stood erect like green soldiers, as if to mimic their dark keepers. She was to assist Doctor Joachim Fischer, a veterinarian who'd succeeded another inmate, a French doctor named Marcel Levi. He had himself contracted *Korperschwache*, an organic decay which claimed the majority of its victims.

It was nicer to work in the infirmary than in the workshop where she'd made crude spoons out of the iron sent to them from Berlin. The infirmary was warmer, the food was more plentiful, and Marta was treated respectfully by Dr. Fischer and by the patients, who thought that she had more influence with the authorities than they had. It was here the red triangle insignia, which marked her a political prisoner and distinguished her from the lower caste of inmate, made all the difference.

More importantly, the eyes of Auschwitz were not always on Marta, and she could work her magic here, dishing out extra half bowls of soup to patients who needed it most, not always reporting a patient's temperature, because a fever sometimes condemned the patient to death in the gas chamber, reassuring inmates that their lives would get better even when she knew they couldn't.

Dr. Fischer frequently asked Marta to supervise the doling out of scarce medication, telling her she was better at it than he could be. "I have to keep reminding myself it's not a horse I'm injecting, and that takes more moderation than I am capable of."

Libuse didn't return to the *lager* as Marta had hoped, and Marta began to wonder if Schlink had had a change of heart and condemned her to death after all. Marta found herself telling a new woman from Hungary one night in German to "have a dreamy night." But then a few weeks later, unaccountably, Marta was asked to change *lagers*. She was moved to a creaky wooden *lager*, one of a series which had once been used by the Polish cavalry as stables for its horses. The crowding here was worse. Over five hundred women were crammed into a building originally designed for forty or forty-five horses.

But here in this stable she met up with Libuse again. The Princess looked gaunter than ever and had lost some of her irrepressible lustre, but Marta was thrilled to see her again. Libuse had a streak of red across her right eye and halfway across her left. "What happened to you?" Marta asked her as the Princess lay in her bunk. The woman behind her snored. "Was it the clubbing a few weeks ago?" She was whispering now. "In the yard? Have you been hit again since?" She didn't want to say the name of Schlink but pointed with her head to some indefinite place outside the horse *lager*.

"I don't know. It's been itching terribly."

"It's an infection, then, maybe."

"I thought you were a dental assistant," Libuse said.

Marta noticed a red blotch at the base of Libuse's neck peeking out of her collar. She placed her hand on her forehead. The woman was on fire. Libuse's eyes were closed. Marta unbuttoned the top buttons of her shirt and saw the blotches continue over her chest. Scarlet fever. She knew it instantly—she'd seen it in the clinic—but she didn't say the words. "You have to come to the infirmary, immediately. I'll speak to Dr. Fischer. You need to be treated."

But Libuse was asleep already, taking in great ragged drafts of air. Marta stood by her for a minute, not knowing what to do. She decided she must tell someone. The *kapo* in this *lager* was a Hungarian woman named Manci. She was not mean to those who let her know she was in charge. Marta had heard the same observation from a number of the women in the stable. She found the *kapo* and told her Libuse had redness of the eye and wondered what to do. Manci rubbed her stern chin, as if there were numerous options, and then ran her hand through the bristle of her scalp. Manci must have thought she was Solomon when she declared that Libuse should be transferred to the infirmary to have her eyes attended to. "I'll arrange it first thing in the morning."

"Good idea, ma'am," Marta said. "Thank you."

The woman smiled tightly, then said, "Get to bed."

In the infirmary the next day, Dr. Fischer examined Libuse's whitish tongue and the red blotches all over her chest and back and concurred that she had contracted scarlet fever. But he said he didn't have enough experience with human disease. He couldn't make sense of the redness of the eyes. "She took a blow across the back of the head from an officer with her stick," Marta said.

"Is that a complaint?" Dr. Fischer asked.

It was the first time the doctor had turned on her. She stepped back a bit, felt she'd taken a blow herself. "No, of course not," Marta said.

It was not until she'd answered that the doctor continued his examination. He prescribed sulpha drugs and quarantined Libuse in a room with two other inmates with scarlet fever, a half-dozen cases of diphtheria, one of typhus and two of dysentery.

"Where am I?" Libuse asked, "the Grand Hotel Europa?" Marta tucked in her ailing friend. There was only one person assigned to each bunk, the room was warm, there were extra rounds of soup, and Marta got to look in on Libuse several times a day. Marta even read to her from a book that was given to her by a male nurse from an adjoining infirmary when he had learned that Marta had come from Szeged. The book, by Mor Jokai, was in the original Hungarian and was called *Eyes Like the Sea*. Marta noticed the other quarantined patients listening to the sounds of the lively nineteenth-century prose, although no one else was from Hungary. So Marta read the novel with extra relish. Jokai was the grand Romantic in her homeland, after all, and she felt happy about giving him the extra push, even if no one understood a word. She felt like a singer with a lovely song.

While Libuse's condition improved over the course of a week, her eyes had taken on a cloudy sheen. Once, when she lay in her bunk awaiting Marta, her eyes wide open, Libuse didn't notice that Marta had arrived and didn't smile until she greeted her. Marta took the single lamp in the room and held it up to Libuse's face. "It's warm," Libuse said.

"Can you see its light?" Marta asked.

"Move it away," Libuse said. Marta moved the lamp back and forth before Libuse's face, but not close enough for her to feel its warmth. "I can see the light," she said.

"How many fingers am I holding up?" Marta asked.

Libuse paused, groped with her eyes across the room. "Twelve," she said.

"You're going blind." Marta dropped her hands to her sides. A couple of the other patients watched her. "You've got scarlet fever, you're going blind, you're in Auschwitz and you're making jokes."

"You're in Auschwitz, too," Libuse said.

Dr. Fischer came to examine Libuse and noted that her fever had broken. He saw the cloudy eyes and didn't know what to say. He summoned a doctor from the adjoining clinic, a family physician from Lodz who spoke only a little German. A day later, the man arrived in the restricted room with his face covered. He watched Dr. Fischer tie up his own mask before proceeding. Marta joined them, holding a mask to her own face. She'd been careless about doing so until then, but she'd washed her hands as often as she could, particularly after cleaning up the dysentery patients. She'd used chloramines blended with water that the male nurse from next door had provided.

"What happened here?" the Polish doctor asked. Fischer shrugged his shoulders and turned to Marta. She didn't dare mention the truncheon again. Even if she were right, they could only now speculate. The damage seemed profound, but she prayed it could be reversed. Perhaps the film over her eyes would lift of its own accord. The Polish doctor couldn't help. He said in broken German, directly to Libuse, what Marta had hoped he would say: that maybe she would mend on her own when she got stronger. Libuse understood the gist of his words. She asked whether scarlet fever caused blindness. "Not that I know of," he replied and patted her hand before withdrawing. "Deafness sometimes."

Much depended on timing. Libuse would not survive outside the infirmary as a blind woman, not even for a day. If Fischer checked her out, she was doomed.

But the scarlet fever lifted a few days later, and Fischer had little choice. "I'll suggest they give her light work for a short time. We can only hope."

That night, with Libuse back in the *lager*, Marta couldn't sleep. The moon was full, and she snuck over to Libuse's bunk to see how she was doing. Libuse sensed her presence and groped for Marta's hand. "It'll be all right," Libuse said when she found it.

On the way back to her bunk, Marta paused at the window to gaze at the big moon, wasting its glamour on the Auschwitz yard. She remembered Istvan. She couldn't bear to think of him, shrivelled in the cellar, now gone possibly, waiting up ahead maybe.

Sixteen

LILI AND ROZSI SHOT OUT of the doors of the Dutch insurance company. They hustled along Ulloi Street, the rope of Lili's blond braid gleaming in the bright morning sunlight, Rozsi's dark hair tucked beneath a baby-blue bonnet, calculated to draw attention away from her hair and to her eyes. They carried with them their Swedish papers and worried less about the Germans, who would likely honour the papers, than the Hungarian Arrow Cross, who wouldn't. They also had a bracelet and ring to barter with.

Lili had wanted Rozsi to stay put at the safe house, but she said she'd go utterly mad if she couldn't have a break from staring at those godforsaken walls. "My best friends have become those stiff wooden chairs and desks." They'd now lived in the Swedish house office together for almost three weeks.

"There are worse friends out there in the world these days, believe me."

"I don't mean to be ungrateful. But I can help you, Lili. I'm not Paul, but I am his sister."

"All right, come with me. We'll manage something, I'm sure."

Rozsi had kissed her Uncle Robert while Lili hugged Klari, and then they switched. Simon looked guilty and anxious, but they all knew he could not leave. Simon could have posed for one of Josef

Goebbels's propaganda figures of Jews, whose cartoonish dark eyes and hooked noses looked down from posts and billboards around the city.

Arm in arm, the two women rushed eastward, past the sharp shadow of the Hungarian National Museum. "We can go to Baross Street," Lili said. "If we make it to Jozsef Crescent along Baross, we can get food at the Madar Café. My friend Maria will give us some without question, just as long as no one's watching her. If there's a particular German officer there, the one I told you about, then we can't go in— that's the only thing."

Rozsi was almost out of breath. "What would we do without you, my darling?" she asked. "What would *I* have done without you? How would we have eaten anything at all? Zoli has been gone so much since he took it upon himself to stand in the line of fire holding up a camera." Rozsi's eyes shifted left and right as she spoke. She was startled by every bird taking flight and every car zipping by behind them at Kalvin Square or up ahead on Jozsef.

Lili, the more experienced and daring adventurer, was much more accustomed to wading in among the crocodiles. Without her scavenging expeditions, the Becks and the group of mysterious nuns who'd just moved into the building annexed by Wallenberg would surely have starved. They'd been transferred from another building that had been raided by the Arrow Cross. As it was, even the portly Robert had become thin. Klari had skilfully pinned the shoulders and waists of the two suits of Robert's that Paul had managed to rescue from their home, and Lili similarly had to alter the three dresses of Klari's she had smuggled into the Swedish compound and which the two women were to share for however long they remained there, despite the billowy look they gave Lili. And the nuns, who'd kept to themselves to the point of seeming secretive, even arrogant, with their once-solid frames filling out their habits, all now stood shivering like thin winter branches as Lili brought back turnips one day, rice another, radishes a third.

Only yesterday, she had come back just before nightfall after a long, worrisome afternoon during which, repeatedly, Simon despaired of ever seeing her again, bearing a sack with two giant cans in it. Lili grunted as she set down her booty with a clump and smiled broadly. She scanned the faces, first Klari's and Robert's, then Rozsi's, the nuns' behind her, not wanting to appear too eager; finally, Simon's. He had the look of a wolf again, and he frightened her. Had he been worried about her? Had he feared he might never eat again? If she had not returned, which alarm would have sounded first behind those fangs?

A chill juddered down her spine. She lost her smile. They were all waiting. She didn't want to be cruel, so she opened her sack and withdrew the great cans with another grunt.

"Tomato paste," she said. "Can you believe it? All this tomato paste. I found the cans in the larder of a badly damaged townhouse. Terribly damaged. And forgotten. Looted already. The paintings were gone as well as the porcelain and silver out of the china cabinet, the rugs off the floor, even the books from the shelf. But these cans were overlooked, somehow, in the dark. They looked like restaurant cans they were so big. Maybe someone had startled the looters or conquerors—whoever they were."

Smiles lit up the room all around Lili now. Imagine. All that tomato paste. A nun said through a dry throat, "And the sack? You even managed a sack." Lili did not even know the woman's name, the nuns spoke so rarely, not even a greeting of good morning, not a thank you, not a "Bless the Lord."

Lili handed the nuns one of the big cans. They all rushed forward to take it. Lili said, "From the brickyard a half block away. There were sacks at the abandoned brickyard. I just took one."

Simon opened both cans as quickly as he could. The nuns sat on the floor all around their tomato paste each with a spoon, like young girls around a great Christmas pudding.

Today, Rozsi and Lili saw a convoy of German vehicles ahead. They could not make it all the way to the Madar Café. They'd have to take another route. Rozsi had just begun to loosen her grip on her companion's arm. She said nervously, "You will be my cousin soon, Lili, and what a delightful cousin you will be, the best of an excellent lot. You'll be like a sister to me."

And then they heard a gunshot. The women ducked into the doorway of a courtyard on Baross Street. There appeared to be someone working inside, pounding leather, two people, a man and a woman at least. Could the workers see them lurking in the shadows?

"Maybe it was a car backfiring," Lili whispered.

"Can these people be trusted?" Rozsi's face blanched with panic.

"Quiet."

Another shot rang out, causing the women to crouch lower. Rozsi covered her head with her hands and whimpered.

"Wait here," Lili said. She dashed out and peered around the corner into the street. She could see clearly down Maria Street to Ulloi, where she spotted a line of people and a single SS officer. Even from a good block away, the yellow star was evident on the chests of those in line. A strange silence hung in the air. And then came a third shot.

Lili rushed back to her blue-bonneted "cousin," now stricken with paralysis. She urged her out, and the two galloped off together in the opposite direction, northward toward Sandor Brody Street, ducked into another courtyard and shrank down again to the cobblestones.

They could hardly be detected from the street. They held still, panting, Rozsi's arm painfully clamped in her companion's. A wooden door clapped open against a wall. Rozsi squawked, then covered her mouth with her hand.

The women turned to find a quiet courtyard behind them, the floor covered by grey cobblestones, rounded and polished as if by the sea. They crept forward, and the door clattered again. They gazed up to discover that it was not a door at all but a wooden shutter. High above it was a skylight trimmed with purple bevelled glass.

More alluring than the scene, however, was the air itself, for it was filled with the smell of soup: onions, garlic, peppers, beans. Where had such riches come from? Lili signalled to Rozsi to hide in the shadows with her. She whispered, "Let's offer them something for some of their soup. My bracelet—your ring."

"No!" Rozsi said, too loudly.

"The bracelet then. They'll take the bracelet."

The two advanced across the smooth cobblestones, still in a half-crouch, like prowlers. They passed under a gothic doorway crowned with a stone garland of freshly painted white lilies on green leaves. The heavy door facing them was as shiny and white as the stone blossoms.

Rozsi knocked gently, and the visitors waited a long, respectful moment before Lili tried more forcefully. Still no answer. Above the women's heads hung a cheerful old chandelier, with white glass stems supporting purple heads of hyacinth with green glass leaves. The light was switched off.

Lili tried the doorknob and, to her surprise, found that it yielded. The intruders thought they would find a genial, warm room, but it was virtually empty, except for a crocheted doily folded over on the floor, an overturned palm, a couple of small chairs and a walnut side table piled high with two towers of books.

And yet there was the robust smell of soup. Rozsi squeaked out a "Hello" in the direction of the kitchen at the back. As they skulked along the corridor covered by a soft Persian runner, they passed into the sphere of the soup and could hear it bubbling.

A corner of the burgundy rug just before the entrance to the kitchen was turned over, and glass crunched beneath the women's feet. Both looked down, slightly alarmed, before taking the next bold step into the kitchen.

The larder was empty, the cupboards open and bare. A pine china cabinet stood bright with white plates printed with lilies. Three chairs sat around a blind table and a fourth was overturned. A pair of green tortoiseshell spectacles, its arms folded, lay on the tabletop by a linen tea towel. The thought of the empty house next door to Lili's home in Tolgy glanced across her consciousness. On the floor lay a maid's white cap, half encircling the hairpin which must have held it in place, and beside these, across the pine floorboards, was a dry maroon smear, which must almost certainly have been soup. A similar smear had dried beside the spoon rest on the stove, but no spoon.

Rozsi drew her companion's attention to an imposing photograph in an ornately carved wooden frame hanging next to the china cabinet. It was of a clutch of four proud hunters, two with handlebar moustaches, one with his foot resting on a vanquished wild boar.

Lili took the linen towel and lifted the lid of the fragrant pot. Rozsi turned off the gentle flame beneath it.

"Let's take the pot with us," Lili said.

"The pot?"

"We'll manage."

"Let's check first—"

"No," Lili said. "They're gone. Recently. *Very* recently. But gone."

Rozsi looked back at the picture of the hunters. Which one belonged to this household? "Let's leave the bracelet for them," she said.

Lili took her companion's face in her hands, tucking the ends of her fingers inside the blue bonnet. "Rozsi, that bracelet is currency for another meal. These people won't be back. I don't know who took them. The Germans. The Arrow Cross. Help me with this."

"This huge pot?"

"Yes, it's wonderful soup. Look!" Lili reached into the steaming pot for the wooden spoon and offered Rozsi some to taste.

"Oh, dear Lord," she said, licking her lips, forgetting herself briefly, then covering her mouth. "We'll try," she said.

The pot was heavier than even Lili had thought. It would be a feat to carry it back the five blocks to the safe house, particularly without arousing suspicion. But then it wasn't only Jews who were hungry these days.

"Maybe we should eat some," Rozsi said, grunting as they transferred the pot to the table. "We'll carry our dinner inside of us."

"We can make it back with the whole pot," Lili said.

They managed to get the soup all the way to the Ervin Szabo Library, where they set the pot down on the stone steps and paused to catch their breath. It was especially hot now. Lili's back was drenched.

"No one saw us," Rozsi said.

"I don't think so."

"We'd be dead by now, wouldn't we?"

"Maybe not dead, but well on our way to it, I'm sure," Lili said.

"My shoulders are coming out of their sockets," Rozsi said as she rubbed them.

"I think I can manage the rest of the way now," Lili said.

Rozsi looked hurt. "Don't be ridiculous. I've held up until now. I'll survive another two blocks. If I don't, you'll never take me out with you again, and it'll be me and the furniture and the nuns with their vow of silence."

They saw a man in uniform a couple of blocks behind them, hurrying in their direction. He hadn't passed Maria Street yet, so if they rushed they could elude him.

The women hopped to their feet, lifted their pot, and marched northwest on Ulloi Street even more briskly than before, the soup sloshing around in the pot. As they approached the last leg of the journey, Rozsi glanced behind her. The uniformed man had passed the steps of the library and turned, gaining on them.

They were almost there. They were almost back at their building, soup and all, but they could live without the soup if they had to. They could heave it at their assailant.

The thought shot through Rozsi's mind like a bullet: "I want to see Zoli again, Lili," she blurted out. "I live for him. I need to see him again." Rozsi's cheeks glistened with tears.

Lili smiled in response. And then the man was upon them. They'd arrived at Number 2, the building Wallenberg had annexed for Sweden, but they still stood on the sidewalk in Hungary. It was like a child's fierce game of hide-and-seek, and they were not home free just yet.

They heard his voice as they turned, still gripping the great pot. "I have an envelope for Dr. Robert Beck," the man said. He was a mailman.

"An envelope?" both women said simultaneously, breathlessly. They set down the pot and broke into wild laughter.

When they finished, the mailman, smiling now himself, said, "Yes, his neighbour on Jokai Street said I could find him here. It's his last paycheque."

"His *paycheque?*" This one was even better. Now Rozsi and Lili were doubled over and howling.

"Do you need help getting that inside?"

"I don't think so," Rozsi said, "but we'll give you some, if you're hungry."

"No, thank you, ma'am," he said soberly and handed over the envelope. "Have a good day." The man moved along in the direction of Kalvin Square.

Seventeen

PAUL MET WITH RAOUL WALLENBERG in his office at the end of an exasperating day. At Nyugati Station that morning, Wallenberg and his team had managed to liberate one hundred and thirty newly minted Swedes from the transports, only to have them apprehended once again by the Arrow Cross, taken to a nearby brickyard and shot. The Arrow Cross didn't like the Germans to take their Jews, didn't accept the notion of Swedes with Hungarian names, and liked to carry out their own killings.

That same day, an unscheduled deportation by the Nazis occurred on the other side of town, the east side, and the Swedes and their lieutenants couldn't act quickly enough to save anyone.

Paul and Raoul were talking excitedly in English. "So what do you propose?" the Swede asked.

"Our agents need to communicate better with one another and with *us*. They're running amok. We need better intelligence, coordinated intelligence."

Wallenberg was about to answer but didn't. Paul thought for a moment that he'd missed something and moved in closer. Wallenberg looked awkwardly at his companion and the two found themselves blushing.

After too long a pause, Wallenberg said, "No, we need to visit Eichmann."

"*Visit* him?" Paul said. "*Adolf* Eichmann?"

"We can cut a special deal with him. The Germans need deals here. Hungarian Jews are still a powerful economic force."

"Not anymore," Paul said.

"They are—you are. Believe me."

Paul looked into Wallenberg's walnut-brown eyes. They were quiet eyes, calming.

"You've actually gone mad," Paul said.

"Madder than someone standing in front of a transport train to stop it—not to mention parking *my* car across the tracks?"

"They needed to see me."

"What, the hat and cape weren't loud enough?"

"Mad like that, yes. The suit and cape were the maddest part."

The Swede walked to the window. "Eichmann can help us, you see," he said. "He *is* mad. But he needs things. War machinery, slave labour."

Someone knocked at the door. Wallenberg was distracted. He was standing at the window, looking out into the rainy night. He looked down Gellert Hill toward the Danube. He could see someone in the wet light across Minerva Street, but whoever it was saw him, too, and ducked into a dark alleyway.

Paul opened the door. The man in the hallway wore a blue fedora and his ears were blazing red. Though the man was Hungarian, he said in German, for the benefit of Wallenberg, "Sir, there's a pregnant woman downstairs."

"Yes?" Paul said.

"She's going to de-pregnate herself at any moment if the pool at her feet is any indication."

"A Jew?" asked Paul.

"Yes, a Jew. No hospital will take her."

Wallenberg turned from the window. "Bring her up," said the Swede.

"Up? Bring her up where?" the man asked. The redness from his ears spread to his cheeks like electric bulbs. He took off his blue fedora and combed back his hair with his fingers.

"Yes, up. Bring her to my bedroom." He turned to Paul and switched to English. "Let's get Dr. Molnar up here again. He's on the night shift downstairs."

The man replaced his hat and said, "I'll prepare your bed, sir."

The woman said her name was Ilonka Nemet. She could barely make it up the stairs on her own, so Dr. Molnar and a strong woman who'd been helping with the *schutz-passes* all but carried the bursting woman up to Raoul's bedroom.

Ilonka Nemet saw Wallenberg and, attempting to be mannerly, tried to say something but began to pant instead. She was pale and perspiring. The group, including the messenger in the blue hat, got her onto Wallenberg's bed.

"The room is too crowded," the doctor said, and Wallenberg and Paul awkwardly shuffled out. The man with the blue hat, who'd once been a printer, left, too, but continued all the way down to the first floor.

Back in Wallenberg's office, Paul and the Swede listened to the rain pattering against the window and didn't talk. They seemed to be expecting another cue, and they didn't have to wait long.

They heard a wail above their heads, followed by moans. They both looked up at the ceiling. To the unwitting ear, Ilonka Nemet might have sounded as though she were alternating between pleasure and intense pain.

Wallenberg whispered, "I hope we've made ourselves useful."

Paul nodded.

"Shouldn't you call it a night?" Wallenberg asked.

Paul shook his head. "I'll wait to see how she makes out." Paul had his own room in a Swedish building adjoining this one.

Raoul and Paul wanted to talk some more but found themselves drawn to the drama of the primal sounds, muffled by the ceiling. The woman cursed and wailed again, a wild sound to add to the rainy night.

And then the noise stopped. Just the rain persisted. Both men looked at the ceiling, waited for the cry of a baby and, when it didn't come, headed upstairs.

Dr. Molnar greeted the men as they arrived. The doctor was wiping his bloody hands in a towel. "Hope you don't mind," he said. "We raided your linen closet."

The Swede shrugged his shoulders. "What about the baby, and the mama?"

"She's fine," the doctor said. "They both are. A little girl."

"Thank you," Paul said.

"Why would you thank me?" the doctor asked. "This is what I do."

Three women were now attending to Ilonka Nemet, one from the embassy, the woman who had been working on the *schutz-passes* and another Jewish woman from the Swedish compound. They cleaned and freshened the bed as Ilonka and her baby lay in the middle of it. They worked with great skill, gently turning mother and child this way and that, cleaning and tidying them up, too, as if they were part of the bedding.

Finally everyone withdrew, except for Wallenberg, Paul, mother and child.

The men stood on either side of the bed. The Swede said, "She's very pretty."

Ilonka raised her head to look and then spat at the child. Paul burst out laughing.

Wallenberg said, "Have you picked out a name for the little girl?"

At first Ilonka didn't answer. Wallenberg wondered if she'd understood his German. He glanced at Paul, who put the question in Hungarian.

"Yes," the woman said in German, "but I don't know what it is."

Paul looked at the woman and asked the question again in Hungarian. She simply smiled.

"Are you the Sphinx?" he asked.

She shook her head and smiled again. The woman's dark eyes, like Greek olives, glowed out of the half-darkness. She looked tired but very alive.

She turned to Wallenberg and asked, "What is your mother's name? I want to give my daughter your mother's name."

Wallenberg took Ilonka's warm hand. The child murmured. "She's a good girl," Wallenberg said. "I can tell already."

Ilonka nodded.

He took the baby's clutchy fingers. "But I won't mention any of her other attributes," he said. "I don't want the spit to start flying again."

Ilonka smiled.

"My mother's name is Maj," Wallenberg said.

"Maj Nemet," the woman repeated at her little girl's head. The baby had curly black hair. "Maj."

The men stood tall beside the bed.

"Stay with me," Ilonka said. Her voice was tired.

"Where is your husband?" Wallenberg asked.

"I don't know."

"Was he taken?"

She was crying. "I don't know."

"I'll stay."

"Just a short while."

"No, a long while," Wallenberg said. "I have nowhere to go. This is my bedroom."

Ilonka laughed, a good throaty laugh she drew up from her belly. "Aah," she said, remembering her recent pain, and she pressed her hand down on her abdomen. She repeated the name of the child, Maj Nemet, and drew the baby up to her breast, but the little girl slept on.

It was an impressive bed, with the three golden crowns of Sweden at its head bestowing a benediction on its occupants.

"I'll go," Paul said in English.

"Where will you go?" Wallenberg wanted to know.

"To my room."

"You'll have to go out to the street to get around to your room. It's not a good idea at 2 A.M. I know we've been reckless, but let's not be reckless when we don't need to. You heard the lady, stay."

"Where?"

"The bed's big enough for a family of six—eight during wartime. Stay. We'll have breakfast together."

The baby was suckling, now, with its eyes closed. Ilonka, too, had closed her eyes and seemed to be sleeping.

Paul marvelled at people's ability to improvise and adapt. He marvelled at the world's ability to reconfigure itself, like magic, taking on whatever shape it needed to in order to preserve life. Without being fully conscious of the thought, he sensed that he stood near the centre of the universe.

Paul took off his shoes, laid them neatly at the foot of the bed and made himself comfortable on one side of Ilonka and Maj. Wallenberg watched before removing his own jacket and shoes and carrying them to the closet. He then made himself comfortable on the other side of the woman and her baby. Soon, everyone was asleep.

Eighteen

WATER NO LONGER POURED from the tap. There was no wood for the stove. Istvan could collect rainwater in a pan, but only at night when no one would notice. He'd eaten the dozen tomatoes from the garden ten days before, shared three green ones with Smetana. He'd eaten the grass with Smetana, every blade, but he didn't want to touch the blooms of the lush angelica in case they were poisonous. Smetana must have caught a mouse. The blood was still around his mouth, and he gloated unremittingly, purring his head off. And then Smetana had brought him a mouse, too, and deposited it on his threshold as an offering to him. Istvan took the little beast and cleaned it and roasted it over a tiny fire—a toy fire, it looked like—out back in the middle of the night.

Smetana knew, now, not to come home during the day, because Istvan could not let him in. The cat was probably arousing enough suspicion as it was, wandering the precincts, scrapping with the surviving stray cats who'd weathered these years when the humans hardly shared.

Istvan told Smetana one evening about another cat, named Tiresius, who lived in St. Agota Old Age Home, around the corner from his dental office. He was a special cat, a tuxedo cat, all black with an elegant white chest and paws, like spats. But what set him apart was his ability to foretell the demise of the residents at St. Agota. "The nuns at first thought Tiresias was the devil," Istvan said, as he ran his hand through Smetana's belly fur. "But Tiresias was too angelic to be the devil. You see, he performed a service for the elderly. He would make the final voyage as warm and comfortable as could be. If the patient's door was closed, he would call out to the nuns to let him in, and then he would wind his warm body around the old person's cold feet. If they hacked with a cough, he would stretch himself out by their side, soothing them with his soft purr, until the rumble in their chests softened, too, and their last breaths were calm ones. On one occasion, when old Mr. Farkas appeared to be going, Tiresias sat by his daughter's side instead in the common room, never leaving her. The nuns opened Mr. Farkas's door and beckoned to the cat, but Tiresias held his post. They believed his distinguished career was at an end. He had foretold the passing of some fifty people just hours before their passing and had not slipped up a single time. They were disappointed with him and turned their attention elsewhere. When they returned, Mr. Farkas sat crying by his daughter's side in the common room. She had passed away, with Tiresias sitting in her lap."

Smetana purred now, too, and curled himself up in Istvan's lap. In a second, Smetana was asleep. "Tiresias himself never died," Istvan whispered, "or at least no one saw him, confirming his status as a divine messenger. He simply walked out the front door of St. Agota one morning and never came back."

Smetana woke up and looked at Istvan, his thorny paws making themselves known to his lap. He purred again. "Of course, you are not Tiresias reincarnated, are you, Smetana? You predict continuing life, not death—or is this Tiresias's next task?"

The time had come for Istvan to get out, too, at night. He'd managed a couple of times, just to steal pears and apples from nearby trees. Could the authorities be watching the house, he asked himself, after they'd murdered his Marta or sent her away with the others? His heart pounded in his head. He pressed the ache in from his temples, tight as a vise. And then he took a deep breath and held it within him. The southern Hungarian air was still free for the taking and abundant and smelled the same to everyone.

His Marta had sacrificed herself with a look that said, "I am hiding something; I do have someone; I have swallowed the canary." And in sacrificing herself, she drew the eyes away from the little house in the old paprika district. No one came around anymore. No one counted the tomatoes on the vine. They'd cut off the water, crossed the place off some list—one of many, no doubt. And now he could roam about in the dark. The time had come to travel farther afield, become Man the Forager. Better to die from a sudden blow than from endless starvation. He could no longer die quickly. He'd been doing it steadily and diligently for months. Better the blow—better the risk—the only thing at stake was what remained of his life. Life without Marta.

He'd abandoned the library of his mind, the books he'd been carrying around with him in his small dark circle, the individual volumes, the individual chapters he'd been mentally thumbing through, and the verses he recollected, especially the lines of his friend Miklos, the fictional characters Istvan had gathered around his fire, the characters he loved as well as the people he loved, some better. The wandering Odysseus sat there glowing, recalling the lure of the Sirens, the horror of the Cyclops—had Istvan become Penelope and Marta the unwilling and unwitting adventurer, Smetana their Telemachus? Or had he been the dupe, Docteur Bovary, turning away as Emma cast her eye abroad, now to Rodolphe, now to Léon, the solicitor, with "the ruins of a poet" in his heart? Or had he become the madwoman, howling down from the attic as Rochester courted Jane Eyre, except Istvan howled up through the floorboards—surely not as a spouse, surely not that secret, a secret inconceivable, no, just a lover, enough that he should be a lover, the howler with the prodigious profile calling up from the hole.

He'd stopped playing the music, too, late in the night, almost inaudibly. It was too painful at first, but then he'd forgotten, the hole in his stomach that could not be filled drawing everything into it, the music, the love, the air, Budapest, Szeged, his dead parents, his living brother and sister, he hoped, or maybe not by now, drawing them in and grinding them up, unrelentingly, the new ruler, greater than the Germans, greater than the war, demanding more every day until one day, suddenly, and for a few days after, it settled down and accepted its state, revelled in it, found peace, and then forgot, until Smetana showed up with the mouse.

But it was not his stomach, briefly soothed, that had pulled him out of his despair. It was his heart, fuelled again by red blood. He'd felt ashamed of himself that his love had been blurred by his need, his egotistical need at first, then his animal need. Against the woman who never spoke his name outside these walls, at pain of death, not to anyone, not to the Cyclops who did not blink even as Dr. Janos Benes dangled from a meathook before them.

And now, damaged, knowing more than he needed to know, knowing as much as those who got to visit the edge of the Earth to peer into the chasm, did he even want to be found? Whatever would happen if he were found? Would he have that look in his eye of the touched, the traveller returned from the East, the visionary down from Mount Sinai, having stared too long at the Burning Bush? Did he *want* to be found? Had he wanted to be saved? Not by his brother, certainly, not by Marta. Especially not by Marta. It would strain his capacity for gratitude, imperil his ability to love. The cat gives back only as much affection as will earn him his next meal. How much better could he be at the end of these years? How much better had his species proven to be?

But then there was Marta. How does one repay a sacrifice so great? Whether Marta was dead now, or forever gone, or back home for the holidays, he would not be free of his debt even unto his own grave. At best, he would be married to the debt and to her, a bigamist—at worst, a celibate but for the debt.

Celibate but for the bars of light, parallel and perfect, never to meet, travelling someday soon over his recumbent bones, by day the children of the sun, thin but still glowing, by night the children of the moon at full blast, skiing across the fleshless bones, the grinning skull, adventurers like the Musketeers, voyagers that light their own path, the glowing needles of Madame LaFarge, weaving out destiny, wasting destiny on grey limbs.

And yet Istvan would go out. Give the world another chance, if only for her, for the sacrifice she made, a destiny not to be wasted—the ultimate sin: an ultimate sacrifice wasted, a destiny discarded.

Istvan waited until nightfall, but only just. He took what seemed at the time a terrible risk. He carried his pan of water, now just a third full, to Marta's little bathroom, lit the second-last of his candles, stood before her mirror, gazed at the skeleton jailed within his skin, found a bar of soap by the sink, stared at the single strand of black hair embedded within it, brought the bar to his nose to smell the hair but detected only the perfume of the soap, took off his shirt and pants, dunked the soap in the last of his drinking water and washed himself, top to bottom.

He could not wear this dingy shirt anymore—not out. But why not out? Was he going dancing? Was he going to take in a sumptuous meal at the Rosenkavalier? He was going out. *Out*. He had not been out for months, out on the street, out where other humans roamed. Should he dress for them, dress his body? It was the same body he'd dressed in the morning and undressed at night, the body that had receded from its clothing, receding to the time before its lungs had formed and its limbs could carry it, before it slipped into the world and had to learn for itself how to breathe, walk and dress itself. And now unexpectedly he got to revisit that time, recede until he dissolved into the genetic materials that met in him and which he could share with the planet that conjured him up.

But he didn't want to arouse suspicion. As it was, the curfew was upon him. The streets were to be cleared. He wanted to be someone just blundering along, running late in getting home.

Marta had a big Alpine sweater she'd worn on a cold night walk not long after they'd met. It was the biggest of her sweaters and the least feminine until she put it on. He found it in her closet in no time. In the heart of this generous sweater, where two white Alps formed a valley, he was sure he could make out her scent. He hesitated a moment, considered preserving her fragrance in the garment but quickly saw the other garments hanging there. He had plenty from which to sip her memory, if ever he made it back to this sweet jail and sanctuary.

It was a clear night when he slipped out of the front door. The sky was crisp, the moon half full, the air cool. He thought right away of the water he'd used up to wash, wanted clouds, wanted to smell moisture. Smetana was nowhere to be seen.

Three doors down, a light was on in the window. He ducked the second he saw it. He had neighbours. No one next door, a poor old woman in the next, he knew from Marta, possibly even gone by now, passed or departed to a friendlier place, but here were neighbours he didn't know about. Who were they? Would they turn him in? Had Marta mentioned them? Why had they kept to themselves? Were they squatters from the city?

He found himself huddling close to the ground, next to a dense bush, more suspicious than if he'd stood upright on the sidewalk and casually smoked. What was he to do out here? The open air and the bright half-moon didn't buoy him up, they shut him down, turned him into a criminal, a paranoid. Who lived here? Who stood there in the shadows? Who made that noise?

He should have been a bat, he thought, vacuuming the air of its bloody-minded insects, quieting the buzz, peering in with blind eyes at the menacing forms in the light, the evil designs plotted out in their warm and quivering glow.

Could he do just that—go blind?—go nearly blind?—shut one eye and close down half his brain? He could not bear his thoughts anymore. Five months of thoughts, an over-exercised brain within the ruins of his body. Or cut the wires between his senses and his mind. Use them to alert, use them to attract, use them to sense surfaces, but not to feed his battered mind.

Istvan wasn't sure where he wanted to go. He was sure he knew of a few farms on the road into Szeged. If he could make it there, he could help himself in the dark to some pears, this time of year, possibly, or peppers, or corn. But it would take him much too long to get there by foot, and he was sure to be detected by someone during so long a trip. How would he explain his wanderings then? What was worse, he was not very good at being furtive. He knew he didn't want to galumph through the bushes and up walks like the mad marauder of the night, so he would try to be subtle, do the very best he could.

He also remembered the address of Mrs. Ella Brunsvik, his very last patient, remembered it from the card he himself had drawn up when she first became a patient, before Marta, before the fancy equipment from Rochester, when Mr. and Mrs. Brunsvik were still able to pay a little something for Istvan's work, not just chicken and dumplings. He'd made his notes about their mouths on that card a couple of dozen times, knew their addresses and their mouths better than he could know them. But how kind Mrs. Brunsvik had turned out to be the last time Istvan had seen her in his office. She'd pushed him to flee almost as urgently as Marta had, just before the goons had arrived.

He thought often in his warren of Mrs. Brunsvik, not only because of her kindness, but also because she lived in the same district as Marta, Tower Town, in a little cottage on the other side, at 17 Lovas Street, not that far from the impressive twin towers of the Votive Church. Istvan used to love the concerts in the square in front of the church, and the ancient Greek plays. He saw *Lysistrata* just the summer before, it seemed a century before. Inside, the Madonna stood near the altar, dressed in a fur coat and wearing red slippers she could have got only in Szeged.

Istvan wondered what the Brunsviks were doing now in their little house, why they hadn't visited Marta in all these months, whether they'd continued with Dr. Janos Benes in Istvan's absence, or if the war had come between the Brunsviks and the new doctor. He would find out now. He'd visit them, though it was late, and ask them for a little help.

But what lured him first was this light coming from the cottage three doors down. He had to peek, just to know who shared the shadows that fell on his house and the sounds all these months.

He crept toward the cottage. The honey light poured out unabashed through the window, beckoning. He found he could not take another step, turned away, and instead looked up at the sky. He was gawking at Venus, nestled brightly among the stars, impersonating the stars. He remembered once, many years before, lying in a field by Lake Balaton with his brother and sister. It was very late at night, or it might merely have seemed that way to him as a child. Istvan lay in the middle as befitted his years. He was fourteen, Paul, to his right, was almost three years older, and Rozsi, to his left, nine years younger. She'd been having lessons at home with a private tutor and was about to begin school. Paul pointed straight up at Venus, and Rozsi asked why it was so bright. Paul said it was a star with special powers. "She's so greedy she has the power to swallow the light all around her, causing her to reign alone in the dark bed she makes for herself."

"She's a lovely star," Rozsi said. "She's very good at sucking up the light."

"Venus is not a star," Istvan said, already the scientist. "Venus is like us, like Earth and the moon. We merely reflect the sun's, our own star's, light. We must look like that to the Venetians, too, except there aren't any."

No one made a sound, and when Istvan turned toward his young sister, he saw that she was crying. He looked at Paul on his other side, and he was still staring up into the sky. Istvan got up onto his knees and said to Rozsi, "Do you want me to turn Venus back into a star?"

"No," she said. "You can't. You were the one who took away her starhood in the first place."

As he looked down again, Istvan wondered about his young sister. He wished he could ask her how she was doing this night in Budapest, if she wasn't with Marta. Could they have met up wherever they were taken and introduced themselves? He gazed all around again at his street, felt momentarily exposed, but saw the window that beckoned. He didn't want to be detected as he approached, and he was lucky. A weeping willow stood before the window, so he could hide under it. His breath left him as he looked in. A woman sat at a white dressing table with an oval mirror, brushing out her long russet hair, brushing languidly, unleashing the golden oil of her scalp into her hair. She had fleshy lips, pouty full red lips. Istvan found himself trembling inside his Alpine sweater. He was faint. Hunger and deprivation had made his appetites run together. He'd developed an Impressionist's eye. The woman was suddenly half red lips and half red hair, the hair long as a garment. He saw now she wore a silk nightie, nothing more, one long leg slung over the other, the upper foot bobbing as if to music, urging its owner onto a dance floor. The woman ceased her operations, set down her brush on the dressing table, arrested her bare, rhythmic foot by planting it on the floor. She looked directly into the mirror, took a violet cloche hat that sat like a straw helmet awaiting her, and fitted it onto her head, wiggling the hat until the posy of straw flowers at its front stared straight back at her in the mirror. She shifted the flowers off to one side for a second, then tried the other. All that was missing was a flapper dress.

How could Istvan visit with her without setting off some alarm? Where could he have come from after all this time, and how must he look? Like someone dredged up from the bottom of the sea, full of seaweed and silt. If Istvan longed for a little lamplight and tea, if he tapped at the window, would she lunge at his throat, plunge a knife in his heart, lunge at the darkness and formlessness of night outside her window?

Was it too late to call? Was she getting ready for bed already? He knew the exact time, 9:13. He always did, now, without checking. With nothing but a cat and clock to tutor him over these months, he'd internalized the ticking as surely as the desire and need behind the scratching on the floorboards.

There might be a man. There was surely a man—she was surely not alone—not with so alluring a nightgown and so ardent an effort at brushing her tresses.

He would be neighbourly—not *too* neighbourly. If this neighbour was a surprise to him, imagine what he would be to her. And he couldn't tell the truth. He didn't want to implicate Marta, not after all she'd been through.

Istvan was at the door now, and he knocked. For a moment, he could not hear a thing and then the door opened a crack. A wedge of light fell out. The woman looked at him, just a nose and eyes, sizing him up. He peered in. She hadn't bothered to conceal herself. She was still in her nightie, without shoes.

He said, "My car broke down a few blocks from here. May I come in?"

"Your car?" she asked. "I have no phone, not anymore." She kept looking him over as she spoke. He took half a step forward, and she didn't flinch.

Who would he have phoned if she'd had a working phone?

"May I come in for a moment?" She didn't answer. "Would it be all right? Is your husband here?"

"No, he's not. He can't help you. He's an officer, and he's on duty tonight. He could come back any time. But even if he was here," she continued, "he wouldn't help. He's not mechanical."

"I can wait a little. Maybe your husband could help me push the car off to the side." What was he saying? What if she agreed to his request? The car could have been stolen, then, gone from where he left it, that's all.

The woman said, "I don't know when my husband will be back. Marton's his name. He's a corporal."

Istvan said, "I was heading for an evening meal when my car conked out." They both knew about the curfew. "It was hours ago. I tried to fix it myself but couldn't." She looked at his hands, his Alpine sweater, looked him over again, top to bottom.

He was ready to back off and maybe run. If she didn't have a phone, she couldn't have him pursued, not right away. He could make it away, but he didn't want any authorities scrutinizing the neighbourhood. He would have to stay away for days. He had backed up several steps when she opened the door wide. "Come, sit with me. We can talk a little and maybe solve your problem. There's someone a block or so away." She stood absurdly exposed in the doorway, her long hair acting as a russet scarf as the night air flowed in. She rubbed her own shoulders. "Please, come in. I'm Piroska." She offered a single warming hand to greet him, and when he took it, she tugged gently, and he was inside in a second with the door closed behind them.

It was warm in the little house and comforting. He saw a bowl of fruit on the wooden table beside them. He expected her to withdraw, put some more clothing on, allowing him to steal a pear, but she asked him to sit as they were in the parlour, a room not much bigger than his own, three ancient doors down the way.

He'd barely sat in a wooden chair opposite her, barely settled back, when she said that Marton would not be coming back that night. "He's not on duty. He's a gambler and a drunkard." Her eyes welled up. He looked across the little room at the mantel. They had no clock. In its place stood a photograph in an ebony frame of an officer, a handsome young man with dark hair and eyes, proudly holding a rifle with a bayonet. She saw what he was looking at and made no remark.

"But he could come back, couldn't he? He *could* be back any second."

She shook her head. "He's been gone three days." She began to sob in earnest now, stood a moment, glanced through watery eyes at the mountains on Istvan's sweater, came over to him and stood before him, her bare knees knocking against his knees as she swayed her distraught form. He thought she might faint. Her eyes were closed. He thought she might throw herself at him, throw herself at a chance, believing in his kindness the way he was hoping he could believe in hers. She was rubbing herself again as she swayed, rubbing her upper arms, then she let them fall to her sides. Was the warm heart of a mouse enough to give him potency? Before he knew it, he was on his feet and she was in his arms, both of them benefiting from Marta's generous wool sweater.

She opened her wet eyes. They were purple in the honey light. He thought she might kiss him with those ample red lips. He glanced again at the fruit, toward the dark little room at one corner, then the other, the one where he'd first seen her. What a world away were these rooms, just three doors down from his own hideout, the table laden with food, the wayward officer, the friendly, needy woman Marta's age. What house was this, centuries before? The home of a carriage driver? A stable hand? The royal florist? And whose ancestors creaked upon these little floors? Piroska's? Marton's? Did their ghosts still hover about the place in the hulking shadow of King Mathias's ghost, the fragrance of fresh flowers awaiting arrangement and delivery?

He found himself plunking backward in a soft chair, Piroska on top of him, straddling him like a jockey her horse. She kissed him, and he felt himself sink into those luxuriant lips. He held back. "Please," he said, feeling queasy.

She pulled her head back, her arms still around his neck. She looked at his eyes, lips and neck, as if she were sizing him up again. "What do you do?" she asked. "Are you from here?"

"Yes. I'm a dentist." He immediately regretted telling her. What if she told Marton, or anyone?

"I don't believe you," she said. He was relieved. "You don't look like a dentist."

"Then I'm not," he said. "I'm a car mechanic."

She looked him in the eyes, surprised, but then she giggled. She got off him for a second and lifted her nightgown, exposing herself, the damp triangle of auburn hair, then mounted him again, began to fumble with the buttons of his pants. He didn't want her to take off his sweater, didn't want her to see how scrawny he'd become. How warm she was in the cool night air. They made love like crazed people.

She bathed the whole lower half of his face with her mouth. Her hungry tongue jabbed at his throat. And then she became rigid and pulled her face away. Her eyes blazed at him. She concentrated all her energy below. From deep within her throat, she released a strangulated cry, chilling. She seemed to swoon away before him, and he clung to her, but the chill froze over her, too, as it had him, enveloping her.

He was not finished as she raised herself off him, crumpling to the floor. He got to his knees and tried to lift her. "Please," she said and raised her hand.

He slid to the floor beside her. He had used the last dram of fuel left within him. He lay exposed, still, as did she. He wanted to get them something to cover them, a coat, a shawl, but couldn't see anything.

She turned her face toward him. "Where are you from?" she asked again as if they were just meeting.

"Why do you ask?"

"You're missing something?" Her eyes had turned to ice with the rest of her.

He put himself together again, pulled up his pants, buttoned up. "Why do you ask?" he said. "Is there a place such a feature is required?"

"There should be," she said.

He looked at her for a few seconds more. He used the chair to pull himself to his feet. She turned away from him and was crying. On his way out, he paused by the fruit bowl but felt he couldn't take one in case she was counting.

When he got outside, he was half as sure about whose house he was going to visit as before he'd left. He hobbled around like a skunk ready to turn foul on any takers. He looked up again for Venus, but she'd hidden herself behind a cloud. He thought later he might catch rain. He kept gazing, happy to be able to look up into something other than a ceiling. For a moment, he thought he might have seen

Mars, blushing through the clouds, but the light moved on, like an airplane, followed by its roar, followed by the lights and roar of another dozen planes flying—where?—northwest toward the Reich? He ducked into a bush, but couldn't think why. If they'd spotted him, would they waste a bomb just on him? Would they brake in the air and descend to apprehend him?

He walked smartly out into the street again. He was better off holed up in his cellar awaiting his Marta, he decided, than a free Piroska awaiting her lover, complete with bowl of fruit—better to be Penelope than jilted Charles Bovary.

A single strong light turned a distant corner and came toward Istvan, beamed at him—a searchlight, it looked like—but as it approached, Istvan realized it was a car with one headlight out, past curfew, possibly a German, probably, the Cyclops approaching. Istvan fell to his stomach beside a bush. There was no time to scramble behind it. Maybe this was the broken-down car he never owned coming at last to collect him. He held his breath, buried his face in the grass.

Nineteen

SIMON HAD BEGUN TO FEEL as useless as he was helpless. He had never returned to work after he was injured, and no one came looking for him, even though letters found their way to the Becks. He couldn't go foraging for food with Lili, or Rozsi, who was becoming more daring and insistent lately. Paul wouldn't have him on the campaigns with Wallenberg, because Simon wasn't convincing as a Swede. He couldn't write a great poem to Lili, though he certainly tried, and it wasn't enough that he could recite poems to her, though that did impress her. He couldn't invent anything, though he certainly tried that, too: he made drawings for a streamlined version of the innards of a butane lighter; he tried to concoct a mixture for an adhesive to be used by airplane manufacturers that would be strong enough to withstand high air pressure, but he couldn't find the chemical ingredients to try out his hypothesis; he designed a disposable stomach for times of plenty, so chubby people could gorge themselves in cafés on meat and bread and cakes and then toss the full stomach in the bin on the way out; he tried to find a cure for something, anything at all, but couldn't, even though, for a week, he pestered his father with questions about how various parts of the body worked. Why did the body attack itself with its green, cancerous army? he needed to know. What was giving the orders, and why? How could the orders be intercepted? Was surgically removing the conquerors as well as the conquered the way to go? If the heart was sending out the green soldiers, why couldn't some kind of filter be installed to stop them, or a ditch to trip them up? If it was the brain that was to blame, why couldn't it be sat down and persuaded to desist?

Simon began formulating a theory of evolution based on a group of humans confined to an office for ten thousand years. He made drawings. In the first set, the people had become as translucent as jellyfish and were vegetarian, sucking the ivy off the building's walls and then the leaves from the potted plants, which had overtaken the top floor. Some were boxlike, and some had heads that craned over and took the shape of desk lamps. Some were flat as floors and striated, to suggest the grain of hardwood. In the next set of drawings, the humans were entirely transparent. Really, all one could see were the offices as they were now, with the occasional indentation apparent in a pillow and in the cushion of a desk chair, where people appeared to be lying and sitting.

Little news streamed into the safe house on Ulloi Street, except what arrived second-hand from Paul or Zoli or, occasionally, Lili. Sometimes the lack of news suited Simon fine. He was content to cocoon himself with his family and with the nuns. He allowed himself to feel immune for hours at a time, sometimes days. And even when there was news, Simon didn't want to know about personal stories. He wanted to hear where the Russians were and how the Americans were doing; he preferred not to think of what had become of his frail cousin Janos, the mathematician—he couldn't bear even to hear his name—he'd wince and turn away—or even Istvan, whom he'd written off, or his uncles and aunts, even Hermina and Ede, who had been kidnapped mysteriously years before. He hoped they were taken for a reason other than for execution, but he didn't want to imagine what it was.

One day, Klari played a record Lili had brought for her, Brahms's Clarinet Trio in A Minor. The honey-dark music was the essence of regret, and Simon had to leave the room or be stricken with it for the rest of the afternoon.

That same day, Lili brought the news that Horst Immel, the lieutenant who'd walked Maria and her to the Church of St. Margaret, was gone and was probably dead, one of his comrades had said. Simon said, "Good riddance."

Lili didn't respond.

"Isn't it a good thing?"

"I don't know. He seemed like a decent man. He had family back in Germany."

"So it's not a good thing? I don't recall sending him an invitation to visit us in sunny Budapest." Simon's ears had turned crimson. "He's an *invader*. He's deporting Jews somewhere. Your family's been deported."

Lili ran to the washroom in tears, and the subject never came up again.

Simon tried to speak to the nuns, but they would turn away. They behaved sometimes like deaf-mutes. He asked a couple of them questions about the Church in Rome and what the Pope's position was on Hitler and Mussolini, but they looked offended and walked away from him. He encountered a young nun one morning by accident in the washroom, and was surprised at how curvy she was. He had accepted, as completely as they themselves had, that they were without shape and appeal. The nun screamed, and Simon ran out of the room.

Simon was least like his former self when it came to food. He paced the floor like a dog, Klari had told Lili, all the time Lili was out on her scavenging expeditions. His anxiety was such that he carried it with him to the door when he kissed Lili goodbye each day. When he finally did have the food in hand, say a piece of bread, he tore at it and seemed to swallow it whole, or, if the Becks were fortunate enough to get butter for their bread, he'd slap a lump of it on one corner before gulping the whole piece down. He had to be eating immediately, his mouth working, as he got ready for the next morsel. And then he would be calm again, his stomach having received its reward, calm and ready to talk about love or poetry or evolution—but not until.

One of the cleverer nuns, the young one Simon had caught half-undressed in the bathroom, began growing African violets from seeds someone had given her. When she showed her colleagues and the Becks that the flowers were coming up, pink ones and purple ones, Simon yelled, "What good are those? Grow tomatoes or peppers or cabbage. What the hell are you growing flowers for?"

Lili was the one who saved him every day and gave him hope. He and she talked often about starting a family the day the war ended. "And we should come back to this building," Simon said, "so our first child can be a real Swede."

"Just as long as we don't become jelly people," she said affectionately.

Zoli happened by that day with a bag of fruit for them all, and the four young people sat together. Simon asked Zoli about his plans with Rozsi, and he said he didn't know—he lived from one assignment from Wallenberg to the next, relieved when he made it to the end of each one, glad he could report back that he'd made it. He looked stern and serious.

"What do you mean?" Rozsi had said. "Don't we have plans, like Simon and Lili?" She wiggled her ring finger. "What happened to our plans?"

"You know nothing would make me happier," he said, "but right now we have what we have."

"Look," said Simon, "I have been rendered little more than an eater of scraps and a wearer of clothes. Let us dream a little, if we may."

"Of course," Zoli said, but he didn't add anything else.

Simon and Lili talked about where they'd live, what they'd do, whether they'd stay in Hungary. He said no—he wanted to go to America or Canada—but she said they couldn't leave his family behind, and Dr. Beck would never leave.

"Then Dr. Beck should stay," Simon said. "He's stuck in this place, physically and mentally."

Simon said it loudly enough for his father to hear. Robert had not returned to work, either. He'd been told his services would not be required any longer.

"Do you think other places are better?" Robert asked Simon. "Don't you become a missionary too, please."

"What's that supposed to mean?" Simon asked.

"Leave it," Lili told Simon. "Please leave it. It's his home you're describing."

Then Klari was there, too, to ward off evil spirits. "Please, boys. Every time this subject comes up, there is a battle. It's not your fault, Simon, darling, that you were born when you were born, any more than it's ours, as you seem to think. People live where they can live. They can't be criticized for it."

But Simon continued. "Father, are you calling Paul a missionary? Is that what you think he is, just because he has strong feelings—*justifiable* feelings?"

Klari tugged on Robert's arm. He didn't answer.

"Who's a missionary? Zoli? Wallenberg? Lili? Regent Horthy? *Me?*"

Klari escorted her husband out into the hall. Just then the front door burst open and several police walked in. Simon was relieved to see they were not the Arrow Cross, but they startled Klari and Robert all the same.

"We're looking for Simon Beck," one of them said.

"We haven't seen him," Klari said, looking at the wall.

Simon stepped out to join his parents and identified himself. Lili was by his side.

"What do you want with him?" Robert asked.

"He's a skilled worker." It was only the one officer who spoke. "We're taking him for the war effort. We need him." Everyone looked at Simon. "He'll be at a labour camp in Transylvania. We understand he has some skills as a tool and die maker, and we need those. It's not a death camp, unless he misbehaves." They all looked at Simon as if at a boy. "If he behaves," the man went on, "then he'll come back to you, most likely."

Robert said, "Please tell me, what can I give you?"

"Not much, it looks like," the officer said. "How about a nice desk chair, boys?" They laughed.

Simon couldn't stand to see his father humiliated. He looked at Robert, believed he would take this as a failure, his own personal failure, and the failure of his country. Everything would be all right for Robert just as long as they could hang on, wait this through.

Simon put his hand on his father's shoulder and thought Robert might cry.

Even the intruders seemed touched. "He heals people," Simon said. "It's what he knows. He doesn't contribute well to a war effort."

"Too bad," the officer said.

"Wait," Klari said. She dashed into the office, dug out a necklace she'd been hiding under the base of a lamp and returned. "Take this instead, please. Don't take our son."

The policeman took the necklace and looked it over. "Thank you, ma'am. I'll take both." And he pocketed the necklace.

"But we're Swedish nationals," she said.

"And we're Martians," the Hungarian said.

"Leave it," Robert said. He looked defeated.

Klari looked around her, as if to seek help. Rozsi was in a corner in the office, cowering on her cot. The nuns were nowhere to be seen. Simon had begun to perspire. Robert could see his son's heartbeat at his temple. What would he eat? he wondered.

"When are you bringing him back to us?" Lili asked.

The officer smiled at her. He looked lascivious rather than kind. She shrank back behind Simon's arm. The man said, "He'll come back when we all do." He smiled again.

"Please let me give him something to take with him," Klari said.

The policeman impudently took Klari's chin in his hand. "He'll have everything he needs where we're sending him. Don't give it another thought."

"Enough," Robert said.

The policeman looked around, as did his men. "Nice place," he said.

And then they were gone. "Oh, poor Lili," Rozsi said, and now she followed her Aunt Klari to her cot to comfort her.

But Klari said to her, "He'll be safe in Transylvania. It's safer than Budapest, safer than taking forbidden pictures." It wasn't a kind thing to say, and Klari knew it. She didn't know why she'd come up with the remark. She sometimes wished her niece could be Paul. She gazed through her tears at Rozsi. Rozsi offered to get Lili, but her Uncle Robert was there first.

Twenty

IT WAS 10:08 WHEN ISTVAN ARRIVED at Mr. and Mrs. Brunsvik's house, a mere fifty-five minutes since he'd knocked on Piroska's door, not too late to call under the circumstances. They were old patients who'd once come to him for help, could pay him only with chicken and dumplings or baked beans. Now he was coming to them. It was not too late. He'd recovered some of his confidence, felt he could tap sharply on the dark window.

The light came on quickly. Istvan met Mrs. Brunsvik at the door rather than greet her at the window where she naturally went first. When she opened the door, she shrieked and slammed it in Istvan's face. A second later the light was out. Istvan rapped again on the wooden door. No one answered. Now he slapped at the door. The light flashed on again.

He heard her voice through the door. "Dr. Beck. You've been gone. You're dead. Marta told us."

"Mrs. Brunsvik—"

"You're a ghost. You . . ." She couldn't finish. He could hear her gasp. He was afraid he'd harmed her, made her faint.

"Mrs. Brunsvik, are you all right?" She didn't answer. He heard more footsteps, agitated shuffling inside. "Mrs. Brunsvik, I need to speak to someone. I need to come inside, but I won't stay."

"You can't come in." It was Mr. Brunsvik's voice now.

Then hers again. "Oh, saintly Mary, what have I done to deserve this? What have I done to bring the Angel of Death upon us. Praised be your name, sainted Mary; praised be your blessed incarnation."

"Mr. and Mrs. Brunsvik, I won't stay. I'm hungry. It's been—" he stopped himself. "I'll go right away, I promise. No harm will come to you."

Mrs. Brunsvik wailed with Mr. Brunsvik by her side. Istvan waited. He glanced all around him at the dark windows. He felt a wind blowing; he sensed the dampness now in the air, even through the warm sweater. He checked his appearance, looked down at himself foolishly to see the wind yodelling down his Alpine valley, wanted to be sure he was presentable—Istvan, the friendly ghost, Istvan, the amiable Angel of Death.

The door still didn't open. They were quiet now, waiting for him to go. He could feel their anxiety, was a greater criminal for drawing attention to their house than a burglar or kidnapper would be, a criminal who could bring death to people who hadn't intended to finish life so abruptly.

He was about to withdraw, had resigned himself to their verdict, when the door flew open again and old Mr. Brunsvik was upon him with an iron skillet, banging him on the shoulder, hitting hard. Istvan fell forward to the ground and covered his head. He took another blow to the back, which clanged, and another to the fingers covering his head. The blows rang around the neighbourhood.

Istvan wanted to throw off sparks like flint. He wanted to become the preternatural creature Mrs. Brunsvik had thought he was when he first knocked, wanted to dissolve from this dimension rather than take blows from the very skillet the couple had used to cook up the dumplings and beans they brought to him in payment for repairing their smiles, brought like offerings from supplicants.

The blows ceased. The door slammed. The light went out again. His breath had been knocked out. He hoped a rib hadn't been broken, felt a sharp pain in his back as he tried to move. He looked all around. A light had come on in a house two doors down. Istvan would have scrambled away, but he needed to get back his breath. One minute more, that was all.

The Brunsviks' door opened swiftly and two objects were flung at him, one striking his tender back. He lifted his head to see that one of the projectiles was an apple. He groped around and found the other, something gritty. A potato. New offerings. He put these in his pockets.

He pulled himself to his knees. He needed to get away. He could feel jagged pain at the end of each breath and knew he couldn't run. He checked the light in the neighbour's window and saw a figure there but doubted he or she could see him. He didn't want the authorities called. He had to move on. He could feel the Brunsviks still on the other side of their dark door, listening for his next move. He rose and tottered over several front yards and a hundred steps away he slowed to catch his breath.

All was quiet. He had to make one last stop in the district, one last attempt to pry open the heart of a stranger. The only other person he could reasonably reach was Anna Barta, the woman who'd made it possible for him to discover *The Trial*, knowing the book was banned, risking her own safety. She was a better bet, even though calling upon her was the greatest risk. Anna would quickly surmise where he'd been holed up—or, if not, where he *would* be holed up.

Istvan remembered Marta's description of Anna's place, here in the northwest corner of the city, a red stone house smaller even than theirs, a house on Arany Street, the so-called "Golden Lane," a lane so narrow that if Anna kicked up half the fuss the Brunsviks had, Istvan would have to dash home as fast as his injured rib would allow. Istvan remembered that the flower shop Anna used to run was directly across from her house. She used the shop now to dispense food stamps and gossip, but he'd be able to identify it still by a sprig of bronze fig leaves over the door.

It took Istvan less than half an hour to work his way over to
Golden Lane. Some of the houses had been built directly into the
arches of ancient walls that might once have been part of the palace
of King Mathias. It was here that late-Renaissance goldsmiths
created their royal pieces and plied their wares, and it was here that
writers and artists moved in, as the years passed, to replace the poor
of the nineteenth century, though they were just as poor. Marta said
that according to Anna the great poet Sandor Petofi and his father
once stayed in one of these little houses. Everyone who lived here
spoke of this greatest of all visitors. Istvan decided that nationalism
could be as parochial as a street sometimes. If this little place were
where the almond had been discovered, they would always have to
have almonds here, even if they were forbidden. If it were where
light was discovered, they would always have to have light, show
them who they were. Maybe he could one day provide Tower Town
with its own claim to glory: the World's Longest Lasting Fugitive
resided here until he was killed one day with a skillet; the World's
Last Jew thinly prowled this neighbourhood with the World's Last
Half-Jewish Cat, perversely named Smetana. It was said the Jew
controlled Two Beams of Light like a Baton Twirler, the Only
Specimen to have been so Peculiarly Gifted in History.

Golden Lane was as narrow as could be. Those who built it never
anticipated modern vehicles. It was easy, even in the dim light, to find
the bronze fig leaves and to look directly into Anna's little row house
opposite, red stone as promised, the only one, Number 16. The door
was too low for Istvan to walk through without stooping. He wanted
to get in—get in or get caught.

He took a deep, splintered draft of dark air as he stood before the
door. The houses were far too close together. What would they be
thinking their Anna was up to if they heard her talking at this hour?
Would they not want to know, want to check?

He raised his hand to knock on the irregular goblin's door but turned
first to look at the flower shop, the food-stamp depot. He would make

this last stop as quick and painless as he could. He tapped so quietly, he was sure he wouldn't rouse a mouse, but he did rouse Anna, who must have slept like one. He saw a match flare through the window, followed by the dim glow of a lantern, and then Anna herself appeared at the window, peering out at him. She could make out little more than a tall, thin man, but decided to take a chance, as he had.

She opened the door more widely than either of his previous hosts. "I'm Istvan Beck," he whispered.

She gasped, put a hand up to her mouth, held the lantern high, so each could see the other's face. To his astonishment, she yanked him into the house so quickly he banged his head on the doorframe. She checked around outside, eased the door shut and looked at him some more, continuing the gasp as long as it was possible to draw it out. He felt his hair brushing the ceiling, felt the stab of the rib in his back.

The room served both as kitchen and bedroom, with a stove in the middle and two beds on either side of it against the walls. She sat on one and urged him to sit on the other. She then changed her mind and joined him on his bed, where she could see him better.

"You're Marta Foldi's Dr. Beck?"

He nodded solemnly.

"Where have you been?" she asked.

He shrugged his shoulders. "Around," he said.

"*Around?* She's been worried sick about you. She went to work for another doctor in *your* office—did you know that?"

He hesitated but shook his head.

"Did you try Marta at home?"

He hesitated again, but this time nodded. He caught her looking at his sweater, wondered if she recognized it as Marta's. He scratched his chest through the wool. He could feel his rib, though not as sharply in the warmth of the little room, and he could feel prickly dry stickiness below and remembered Piroska.

"She's gone. They sent Marta away. Poor darling." Anna took Istvan's hand in hers and patted it. "She waited for you, poor thing.

She may even have been in love with you, I can't say for sure. She had that look. But she waited. She had a glow when your name came up—that I can tell you." She looked at Istvan, who turned his head down and away. "I don't know where they took her," Anna said. "They've taken some people, and they haven't come back. But it doesn't mean they won't. They must all *be* somewhere. You can't just go off and kill that many people. I thought *you* were dead, too, and now look at you. You're not. Here you sit, praise be to Jesus-Maria."

She stood up and studied him in the light of the lantern. She was half his height, a perfect size for this little cabin. She was wearing a full-length flannel nightgown topped off with a heavy wool tartan jacket. To the outfit she'd added thick wool socks and men's leather slippers. He thought, as he looked at her, that she was gazing at his sweater again and wondering. Instead, she stepped up to him and felt his shoulders and chest. "Look at you," she said again. "Where have you *been*? Did they not feed you a thing?"

Istvan felt the apple in one pants pocket and the potato in the other. "Not very much," he said. "I've been all over."

She was already stoking up the wood stove, causing it to blaze. The room began to feel too warm. He hadn't felt such warmth in years, hardly remembered the sensation.

"I'm going to have to feed you now before that meat of yours, whatever's left of it, falls off your bones."

"You have something for me to eat?" Istvan was conscious of how pathetically the question had come out. He tried to compose himself. He sat up straight.

"Of course I've got something to eat," she said. "I'm the food-stamp person." She smiled at him, and he smiled back. "I've got some nice stew," she said. "Rabbit." She went to the back, through a dark curtain, and returned with a pot. "A fella brought me some rabbits he shot some days ago. I've got far too much. I'm grateful to have you to share it. It's got luscious stuff in it, too: potatoes, beets, parsnips, celery—um-hmm—imagine all that bubbling together in a pot to keep the rabbit company."

Istvan's mouth watered. He could barely maintain his dignity. His heart was beating a path out of his chest, looking for a new home. She didn't ask more questions. She just said, "Go on in the back, there, and splash some water on your face. Wash up, feel free." She was pointing to the curtain. She bent down, doubled right over, and from beneath the bed fished out another pair of men's leather slippers. "Take off those shoes of yours. Put these on. Go, wash up."

He did what she told him and set his shoes just under the bed he sat on, their noses poking out still. He put on the slippers and stepped through the charcoal grey curtain to the back, where a little water closet greeted him on one side and a cool pantry on the other. Another lighted lantern awaited him in the water closet. He looked at himself in the mirror, saw his gaunt face repeated there. He had the eyes of a wren, quick, dark and alert. He felt he'd travelled from Outer Mongolia and finally come to rest in the land of his keepers, felt he could play the role she'd imagined for him with ease. He even found himself hoping, as he brushed his teeth with his finger and some baking soda he'd found in a jar by the sink, that Marta would reappear from some obvious place the way he had.

Istvan stepped out from behind the curtain. The aroma of the stew and the light of the lamp must have rung out over the neighbourhood. He paused where he stood, watched small Anna set out a nesting table for each of them—a cup and saucer for her, a great bowl, a spoon and a crust of bread for him—and he was overtaken with feeling, considered retreating again to the water closet.

She felt his presence behind her. "Sit on your bed," she said, pointing, urging—*his* bed. "Sit, go on." She turned to make sure he was doing it. She had the scheming eyes of a fox, but he felt sure they'd be scheming on his behalf now.

She looked back at her stew and tasted it. With a full mouth she said, "The Russians are going to be here." He didn't answer. "You must know that," she went on. "Maybe you brought them with you." She laughed heartily. "The cockroaches have come to drive out the shits." She laughed again uproariously, pleased with herself. He tried to laugh as she took his bowl and ladled out a steaming helping of the stew. "Anyways, maybe you didn't bring them, but you're here with us now. You made it home—that's what counts."

Home, she'd called it. The word seemed too corny to be true, the place too warm, the steaming bowl too fragrant. But surely even interlopers had a home. Even cosmopolitans had a resting place. A watering hole. A hitching post. Even rapscallions. Even dentists with renegade noses and telltale surgery scars.

He tried to control the speed at which he gulped down his stew. He was full in a minute, bursting, but he pressed on. "You're starving," she said, watching him. She got up to pour boiling water into a teapot and sat with him again as he ate. She took a small tin out of her jacket pocket and stuffed a little snuff into a nostril. "Didn't anyone feed you in that big country?" He shook his head. "I heard it on the BBC." He looked at her, puzzled. "The Russians." She pulled a small radio set out from beneath her bed. What *else* did she keep down there? "I heard about the Russians on the BBC." He looked at her. "I heard some other things, too."

"You did?"

She adjusted the snuff in her nose, snorted, then nodded. "They tried to kill the man—the *big* shit."

"Do you mean Germans—you mean the *Fuhrer?*"

She nodded. "They tried to blow him up, but they missed somehow, the dumb asses." She chuckled at her own wit. "It's not the first time people have tried. And they've paid. They got strung up themselves. I hear he even has a poison tester. Next thing you know, he'll be wearing a suit of armour like an old knight." Istvan nodded. "I guess he'd have to wear it even when it got hot in the summer," she said. "It'd get just a tad sticky in there, I imagine." She snorted again, attended to her snuff.

He had no comment. He was imagining how the Germans dealt with would-be assassins. Death would have been too simple.

"Do you have family?" she asked.

"Not here."

"Where, then? Back in Russia?"

"No, Budapest. I have some in Budapest."

"Look," Anna said, excited. She was pointing to a shelf of knick-knacks above the foot of her bed. She dashed over and fetched down a bowl to show him. It was a fruit bowl from Lake Balaton. It had "Memories of Lake Balaton" spelled out in seashells embedded in its blue ceramic base. "We were there," she said as he held it, "Arpad and I. We visited the lake in 1933. It was not a good year, but Arpad needed to get away from some men here, so we went to visit a cousin of his, who'd married a nice fellow, and they took us to lovely Lake Balaton. Our only holiday in years, and so lovely. We were lucky. We could've had our only holiday somewhere crappy, but our Lake Balaton isn't that at all."

Istvan looked at the blue bowl with its loud shells and smiled. The bowl was hideous, but at this moment he sincerely felt it was the most pleasing object he'd held in years. "It's very nice," he said.

She took the bowl back from him and replaced it as though it were fine porcelain. "They're coming into all the occupied countries," she said. She was pointing to the radio this time.

"Who—the Russians?"

"The Russians on the one side, the Hitlers on the other. The Hitlers came in to clean out the Jews and Gypsies, and I hear they've done better than expected under the circumstances, working from the frontiers in toward the capital, like a vise."

Istvan wanted to get to his feet, as if there were somewhere to go. He felt the stew in his stomach curdling. He excused himself, bolted back through the grey curtain to the water closet and vomited the good dinner into the toilet bowl.

"Are you all right in there?" she was asking.

When he didn't answer right away, she came in after him. She prepared a wet cloth and, when he finished, when he'd stopped heaving and grunting, she wiped his face vigorously with the cloth as if he were a small boy who'd come in from the dirt. "I had a husband once," she reminded him. She rinsed the cloth and wiped him over again, going all the way up to his hair and through it. "He threw up his guts in this very bowl, damn fool—turned himself inside out. 'Course, he was yellow by then, drank himself yellow. Then his insides revolted and burst out. Damn fool."

Istvan felt much better. He'd got a brief taste of what it was like to be full, and now he felt better. She flushed the bowl and helped him to his feet, added a little grunt herself to the proceedings. "You're lighter than I am. You're a feather. When you feel better, I'm going to have to give you some more stew. I'm sure your family is all right back in Budapest. Marta's all right, and your family's all right, the same way you're all right, or you will be soon. It's a rough time for you people."

When they returned to the warm kitchen-bedroom, Anna urged Istvan to lie down and rest. She took his slippers off for him, helped his head to the pillow. "I have some nightclothes for you if you want. They were my husband's, but I washed them through, don't worry."

"I'm not worried," Istvan said, "but I can't stay."

"Arpad—that was my husband—did me a big favour, damn fool. He died for me on a Sunday. We were getting all set to go to church, so he dolled himself up—as best you can when you're yellow. He scrubbed himself top to bottom, shaved nicely, put some grease in his hair, shined his own shoes and got on his three-piece blue suit. Then his innards rebelled like always and, holding a towel to his front to save his suit, he ran to the toilet and let fly. He came out again, feeling relieved, sat on the bed right there where you are, closed his eyes a minute, and then he was gone. I called over the undertaker, and Arpad was all set to go into the box just as he was, poor darling. All I had to do was cover his yellow cheeks with a bit of rouge and away he went."

Istvan was about to laugh when he saw that his hostess had begun to cry quietly and blow her nose. He buried his mirth along with the image of Arpad in his suit in his box, and told Anna he was sorry.

She sniffled before saying, "If you stay, I'll keep you safe." She was sitting down now on her bed.

"I'm sure you'd try, but *you* wouldn't be safe."

"I'll be fine."

"The lane's too narrow; the place is too small. I'm sure there's traffic, visitors, busybodies."

"There are those," she said, quick to chuckle again. He was sure she was familiar with the species.

Her offer was more than tempting. Here she'd been, all this time—the food-stamps lady—and all this time, he and Marta couldn't be certain of *her*. He propped himself up on an elbow, his stomach still a little queasy, the pain in his rib sharp, and studied the floorboards.

She looked where he was looking. "Something wrong?"

"No," he said. "I've been back a little time. I didn't just get back. I've been at Marta's."

"Well of course you have," she said without hesitation. "Where else would you go first? But she wasn't there—am I right? You've been waiting for her."

"Yes, and I have to go back and wait some more there."

"You'll be safer here, and you'll get fed."

"*You'll* be safer if I'm there." He was sitting up now.

She gave it some thought. "I'm sure we can manage it."

"I'll go back to Marta's. It's good to know you're here."

"Well, then, take some stew with you. You'll need to eat some more, first thing tomorrow, when your stomach settles. And then I'll bring you something else."

The comment got him to his feet. "I'm worried that—"

"Don't worry," she said, interrupting. She got to her feet, too, and looked at the stew. "I'll be careful. No one will know. It'll be at night, like tonight."

She went out back through the curtain and returned with a preserving jar. "Is there anything else I can give you for now?" she asked.

"Marta has a cat, too," he said. "Smetana."

Twenty-One

PAUL WAS WONDERING ALOUD how long the Swede planned to continue his campaign. "I'm not alone," Raoul said. "There are others: Carl Lutz, the Swiss vice-consul, Per Anger, Angelo Rotta, the priest, Giorgio Perlasca, the businessman."

Paul held up his hand. "Very few. You could probably name them all in a minute."

Wallenberg took a sip of his espresso and frowned. The coffee was bitter. "How about you?" he said.

"I'm fighting for my own people. Because of the circumstance we've found ourselves in."

"Would you have come to my country to do what Carl Lutz and I are doing?"

Paul thought about it for too long. Wallenberg reached out to pat Paul's hand. "Possibly you would," the Swede said.

What the two men no longer needed to discuss was the aim of the operation, merely the operation itself. Raoul Wallenberg and his half-dozen lieutenants were ferreting out as many Jews as they could and issuing them Swedish passports. Finding Jews was easy. Many were wearing the Star of David. They found them clustered in the ghettos or in the long lineups being loaded on trains for export to concentration camps.

Wallenberg sometimes wondered aloud what would happen if the Jews simply hadn't worn their cloth stars. What confusion! The news had filtered through to Hungary the previous year that when Danish Jews were asked to wear the star, most other Danes did so, too. In the midst of the chaos, Danes organized clandestine flotillas to transport their Jews to safety in Sweden.

Paul Beck never wore the star, not even in the beginning. He might as well have been asked to put on rabbit ears. Neither did Zoltan Mak. What Zoli always did wear was an ingenious cape, like Paul's, given to him by Wallenberg. Zoli could not have taken photographs otherwise. The cape closed at his chest with a sturdy leather lace, and Zoltan could rest the chin of his lens directly on the lace itself. Sometimes he snapped photos just a stone's throw from the SS or the dreaded Nyilas before they could notice him. When they did, Zoli nimbly yanked on the camera strap inside, thereby shifting the Hasselblad to the back.

On this day, as Zoli was getting his gear arranged and his cape on, Rozsi watched him. They'd had a rare night together away from the others. He'd moved her cot to the basement.

She followed him to the front door of the Dutch insurance company building. She didn't want her relatives to hear. He said, "I'll see you."

She took his hand. She was wearing the ring he'd given her. She put her arms around him, around his ridiculous cape. "I'll wait up for you," she said, and he kissed her.

Today's destination for Wallenberg and Paul was the Jozsefvaros train station, at the far end of Ulloi Street itself. Zoli had planned to meet up with Wallenberg's group, but this day he was determined to photograph the herding of the Jewish deportees. Halfway up Ulloi Street, he hovered across the way from the Jews and their captors, acting uninterested, acting like a businessman on the way to work.

Some four or five hundred Jews had been rounded up on this fall day, and other than the shuffling of feet, the street was painfully silent, the march remarkably orderly. Except for a look of anxious apprehension on some of the faces, one might have thought the throng was off to the fair, complete with a military escort.

Zoltan realized, just as he managed a quick photo, that he was the only bystander, the solitary onlooker. When someone fell out of a tree and broke a leg, or was hauled drowned out of the sea or from under the wheels of a bus, broken and bleeding, a hungry crowd always gathered to feast on the spectacle. This time the reverse was true. He stood alone to watch as the hundreds marched.

But only for a moment. One of the Einsatzkommandos turned to look at Zoli, as did some of the Jews nearest the German officer. Zoli was glaringly out of place: a Jew with Swedish papers and a camera behind a conspicuous cape, gawking across the street at a lineup of Jews heading for deportation. The officer continued to watch him. Zoli felt sheets of sweat flowing down his back. The only way to become invisible was to fall into line. Zoli hesitantly crossed the street, merely as if curious to see what was going on. He wanted to be brushed aside, told to go about his business.

And then into the quiet of this quaint street with its elegant stone townhouses and apartments, their façades proudly recalling their allegiance to the Austro-Hungarian Empire, Franz-Josef's crown on one, the grey stone double-headed eagle, fierce and watchful, on another— into this setting was dropped the sound of soothing music. The notes fell from a window above the heads of the marchers.

Why did the officer at the front stop the line? Why was the scene so preposterous, this lovely adagio drizzling down on the walkers on their autumn march? Was there a place for music aboard a sinking ship, like the little orchestra that played on the deck of the *Titanic* as she slanted into the sea? Was there a place for an orchestra to play Mozart a hundred paces from the crematoria—or here, not three blocks from the Jozsefvaros train station, where all was ready to take these people out of the country of their birth to the country of their—*what*?

It seemed incongruous to the throng below, to Zoli, who fell in behind an elderly gentleman wearing a handsome grey herringbone suit, strange even to the German officer who halted the line.

The music was as sweet as pastry, but touching, the essence of sadness.

The officer who'd spotted Zoli across the street asked, in German, "Who is the composer of this music?"

The gentleman in the herringbone suit in front of Zoltan said, "It's Dvorak. Antonin Dvorak."

The officer's gaze fell on Zoli's face and detected something there. "We'll see," the officer said.

He parted the line with his rifle and strode up to the door below the musical window. He pushed open the door and stepped in. The heads craned from the bright street to look in to the shadows of the dark room. Those nearest could see on the ground floor an elegant red-plush Queen Anne chair and a baby grand piano. All they could hear, now, was the music, not another sound. Lovely music. As suited to the street as if it had been written in the very room from which it emanated.

A shot rang out, killing the music. Then the throng heard one syllable—"*De*"—Hungarian for "But"—before another shot cut the speaker short.

A moment later, the German officer rejoined the line where he'd left it and said to the gentleman in the herringbone suit, "What is your name?" The officer was reloading his rifle.

"I'm Laszlo Zene."

"Mr. Zene, the composer of the piece we were just listening to was not Antonin Dvorak. It was Gustav Mahler. The adagietto from his Fifth Symphony."

Laszlo Zene nodded his head and shrugged his shoulders.

"Gustav Mahler is forbidden," the officer said. "*Verboten*."

He set the warm muzzle of his rifle against Laszlo Zene's chin and fired a third time, sending up a fountain of brain, blood and bone to drizzle down on Zene's neighbours in line. No one dared make a sound.

The gentleman fell back against Zoli, a button on the back of his collar snagging on the lace closing Zoli's cape. The lace snapped. As Zoli set the man down on the sidewalk, his cape pooled around him at his feet and his camera dangled free at the back.

The officer at the front had ordered the line to advance. As it began to move, the officer who'd shot Zene waited, his back to Zoli. Frantically, Zoli began to pull the dead man's jacket over the wet stem of his head, struggling to free a lifeless arm. The officer was poised to turn back toward Zoli. He was half-turned, still watching the advancing head of the line. The column of Jews was filing past Zoli and the dead man, each one pausing in horror as he or she glanced down. A young girl came face to face with Zoli, still down on his haunches pulling at the jacket, glared at him and slapped him, then moved on. The officer turned forward, away from him again, though he still did not move ahead.

In a flash, Zoli had the dead man's jacket on his back, one arm in one sleeve, the second tunnelling through the other, his camera buried in the heap of cape on the sidewalk. Beside it lay the gentleman in a stained but elegant shirt, his arms spread out to embrace the cool sun.

Would the officer look at Zoli as he marched forward with the throng? Did he have the composure to single out another Jew for execution, or had his point been made, the example set? Step by step, Zoli moved onward, unnoticed, from instantaneous death on the sidewalk to possible death in a train yard, or probable death down the line in the Polish countryside, where a tidy camp had been erected to receive visitors. Zoli's Swedish papers were buttoned into an inner pocket of the cape. They were gone with the camera.

Glaciers of sweat and blood oozed down Zoltan's back beneath the warm grey jacket, worn customarily for afternoon teas, no doubt, and Sunday walks. Proudly, shamefully, sewn to the expensive garment's breast pocket was a yellow six-pointed star with "*Jude*" marked across it.

A few steps more, and the Jews, together with their captors, arrived at Jozsefvaros Station, where they were greeted by their own Nyilas, the Arrow Cross.

Zoli was forgotten, now, as he was hustled along with about fifty others toward a particular boxcar, usually employed for hauling bricks. And then out of the hubbub Zoli heard a whistle blow, and he was gazing at the familiar face of Raoul Wallenberg. Behind him, carrying a folding table and chair, was none other than Paul Beck. The duo waded right into the middle of the crowd, Paul unfolded the table and chair, and Wallenberg took a seat. The noise persisted for another minute until another whistle blew. It was Paul, now on top of a boxcar, pointing to the Swedish diplomat. The crowd quieted down.

Wallenberg unclasped his briefcase and declared, "You have a number of Swedish nationals here, and I'd like them released to my care immediately."

"Like hell!" one of the Nyilas men shouted and, using his rifle, he bashed out a path toward the outrageous table. Switching to German, he said, "These are not Swedes! They're not even Hungarians. They're Jews! Get them on these trains."

The German commander stood between the Hungarian and Wallenberg. "We do not deport Swedish nationals," the German said.

"These ones you do!" the Nyilas barked.

Few could have imagined such a scene unfolding, though Zoli had heard of such confrontations. Two Einsatzkommandos quickly disarmed the big Hungarian officer and locked his hands in hand-cuffs before he had a chance to react. In response, the other Arrow Cross guards started shoving Jews onto the trains. It took several minutes before the whistle rang out once more.

It was Paul again. The noise died down. The Swede still sat at his table. Wallenberg said, "These are in no particular order: Kepes, Robert! Kepes, Klari! Felix, Dr. Janos! Zene, Laszlo! Enekes, Aniko!"

As individuals in the crowd jubilantly shouted out "Here!" they were plucked from the crowd and brought to stand behind Wallenberg. It was Zoli himself who had taken their pictures for the papers Wallenberg had brought. On this occasion, though, the Swede had no more than forty-five *schutz-passes* to distribute. It was difficult to keep up with the pace of Eichmann's deportation machine. Sometimes, in just one afternoon, Wallenberg and his deputies forged and stamped papers complete with photos for a couple of hundred Jews. At other times, Eichmann's people outfoxed their opponent and cleared out ghetto buildings not yet scheduled for evacuation, buildings the Arrow Cross had stocked with Jews. The makeshift ghettos themselves had been created as quickly as they'd been emptied of their original occupants and their possessions.

Just as the list ended out, Paul spotted Zoli. He regarded the younger man impassively, betraying no familiarity to the guards. But then the thought raced through Zoli's mind that there was nothing whatever to be done. He was standing by a deportation train wearing a Star of David affixed to his chest. Paul's darting eyes asked, "Where is your cape? Where are your papers?" And Zoli's eyes reassured him: "It's all right." Paul tried to attract Wallenberg's attention, but he was too distracted to pick up the signal. When Wallenberg did catch on, he stood up, as helpless in the circumstance as Paul, or Zoli himself.

"*Genug!*" the German commander barked. "Enough!"

His soldiers, eagerly assisted by the Nyilas, resumed hustling their captives onto the trains. Zoli found himself no more than an arm's length from the young girl who'd slapped him, but a man stood between them. She was wearing a green velvet dress and clutching a small white patent-leather purse that perfectly matched her white socks and shiny white shoes. She looked terrified at first, but now for some reason, once she saw that Zoli was being hustled aboard a boxcar, too, she calmed down and even smiled as their eyes met.

Then Zoli looked back at Paul on the crowded platform. Wallenberg, standing beside Paul, had a pained, pale look on his face. He ran his fingers back through his thinning hair. Paul turned away from the sight, a first for him. Then the door of Zoli's car was clamped shut.

Zoli lost his balance for a moment in the dark as the impact of what had just happened struck him. To steady himself, he grasped for the basic elements of his life, as if he were grasping for the fundamentals of earth, air, fire and water. These were his Rozsi, his camera and the image of his parents on their last morning, his father getting set to go into his darkroom, his mother asking Zoli to hurry, come see the oriole in the back garden. Someone behind Zoli spoke the name Rozsi, and he turned, his eyes groping in the dark for her, though he knew that it had to be another Rozsi.

Wallenberg turned boldly now on his heel and asked one of the brand new Swedes, Dr. Janos Felix, to help him with his folding table and chair. Dr. Felix happened to be staring proudly at his papers, his own photo looking confidently back at him, the words "*Schweden*" and "*Svedorszag*" below his description and photograph and a triangular arrangement of three crowns to protect him.

"Is everything all right?" Wallenberg asked, as he handed the folded table to Dr. Felix and hoisted up his briefcase and chair.

"Yes, of course," Dr. Felix said. The two joined the others to retrace their steps up the same street they had just come down. In a moment, they came upon the dead man, Laszlo Zene, and several of the Jews now felt free to sob. The gentleman lay peacefully, his arms out and inviting. Bunched beside him lay a familiar cape.

Paul bent to retrieve the garment, and the camera tumbled out. He folded the Hasselblad back in the cape and took it with him under his arm.

As they resumed their walk, Dr. Felix spoke in German. He said he had one question.

"Yes, anything," Wallenberg answered.

"I'm wondering, sir," said Felix, "because I haven't been able to go for a while, if my Swedish pass entitles me to admission at the opera."

Wallenberg paused, turned to look down at the pavement and the fallen man and the train yard beyond. He glanced at Paul, sighed, then continued walking.

PAUL WAS INCONSOLABLE. He paced for an hour in Wallenberg's office, then sat staring out the window, chewing on his pencil. Wallenberg came in with some more espresso. He put his hand on Paul's shoulder and told him, "We'll do what we can to get him back. He's a Swedish national."

Paul acknowledged the hand with his own. "We haven't figured out how that part of the operation goes, have we? We can prevent some from going, but we can't get them back. Except—"

"No, Paul," Wallenberg said. "You're not going with the car again. I can't afford to lose you. Or the car."

"It worked once."

"Yes, once and once only. We can figure something out. I have been lobbying."

"I know," Paul said. He patted the comforting hand. "It's just difficult continually taking the tally: I lost my mother before the war, then my father—I know you never even *met* your father, Raoul—then my brother, Istvan, in Szeged. I have no idea what became of him. I have aunts and uncles and cousins in Miskolc and Debrecen who appear to have vanished. Even that friend of Istvan's, the poet, Miklos Radnoti, has disappeared. Now my future brother-in-law—what a good young man he was."

"*Is.*"

"Is. Of course, *is*. We'll have to get his film developed. My sister knows where his place is, where the other films are hidden."

"Good," Wallenberg said. "And I have news for you."

Paul turned to look at the Swede.

"Adolf Eichmann has agreed to see us. He wants to talk—bargain, maybe."

"When?" Paul stood.

"First thing in the morning. Stay with me, we'll talk strategy and go together in the morning, only the two of us—that's the deal."

Paul bit down on the end of his pencil, tapped it against his forehead, and then snapped it in two. Wallenberg watched him. "Steady now," he said. "We have to do this right."

"Shouldn't I go tell my sister tonight what happened?"

"She'll sleep better if you don't."

"I want to take a pistol."

"They'll confiscate it and shoot you with it."

Twenty-Two

Budapest – October 10, 1944

EICHMANN WAS HEADQUARTERED in a grand white house surrounded by iron railings behind the Octagon, off Andrassy Street.
Wallenberg and Paul took the Alfa Romeo and made an impression
as they glided along the wide avenues of Budapest. When they came
to the house, it was guarded on all sides.

Paul and the Swede disembarked and special guards came at them
from both sides while two more created a barrier with their crossed
rifles in front of the visitors. The men were frisked. Then the two
rifles were uncrossed.

"You are?" an officer asked in German.

"Swedish diplomats, both of us." Paul offered their papers.

The soldiers lowered their rifles altogether, and the officer trotted
to the front door, tapped lightly and was admitted. Wallenberg and
Paul waited with the other guard. The two stood facing the house,
admiring its white gabled porch, the generous bay windows admitting
the autumn sun. On how many occasions had this gracious house
received friends and relatives? How often had it been a place of
celebration, retreat, music, love and laughter?

SS-Obersturmbannfuhrer Adolf Eichmann, the special commander
of the region, greeted Wallenberg and Paul with a surprisingly limp
handshake. Paul loomed over the German. Eichmann looked the two

of them over, especially Paul. The unlikely Jew was tall, had sharp, fierce eyes and an impressive head of red hair; he was bedecked in a light wool suit and his camel hair cape, like someone come to call on the lady of the house. The visitors could hear a phonograph from the parlour, playing Beethoven's Pastoral Symphony. How lovely. On whose gramophone? Paul wondered. Whose record?

"Nice house," Paul said in German. "Yours?"

"Yes," Eichmann said. He clasped his hands together. "It was abandoned."

Paul could feel the Swede's eyes on him.

The three were standing in the bright hall before a sweeping blond oak staircase leading upstairs. Two guards stood before them at the foot of the stairs and another two behind them at the door.

The Beethoven was beautiful. Paul's stomach rose to his throat.

"I have a proposition for you, gentlemen," Eichmann said, and led the way into the drawing room. The men followed and each took a seat in a peach-coloured chair. It was too summery a room for the time of year. Eichmann sat facing them, and two guards stood behind the visitors.

"There are wealthy Jew industrialists, like Manfred Weiss. Do you gentlemen know him?" Wallenberg turned to Paul, and Paul shrugged. Eichmann said, "I need his holdings transferred to me. I had underestimated how strong some of these men are. We need the steel, the munitions. For the war effort."

"You mean like Baron Louis de Rothschild, the Vienna Rothschilds," Wallenberg said, "who signed over their steel mills to the Hermann Goering Works in exchange for their freedom? Is that the sort of conversation you want to have?"

"Precisely."

Eichmann was a surprisingly unimposing man when he sat. He had thinning hair, like Wallenberg's, and small bones to go with a small voice.

"Why are you asking us?" Paul asked. "What makes you think we have any sort of power over such people?"

Eichmann paused. At first Paul thought he might be listening to the Beethoven. The symphony's country carnival celebrations were being played out.

"You Swedes are the people everyone listens to now. You have attractive powers of persuasion. We want the holdings of a number of people, and we're prepared to trade safe passage for their families to Switzerland. I've already spoken to Carl Lutz about the arrangements."

"What about the other deportees?" Paul asked. Wallenberg glanced at his companion. "What happens to them?"

"No one is being deported, merely relocated."

"Call it what you will."

"Well, you gentlemen, I take it, seem to show up at some of our relocation launches, and you skilfully sniff out Swedes among the Jews."

Paul noticed a large, dark rectangle on the wall where a painting must have hung. The wall looked strange, undressed.

The German lieutenant colonel looked toward the parlour where Beethoven's soft sun was coming out after the celebrations. The birds of the countryside outside Bonn were twittering sweetly.

"Maybe some of the people you describe are actually Swedish," Wallenberg said. "We'll have to check. There are some very powerful Swedes who have invested here in Budapest."

The commander rubbed his chin. He looked into the parlour again. Beethoven's fragrant countryside was ablaze with colour now. "You are students of contemporary history, Mr. Wallenberg? Mr. . . . ?"

"Beck."

The German ran his soft hand over his chin again in exaggerated contemplation. "My good Beck. Good Swedish name, Beck."

Paul nodded his appreciation. He didn't dare look at Wallenberg; he didn't want to read the anxiety in his face. Paul thought he could hear his own heart beating.

One of the guards took a step toward his commander. He stood beside Paul now. But Eichmann lifted a pale hand, and the guard stepped back obediently. "I asked you, gentlemen, about your awareness of contemporary history."

"Yes, we are quite aware," Wallenberg said. "Paul studied at Cambridge, and I studied at the—"

"University of Michigan," Eichmann said for him. "Yes, I know."

Paul's thoughts fell on Zsuzsi in Philadelphia. She seemed planets away, galaxies. Paul remembered the photograph of Rozsi, Istvan and him, dressed as the Three Musketeers. How would he tell Rozsi what had happened? What words could he use? He found himself flying out of this room, every which way his mind would propel him.

The commander stared at both men, looked each straight in the eye, but then looked away, stood and turned his back on them altogether. "You will lose this war," Paul wanted to tell him, "and you'll lose the whole century with it, maybe more."

What would the weasel say then? Was he the one who'd ordered Paul's father to be executed? Would the weasel say, "I was merely following orders. I'm a good soldier."

"Is that all you are," Paul would answer, "a good soldier, neutral on all matters—Jews, Gypsies, communists—a good soldier awaiting a promotion?"

"Yes."

"And it doesn't matter what your boss asks?"

"Not at all."

"Would you kill Germans the same way, if asked—grandmothers only, if asked—all pet dogs?"

"Yes, the content of the order doesn't matter. I have my superiors."

"I don't think they're all the same to you."

"Think what you want."

"I think you like German grandmothers better than Jews. I think you like dogs better."

"I do like dogs."

"You'll lose this war," Paul would say.

"Yes, Swede, possibly," Eichmann might reply. "But we won't lose in the way you have in mind. We'll lose the war in a way even we could not have foreseen. I am and have always been an ordinary man with ordinary ambitions, like the Jews. But the Jews have always been victims. It's a great racket. And no one else comes close to the Jews for playing it up. For two millennia, maybe longer, the Jews have been victims. Did you know that, Swede?"

"Are we on some sort of philosophical cliff here, German, our claws hooked into each other's necks?"

"Do you know what we'll do, Swede? We'll turn each and every Jew into a martyr. We have nailed them to a cross as big as Europe, and the hammering has been loud enough to attract the attention of the whole galaxy. The Jews have always been despised; you might know that. Maybe you have even felt a touch of hatred yourself. Even when people *like* Jews, or appear to, they despise them. The Jews of my home town of Cologne despised themselves—what do you think of that? They wanted always to be German. They begged to be German. And for a time we let them."

Might Paul ask, "Is it possible for us to have an idea between us that is not profane?"

"Let me try," the little German with thinning hair would say. "We were only doing the world a favour. But it will backfire worse than any punishment ever inflicted upon the Jews. Jews have always been inventive. Now they will become the world's greatest inventors. They'll become our best scientists, our best poets, our best composers—oh, how they'll sing like the lark soaring above a flaming countryside, unable to land." Here Eichmann would spin like a dancer, as he himself sang out the words to accompany the music coming from the other room. "We will lose this war if a mere dozen Jews survive, because we will turn them into warriors, Jews seeking justice, Jews on a mission. Oh, may the God of the Jews save us all from the furors we unleash today."

"So what are you, then, Mr. Eichmann? Are you merely the sounder of the sirens? Are you the one who points to the fire but can't put it out? No, you are more than that. You're the one wearing the uniform, so it is you who are on a mission. And you are possessed by your mission, ready in a second to blame your bosses. You'll lose in yet another way— do you know that, commander—lieutenant colonel, is it?—not quite colonel? You'll lose because you are a soothsayer, and that is the worst curse. You'll lose because you're sharp enough to foretell your own downfall, yet not courageous enough to subvert it while you still can."

Beethoven's tremulous countryside flowed into the room where the men were meeting.

"Is it courage you're describing, Swede, or is it determination? Or better, is it cunning?"

"It's courage."

"The sanctimony has already begun."

Beethoven's storm clouds gathered.

WALLENBERG SAID, "If I can persuade Manfred Weiss and some others to sign over their factories, what then? Would you stop the transports?"

"I am under orders," Eichmann said. "But I can stop the *surprise* transports. You can know when each one is occurring."

"So there will be no surprises?" Paul asked.

"Please, gentlemen, I am a soldier who receives direction from Berlin. I am not Berlin myself."

Paul looked to see if there was a blunt object nearby. The Beethoven was finished. Wallenberg took Paul's upper arm sharply, painfully, into his clutch. The man was as instinctive as he was brave.

IN THE BACK OF THE CAR, Wallenberg told Paul, "I felt your intensity in there. I know you didn't say anything, and yet I'm surprised we made it out alive. I shouldn't have taken you with me. I can't take you along everywhere."

Paul threw his cape back off his shoulders. "Of course I was intense. Do you know who that was?"

"I know who it was, but you're making him into much more than he is. He's a man of a single note. When birds sing and sing again, they're not driving home a point. They're singing. Eichmann is that bird. Even Beethoven in the background doesn't give him an additional dimension."

"Maybe birds are saying something to one another," Paul said, "not singing for *our* benefit."

"Maybe they are, but their message is simple: danger, food, rain. Not, *Why are you over in that other tree?* Not, *Why do you insist on ignoring me?* If we psychoanalyze the Reich, we'll get nowhere. We'll kill ourselves with despair, or stand in the line of fire. If we concentrate on figuring out how to save lives and then *save* them, we'll beat them. Sometimes. *Occasionally.*"

Paul threw himself back against the seat. "Yes. Occasionally."

"Look," Wallenberg said. He turned to face Paul. "I'm a simple man. I'm like Eichmann, but with different values."

Paul looked at the Swede. "You are much more complex than you know."

"Not today. Today we have a job to do. Tomorrow, if we survive, we'll reflect."

"Tomorrow," Paul said. "Yes."

Twenty-Three

LIBUSE HAD RECOVERED her eyesight well enough, miraculously, that she could make out figures of people in front of her, even if she didn't recognize who they were, necessarily. She was very good at faking what she needed to fake: working, eating, getting ready for bed, answering questions.

The *kapo* announced a dreaded *selekcja*. Marta awoke with the word waiting in her ear. The word spread around the *lager* and the yard. Latin married to Polish to produce a devil child: *selekcja*, the selection. It was to be more formal this time than last.

The inmates had a day to prepare. How could they prepare? They needed to puff themselves out in a day, make themselves look more robust, clean themselves up in the scarce seconds they had in the latrine. Women asked one another whether they'd be picked or spared, and their kindness, whatever was left of it, flushed to the surface. "You look good," many said. "You look strong." No one said pretty. The lustre was gone. Those who were still standing were starved and grimy. Their skin seemed to cling to them as if to a coat hanger.

The exception was Marta. She hadn't starved for long enough yet, had been spared much of the heavy labour forced upon the others, felt her work had a *purpose*, had got more to eat in the infirmary, and she was lovely to begin with. So everyone sought her opinion and approval. And she tried to give it and make it sound fair, though she had to lie to many.

"What number am I again—the last three digits?" Libuse asked Marta as they stripped bare in the *lager*. The taller woman held out her arm.

"You know your number," Marta said. "705."

"Just checking to be sure," Libuse said as she removed her wooden shoes and was bare before Marta was. "I was in the pink of life when I got here, and now I can barely even see pink. How do I look?"

"Strong as ever. Just look ahead as though you're at attention."

Manci, the *kapo*, circulated through the bony throngs, handing each woman a card with her name, number, nationality and age written on it. When she said, "705," Libuse smiled and held out her hand. Manci didn't notice anything unusual and asked Libuse if she was feeling better.

"Much."

Manci gave Marta her card, 818, and moved on, hustling the naked women out to the yard when they were ready. Just as soon as the *kapo* was out of earshot, Libuse whispered, "Must the Germans persist in proving to us who they are? Must we persist in proving to them who we are? Why the same exercises every time?"

A small woman hiccupped, folded herself back on a bunk and vomited all over herself, another woman's foot and the floor.

"You bitch," the other woman said and tried to fling the vomit off.

Manci was upon them in a second. "Wipe yourself clean, both of you, and get outside!" Manci booted the one who'd thrown up and the woman fell over, but she leapt back to her feet and ran out past the others.

The other inmates stepped aside to let her through. They didn't want to be infected with an illness, not now. The stench was worse than usual. In the next narrow aisle between bunks, someone said that the Russians were within a hundred kilometres of Auschwitz.

"How's that possible?" someone else whispered.

"There's been bombing in the countryside. They're coming for us."

"Not today," Libuse said as they stepped outside.

"Didn't you hear the planes? Those weren't German planes. They're coming."

Manci came up from behind. She punched the woman, who fell in a heap to the floor. "Outside," Manci said.

The woman rose and staggered toward the door. "Don't you want for us to be liberated?" the woman said. And Manci hit her again, harder, so that this time she stayed for a spell on the floor, and women had to step over her scrawny legs.

"There are new recruits," Manci announced as she stood by the door and herded the women out. "We need to make room for them. There are many of them, and they're from my Hungary. *Selekcja*," she said again as if she were calling people in for tea. "Come along. *Selekcja*."

They were greeted outside this time by a senior SS commander, Romeo Stern, and four guards. Manci would trail along to answer questions as they arose. The officer would inspect each woman, sometimes merely by glancing at her, sometimes by circling her, sometimes by asking a question. Then Stern would call out "Right" or "Left," the right possibly meaning death by gassing today and the left a reprieve—until the next selection. The last time, it was the reverse; left meant death, while right meant life for another day. No one said openly that one side was death by gassing, of course, merely that some people were once again being relocated and were to be given a special shower, so clothing would not be necessary. The clothing was then piled on a cart or truck for laundering for the incoming prisoners, or for disposal, depending on how ragged the garment had become.

The five hundred women stood in rows, wretched and naked, but also stalwart, like soldiers in the breezy autumn air. It had not rained in a week, so the ground was dry. Stern looked the women over as he made his rounds. "Left," he said to one woman, and "Left" to the woman beside her, who was larger and still robust. The card each woman was holding was placed in the left hand of Stern's junior officer.

Immediately, everyone was trying to discern a pattern. Why did the robust woman's card join the slight woman's card in the guard's left hand? Was he looking for a particular posture today, the more erect the better, or a particular light about the face, some responsiveness? Did Romeo Stern have a quota? "404, right," he said to a puny thing; "203, right," to a woman who stole bowls and always wanted to trade something for bits of people's crust of bread. But here was the woman who'd vomited: "387, left," Romeo said. Had she cleaned herself up? Did she not look so green? "675, right," to an inmate whose hair stubble had turned white in the short months she'd spent in the camp, a woman of twenty, no more; "662, right" to the oldest one in the *lager*, forty-five, but strong and tough, a bull of a worker.

The infernal band sounded again nearby, where camp insurgents were to face the firing squad. They played another marching song, "Flieger Empor!," a song exhorting the German air forces to triumph, followed by "75 Millionen, ein Schlag!" This one brought a smile to Romeo Stern's face. He even conducted for a moment as he turned to his junior officer to say, "Seventy-five million Germans—one heartbeat." The song cheered Stern up, and while it played he said "right" more often than "left," much more often, giving the inmates a hint as to which was which.

"The bogey man has come," Libuse whispered as the band played on, "not for you, beautiful Marta, beautiful Snow White, but for me, the water spirit, washed up here on the land."

"Wherever you go," Marta said, "I'm going, too."

"I doubt it," said Libuse.

But Stern was approaching, so Marta begged Libuse to keep quiet.

Marta glimpsed his face from over the women's heads. Romeo Stern. Who'd given him the name of Romeo? Who'd given her northern boy that sunny southern name? Who'd looked into his blue eyes and decided he would seek love? Who looked into his eyes and sought love herself? And who was his fair Juliet? From what sad balcony in what German town did she beam her love to this distant yard where the inmates burned daylight, where Juliet's Romeo was beating the dancing days out of the knobby knees of his charges, where he was turning swans into crows into ash? Or was there no balcony after all, Marta wondered, and no Juliet waiting? We are your Juliets, we star-crossed lovers, we brides of Frankenstein, we five hundred nymphs, shorn, starved, bare and barren, unable to express our modesty with sultry striped and numbered uniforms. Wherefore *our* Romeo, tough Star of the yards? Gone to cellars and wet trenches? When we are gone to unseen balconies, our sweet southern love, will you cut us out in little stars, or will you turn us instead into black cloud to smudge out the day and fill in the night, so that we will show your conscience the way to its own grave?

And then to the women's surprise, but in particular to Libuse's surprise and Marta's, the band played a beautiful Czech song.

"It's a sign," Libuse whispered. "I'm half-Czech, don't forget, like the whole Czech Princess Libuse."

"Quiet," Marta said.

"My time has come."

"Don't talk, please," Marta whispered. Stern and his entourage approached. Libuse had begun to sway, to mouth the lyrics. "Please, Libuse," Marta whispered.

And then the two were in front of them. Stern took the card from Libuse's hand. "Are you enjoying the entertainment we've arranged for you?" he asked.

He was looking directly into Libuse's eyes, Marta could tell, and Libuse turned her head directly toward the voice.

"Yes, sir," Libuse said. "It's a song from *Rusalka* by Dvorak, my favourite opera."

"What appeals to you, exactly?"

"It's never easy to explain why music appeals."

"Still," he said.

"It's Rusalka's call to the moon, we're hearing." She'd begun to sway a bit again. "'*Rekni mu, stribrny mesicku, me ze jej objima rame*'—'Oh tell him, silver moon, that my arms enfold him, in the hope that for at least a moment he will dream of me.' She is the little mermaid, the fairy-tale mermaid in love with a prince," Libuse said. "She wants to become a creature of the land. The prince doesn't know, when he goes to swim in the sea, that she envelops him, stirs up the waves to caress him." Libuse paused, but Stern didn't respond.

At the conclusion of the aria, the band bounced on immediately to another soldier's song, "Es war ein Edelweiss," Herms Niel's paean to the elite mountain troops, played repeatedly on Heinz Goedecke's *Request Concert* radio show, broadcast over Greater German Radio to the armed forces.

Libuse heard nothing but the marching music. She saw a presence still before her, so she took a chance and proceeded. "Rusalka is neither woman nor fairy, neither living nor dead. She wants to be set free from a watery grave. She sees a devastating beauty she can't attain—more than a prince, more than the land—*beauty*, a life."

The officer still didn't answer and didn't move. She couldn't see him. Was she supposed to keep talking until he asked her to stop? Maybe she should talk about other arias, other operas, her feelings about music. She said, weakly now, calmly, "It seems to be a story about the earth and the sea, but really it's a story about desire. In the song, Dvorak is really bringing us news from heaven, if you listen."

"I see."

"But that's not why I love the music."

"It's not?"

"No, I love the music because I want the same thing Rusalka wants. I long for beauty. The song is beautiful, and you've asked me to explain beauty, to rationalize my love. It's not easy. It's much easier to rationalize hatred."

Stern waited another moment as if to see if Libuse was finished. Libuse kept her head aimed at the place his voice had been. "705, to the right," he said, finally, and placed Libuse's card in the hand of his assistant.

Libuse was just then overcome. She sobbed, tried to hold it back, but sobbed again. She didn't know how to stop herself. Stern was still half in front of her. He waited. Libuse clutched herself around the ribs and breasts, shuddering with the fall wind and with the final triumphant notes of "Es war ein Edelweiss."

Stern stood before Marta now, but waited for Libuse to finish before he continued. He was grinding his teeth, his jaw rippling as he gazed at Marta, held her card, glanced down at it and up again. Finally, though Libuse had not finished gasping and hiccuping, Stern said, "818, right."

He moved on immediately. There was a woman standing next to Marta whom Marta had never seen. She didn't know what nationality the woman was and couldn't even tell her age, and yet it was plain she'd been in Auschwitz a long time. The ravages showed in her body and face. When they'd first assembled in the line, Marta had wanted to acknowledge the woman with her eyes, touch the woman with her health, but she'd seemed out of reach, untouchable. She was a woman utterly deprived of the means to express herself, not with a jaunty dress, not with the copper ringlets of hair quickly sprouting from her scalp, not with an extra handle around the midriff to say she enjoyed her cakes, not with so much as an expression on her face—not a smile, not a scowl, not fear. She was a woman in whom even the pilot light had gone out.

Romeo Stern took this woman's card, noted her number, "344," and added, "right."

He hustled down the line now. A spate of lefts was followed by a long succession of rights. It seemed almost indiscriminate, rushed. Then the small group in charge marched to the front where they'd begun.

Stern was matter-of-fact when he turned and spoke. "Those of you on the left, return to the *lager* and retrieve your clothing. Those of you on the right, you won't be needing anything for the time being. Please stay in the yard until the others have left."

The words clung to Marta, constricted her throat. As the chosen women filed back into the *lager*, Libuse leaned toward Marta and said, "I'm sorry. I lost my grip on things. I—"

"Do you ever shut up?" Marta asked. "I mean *ever*?"

Oh, dear Lord, my dear God, thought Marta, as the reality of her situation circulated through her body. What had happened here? To stand before an accuser in a court of law after taking the life of a child or an innocent bank clerk or a political leader—to butcher a sworn enemy at an inappropriate time and in an inappropriate place—was one thing. At least you could fathom why you'd been sentenced to death. Even if it didn't thrill you to be so sentenced, something in you, a sense of balance, would have been satisfied. Even here, even in Auschwitz, to stand before a firing squad with an idiot orchestra playing after organizing an insurgency and strangling a guard, or even *not* strangling a guard, in some demented and satanic understanding of the universe satisfied a sense of justice. But to have been a dental assistant in Szeged who wanted nothing more than to make visitors comfortable, relieve every patient's toothache, to have attended mass and confession more often than Jesus or Mary had any right to expect, to have sought extra cabbage for her man and her cat, to have grieved her parents' passing and written loving letters to her one brother in Chicago, to have confidently played Juliet in her *Gymnazium* opposite another Romeo, a sweet but fumbling one with blond curls coiling from his musketeer hat— where in this *vitae* did a visit to the gallows satisfy the laws of humanity or nature?

Libuse turned to Marta and clasped her fleshy body against her own bony one. Libuse's nipples were hard and cold as sea pebbles. The two cried together briefly until the *kapo*, Manci, told them to break it up.

"Why?" snapped Libuse, pulling away from Marta and turning toward Manci, her nearly sightless eyes reaching through the fog. "Are you going to shoot us if we don't?"

Manci didn't answer but waited for the women to finish. When they did, she said softly, "You can walk together. Stay together as you walk."

The women of the right took their walk of a quarter of an hour toward the gas chambers. Marta glanced behind her at the inmate who'd been beyond reach. Her eyes had no function other than to find the way. A twinge of envy shot through Marta. How much better to have been this woman now, in these last steps of the journey.

As the inmates approached, they heard many more voices. "New recruits," Marta told Libuse. "Hundreds of them, several hundred. There are children and—"

"Please," Libuse said, "I can hear them."

A boy was speaking in Yiddish about Transylvania, but he stopped as the women of the *lager* came near. "Why doesn't he say more?" Libuse asked.

"He's staring right at us," Marta said.

"We must look like subterranean creatures," Libuse said. "I don't blame him."

Libuse said in Yiddish to the boy, pointing her voice where she believed he was standing, "Where in Transylvania are you from, what part?"

The boy said, "Not the part where the mountains are lying down and are smooth, but where they're standing up."

"Oh," Libuse said. She was smiling.

"We came on a stinky train," he said. "Now we're having a shower."

The smile withered from Libuse's face. "Of all the planets in the solar system," she whispered to Marta, "I think this one's my least favourite."

"Are you blind?" the boy asked.

"No," Libuse said. "Are you?"

The boy thought this was the funniest remark he'd ever heard and erupted in wild laughter. Libuse laughed with him.

The new arrivals, many of them women and children and grand-parents, most from Hungary this time, saw Marta to be rosy and alive—scared, yes, and baffled, but spirited, animated. A woman stepped toward Marta and Libuse. She was wearing a grey cloche hat with an absurd violet ribbon tied around it, and her white hair puffed out from under the brim, light as cirrus clouds. Otherwise, she was naked. Everyone else was naked and shaved as always, the hair sent off for mattress stuffing and other products. The guards had overlooked her. They'd forgotten the part about the hair and the hat. Marta rejoiced at the mistake. She whispered the news to Libuse.

Libuse said, "Maybe by accident they'll scatter our ashes in Canada and we'll be shipped off with the gold fillings and earrings to Switzerland and be turned into gold bars."

"Who knows?" Marta said.

"And you are a red triangle," she said to Marta, "a political pris-oner—not a Star of David. What are you even doing here among us?"

Marta took the blind woman's hand in hers and clutched it, feeling the thin bones shifting.

A woman nearby, one of the new recruits, said, "What's going on here? It's cold." She rubbed her upper arms and shoulders. "This is ridiculous."

"Don't worry," Marta said. "It won't help to fret."

Another woman, a younger one with small pancake breasts and wide hips, watched with wild eyes that darted from person to person. She was with a young man with a long, thin penis jutting straight out from his loins. How odd, Marta thought. Had it been impelled by lust or by a bursting bladder? Would it outstand him? Would he die before he could satisfy whatever urge made it rise from its seat, the man's heartbeat frozen in the standing column? What thoughts possessed her. The man saw Marta staring and concealed his genitals with his hands. He was looking at her, too, her breasts and her black triangle below. Marta didn't hide from his eyes, so he turned away altogether.

The women from the *lager* were herded to one side of the gas chamber, and the new arrivals were ahead of them, so Marta and Libuse were at the very end of a long line. The *kapo* came by and said something to them in Ladino. He was a Greek Jew and tried some German now. He spoke harshly, pressing people into line, shoving one or two. A man asked him a question about the proceedings, and the *kapo* slapped him roundly across the face, then hustled up the line, waiting to be challenged again.

To make sure the inmates had understood the *kapo*, a German guard, an SS, now walked down the line of naked people. Marta warned Libuse that he was coming. As the soldier moved along, he jabbed people in the ribs with the butt of his rifle, reminding them what order meant, saying in German they were to enter the showers quietly and co-operatively so that they could all get on with their day.

"Who is this one?" Libuse whispered, her head down. "Is this Cerberus—*Kerberos* for our Greek friend? Is this the monster dog with three heads and a tail made of writhing snakes?"

"He's coming," whispered Marta.

The guard paused deliberately at someone ahead of Marta and Libuse so that Libuse could hear him approach. "What's with Hell Hound?" Libuse whispered. "Maybe at an early age he was dropped on his heads."

Libuse took a rifle butt to the ribs that made her cough. "Where is Hercules when you need him most?" she sputtered out. And the goon struck her again.

He waited for her to stop coughing and straighten up. She was nursing the place at her side where he'd struck her. She started to say something more, but Marta grabbed one of Libuse's hands and squeezed hard, begging her to stop. At first Marta was sure the goon was going to strike her now, but he was gazing at her instead, not fiercely, as he had been a moment before. Marta didn't back down now. She stared back into his dark eyes, eyes the colour of her own. His hair was as black as hers, when she had some. He seemed disarmed for just a moment. A young girl up ahead called out to someone, and the goon hustled back up the line and clubbed the child with his weapon, and clubbed her again, so that she fell unconscious to the ground. When her mother tried to lift her, the goon bashed her head, too, and added her to the heap.

In a flash, the *kapo* was there to help clean up the mess. He made a couple of male inmates lift the woman and girl and carry them to the front. The door of the great chamber opened then, and they deposited the two inside against the far wall.

Libuse's stomach growled audibly. She was still clutching her side. "We haven't had breakfast yet," she said. "I guess they didn't want to waste any gruel on us."

The clang of the gas chamber door sent a shudder through Marta's naked form. The end of her life was as far away as that door. She had planned to have children. She'd wanted a boy—or either—a child with Istvan. It would have been a good marriage, if he'd agreed to have her. The subject had never come up. In all that time, it never came up. Where would the ceremony be held—in the dark cellar under the floorboards? It would have been a comfortable life with Istvan and their son or daughter. What a twist. She'd had so little time to ascertain what they were doing here, on Libuse's least favourite planet, and no time now.

"I could have got us some sleeping pills," she said to Libuse, "from the infirmary. It would have been much easier—we'd doze, fall asleep, and then . . ."

Libuse gripped Marta's hand ever more tightly. For once, the tall woman was speechless. She was trembling. As they heard the barks of the *kapo* and the goon and began to move, Libuse said, "Whole cities will go down with us today—do you know that?—whole civilizations."

Marta looked all around her at her companions, the woman up ahead with the cirrus hair and cloche hat, the Transylvanian boy, the woman with vacant eyes from the line in the yard—344, she thought it was. She wondered what it would be like to stand in line with hundreds of people who shared her birthday, June 16, the way she now stood in line with hundreds who'd share the day of her death—what was it today?—October something—she'd lost track. "What's the date?" she asked Libuse.

"What does it matter?"

"Because I want to know. I'm just thinking. I need to know."

Marta put the question to the people ahead. She put it in German and tried halting French, but no one said a thing. They were all shuffling forward. She thought she might arouse the wrath of the *kapo* or the goon. She called out the question more forcefully, frantically, until someone turned from way up ahead, near the young man with the erection, and said, "November 7."

November 7. She felt calm all of a sudden. November 7. *16 June 1917–7 November 1944.*

She imagined the graveyard with her companions:

12 May 1931–7 November 1944
15 March 1912–7 November 1944
6 December 1880–7 November 1944
11 November 1939–7 November 1944
23 September 1907–7 November 1944

How quaint—but of course there would be no graveyard. Or, if there were a graveyard here, her stone would read: *181818—16/6/17–7/11/44.*

What a lot of handsome numbers. And if you wanted a blessing from the Lord on the stone, what number would He be? One, surely. And His number would have to be spelled out: *One. Ein.*

Half the line had been swallowed. Hundreds were inside already. For a moment, Marta was able to see what lay beyond the chamber and above the smoke, a certain peace, like good music, as Libuse had described it, the "Lacrimosa" from Mozart's *Requiem*, the "Marcia funebre" from Beethoven's *Eroica*, the symphony that always loomed there, whether played or not played, remembered or imagined—it presided over all other music—its perfection waiting to make companions out of us, waiting to make us whole—the poetry of *Romeo and Juliet* waiting, too, and Homer and the Ancient Mariner—and—no—music above all else, at the fore, kind Mozart, solid Beethoven—his music so impossibly beautiful he himself must have been influenced by it, fallen into the groove of his own good work so that he had to pull himself out, dream of something new each day—and steady Bach, discovering beauty in his mathematics—their angelic German souls gazing down on this chamber and this yard and these shorn heads.

They were near the door, now, and Marta's heart quickened. "We're going to this place together, Libuse," she said, "and I don't know you. I don't even know what you do. I know one of your parents was from Brno. I know you're tall."

"I play piano—I *played* piano. I gave lessons, and I played in the Prague State Opera Orchestra, and then the orchestra in Miskolc," she said. "And where do you plan to take this knowledge now?"

"Where? I—"

"And I have a husband and a young son. We came together on this journey."

Libuse and Marta were the last two naked inmates herded through the gas chamber door. A boy inside, a boy from Thessaloniki, possibly, or even north of it, Kastoria maybe, said his feet were cold—that much Libuse could make out from her passing knowledge of Macedonian, and she passed it on to Marta. His mother said they would warm up soon in the shower.

Marta turned Libuse toward the open door and hoped for sympathy. What else could she do? The two women had one tiny advantage: they were nearest the door and their executioners.

Once again, she caught the goon's gaze, his features much like hers, his black hair, his dark eyes—he would have passed more easily as a

Jew than an Aryan, as would she—as *did* she. But he wore the uniform, and his eyes were glassy. They must have seen too much, Marta sensed in that moment, and she was just one of the huddled, herded masses he had to jab along into the showers every single day— and this was his life—he on one side of a fence and she on the other, just a few steps away. She knew that then, and he might have known it, too. That was the kind of world she'd stepped into. She was grasping Libuse's hands too tightly and glanced down for just a second to see the whites of their knuckles. Then Marta looked squarely up into the glass eyes of the goon—they might as well have been glass—they had no life, no spark, no gleam of recognition, just the gleam of glass—and she stared at him, just to penetrate his face, warm the glass. Marta wanted him to remember one single face out of the hordes—it might as well have been hers—why not hers?

Then she saw the *kapo*, the aggressive Greek Jew, step up in front of the goon to close the vault. The goon would have had to bend around him to maintain eye contact, and he didn't. Of course he didn't. She'd almost managed to pull a glimmer of recognition up through his eyes like rope.

And now Marta's eyes were adjusting to the darkness of the chamber. She looked up into the showerheads to see what she might ascertain, to wait for it to begin.

A dread silence filled the room until she heard someone, an old woman, moan, and a young boy or girl say, "I want to get out now. I need to go." A child said, "The showers don't work." Then lots of small, quiet sounds, solemnly spoken, reverentially, it seemed, not loudly, not intended for the outside, small squeals, mostly, yelps, ohs, strangely reassuring to Marta instead of unsettling, strangely comforting, reminding her at least that they were all going into this together, and it was November 7, a day to etch on the dissolving brain. They were standing in this great chamber, like some great elevator, like a cattle elevator, and Marta found that blind Libuse had wrung the life out of her hand, but the taller woman was standing stiff as a trooper.

"Hit me," she was saying, as though she were standing in a boxing ring, or before a firing squad. "Hit me."

"I won't hit you. Think of music instead. Think of Rusalka and the moon."

They heard the sound of a canister, then a hissing above the little grunts and caws. They both faced upward. "What was his name?" Marta said. Libuse didn't answer. "Your son." Libuse still didn't answer. Marta was holding her breath with a force equal to that of Libuse's grip. Someone bumped into Marta, stumbled back against her, the naked flesh cold and stubbly.

Libuse said, "Emile. He was nine. I was giving him piano lessons, and I made him practise his little heart out—you can count on that."

Marta heard what her friend said, but the voice was muffled, distant. Everything in her was closing down. She clamped her eyes shut, her ears, tried to shut down her mind, and the beast between her ears had begun to cooperate. She was wobbly and light-headed as she took in a first delicious draft of air. She imagined Istvan, waiting for her in his hovel with Smetana, or maybe not—maybe they were waiting just up ahead—how nice that would be, how quick and nice. All he'd wanted to do was survive, like Libuse, like her, like Smetana—like her pretty angelica out back, like the walnut trees and apricot trees that were clever enough to keep Marta alive so she could propagate them, harvest their fruit to bake her cake and keep her vases lush, waiting to be appreciated, the fragrance so sweet, waiting to be adored, waiting to be rescued, waiting to mask the scent of human fear—when—when what?—a clanging sound from behind Marta roused her from her reverie.

The door of the death chamber swung open. Marta felt a cool draft. People started to heave like one mass of flesh out through the chamber's opening. The goon shoved them back with the butt of his rifle. He was all by himself. The *kapo* was nowhere to be seen. It was Marta's goon, the one with the glass eyes. It was like some kind of hallucination. He reached in and took hold of Marta's free hand.

Marta heard a whimpering sound bubble out of blind Libuse's throat beside her. The goon was pulling Marta outward, and she felt clothed in her reverie. She forgot she was naked, a fleshy young woman being pulled out through the ribby flesh pressing in at the opening, the gash in the chamber—the Air—out from where the gas itself was already flowing, and the goon was trying to cover his own nose and mouth with a handkerchief as he yanked at Marta. He had hold of her hand and was much stronger than Libuse. "Go," Libuse was saying. The blind woman saw what was happening before Marta did. "Go." And she released her, let go, gave her permission, a mother setting her child free. He had her hand, and Libuse's was gone now. He yanked her out of the chamber and tried to force the door closed—old limbs tangled up with new ones, and the goon fired his rifle and fired again into their midst, and Marta's naked breasts were splashed with red blood.

Marta heard, "No," in Hungarian. That one utterance just as the door was clamped shut behind her, and she could feel the air again, the autumn draft, the seasons continuing, November 8 waiting ahead, and she and the goon turned to see the face of the stupefied *kapo*. He glowered at Marta, then the SS guard, the goon, and the goon turned away from the glare, unlatched the chamber door again, flung the *kapo* inside with a single whipping motion of his arm and slammed the vault for the last time.

Marta stood naked and alone with the goon in the air. The first thing she felt was shame. All she wanted to do was cover herself. A moment before, she'd wanted to survive like the walnut tree. Now, she'd moved beyond survival into shame. Next, she might consider her forthcoming meal, her sleep that night, the damp, and the next episode of moonlight. But the first thing she remembered was shame, like Eve exiting the Garden.

She covered her blood-streaked breasts with one arm and her vagina with the other hand, the hand Libuse had been holding, the hand her own blood was rushing back into. It was the first thing she felt as the goon looked at her with those same glassy eyes, now warmed over, a hot-blooded killer, a discriminate killer. Not very much more, but at least a person now.

And the goon, too, felt shame. He turned away from her and said, "Go," from under his breath. "Go, before we both end up in the chamber." He pointed with his rifle to a flatbed truck parked near the gate, the electrified fence and the barbed wire. The truck was piled high in the back with the filthy uniforms of the women of the *lager*. Those stinking grey clothes, their broad stripes grimed away, were the most beautiful sight she'd ever seen—the stink of life—and now they represented her exit from shame and cold.

"Put on some of those clothes," the goon said, "and hide away in the pile. "The *kapo* and his minions were supposed to move the pile away to have it laundered for the new recruits, but I will arrange for it to be incinerated and drive the truck outside the gate myself. We do that in a pit outside the gate. You get into the pile, and I'll move you away, too." He was speaking slowly in German for Marta's benefit, speaking as slowly as he could, though his voice was excited. Then she could detect what she thought was a smile on the face of the goon, or something approaching one, and the beast between her ears growled alive, bounded away from the gates of shame, noticed the goon's white teeth, his black hair, his boiling black eyes.

The chamber behind Marta was quiet. Up until a moment before, it had sounded like lobsters in a pot, but now they were good and cooked. The pot was quiet. The red claws had stopped clattering. The pot didn't even simmer. Kosher lobsters.

The goon and Marta rummaged for clothing together. "I can manage," she said. "You certainly don't need to help. You've done enough for me already. I'll just get into the truck if you'll let me." And he took her at her word, stepped aside, waited.

It felt like evening when Marta got out into the cold damp air of the world again, but of course it was still just morning and dark for her beneath the grime of the bodiless clothes. She wiped herself raw to get off the splash of blood. She was not sure it was gone, but she kept rubbing, using the abandoned clothes all around her in the flatbed truck, the clothes and the rubbing making her warmer than she'd been in months.

Marta was still panting from her unexpected encounter with the goon and had just got dressed, selecting garments at random, a top, bottoms, when she felt him close again through the bodiless clothes, the foul garments whose clean ghosts had flown off, though some might still have been hovering above this truck. The goon tugged down the big pants Marta had pulled on to hide her shame, and then she felt his hot flesh. His eyes were silver in the dim light. "Happy birthday," said the goon, and except for his breath and a single gasp, it was the last thing she heard coming out of his mouth. When he was done, he slipped away and out.

She heard the front door open, the truck bounce slightly, the door close, the engine start, felt the truck lurch forward, squeak to a stop, then the door again, some voices in German, the truck bob, the door close, the truck shift into gear and lurch again as it sputtered for two good minutes before it halted, the engine was shut off, the door opened, the cab bounced, the door closed, the sound of footsteps walking away on gravel or dirt. He was back inside, past the barbed wire and in through the gates. And then Marta heard nothing at all, though her ears were alive to the world. She waited. What if they came for the clothes before nightfall? She could not climb out before nightfall—not in view of the gates. The goon had been thinking like a furtive guard, not like a furtive prisoner.

Seven hours of silence ticked by, eight, until it was night outside the gates of Auschwitz.

Twenty-Four

Budapest – December 6, 1944

A LETTER CAME to the Dutch insurance company on Ulloi Street. It was over three months since Simon had been taken and almost two months since Zoli had gone. Lili met the mailman and rushed to her cot to open the letter.

Bereck, Transylvania
December 2, 1944

My Dear Lili,

Since you are holding this letter in your hands, it means that Imre Vollman made it back to Budapest and managed to post it without the beady censors looking over my shoulder here at the labour camp. We can rejoice at the coming of Christmas finally. There's been a break here, some talk of the Russians moving in and our having to clear out. A couple of dozen of the inmates have moved to the Ukraine, including my friend Laszlo Kis. He wanted me to go too. We had a choice for the first time: we could stay here under confinement, or we could move to the Ukraine and be confined there, which may be even worse. Laszlo thought we'd be safer there from the Russians and Germans both. I had my doubts. You could be safe from the

Russians and Germans, but would you be safe from the Ukrainians? Laszlo asked us, rightly, I guess, "Are we safe from the Hungarians?" We had a heated discussion in our barracks— it was about the only heat there was in this hole. Anyway, I'm still here, as you might have gathered. Most of us are still here. The commandant sent that bastard Erdo, the sergeant, up ahead with Laszlo and the rest. He's supposed to report as soon as he can.

My dear Lili, your precious package arrived here at the camp, but it contained nothing but your letter, which, ironically, helped incriminate the packet's violators. The biscuits you must have pilfered from somewhere left their remains in the form of a couple of crumbs among the bits of tobacco from the tin you mention in your note, a cruel fiction, it became. The "fruit" would have been a special treat, whatever its rosy colour, in this bleak and forgotten place—no, I should say not quite forgotten enough, I'm afraid. Was it an apple? A yellow pear to add to my nightly fantasy? I don't know which image to entertain first as I sink into my frigid slumber in the Transylvanian mountains. You or the fruit? And where did you procure whatever that treasure was? Did you manage, on your brilliant scavenging expeditions, to persuade someone to part with an orange—oh, my God, a holy orange to light this night!

The mere thought of your package and their author warmed me all the way out to my frostbitten extremities. The winter has been particularly merciless in this godforsaken place. No wonder Dracula arose from these chill Transylvanian highlands hungering for warm blood.

Do you remember Elemer in the bunk below me, the one I told you about last time? He was permitted a visit by his sister, Margit, and only with a bribe I cannot even mention here. Margit gave her brother the scarf from her own neck and some woollen socks she'd knitted. She tried to be cheerful for the sake of her sick brother, but her anxiety showed. At first I thought she was just worried about him. Then I believed she was upset about what it took for her to get in here. But now I believe it was neither of these. She looked like people on the inside here: grim and beaten, a generation that feels it will not produce another one.

Sweetheart, a glimmer of kindness revealed itself to me like a religious experience in the middle of this dark season. As I was being hustled off to my trusty lathe machine this morning while it was still dark—you should see me on that thing, that lathe—I've produced enough dies for munitions to start my own little army, and I could lose my life just for uttering such a thing now—as I was being hustled off, to get back to my point, Elemer was coughing and hacking—I thought he was going to turn himself inside out. The commandant stepped in and told Elemer he could be excused from duty for a day and could stay in bed. His right-hand man, Erdo, that sergeant, the bastard, would never have allowed it. The commandant even had a pot of tea brought to him. Imagine.

I feel sometimes as though we were made by a dark, insecure god. Did you ever read the poet Endre Ady? Did you ever get to him in your school in that small town of yours? A singular poem of his still stands out for me. I remember it often in my bunk here in the night. Its title asks, "Am I Not a Magyar?"

The ancient Orient dreamed him
as I am
heroic, sombre, proudly extreme,
ruthless, but one who bleeds
pale at a thought.

The ancient Orient dreamed him
bold and youthful,

a noble, eternally big child;
sun-spirited, thirsty, melancholy,
a restless warrior;
the pain-wrought tested masterpiece
of a true unhappy god,
the child of the sun, a Magyar.

Thoughts of you, my Lili, keep me going.

Simon

Lili looked distracted when she went to tell Simon's mother that her son was all right. Klari was sewing, taking in one of Robert's two pairs of pants. She and Lili were often taking in garments these days, whichever ones they could. Paul had brought them a sewing kit, and they made good use of it. It was a chore even to find thread that winter, and Paul said he had to trade a silver sugar box for the kit, including six spools of thread, four brown and two black.

"What did Simon say?" Klari asked, looking up.

Lili looked over at Rozsi, lying on her cot, her arm shielding her eyes from the light.

"He said he is managing—surviving, but he is very cold." Lili did not want Klari to know about Elemer or Laszlo, in spite of the moment of kindness Simon mentioned.

"Poor boy." Klari put down her sewing and rubbed her own arms and shoulders. She felt cold, too, but lucky to be in a refuge like this one, even in diminished circumstances, particularly diminished since her son was taken. "Poor cold boy. Did he say anything else?"

Lili had left the letter under her pillow, tucked in its envelope. "I didn't understand every word," Lili said meekly. "He recited a whole poem in the letter."

"My poor little windbag," Klari said. She was smiling and shaking her head. "My poor cold windbag."

"He said a girl was there to visit her brother."

"At the labour camp? They let her in?"

Lili nodded. Klari looked down.

"I'm going to go to him," the younger woman said. Klari put down her sewing and got to her feet. "No, please," Lili said, "I know you'll try to dissuade me, but I'm going. I've got to go. I'll make it. It will be all right."

Klari had watched this young woman's determination, had marvelled at the food she was able to scavenge for them, the supplies, and the comfort she'd brought to the Beck family since the Germans had invaded. She thought often, too, about what young Lili had endured to see her own family deported. She'd often seen Lili twirling her mother's wedding ring in her fingers—or at least the ring she'd salvaged from the deportation train, the one inscribed "*Ivan.*"

Klari said, "I'm going to do something. Please let me, and please don't ask." She approached her niece and sat gently on her cot. "Rozsi, my darling," she whispered. Rozsi kept her arm folded over her eyes. Rozsi had turned dark. She hardly spoke to anyone, barely accepted her scarce meals. Her darkness was so apparent, even one of the nuns tried to help. Klari heard her trying to talk to Rozsi in the bathroom. It turned out the young nun's name was Beata. She was the one who'd been growing the African violets.

Klari said, "Rozsi, we've been cooped up too long. I want you to come with me."

Rozsi didn't answer.

"I'm not asking," Klari said. "I insist." She was losing her patience.

Lili saw what was going on and wanted to intervene, but Klari held up her hand for her to stop. "We're going to go back to our old place on Jokai Street. Just for a bit, just quickly."

"Zoli?" Rozsi asked, uncovering her eyes. Dark circles had formed around them.

"No, not for Zoli," Klari said. She spoke as if to a child. "We'll have to wait patiently for Zoli, as we're waiting for the others, too. Lili's waiting for her whole family." Rozsi looked blankly at Lili. "Come with me," Klari said again. "We'll put on those nice wool coats Paul got for us from the Red Cross. Come."

Robert was out. He'd become increasingly despondent as his son's absence grew long and as the winter settled in. His assistant had come to take him to his home for the morning. It was a nice surprise—a little risky, but nice. It was never easy to venture out, but it had become necessary for the well-being of the Becks. Klari had told her husband she wanted to stay with the girls.

"We need to go while Robert is still out," Klari said, "or he'll never let us leave. Come, Lili, help me."

Lili didn't argue. She got their coats and helped Rozsi on with hers. "Do you have your papers?" Lili asked.

Beata was behind them, wanting to help. She patted Rozsi on the shoulder.

Klari nodded, and the two left. Rozsi trudged along the sidewalks like an injured woman, but Klari kept her going. The familiar sights and the cool air seemed to liven the younger woman up a bit.

When they got to their Jokai Street home, Klari rang the bell repeatedly for several minutes. She was sure she saw the curtain move. The courtyard door, surprisingly, was open and they made it all the way to the Becks' front door and knocked.

Vera answered. "Oh, Mrs. Beck. You're all right." Vera looked a little pale but otherwise healthy, better than she and Rozsi must have looked, Klari was sure.

Someone inside, a man, said, "Who is it?"

Vera said, "Don't worry." But she didn't budge.

"May we come in?" Klari asked.

"It's not a good time."

Klari's hand was on the door. "Not a good time? No, it's not a good time, is it." And she gave the solid door a hard push. She pulled Rozsi in after her. Rozsi stumbled. The place had a different smell, something cooking, something they hadn't had before. Was it another zoo animal?

Vera's mother was living in the Becks' home now, as were her uncle and aunt and three of her cousins. Klari noticed right away that the Ziffer in the living room was gone, the painting called *Yard with Trees*. The hook it had hung from was still on the wall.

Klari didn't want to inspect the place. She might have if she'd been alone. But it was full of people, and she didn't want to be challenged. "We're not staying," Klari said. She pushed through to her old bedroom, and Vera didn't follow.

A young man was lying on her bed with his shoes on. He looked as if he hadn't shaved in a week. Rozsi said, "Oh," as if she'd been expecting someone else, but put her hand up to her mouth. The man sat up. Rozsi leaned back against the wall.

Half the clothes in her closet were gone, but not her mink coat. It was what Klari had come for. At the front door again, Vera was about to say something. She reached for the coat, but Klari's look told her to back off. For a moment, Klari wondered if Vera would call the authorities, but she'd feel confident enough only to call the Hungarian authorities, and Vera didn't know where the Becks were staying.

A cold wind had blown up by the time Klari and Rozsi made it outside again. Rozsi began shivering immediately. Klari threw the wooden hanger down clattering onto the courtyard floor and wrapped the fur coat around her niece's shoulders. She saw Vera watching them through the window.

Klari was jubilant by the time she got back to the Dutch insurance company. "Look," she said to Lili as she showed off the fur coat Rozsi had on. Klari wanted her niece to model it for her, but she had to force her to turn this way and that.

"We'll sew it together, the bottom, I mean. We'll turn it into a sleeping bag, and you'll take it to him. With luck, he'll stay warm and alive, and we'll feel better, you and I, knowing it."

A strange man appeared behind Lili. "Who's this?" Klari said. Even Rozsi looked.

"Paul brought them while you were gone," said Lili. "They're the Ganzes, saved from the transports."

"We're in the offices on the south side," the man said. "I'm Vilmos Ganz, and my wife is Kati." He came closer. He looked scrawny in an oversized navy suit. "What are the sisters doing here?" he whispered.

"Who knows?" Klari said. "They don't say. Don't worry," she added. "Have you lost people?"

Vilmos nodded and shrugged. "The Forgacs family is coming tonight, too," he said. "And the Szents, possibly, probably." Then he bowed and backed into the far office.

With a simple needle and thread, Lili set to work immediately on the coat. She had some difficulty because the coat was thick. Klari noticed that Lili had a habit of sticking out the tip of her tongue the way a child might as she struggled with her task.

By afternoon, the luxuriant sleeping bag was rolled up and strapped into a leather satchel, which sat by the door. Robert arrived back at the safe house carrying some pickled tomatoes, pickled peppers and eight apples his assistant had gladly parted with. He also had with him a couple of records, one by Glenn Miller and a forbidden one, which he had concealed in a pillowcase. It was by Gershwin. He headed straight for his niece, who'd returned to her cot. "Look what I have for you," he said. It was *An American in Paris*. For the first time in weeks, Robert and Klari saw the beginnings of a smile.

Robert's clothes hung from his shoulders too loosely. The good cakes from the café he used to relish had become a rare treat, and his favourite, *silvas gomboc*, the dish he sometimes dreamt about, was only a distant memory: a plate of plum-filled dumplings mounded with ground walnuts and powdered sugar. But he felt grateful to be adding to the dried beans Lili had scrounged a couple of days before in exchange for a small painting of a child standing by a haystack that looked more like a whirling dervish. They'd found the work in a cupboard in the storage room downstairs.

Robert said he'd asked his assistant to stop at their home on Jokai Street. "*When?*" Klari shouted.

"Just a half-hour ago."

"No," she said. "I was there, too, today."

"You went out?"

She nodded. He looked unhappy. She changed the subject. "So you saw Vera and her people."

"Yes, I saw them. I managed to talk her uncle into giving me back a painting of ours, the one by Rippl-Ronai, the smaller one, *Christmas, 1903.* It was behind him, up against the wall by the entrance. I don't want to part with it, though, at least not yet. I'd trade it for our son, naturally, or for safe shelter, if we're forced to leave, or some kind of legal immunity I've been trying to arrange through Paul, but not for a sack of beans, or a dozen sacks."

As Klari and Lili embraced Robert again, he kissed each on the cheek, held up his booty once more for them to praise and then asked what was in the satchel by the door.

"My fur," Klari said, meekly.

"Is that what you went to get from Vera?"

"Yes, sir."

"Why? You *have* a coat now." She nodded. He said, "Why then? We're not ready to trade it, surely—or are we?"

Klari looked down. Lili stepped forward. Robert had set down his jars of pickles, and Lili took the fruit from him while he removed his coat.

"I want to take the fur to Simon. He's cold. He'll get sick. Only I can take it to him. No one else can."

"Yes, only you can, but you may not," Robert said. "I cannot allow it."

The women gazed at each other as Robert went to the bathroom to wash up. They followed him. "I'm famished," they could hear him saying from behind the door. "I want so much to sit with my ladies and eat. No amount of cake will equal the beans

and pickles we'll eat, because there's nothing like hunger"—
Robert opened the door dramatically—"and nothing like satisfy-
ing it. I would never have known that if our friend Hitler hadn't
taught us the lesson."

Within minutes, the diminished, makeshift family of four had
taken their places around the desk they'd been using as a dining
table. Rozsi didn't want to eat just then and held her stomach as
though she were ill. They gave some of their food to the nuns and
some to the Ganzes. Lili sat and watched Robert smacking his lips
with relish. She had less than half his portion of boiled beans. "Sir, I
ask you, please, to reconsider for the sake of your son."

"And what about for the sake of my future daughter-in-law, I hope,
I pray, if the Lord sees fit to release us from this grim joke?"

"You'll have no daughter-in-law if you have no son."

Robert stopped chewing. They were all surprised, even Lili, by the
sharpness of her tone.

"I have you at least for now," Robert said warmly, "and with any
luck I'll have my son back, too. My arithmetic is different from yours,
that's all."

"Not arithmetic," Klari put in. She set her fork down. "Your
outlook is different, dear. I care just as much for this girl as you do, and
as much for our son, naturally, but she's determined. She's here with
us, the only one left from her small town. And she wears the perfect
disguise with that blond hair of hers."

"To be sure: our perfect Aryan."

"Robertkam," Klari said.

"Well, that's what you meant, wasn't it? All I meant," Robert said
good-naturedly, "was that you are a girl of many disguises."

"And?" Klari asked.

Robert was cutting into a pickled tomato. "And you've kept us
alive. It's incredible what you've managed. You were sent to us by
heaven."

"We found each other," Lili said sternly.

"And if we hadn't, you'd be dead," Robert said, "and we'd be dead. But we're all still here—or some of us—and we can't risk losing you, too."

Klari said, "Robert, no one can succeed like this girl. We're talking about our son."

Robert set down his fork. "Think about what you're asking, what you're proposing."

"I don't want to think," Klari said. "It's not the time for thought—that much I've learned."

"Exactly."

"I'm sorry," Lili said. "I don't know." She felt ashamed. Her face was red.

"No, *I'm* sorry. I don't mean to be pompous."

"No," the young woman said. Klari reached for the girl's hand again. Lili said, "Please, I don't want to be dramatic either. I like to keep my wishes simple. I don't question as much as you people seem to."

Lili sat back and smiled disarmingly. She hoped she'd made her point. She hoped she hadn't contradicted herself or offended anyone. The warm smiles of Klari and Robert told her she hadn't.

Robert said, "You are so smart and serious for someone who cheerfully dismisses thought." She didn't understand what he'd meant, entirely, and didn't want to ask. She didn't want to disappoint him. She'd thought just enough about herself in her short life to know she was more earnest than smart, more honest than able to apprehend truth or anticipate the larger realities. Or perhaps she'd come from too insignificant a place to see the bigger whole, and insignificant as it was, the place she'd come from was not even a place anymore.

Robert ate the last half bean on his plate and set his fork down before saying, "You can't go, Lili, and that's final—not on my watch." And he rose out of his chair and went to lie on his cot. He felt weak and sorry.

Lili got up to tidy up, but Klari stopped her. "I'll take care of everything."

Lili wouldn't hear of it. "It'll only take a minute."

Klari clutched the girl's strong, insistent hands. "Go, rest, let me. Offer a bit of food to Rozsi again."

Lili bowed her head and went to sit with Rozsi. Rozsi gave Lili her hand, but kept her eyes closed. Lili sat with her back straight, determined, like Joan of Arc, but not rebellious. She could not rise up against her adoptive parents. Robert was as wise as her mother. She remembered the white wardrobe back home in Tolgy, how her mother had hidden her behind it. She was asked to stay put then, too, so she stayed put. At the time, it was the right thing to do.

When Rozsi fell asleep, Lili crept up the stairs to the window out of which all the Swedish inductees spied the Hungarian streets through a chink in the shutters. The spot was ideal, because the stairs provided a place to sit. Lili made herself comfortable on a step and looked out at the dark winter street.

A single gas lamp stood before her building, the flame flickering in a glass globe. She was mesmerized by its undulating glow. She thought of Simon for a time, but then a young couple appeared. The girl was barely older than Lili, barely past her teens. The two stopped beneath the lamp. As they kissed and giggled—Lili could see them giggling even if she couldn't hear them—a parade of people appeared just as magically as the lovers and marched by on the far side of the street. Lili rose from the step to watch. Some looked unreasonably young, others unreasonably old, out of their beds at this ungodly hour. And there it was now: the marchers were being led by the Germans. A night march.

Lili slipped to her knees on the floor but still peered out the window. Above the marchers' heads, other windows had been shuttered. Had they been shuttered all along? Lili's eyes darted all around.

The lovers stopped what they were doing and turned their backs to the marchers, resuming their embrace. They struggled to recapture the mood beneath the little globe of light. But the young man slapped at his sides. The moment was ruined, the magic gone. He flailed about until the young woman got hold of his arms and clamped them to his sides. The man turned away from Lili as if to say something to the marchers.

Someone stopped across the street from the young couple. He had to be a guard. He unhooked the strap of his rifle from his shoulder as the people flowed on behind him. The guard took aim at the young man, but his girlfriend gave her man a great push. The young man almost tripped. "Go," she was saying, "*go.*"

Lili ducked for cover and stayed that way for several minutes. When she peeked again, the couple was gone, but the soldier was still there. He was hanging the strap of his rifle back over his shoulder and turning to rejoin the stream of walkers heading toward the train at Nyugati Station.

KLARI FOUND LILI before dawn, still dressed as she'd been dressed for dinner, still sitting determinedly on the step. She sat down beside the younger woman and put her hand on Lili's shoulder. "I haven't been able to sleep myself, but you haven't even tried." Lili didn't answer. She didn't mention the deportation march she'd witnessed. She didn't mention the lovers either.

"I want to go to him," Lili whispered. "He's cold. He needs some comfort now. I just feel it." A moment passed as Klari stared at the dark floor. "I can manage," Lili said. "I'll get through and back."

"Then you should go." Klari took a deep breath as she felt the young woman's eyes on her. "We'll know in years to come whether or not your choice was the right one, but we don't have the luxury of waiting to find out. You may succeed, or you may not. You may step onto the wrong train and find yourself deported. You may bring him back here and find we have gone. We may be foolish to think Paul's influence gives us some kind of lasting immunity. It could all back-fire. Or you may come back, and we'll celebrate, only to perish, all of us, the following day. Or you may go and not return, either of you, and we could follow and disappear with you over the frontier into Romania, or into the ether. We could become nomads again. Our ancestors were. But we don't have the luxury to wait."

"What about Dr. Beck?"

"I will take care of my husband. Dr. Beck will find it difficult to despise you when you've gone to help his son. Dress up warmly, dear, and go. We'll wait for you anxiously, but I have confidence in you."

Lili leapt into action with the spirit of someone who'd just got permission to go to the carnival. Within a few minutes she was at the door with her bundle, the fur sleeping bag they'd created and a few other things for the journey. Klari had returned to her bed as Lili prepared. At first, Lili thought she could see Robert stirring in the dark. Then she could hear his voice, and the voice of Klari, but he didn't come out to stop her. When Klari emerged she didn't say what he'd said. She said only, "You're a brave girl. I know why my son loves you. He's lucky." She kissed Lili on the forehead and watched her leave. She glided out the door like a cat and was gone.

Lili wanted to walk boldly down to Andrassy Street as though she were on her way to a job at the Madar Café, like her friend Maria. But as she strode down the boulevard, she encountered what she dreaded most: another stream of marchers on their way to Nyugati Station. Had the Germans stepped up the campaign? Paul had been saying they might, because Wallenberg's group was meeting them at every point of exit from the city. Lili was going the opposite way and needed to act confidently as she rushed by. She didn't know how jaunty she should be while passing them. She had seen others—non-Jews—simply go about their business. Were they used to the sight? She pranced by them like a lover on the way to another promising lamppost, and no one stopped her. She wondered what they thought of her, but then sped up as if to help rush the thought along, too. She worried about the bundle with the fur coat. What would she say about it? She'd say she was visiting an ailing aunt with circulatory problems. She had just such an aunt in Tolgy who always asked for medicine from Lili's father, but David told her to bundle up instead, cover her legs with a blanket as she crocheted. Sometimes these thoughts pierced her like a bullet as she came upon lines of deportees or heard Paul talk about them.

Lili passed the line of deportees as quickly as she could. She could not look at a single one in case he or she looked back. She couldn't bear to carry the image with her. She was relieved to find the line was shorter than the one she'd seen through the window.

She walked by two shops, both closed—a shoe repair shop, featuring their handiwork in the window, and a florist—before a man stepped out of a doorway and startled her. "You can't go any farther," he said almost inaudibly, "not at the moment. You might get into trouble up ahead."

"What kind?" Lili asked, taking a single step as if to pass the man. He was much taller than she was and was eyeing the bundle she now held behind her back.

"Trust me," he said, opening the door he had come out of. She didn't move. "Come in, please. Trust me."

Maybe there was something up ahead. She chose to step in. "Just for a moment."

Lili found herself in a dark wood-panelled vestibule with a grandfather clock standing in front of her, ticking. She gripped her bundle and was reluctant to proceed through the French doors into the man's parlour. He was not as imposing a figure, here in the dark, as he'd been outside. He was young, but looked thin and wiry rather than powerful. Maybe he hadn't had much to eat lately.

He sensed her hesitation and looked down as if hurt. Was he an innocent bystander to all the activities in his city? Was he a Hungarian Catholic? Was he a sympathizer? A resister? An Arrow Cross guard? A Jew? He didn't look like one, but neither did she.

The man took a step back as if to invite Lili to come forward, and she did. The smell of cabbage clouded the air. Suddenly there came the croak of a woman's voice from the adjoining room, and the man flinched as if he'd forgotten the woman was there. "We traded the cabbage for the linens," she said, "but we still have the linens."

The young man rolled his eyes. "We haven't traded the linens. We still have the linens, and the cabbage, too."

"What good are the linens when we have nothing to set out on them? Nothing splendid, nothing." Her voice faded. "We traded them with the other girl who was here," she said more cheerfully. "We traded Hermann's chair for the tobacco the young girl brought."

Lili peered in at the woman. The lights in the woman's eyes seemed to have gone out, as if her mind were fading. The woman wanted to say something more, but she didn't or couldn't. Her mind was grasping at thoughts. Then the look of Lili smiling effortlessly registered on her consciousness. "You are such a pretty girl," the woman said, "like someone from a fairy tale, a pretty girl who walked in out of the war. Won't you stay with us for a cabbage roll? It's good. It has rice in it and meat."

"Meat?" Lili said. She took another half-step in. The shelves and china cabinet in the room were filled with ruby glass: goblets, dessert plates, a great fruit platter with a pinwheel pattern cut into the red, a crystal bell. It was like a ruby glass emporium.

The morning sun burst through the window, lighting up the glass like blossoms. Two ruby vases stood guard over the upright piano.

"Do you want me to play something?" the young man said.

"Yes, you do that, Hermann," his mother said. Her look went blank again. Then: "Play a Chopin Polonaise for the lovely girl."

"Should I play Bela Bartok, or how about Erik Satie?" he asked her while he kept his eyes on Lili. "A *gymnopédie*?"

"No," his mother said imperiously. "Chopin or nothing—all right, Chopin or—what was that lovely Dvorak you were tinkling with the other day?"

"It was Sibelius, that's what."

They all gazed at the piano as if to ask if it remembered. The vases stood over it like jars of blood.

"Why didn't the other girl take your father's old chair, son—*your* chair now?" the woman asked. Lili glanced around to see what chair she meant. Maybe the red one, wine red. She held on tightly to the parcel for Simon. "Did she not leave the tobacco?" the woman asked. "I smoked some, that I can tell you."

Lili looked at Hermann, who breathed quickly and smiled awkwardly. "I have to be going," she said. "I have to catch a train."

"You can't just yet." He took a step toward the entrance. "You shouldn't."

Lili paused. The imposing odour of the cabbage filled the room. "Have some cabbage rolls with us," the woman said.

"So early in the morning?" Lili asked. She didn't know why she would say such a thing. Good food was welcome whenever you could get it. She said, "I mean, how did you manage cabbage rolls so early—I mean, the meat?" Lili shook her head as if to shake away her confusion.

The woman got to her feet. She was not much taller than when she'd been sitting. What a tall son she had. Lili felt surrounded. "Pigeon," the woman said. She took a single step. They were like chess pieces, the three of them, taking one step at a time this way and that, hesitating, then moving again. The woman said, "Hermann trapped a pigeon out back yesterday morning. He's done that quite a few days, and you can enjoy some more if you stay." Lili thought of the other girl, the one who'd brought the tobacco, or was it the cabbage? Hermann's mother said, "We have quite a sack of rice, and we acquired cabbage. We ground up some pigeon flesh so we could have cabbage rolls. They're surprisingly tasty."

"I'm going to have to go," said Lili. Her stomach was turning, not because of the pigeon but because her hosts were making her feel ill at ease. She didn't know who they were—didn't know what anyone was capable of these days.

Was Hermann a butcher, a guard somewhere, a glass merchant? Had his shop closed down, and all the glass merchandise been moved to their house? She began to back out, and no one moved. She could feel the cooler air of the vestibule behind her. When she made it to the door, she clutched the handle, and no one came. She heard the piano. Rachmaninoff, she was sure. Klari must have played a recording of it for her one evening. Hadn't she heard it at Klari's? Dr. Beck had so many records.

No one came to stop her. Her foot bumped against something by the door, a soft lump—she looked down—a sack. "*Magyar Posta*," it read in gold letters across it. Hermann was a mailman.

Just as Lili turned to leave, the short woman appeared before her in the half-darkness. She'd put a charcoal-grey wool scarf over her head and ears—for when the door opened, Lili guessed. She could still hear the Rachmaninoff, the feeling swelling.

The woman held up a crystal butter dish with a ruby glass dome beneath which lay a cabbage roll. It looked like a small beached whale. "Take it with you," the woman was saying. She held out the butter dish with one hand and pulled the scarf tight with her other. Lili took hold of the dish with its dark scarlet dome. "Take it." The woman smiled broadly as Lili did so. "Wait," she said. Out of her apron pocket, the woman pulled a packet of Turkish tobacco, labelled *Sophia*, and some cigarette papers. "Take these, too," she said. "You never know." Lili stuffed the tobacco and papers into her deep coat pocket. There was a pause in the Rachmaninoff but no other sound.

Lili stumbled out the door and into the world again. She proceeded for a moment down the street, looking all around her for the danger Hermann had warned her about, or for another line of deportees, but the boulevard was deserted. Lili remembered what time it was, still very early for anything other than early trains but not too early to turn off the city's gas lamps. She ducked under an awning as the winter sky brightened. What was she to do with this lovely ruby dish, which lit up her white hand and wrist like a jewel? She tiptoed further into the entrance of what turned out to be a small bookshop, one she remembered roaming through with Simon soon after she got to Budapest. He had bought her a little volume of the poems of Petofi and afterward read a couple of them to her each night. Lili remembered the sound of the words, lofty and romantic, even though she could not comprehend all of the old Hungarian.

The shop was closed, naturally, and Lili turned her back to the door and set her sack down gently. She opened the red hood of her dish, picked up the cabbage roll with her fingers and ate. The plump little meal was more delicious than she'd imagined it could be—it was still quite warm—and the morsel was gone in a minute.

Lili took out a handkerchief, monogrammed with the letters "KB," Klari Beck, dabbed at her mouth before wiping the dish as clean as she could make it, retraced the few steps to the doorway she had just departed and set the dish back down gently on the step.

She then turned up Andrassy Street again and headed northeast toward Keleti Station. She moved along furtively, worrying still about Hermann's warning. She felt exposed as she stole up the street, felt she could be nabbed in an instant and, like Zoli, made to join a line going the opposite way, or worse, shot instantly. She had her story ready. She was rushing off to visit an ailing aunt on the frontier with Romania, hence the fur sleeping bag and the tobacco for her equally ailing uncle. She hadn't seen them for two years, she would say, and this was her last chance. She'd say her uncle was the pastor at the Church of St. Margaret, and she'd mention him by name, Father Ambrus. The priest had told her to do this, any time she needed. It would be a "benevolent lie," he said.

Lili felt better after she'd scuttled into the City Park past the imposing Museum of Fine Arts on the left and the Palace of Art on the right. Heroes' Square awaited her. It was wide open and made her feel exposed. She dashed for cover toward the monument of the fierce Rydwan, god of war, aboard his chariot pulled by two powerful steeds. Rydwan was pointing the way, but had he lost his way now, here, in Hungary? The proud country had backed Hitler, and now Hitler had turned on Hungarians. She remembered the spring day she'd got here, the Gypsy trio, the blind girl soliciting, the strange things she said. Where would her family find her, even if they wanted to?

Lili could see the fierce statue of the great Arpad, leader of the Magyars, wearing his battledress, his head crowned by a knife blade, a lightning rod, aimed at the heavens. She saw King Ludwig I, his monument completed just a decade and a half before, to remind Hungarians their rulers had led them to the promised land. Were they small men, Ludwig and Arpad, that their monuments had to be so immense? How big was Hitler? How about Stalin? She'd heard that Napoleon was a small man. Did Ludwig and Arpad face in the direction Rydwan had inspired them to face? If you lined up the warriors of the world, horse to chariot to horse, across the planet, would they be pointed in the right direction?

Lili moved on. The Museum of Architecture was not far ahead, housed in the Vajdahunyad Castle, and the zoo, a small one, not the one she'd visited with Maria and her brother. She wanted to walk straight past them, out past the City Park toward Keleti Station.

Winter clouds had begun to crowd the sky and a cool wind blew. She spotted a small group of uniformed men up ahead. They might easily have been zookeepers or tram conductors, for all she knew, but she didn't want to find out, so she turned right. She would duck into Jak Chapel if she had to, if she could, and worship dutifully if she needed to.

She made it all the way to Jak Chapel and beyond, but if she continued now she would be leaving the park altogether. She stepped behind a monument she had not noticed before. It was the Statue of Anonymous, a poet, the plaque said, a life-sized bronze of a calm, ghostly figure seated on a bench, either man or woman, she couldn't tell, holding a bound manuscript in one hand and a primitive stylus in the other. The face of Anonymous was buried inside a deep hood, and like a mole the poet looked out of the darkness into the light of the park, the face barely discernible.

Lili heard steps coming toward her from the street and crouched behind the monument, her heart racing. She seemed to be hiding everywhere, she realized, skulking about like a criminal. Maybe Anonymous was the best person to be, off to the side of the City Park, looking downward, staring at the foot of Vajdahunyad Castle, neither Ludwig nor Arpad, and not Rydwan either. This was the benefit of being Anonymous, Lili decided: your face receded into the darkness behind the folds of your hood, your sex receded. You withstood sun and snow and the comings and goings of monks and killers who had long forgotten you were sitting here—because the minute you became Arpad, the minute you loomed large, you'd better get set to lead; the minute you became a blond Jewish girl who had fled to Budapest, you'd better get set to hide. Better Anonymous than Arpad—you could sit and watch—but either way better bronze than flesh.

Someone crept up behind her. "Who are you?" the voice said. She turned to find what looked like a priest, a monk possibly.

"I'm . . ." Lili said, straightening out.

"Are you all right?" the priest said. "Are you cold?"

She nodded.

"Come," the man said. He was heading for the chapel. "Come, you'll catch your death. I can give you some tea with honey and a little biscuit. Come, you'll feel better."

Lili heard the church bell toll eight times. The city would be getting up and out now—friends, enemies, oppressors, collaborators. And those who would always surprise you, like this gentle soul. For the second time that morning, on the way to a train that didn't leave until five minutes to ten, Klari had told her, Lili stepped into an unknown building to accept the protection of a stranger.

At the doorway to the chapel stood two laughing creatures, boars possibly, or mythic beasts, with all their teeth showing. But instead of taking her through the front, the robed man led Lili around to the rear of the church and made the turn toward the rectory. Inside, he removed his cloak, hung it up, lit a gas stove and filled a cast-iron kettle with water. He did not ask her any other questions, and she felt relieved not to have to make up answers. She guessed the man knew that's what she would do if pressed. He made her tea, set out a few biscuits, a bowl of honey and a yellow apple. Added to the cabbage roll, this was more breakfast than she'd had in months, and more than, in good times, she would have accepted voluntarily.

The priest lit a lamp with a tortoiseshell shade, which gave off a warm glow. He plucked at the shoulders of his brown robe to adjust the way it hung. He had a baby face and generous brown eyes. He could not have been more than a half-dozen years older than Lili. And then he looked up, and Lili realized he was slightly wall-eyed and might have been ashamed of the defect. As his eyes settled on her, she checked beside her to see what else he might be looking at. He was watching her enjoy her tea—of that she was confident—and she smiled appreciatively at him. And then he turned his back to her, opened the lid of a hatbox phonograph, selected a record and switched it on to play. Lili expected Bach or vespers of some kind but heard instead "In the Mood."

"It's a new record," he said, smiling, clapping his hands once, then dropping them to his side. "It's by Glenn Miller, an American, with his American Forces Band."

It might have been the same record Dr. Beck had brought for Rozsi. The robed man then turned to depart, to get the chapel in order, she supposed. "Stay as long as you like," he said before closing the door and leaving her on her own.

And here she was, with her breakfast and record. Why did everyone want to play music for her? Was she expected to get up and dance around the room? Maybe just smile. She could do that easily enough.

For a moment, she imagined the wall-eyed priest calling the authorities while she ate, drank and listened, but her feeling about the man contradicted the thought. She got quite comfortable and warm before deciding it was time to go. She wrapped the remaining biscuits in another handkerchief Klari had given her and tucked them into her bag. She'd save these for Simon. She wasn't sure what was to come next. She didn't know whether she was to receive benediction. She didn't even know what benediction was or if one could receive it on a Wednesday.

She turned to the phonograph as it played its jaunty tune. Was it polite to leave before the song was done? There was a desk to one side, and she thought of leaving a note of thanks, but she didn't want to disturb any important church papers.

She gulped down her tea and used her spoon to clean the honey from the small bowl before getting up. She gazed expectantly at the chapel door one last time. She watched Glenn Miller whirl on the turntable and then left.

Lili made it the rest of the way to Keleti Station easily now. The sky was heaped with cloud and a cool wind whipped at her face. She was grateful she had a scarf and gloves, which Klari had given her. There were many people out and about by now, but instead of worrying Lili, the traffic made it easier for her to disappear among the throngs. People paid little attention to her. Not even a dog she saw paused to look at her.

Though she'd been there before, she'd forgotten quite how imposing Keleti Station was. She was sure the whole population of Tolgy could make itself comfortable strolling along its floors and lounging on its stone benches. From a block away, the building looked like a cathedral with an arched roof, a dome on each of its shoulders joined by an immense arch of window in the centre with more glass in it than in all the windows in all of the houses of her town combined. Who polished these windows and how?

She collected herself as she entered the echoing station. She stood in line for a ticket and withdrew her precious Swedish *schutz-pass*. The ample woman ahead of her at the lancet-topped window finished, signalled to a porter to come to get her small suitcase and moved along toward the trains.

When Lili stepped up timidly to the window and asked for a return ticket to Bereck in Transylvania, the ticket seller took a good look at her, an inquiring look rather than a suspicious one, a good-natured look. She handed the man the *schutz-pass*, together with some coins, and he looked her over again but didn't say a word. In fact, not a word came out of his mouth the whole time. The man, with greying hair at his temples, wore a conductor's cap. He wrote out and punched two tickets without another glance at her. "Track B," he said. He was breathing heavily, panting, it seemed to Lili, as he went about his business and handed Lili her tickets. He looked wan, and hunched over his ink blotter, most of the day ahead of him still.

It took Lili only a moment to find Track B. Her train was not yet there. She set down her leather satchel containing the fur sleeping bag and looked up to see a sign in Hungarian: "NO JEWS PERMITTED ON THESE PLATFORMS."

A set of doors in the distance swung open and several hundred people were herded in, testing Lili's hypothesis about the people of her town fitting within the walls of the station. She recognized, even before she laid eyes on the guards, what the nature of this gathering was. She saw the yellow stars sewn to jackets and coats. There was little hullabaloo, just children whining now and again, and a particularly unhappy baby. They were being assembled, all of them, on a far platform, Track L, one of the three platforms for the freight trains which often stood outside the station in the yards.

When Lili strained she could read the sign now: "JEWS, GYPSIES AND FREIGHT—THESE TRACKS ONLY."

Lili stood self-consciously on the safe platform with just a few others. There was still an hour to go before her train was supposed to leave. Most here looked indifferent to their surroundings. A man read a newspaper. A woman stood with a porter and her trunk, another with her grumpy little dog.

The dog yelped while the baby across the way wailed. Lili could see a guard hovering over its mother, who tried to muffle the baby's cries, bobbed about with the child, covering its mouth with her hand. The guard moved on, but not far.

A fit of fear and anger boiled up within Lili, but she remained immobilized and helpless. A freight train pulled in behind the crowd at Track L, and many of the people were made to turn and face it. It seemed more orderly a gathering, from where Lili stood, than a meeting of townspeople in Tolgy might have been, or an assembly of farmers Lili had once seen. It was oddly subdued, in fact, except for a few children, and the baby.

It was not until the hovering guard returned to the woman's side and seemed to be asking for the baby that the crowd stirred. The mother shook her head, and the guard pulled the child from the woman's clutches with some force, cranking up the baby's cry to a wail. The soldier walked calmly out with the baby toward the door they'd come in, and the woman hesitated but then followed. Another guard was calling after her, but she wouldn't listen. Everyone turned toward the door to watch. The second guard joined the first with the baby and the woman outside the doors. No one inside could really see what was happening and no one dared follow.

And then all of them heard two sharp pops. The noise of the crowd turned into a rumble. A guard barked at his charges, and the little dog on Lili's platform barked back, fiercely and sharply. The man near Lili with the newspaper peered over at the disturbance and then at the dog before hiding again behind his paper.

The dog wouldn't stop its hysterical yelping. It might even have contributed to the rush with which the soldiers began to hustle their captives onto the freight train. The dog's owner tried to quiet the dog by lifting it, but it wriggled out of her arms. Already, several cars were filled. Better inside these cars where it was safer, the people must have been thinking, than outside in the commotion.

And then, as the two guards returned to the platform through the fateful door, they were followed by two other men, dressed in suits, who waded in among the throngs. Both were thin, and one was quite tall. "*Achtung!*" the shorter one commanded. "Stop at once," he said in German. "Many of these people are Swedish nationals, and we demand their release."

Several of the guards kept herding people into the windowless cars of the freight train. And then one of the men in suits, the taller one, climbed the ladder affixed to the engine and blew a whistle that echoed around the halls of Keleti Station. The little dog was struck dumb. The newspaper man dropped his hands to his sides, his paper flopping to the stone platform.

The tall man stood erect on the roof of the train engine and blew his shrill whistle again. This second blast turned the tide on the proceedings. The hubbub in the station ceased altogether.

It was Paul. He was holding a fistful of papers. She watched him, held her breath. He looked taller than ever; perhaps it was the sun coming in through the enormous window and lighting his red hair as he stood high above the distraught throng. He looked as if he'd always performed this function, as if he were born to it and could not be stopped. When Lili made an effort she could act confident, but Paul exuded the trait with every step, every turn. Of course, he was supported by the man still down on the platform. The man announced who he was, Raoul Wallenberg, and said he was here with his assistant from the Swedish embassy. Wallenberg requested calmly in German that all Swedish nationals in the group be released into his care at once. "You have no right nor authority to be detaining— let alone deporting—Swedish citizens. My assistant has documents to prove that a good many of the people you have here today are Swedes."

None of the brown-uniformed guards budged, but the one in grey, the commander with the jagged "SS" insignia on his lapel, approached Wallenberg and took a look up at Paul standing on the engine. The officer accepted some papers from Wallenberg and studied them, then studied the wallet proffered by the Swede, the only genuine Swede in the whole building.

Lili could see the commander gesturing for his men to release the Swedish nationals from among the Hungarians boarding the trains, and Paul began to call out names: "Almasi, Arpad," and the summons went out among the soldiers down the line: "Almasi, Arpad; Almasi, Arpad," until a small man in a salt-and-pepper suit and a grey fedora stepped out happily. They handed him his Swedish papers and sent him to stand by the door. "Apoli, Heinrich." The call went out, the list went on, and one in every three Hungarians was converted into a Swede and plucked from the group at Track L. Some had already boarded the trains; the others stood in front of the cars, awaiting the lottery.

And then Paul lifted his gaze and saw Lili. She was so glad that he did. She wanted desperately to wave. She would have done so, frantically, if not for the others in the station—*all* the others. He did not acknowledge her with so much as a smile.

The train for Romania rumbled in before Lili, pulling a damp winter wind with it. The few others on Lili's platform boarded impatiently. She did, too, and hurried to take a window seat looking toward Track L, but then another train pulled in and blocked her view. Lili wanted to dismount again, if only for a little while longer, to see how Paul made out.

What would Paul have done in Tolgy the day her family was taken? If only someone had interceded—there or along the way—in a station like this one—in a station in Miskolc, maybe, or anywhere.

Lili could see nothing, now, but the train that had pulled in between her and the miraculous activities at Track L. She felt restless but safe at the same time in this warm car. She felt a spell of fatigue as the night of sitting on the stairs looking out the window began to take its toll on her.

A woman dressed entirely in black boarded the train and chose the same compartment Lili sat in. Lili was worried about looking too eagerly out her window at events she could no longer see anyway, and she was sure, now, that leaving the train for another look would arouse suspicion.

The woman in black reminded Lili of women in her town who forever wore black after the death of a spouse or parent or child. When Lili was a child, she knew a woman of twenty who'd been widowed and put on black clothes. She remembered thinking the woman had entered a black tomb, never to re-emerge.

The woman in her compartment could not have been much older than forty, but she looked significantly older on account of her attire and her strangely proportioned shape. Her head seemed too small for her body, as if it had been plonked mistakenly onto the neck of the wrong woman.

As she settled opposite Lili, the woman withdrew a white egg from her ample black bag and set it in her lap as she adjusted her belongings. The egg looked odd there, starkly white in the black lap. It looked as though she'd set it there to hatch—to warm first in her black nest and then hatch into a little black chick, with an extra-small head, bursting out of its impossibly white tomb.

"Where are you going?" the woman asked Lili as she continued her settling and adjusting.

"I'm going all the way to the frontier. I'm going to meet someone. I need to see someone. How about you?"

The woman didn't answer right away, but took out a handkerchief and cracked her egg on her knee, then began to peel it. Her hands were older even than the rest of her. They were hands that had worked hard in the fields, on a farm. When she'd finished peeling the egg, she held it up in front of Lili. "Share?"

"No, thank you."

"Just a bite, a pretty girl like you on a cold day?"

"Thank you, no."

For a moment, Lili thought the woman was looking suspiciously at her, maybe because of Lili's slight accent, but the woman smiled. "What hair you have," the woman said. "Gold. Nicer even."

Lili was surprised as always that her light hair should spread such a halo of virtue over her. All that mattered was context. She would not

have looked the same to any invader in the town of Tolgy. Her family
was the proof of that, her golden-haired brothers and sisters, most of
them. The key in this context was to remain composed, and this was
Lili's second virtue, after her sunny smile.

Her companion's own hair, the jagged wisps that escaped from her
black bonnet, looked like bleached straw.

"I'm going only as far as Szolnok," the woman said. "I need to see
my Uncle Attila in his bed with a fever. He's had the fever too long,
maybe two months. My mother's there already—he's her brother."

Lili nodded. The woman's accent was unlike any Lili had heard.

"What were you doing in Budapest?" Lili asked.

"I'm living there now, looking after some elderly people in a home
out in Buda, on Toldy Street."

Lili felt relieved. She was likely safe in the woman's company. She
leaned forward to offer her hand. "I'm Lili." But the moment was
awkward because the woman was working on her egg and had to finish
the rest in a bite, wipe her hands on the handkerchief containing the
shell and return the handshake while still munching on the egg.

"I'm Mary," the woman said through a plugged mouth. "I'm very
glad to make your acquaintance. Such a pretty girl. Lili. Pretty."

Lili smiled and said it was nice Mary looked after old people.
Mary nodded and turned toward the window as the train between
their track and the far one, the one blocking their view of the terrible proceedings, rolled out. The Germans were loading the last of
the people onto the cargo train. "Look at that," she said, shaking
her head.

Lili looked composed but lost her smile. Raoul Wallenberg and
Paul were gone with their new Swedes, but the others were off to
follow her parents. She took a deep breath. She imagined the people
inside, remembered what it felt like, remembered what she was thinking that day. She developed goosebumps now, all over her body.

"Pity," the woman said, giving Lili permission to sink a little further
into her sadness. Budapest was just like Tolgy. The evacuation of its

undesirables simply took longer and was more complicated. It was Tolgy a thousand times over, every building a Tolgy, every street in the ghetto. Lili didn't know why this simple fact had taken so long to occur to her. She turned away from the window. She wanted Mary to say nothing more, good or bad, on the subject. "Poor sods," Mary said. "I wonder where they're taking them." Lili didn't answer, so Mary went on thinking aloud. "Germany?" Lili still wouldn't fill in the gap Mary had left for her. "Poland, I heard. Camps. They say there are camps. Mary, same name as me, in the home I work in, Old Mary, everyone calls her, said they're camps."

Lili nodded. "Old people must be good to care for," she remarked again.

"They're like young people, really, just bigger, not as nice smelling, not as cute, but adorable in their own way." Mary's voice began to sound philosophical. "Old folks. Old Hungarians." She gazed out the window. "And then there are the old Jews."

Lili's heart quickened. What did she mean? What kind of hierarchy was this? Old Hungarians. *And then there are the old Jews.* Could it be broken down further? There are the old Hungarians. And then there are the old Hungarian Lutherans. And then there are the old Hungarian Jews. And then there are the old border Jews who speak Yiddish. And then there are the old Yemeni Jews who speak God knows what. And then there are the old Gypsies. And then there are the old dogs. And then there's the old luggage. And then there's the old dirt.

Lili could barely breathe. "Excuse me," she said, rising. "I wonder if there's a water closet." She needed to clean up, wash away the night and morning, return to her cabin, show her ticket to the conductor, then rest—nap if she could—shut out Mary, even if the woman meant no harm.

When she returned to her overly warm compartment, Lili felt refreshed but looked pale.

"Why don't you eat something?" Mary asked her. "I have another egg."

"No, I couldn't." Lili began to feel a little queasy.

"Don't be silly—I brought four with me."

"Thank you. I'm full. I ate plenty today."

"You ate plenty. Look at you—you weigh less than my head." Mary rummaged through her black bag and took out the remaining three eggs and offered them to the younger woman, all three smooth white eggs held out to her in a gnarled hand. "Take them. If you like them, I'll lay some more."

Lili studied Mary's face to see if she'd really said what she'd said, as if to get permission to laugh. She received it from the woman's eyes and burst out, as did Mary herself. Lili's sides hurt as she doubled over with laughter, winced with guilt and then laughed some more. "You city people," Mary said between bursts and shook her head, "refusing things. Full, proud, city people."

Finally, the train grunted forward and pulled out of Keleti Station. Lili felt she couldn't have spent much longer facing the cattle cars on one side and the place where she had stood illegally on the other.

Lili said, "I wish I could do something with my brain other than think."

"Do what I do," Mary said, as she patted the side of her head. "Use it to give shape to your bonnet." Lili looked at her companion and smiled broadly. "Think with your heart," Mary said. "It's a little like breathing through your mouth." And now Lili laughed again.

Mary said, "Not all old people are the same—you can count on that." She made a sour face. Lili worried about what was coming next. "Some are nice, but some aren't. Some are nasty. It's like children. They might all be adorable, but some are sweet, and some aren't. They grow up the way they started, and end up the way they started."

"I know what you mean," Lili responded. "Old people are who they are, I guess. That's what you mean, isn't it?"

"Except more so."

Lili giggled.

"I don't mind a little bit of shitting yourself," Mary said. "That's not what I mean. I don't mean I mind that kind of thing. It's just dirt, just shit. I can clean up a shit-ass like no one in the business. What I mean is the types who bark at you when you're trying to help out, and you get the feeling it's not because they're hurting someplace that they're barking, and it's not because they're ashamed. It's because they're barkers. They make *you* feel ashamed, even though it's them that's shitted themselves. I had this one fellow, Mr. Daranyi, who's gone to his rest—Lord, soften his hardened soul to ease his passage." Mary crossed herself here. "Mr. Daranyi said we used up all the water on ourselves and we used up the heat. He'd worked hard all his life for the water and the heat, and we young ones just wasted it on ourselves and had plenty of it because of all his hard work. The whole time Mr. Daranyi was talking, I'd be wiping him up and spending plenty of water and heat doing it, and I couldn't shut him up for the life of me. That was what he went on about every time I checked in on him, poor bugger, poor shit-ass. You'd have thought he created the oceans and the sun, poor shit-ass."

Lili was remembering someone, a Mr. Friedlander from Tolgy, who was like Mary's Mr. Daranyi, a complainer, a blamer, when Mary added, "He was about as pleasant as a slap across the belly with a cold fish." And here Lili was treated to yet another laugh. "Don't you think?" Mary was asking, hardly laughing herself, but waiting for corroboration. "Why would you use up a perfectly good human being like myself to service a perfectly rotten one like old Mr. Daranyi? Does it make any sense to you? It wouldn't happen with old bears or old trees, I can assure you. They don't use up perfectly good ones to haul their old hides."

Lili gave the idea some thought and shook her head in agreement.

"I had some others who were lovely, as I was saying. There's a couple there, still are—Mr. and Mrs. Biro. They've been married sixty-eight years now—imagine that. He's ninety-two, and she's eighty-nine. You should see the two of them, two skinny little things."

Mary held up her pinky in the air. "He makes jokes about her," Mary said. "I ask him, 'What's it like being married all these years?'—yelling mostly, because he can hardly hear. He pulls me by the collar to whisper into my ear. He says to me, 'Honey, my wife and I have been together so long we're starting to like each other again.'" Mary left room for another chuckle, which only she enjoyed this time, and then added, "But I don't believe him. You should see the two of them. She feeds him and he tries to help clean her. I leave them to do it themselves, as much as I can, but you know . . ." Mary paused. "They're such a tidy couple," she went on, "and thin." She held up the pinky again. "Mr. and Mrs. Biro. I can imagine the sparkle on the home they must have walked out of." She stopped again before saying, "Anyways, all I mean is that, if people start out nice, the nice gets bigger, and if they start out nasty, the nasty gets bigger and fatter. Small," Mary pinched her fingers together, "only gets big." She held out her arms as if for a hug.

Lili and Mary sat quietly for a time and, to the younger woman's surprise and relief, it was Mary who nodded off before she did. The conductor came by, looked in, but didn't bother with the tickets. If Lili's appearance was deceptive, Mary's clinched it for the two of them, or maybe the conductor didn't care, like the ticket seller. Lili let out a breath and let down her guard, relaxing, finally, at being in the countryside outside Budapest. And then she, too, fell asleep.

But she had a disturbing dream. She saw Klari and Robert step out from what Lili thought at first was a shower, and so the Becks were naked, but it wasn't a shower; it was a gallows. They were grey and wan, although Klari had clownish circles of rouge in the centre of her light-blue cheeks. She was holding her arms out to Lili, and so was he, as the two approached, beckoning to her to embrace them but looking through her, the whites of their eyes as blue as their skin. Lili wanted to do something for the Becks, bring them back from the brink, so she cried for help, but not a sound came out of her throat. She tried again with greater force and out sprang a song, an aria from

Nabucco, a beautiful song Dr. Beck had played for her one night after dinner. "My girl, be quiet," Robert had said to his wife, who was talking to Lili about something or other. "Either we talk or we listen." So they listened. Lili had loved the Verdi. She felt he was so much less taxing on the heart than Puccini, but still taxing in his own way—he was more composed. The dream music from her own throat calmed into a hum, allowing Lili to lie back in the dark place where the wall met the floor and where it was colder than before. Now Klari and Robert flung themselves upon Lili's shivering form, her train-jiggling body crawling with fear but not revulsion—never revulsion.

Lili awoke to a tangle of sunlight on her face. The train was stopped in a station, and the winter sun shone through the bare branches of a solitary tree, which huddled over the station roof.

Lili was alone in the car. Beside her on the seat, nestled in a clean, red-checked handkerchief, were three eggs. She pulled her satchel out from under her seat and packed away the eggs. Though her heart still thumped from the vision of Klari and Robert in the shower, she smiled.

Lili stood and stretched, but when a conductor on the platform walked by her window, she crumpled to the floor. Her heart raced, but she shut her eyes and breathed as deeply and steadily as she could. If she lived to tell the tale, she'd say it began on her sixteenth birthday, when she ceased to be a passenger and became a stow-away, moving furtively from place to place with a secret in her heart, a lie, the biggest lie going. Lili didn't want to look over her shoulder or flinch at every slammed door. She didn't want to worry at each stop about who'd be getting on and who'd be getting off. She didn't want to keep smiling blondly at the world.

Lili waited until the train rolled out of the station before resuming her seat, never finding out, as a result, what town they'd stopped in. But possibly it was Szolnok, Mary's stop. She watched the rolling hills turn into Hungary's Great Plain, flat and fertile, below what should have been called the Great Sky.

This was the plain traversed by the conquering hordes who formed the nation Lili now herself traversed, travelling in the opposite direction. Lili remembered them from Mrs. Wasserstein's class, had memorized their names. Two and a half millennia had passed since the Scythians had passed over the Carpathian Plain to discover this wild and rich country. They were followed by the Celts, the Romans, the Avars, by Charlemagne, and then, leaving their Volga and their Urals far behind them, the tribes that were to give their name to the nation, the Magyars, under the great Arpad. Many others romped over the fields in the coming centuries on the way to the throne, the Turks, notably, and now the Germans. But these Germans bore gifts. Just as Lili's land had been returned by the Third Reich to Hungary, so had the lands up ahead, the Transylvanian Alps—Transylvania—where Simon was being held and where he slept in the night near Dracula.

Of course, one would need a horde to storm across a plain and conquer a nation. It would be difficult to storm on your own. What was it like to be part of a horde? Lili wondered. You would need to forget you were someone's son or husband or father, a son who rode a horse well and excelled at mathematics, a husband who once rescued his dog from a roaring river. In the greater interest of the horde, you would need to be united and fierce. You couldn't be dithering about your daughter's limp or your wife's philandering. If the parts of a horde dithered, they would become horde pie at the hands of their victims. Maybe this was the great advantage of belonging to a horde. You got to be fierce and united. Unquestioning of your aim and ideal. Even if the aim and ideal made you hack down everything in your path. Even if they took you bounding over a cliff. It was safer to be part of a horde even if your life was at risk. There was little to worry about and nothing to question.

Lili felt like a girl without a homeland. Even her homeland was not a homeland, only a place of temporary refuge. The Inquisition had chased the Bandels to the southern border with Romania and the

Becks to the centre of Hungary some five centuries before. And they were the lucky ones, the ones who had been chased and scattered rather than squashed where they were. So where to next? Homelands were a fleeting thing, even for the original homeowners sometimes.

The train remained almost empty. Maybe there was not much call for this particular destination, or maybe the inhabitants of the region could not afford to leave or return to it.

Lili swooned back in her seat again like someone in love with the countryside. Finally, she could feel the air grow thinner and the compartment cooler as the train crossed the Tisza, "the blond river," they called it, because it carried sand downstream to be blown into dunes. She looked out to see the houses of the plain. They were like wagons that had come to rest after a very long caravan—after a nomad had said, "Let's nail our home down for once and have some-place to come back to."

The squat houses looked like mud huts with roofs made of straw, but without chimneys, so that the smoke from the hearths streamed through the roof cracks. As they approached villages, the houses began to look prettier and sturdier, with whitewashed stone walls and slate roofs. Many of the homes exhibited cob-work construction as if another species with other plans had touched down in the region.

The train stopped in Vadas, her stop. A woman approached her window even before the train had come to a halt. She wore colours that defied the drab season: a festive kerchief embroidered with a garland of crocuses and poppies. She had strings of fresh, bright peppers slung around her neck and was offering them for sale—or if not those, what about garlic? She had garlic bracelets coiling up one arm and, up the other, children's knitted woollen mitts strung together as if they were charms. She wore the colours of Christmas—red, green and gold—and then some, adding to them the snowy lace at her neck, the summer flowers of her bonnet, the autumn walnut-tree leaves on her collar and the summer peppers themselves. Where on Earth had she got her hands on freshly grown peppers this time of year? Had she grown them in her window the way Lili's mother had, tending to the little nursery as if they were babies?

Behind the woman was a tableau of a bygone era. No motor vehicles drubbed along the stone roads; they were travelled instead by mule cart and driver, the drivers dressed in handmade coats, boots and flannels. There wasn't an electric wire evident, nor a water source more sophisticated than a town pump being worked by two teenage girls with ruddy faces filling wooden buckets. Out in the fields beyond the buildings were some primitive barns, their roofs sagging, but few animals apparent this late in the day, just a couple of goats and some sheep. Were there more telephones here than in Tolgy, Lili wondered, more numbers than seven?

Lili stepped down onto the winter platform and arranged her coat and bag. She checked to see if any of the travellers from Budapest had made it this far. She had not heard the yelping dog once. Where had it got off, and where was the man with the newspaper? While there were others who disembarked, Lili felt she'd travelled to the farthest remove from the city, as far as she'd been since she'd fled her town, and she felt strangely more at ease here than in Budapest. She felt a thrill, too, in the nearness of Simon, wherever he was.

The festive woman approached Lili with a smile and held out the mittens and rattled the string of peppers as if they were bells. She asked for whatever Lili could pay. Lili offered fifty pengos for the peppers, garlic and a little information. "Sixty pengos," the woman said, "and I'll give you the information free of charge, but no garlic."

"Fifty-five," Lili said, "but you have to throw in the information. And the garlic."

"Sixty-five with the garlic."

"Sixty."

The woman paused. She looked healthy in these lean times and in the failing winter light, her cheeks plump and pink. What a cheerful wretchedness was here, thought Lili. If the woman didn't manage to sell her peppers, she had them to eat that evening, and her children had the woollens to keep them warm.

"Sixty, then," the woman said. She pulled a sheet of butcher paper from a backpack Lili hadn't noticed and quickly wrapped up the peppers and garlic. Lili gave her the coins, and the woman eyed them as if they were jewels. Her lips moved as she counted. She pocketed the money in her apron.

"I need to get to the labour camp," Lili said slowly, as if to a foreigner. "The place where they make munitions."

The woman seemed to turn cold. At first, Lili thought she wouldn't tell as promised. "It's over there." She pointed to the east of the station.

"Where?"

"You can walk through Szemzo's fields back there and take the gravel path that winds to the left and then forks. Keep left. Up into the mountain on the left. Arpad. That's its name, but it won't be telling you that. Arpad. Five hours, maybe, in *summer* five hours." Lili felt the darkness encroaching, felt the chill. The woman turned away. "Or," she said over her shoulder.

"Or what?"

The woman stopped and turned. A shrewd look had come over her rosy face. "Ten pengos," she said.

Lili wanted to be older than she was—with more authority—and bigger. She wanted to puff herself out. "All right. Ten more."

The woman would not say anything until Lili had dug out the additional coin. "Just around the clump of trees," she was pointing the same way, "on the way to Szemzo's, there's an army truck parked at the side of a large wooden place. They'll take you, you can be sure." The woman had a sly look now.

"An army truck?"

"Yup. Hungarians, don't worry. Guards at the camp." The woman winked.

Lili swallowed a cold lump of air. "I don't know Szemzo's."

"Over there," the woman said, pointing again, turning a corner with the crook of her finger. She pocketed the coin and hurried off.

Lili walked briskly around to where the woman had pointed, looking for Szemzo's fields and wondering who he might be. She came to a line of trees between two corn fields but could not see an army truck or any building. She could see several mountains hulking in the distance. She walked the length of a field, still following the route she believed the woman had indicated. At the next line of trees she saw a path and took it.

The day was coming to the end of its light. Crows sat heavily in the branches above her head and called out like weathermen. Snow had begun to fall. It fell in clumps, which looked in the near-darkness like white blossoms. The last sight Lili could make out was a stable to her right—at the end of this field, most likely, but that would not have been the direction the woman had suggested. She walked along the path, feeling the stones beneath her pliant leather shoes. They were sensible, warm, flat shoes, but not boots, and now the snow drove into her face and she had to pull her scarf over her ears and around her mouth. The satisfied crows flew off to tell others.

The truck might have departed, and she could be stumbling through the cold, blindly searching for something that was not there. She could try to hold the path for the five hours the woman had suggested, but what if she made it to the gates of the labour camp after lights-out? She could be turned away, or worse. Daylight made more sense by foot, or by truck, if she were lucky enough to come upon it the next day. The barn looked like a good bet for the night, better than the fields and the rushing snow.

Lili groped around its walls, feeling for the door. The ground was hard, but then Lili's feet encountered a soft patch. She couldn't tell what it was. She couldn't smell anything but the pummelling snow, fresh but fierce. She found a latch and it gave easily, and as she tugged on the door it squeaked and then groaned. Lili shot her hand to her mouth and froze, wondering if the farmer had heard.

She stepped into the building out of the snow and could smell the fresh dung. And then she could hear shuffling and clumping, some snorting and neighing, the sounds of horses. She was in a horse stable. She carefully closed the door, though it yelped again on its rusty hinges, and worked her way across the wall until she came to a stall and then a second one.

She chose the second one, opened the gate and stepped in carefully. The warmth was welcoming despite the dung. A horse nickered as Lili's hand found its rump. She felt more secure now. Lili removed her gloves and patted the great beast beside her, finding the horse's flank, its mane and neck. The animal swung its head around toward the girl. Lili wished she could see it, to check what colour it was, what sex, what age. She guessed from her cursory feel that it was fairly young, well fed and exercised, with a good oil sheen on its back. She groped its tight shoulder, its chest, its thigh. A good animal.

Lili walked up and down in the space beside the horse to determine how much room she had and whether the area had enough clean straw. She found a place in the corner away from the animal's front legs and put down her satchel. The horse gently nickered and grunted. Lili was well-prepared. After feeling with her hands to confirm she had chosen the right place, she took out her fur sleeping bag, unfolded it halfway and settled herself down on it. She felt for an egg in the handkerchief, imagined the red checks of the cloth. She loosened the collar of her coat and leaned back against the planks of the corner. She was comfortable, surprisingly comfortable. It occurred to her she could do with less, and she contemplated leaving the sleeping bag unopened and clean for Simon, but she reasoned that if it was just straw beneath her, she could brush it off easily in the morning. Knowing Simon, Lili also predicted he would tell her he preferred the luxurious bag with her warm scent in it anyway, or maybe he just said those things. And so she ate her egg and tidied up after herself, sprinkling the eggshell in the horse's feed. The horse whinnied quietly, approvingly, it seemed to her. She prepared to go to sleep, using her coat rolled up in the satchel as a pillow and the fur sleeping bag as her bed. She lay back, took a deep and happy breath, satisfied she had made it this far, confident she could complete her mission and make Simon as happy as she was now. She could hear pigeons cooing in the rafters, and something whooshed by her head, a bat, possibly, as it surveyed the barn for insects to eat. She heard the snow brushing against the outside of the wall but could not feel a draft. The stable was well constructed and the horses as happy as she was.

Lili drifted away in the folds of the little fur pallet she'd fashioned for herself. The dung-laden air took on a hint of espresso, she was certain. And Budapest. Gerbeaud. With its glass cases laden with fancy cakes of all kinds. Goodness, Gerbeaud slices and Dobos torte. Hadn't Gerbeaud once been turned into a stable for the cavalry in the Great War? Did the dung still infuse the chocolate air, beckoning the hardened and bitter and dour wanderers of Vorosmarty Square to step into its sugared walls to gladden their day?

How nice it would be down here in the dung with the espresso lava flowing over her—and him—if she and Simon could wait it out in the straw stable among the driftwood horses and the whirling bats as the war and the world went by. How simple it would be and nice, with all that had happened to her in her short life and to him in his, to sink and dissolve into the compost of this far-flung stable.

The Pompeians might never have been remembered if the warm lava had not made moulds out of them, and out of their tables and chairs, their dogs, their vases, their wine goblets, statues and toilets. Warm rock. Warm Italian rock. What a forger of memory. Cooled. Cold Aryan rock. Is the forger of human memory better cold and hurled than warm and flowing?

Who knew, and who would mind in the million-year-old field, except for the lecturer for the sake of her notes and for the photographs in a scrapbook of resurrected human bones, cool and catalogued and curated?

She remembered just then that Tolgy hadn't even a sign to identify the town and no one there anymore to tell anyone who happened by. The town council had been talking about erecting a marker, but never got around to it. So now, newcomers could simply arrive, occupy the houses, and call the town whatever they chose. Or no one could come for a million years, until the lecturer came with her students and formulated a hypothesis as to what this was and where all the ancient people had gone to, all of a sudden.

Lili sank into a rapture as the neighing of her companion in the stall beckoned her upward again and outward. She felt the horses around her, felt them breathing and snorting, pictured them thundering within their stable, waiting to burst out upon the fields all the way to the end of their flat Earth.

Twenty-Five

SOMEONE WAS TAPPING on the door of the little house on Alma Street. In his cellar, Istvan waited for the visitor to go away. But the visitor's tapping turned into an intruder's banging, and the banging went on for several minutes. If Istvan waited long enough, the whole of Tower Town would descend on him and Smetana.

So he rose from his cellar, heard the cat stir above him, pushed aside the planks and peered at the door. Anna Barta was gawking right at him through the window. He clapped a hand over his heart. She'd given it quite a workout.

"Let me in," she mouthed, and she pointed at the door. "Let me in."

He looked through the window beyond Anna and then rushed to open the door. She had brought a big pot of autumn cabbage, potato and pork. "Not kosher," she said to him as she lifted it up from the front step with a grunt and carried it into the house. She had a small burlap sack with her, too, and from it she pulled six apples, two jars of apricot jam, a small loaf of bread and another book. "Kafka," she said. "Your Kafka. *The Castle*. Maybe *your* castle, too." And she laughed at her own wit.

"Probably," Istvan said.

She wiped it across her chest to remove a smudge from the cover and showed the book to Istvan, but said right away, "Hide it—put it away—safe—quick." He put the book down the front of his pants, behind the belt.

She looked back at the door. Then she pulled a big preserving jar from her purse and whispered, "Tea, with lemon and honey—*lemon*, can you believe it? If I had a mother to trade, it wouldn't have been enough for this lemon. Maybe a mother plus a husband—when they still had a pulse. May God rest their blessed souls."

Istvan shook his head and smiled with delight.

Smetana was purring militantly and weaving himself around the visitor's ankles. Anna lifted the pot lid, poked around with a finger inside, pulled out a hunk of pork bone and gristle, found a plate to put it on, and set it on the floor for the cat.

She sucked her finger clean, said to Istvan, "Now you sit down, too," and used the same finger to poke him in the chest. She set out a new plate for him, found a serving spoon and ladled out an ample portion of the stew. He sat on the floor out of sight of the window and ate as ravenously as Smetana. Anna got the hint, looked out the window and slid down to the floor herself. All one could hear was chomping and smacking. Anna watched them both, but then Istvan thought she was watching him too closely. She took hold of his ear and said, "You have a rash." She was breathing down his collar now, then poking. "It goes all the way down here. What is it?"

"Who knows," he said, with his mouth half full. "Scurvy, for all I know."

"Drink the tea," she said. She ran to get a glass. "Right away." While she was on her feet, she said, "I have a skin cream," and set to finding it in her big black leather purse. "It's something a friend cooks up. It's the best cream I've ever seen. I covered my husband's whole back and front with it once when he had a burn in his factory. In two weeks, he was clean as a baby—and hairless as a baby's ass."

She was a walking hospital. She didn't know which good medicine to administer first: nourishment for his stomach, drink for his ailment, balm for his rash, a story for his starved mind, company for his lonely heart.

"You're an angel," he said, as she slathered cream down his neck and behind his shirt.

"Hardly," she said.

"There aren't many angels in this time."

"Achhh." She waved him off.

"Trust me," he said again, "you are an angel."

"As long as you're not the devil, we'll be just fine," she said.

"How do you know I'm not the devil?"

She pointed to her nose. "I suss these things out, and I'm never wrong." She was shaking her head. "No, you're just a dentist, a lonely dentist. In the wrong time. The wrong place." She took a deep breath. "And where is your poor Marta, the poor dear?" She sniffled, and he was surprised to see she was crying. "I hope she comes back to us," Anna said, "to her home. She's not even a Jew, and they took her." Anna sighed.

Istvan paused. He couldn't take another bite, so Anna grabbed his spoon from him and began force-feeding him. "Please," he said through a full mouth, "I'll have some later. I'll be so happy to know it's here for later."

"Oh, it'll be here," she said, "and I'll bring you some more, too."

Anna went to tidy up. She finished the last scraps from his plate herself. She turned on the faucet, but it was dry. "I stole a pot full of water last night from a neighbourhood well," Istvan said. "I keep it covered with a lid under the sink." He was pointing.

"Let me give a sip to the cat." She looked for a saucer. "I'll bring you more on my next visit."

"You can't come back here," he said. "You're endangering your own life."

"What's to endanger? I've lived a life. You still have some left in you." She crossed herself. "Let's hope and pray."

She washed his dish, and she waited for him to finish his tea before taking the glass, too. He felt the honeyed liquid flowing to his very extremities, irrigating the crumbling channels of his body.

He wanted desperately to get to the Kafka, but what was a book, he asked himself, beside real human company? There would be plenty of time for the book. "Is there news of the world out there, the war?"

She thought he meant Marta. "I check for you every day. They post the names of the returnees at the post office. No. Not *yet*."

"Anything else?"

"Yes, Eichmann is still in Budapest. The German army's still there. They're clearing out Hungary the way they cleared out Prague and Poland, too. On the transports. I don't know it for sure, one hundred percent—it's not the stuff you see in the papers, exactly— but Mr. Cermak told me he heard it from a reliable source. And it's in the coffee houses, so he's not the only one who says so. I heard they've taken a half-million. I heard it from Denes Cermak, the newsman, but off the record, of course. He has his sources. They moved from the outside in, clearing the countryside first—every last man, woman and child of Jewish blood—even old crows like me." She brought her hands together like a vise. "And now they've moved in on the capital—they're clearing out the big city, too."

"Jesus," Istvan said.

"They'd take him too," she said. "Do you have many people there still? Family?"

"Yes. Maybe. My brother and sister, cousins, uncles, aunts."

Her vise hands became praying ones and she tapped her lips with them as she looked ceilingward.

"But the Russians are not lying down, either," she said. "I heard they've taken heavy losses, but losses don't mean much to Josef Stalin. He has more losses to give. They're driving toward Hungary and Poland and here. They're not far off now. It's only a matter of time. And I hear they're twice as fierce as the Germans, what's left of them."

"What's left of them?" Istvan asked.

"Oh, yes. They're not on easy street anymore. They're taking losses, too, and they're not as content about it."

"Content—ha."

"I want to see the place you've been living, you poor dear. I want to see that hole in the floor." She pointed. The planks were still laid to the side.

A chill rode down Istvan's spine. No one other than Marta had ever seen his hiding place. He felt an element of his security slip away. Who else might soon know, even if the information were shared with the best of intentions? Anna liked the coffee houses, too, and she liked to tell stories.

His hesitation registered on her. "You won't tell anyone, will you?"

She put her hand on her heart. "Who would I tell?"

"Anyone."

"Do you think I brought you a pot of meat to fatten you up for slaughter, you and your little cat?"

"I don't think you did, but you can understand."

"It's too late for that, to tell you the truth. I already know. Seeing it is just dressing. To me, if it's a piss-hole or a shit-hole it hardly makes a difference." So she *had* been shaping the story in her mind. She was a lovely, kind, innocent old blabbermouth. "You were at my place some time ago. I got the juice out of your life story then. You'd be *dead* by now if I'd run off at the mouth."

"That's true," he said. She looked hurt. "I'm sorry." She nodded her forgiveness. "I'm so sorry."

"I never lived in a hole. I can imagine what it does to people. We're not moles or badgets." She pointed to her temple. "I'm amazed we're still chatting, to tell you the truth. You've got a tough, stone head and a good beater. You Jews are tough bastards, I swear." She crossed herself. "The ones who keep making it through the ages. You're tough bastards and bitches, the lot of you."

He was meant to feel flattered. Anna was beaming. "Well," he said, "we're being put to the test now, aren't we."

"You are," she said quietly, sadly.

"And tough as I am, where would I be without Marta? And *you*."

"Thank you, dear," she said.

"You're thanking me? Come, good lady, let me show you my lair."

She grunted as he helped her down the wooden ladder to his dark cellar. He came up again to fetch the cat, who was happy to accompany them. He'd spent surprisingly little time down here with Istvan.

Anna was aghast at the pallet on the floor, the dusty blanket, the bucket in the corner, the mustiness, the darkness. She crossed herself yet again. "Oh, my Lord. Is this any way to treat a living thing—*any* living thing?"

"I don't think I'm classified as a living thing," Istvan said.

"Come, stay with me," she said. "You'll be safe, I swear. No one will suspect me of monkey business. I'm too old and foolish."

"Foolish you're not," he said, "and not even terribly old."

"You are a dear," she said. "Worth saving. But you have to move to my place, I insist."

"I wouldn't dare. It's not possible." He had to wait for Marta to return.

Anna looked up out of the hole. They heard the distant buzz of an engine, a motorcycle. The sound intensified. It was approaching. Not many motorcycles came to Tower Town.

"Stay down," Istvan said, "and absolutely quiet." Anna crouched. "Not a sound."

He dashed up the ladder with the agility of a trapeze artist to replace the planks. As he did so, the motorcycle stopped right outside the house. Istvan crept back down and put a hand on Anna's mouth to remind her. Where was the cat? He couldn't feel Smetana with them, and then the soft weaving through his ankles reassured him. He could feel the animal purr, his little engine running while the big one roared above them.

Someone slapped the door rather than knocked. Then a voice, not speaking to the door, but to someone else. Then a reply. Two men speaking German. They slapped the door again and said something, but the motorcycle made it impossible to understand.

Then the engine was switched off. Istvan gripped Anna's hand in the dark. She was trembling. The quiet was more menacing than the roar of the motorcycle. There was some fidgeting at the door, and Istvan believed finally that his hour had come. Would they look through the window? Would they see the pot and dishes—the bowl on the floor? The wait was over. And this unfortunate woman had been caught with him.

He wondered about his Marta, home at last when this was all over, tired, hurt but not beaten. She would find three dead creatures in her small house, stiff and decaying, the stink long vanished, the ghosts flown, ready for burial in a single small plot in the back among the weeds and angelica. Home at last, his Marta, her Odysseus to his Penelope, home to her little place with the tiny garden and the prodigious memory, the curled-up ghosts hovering above the diminutive house like a Chagall, the suitors awaiting her, ready in a moment to start anew, unfettered, with his raven-haired beauty.

The fidgeting at the door ceased. Surely these men were capable of blowing off the lock. What were they waiting for? The motorcycle started up again. Istvan and Anna could smell the diesel exhaust seeping in from above. The men said something more in German and then one of them chuckled. The machine growled once and then bellowed as it left the house, transforming itself into a drone and then a buzz before vanishing. The silence burned.

A minute passed. Two. "Let's get up," Anna whispered. She grunted as she prepared to stand.

"No." Istvan held her down forcefully. "We have to stay where we are." They thought they heard a sound—they froze—but it might have been the cat. "One of them might have stayed." She could barely hear him. He put his lips to her ear. "They might suspect something, and one of them might have stayed behind. He might be watching the house."

"Why?" she whispered.

"He might be waiting for us to come out, or for someone to come in."

The two of them listened. Smetana made himself comfortable in Anna's generous lap. "We can't talk anymore," Istvan said, barely audibly. "Let's not take a chance. You'll spend the night."

He urged her back on his pallet. She wasn't sure what he meant at first. He gave her shoulder a firm push, but she resisted. Then she relented and eased back, clutching the cat against her bosom.

They lay together until their breathing was steady. He felt grateful, suddenly, to have been given a reason to extend Anna's visit. She couldn't leave now, no matter what. She was another human being from the world outside, with the world's fragrance and with its provisions. He was someone to care for when no one else needed or appreciated her efforts. Soon her warm shoulder and arm rested against his taut and bony one. The touch unlocked other times in their lives, better ones. He took her hand in his. Anna made a sound that he thought, at first, came from the cat, but it was closer to the burbling of a pigeon than a purr. He was feeling better than he had in weeks, and he was drifting. Come back to me, Marta, if you can. Come back to me is all I ask. Forgive me for the anguish I've caused and come back.

He awoke to her laughing and to the thorny cat using his chest as a pad to launch himself to the darkest corner of the room. "Look at these bars of light," she was saying. They'd spent the whole night together.

"Sshhh," he said.

"Look at them," she whispered.

The celestial beams were making their journey across the two of them on the floor, crossing both of them out, one each. She put her hand under the light to study it more closely and giggled again as quietly as she could. He took the hand and kissed it. She giggled again. "Thank you," she whispered.

She sat up. "I need to go to the toilet."

He pointed to the bucket in the corner.

"Not for me," she said. "What am I going to sit on and wipe myself with, my dress?"

"The toilet upstairs has no running water, and you can't go up there anyway."

"What—*forever*?"

"No, just for now."

"And what if they find me? What then? I'll say I was scavenging for food and picked the lock. Do you think I'm the first who's done that since the war started? I'll make like a lunatic. They want nothing from me, Dr. Beck, believe me. They wouldn't even waste a bullet. I'm going up to piss. Then I'm going to use some of your water to flush. Don't worry, I'll bring you more."

So she did, taking care to replace the planks after she'd climbed out. He waited, listened attentively. She did her business and then she crossed the floor. She was making herself far too busy up there.

A minute later, she said to him, not whispering, "It's safe, come up." She'd lifted a plank and was talking into the hole.

He gathered up Smetana and climbed the ladder. He stole to the window, peered out in every direction until he saw something fluttering from his doorknob, a white tag. It had been tied to the door. "Look," he said.

She joined him at the window. "What is it?" She stood at the window in full view of the world. "It's a piece of cardboard. White. It has something written on it."

She opened the door, took the tag off the knob and read, "*Verlassenen Besitz*"—"Abandoned Property." And now he could laugh, too, with some relish.

Twenty-Six

LILI HEARD A CRACKING SOUND, which echoed through the fields against the mountains. A second shot and she was fully awake. The horses were bucking furiously. Their neighing had turned into shrieks. Lili opened her eyes to see the whites of her companion's eyes in the stall and to see him rear against the wooden constraints. He was a stallion. The horses had spooked the pigeons, who shot into the air and flapped up against the rafters—up but not out, frantically trying to comprehend the new, low, unyielding sky. Lili jumped to her feet, too, and yanked up her sleeping bag to protect it. All the horses were whinnying, bucking and shrieking as they tried to vault over their troughs and smash their stalls. Something whirred by her face like a shot—a sparrow or starling—and spun past a post in a flurry of feathers.

Lili could detect in the dust and smoke the beginnings of morning as its light cut through the far boards. She must have been asleep for hours. She braced herself against the boards of the stall. Her horse saw her now, she was sure, her own boy. He was a noble Arab, smoky white with black tips and black eyes.

Who had fired the gun? The farmer? No, not the farmer. And not the Germans. They wouldn't waste the bullets. Not the Arrow Cross. Who was out there to frighten? The men in the truck? Goodness. The men in the truck.

They fired again and Lili could hear voices whooping. Her Arab kicked and bucked, as did the others, the Lipizzaner in the neighbouring stall, and another Arab, a smaller one. There was nothing to calm them down. They wouldn't hear calm talk, nor receive pats and caresses, even if she could get to each one of them. But she found herself unafraid of the horses. She would brace herself, hold tightly to her small corner and wait out the storm. She couldn't pass by her Arab's bucking hooves in any case. She would wait out the beasts of the barn and the beasts of the field.

It was an hour at least before the stable settled again into snorts and whinnies and some chomping of hay and slurping of water. Lili watched her horse drink with his sloppy tongue. Nothing like fear and hysteria to work up an appetite. Daylight had come and, while the barn was still dark, Lili could make out the sheen on the horses' backs and bellies. How far was the farmer that he had not heard his animals' cries? What if there had been a fire? How far was the truck with the soldiers? Had they collapsed in a heap somewhere or were they waiting for some more fun? Or had they departed? She would not have heard over the shrieking horses. She needed to see, to get out quietly, if she could pass undetected through the squealing door.

Lili straightened herself out, brushed the fur of her sleeping bag, packed it away, buttoned herself into her coat and combed her fingers through her hair. What a sight she must be. How could she make herself presentable for her prospective drivers? How could she make herself pretty for Simon? It had been too long since she'd seen him, and she hadn't eaten well. What a sight she must be, what a surprise.

She patted her horse, and he whinnied for her. She made her way out of the stall and to the door and found a crack she could peer through. She could see little at first but the white field laid out like linen over a grand supper table. She took in a whiff of the horse-fresh morning. The field was abutted by a row of birch trees, which, with their white bark, stood like a line of naked girls caught by the cold.

And then her eye took in with a thrill the blue mountains looming to her right. The partial view barely allowed her to ascertain their dimensions, so she had to step out, had to find her way on this last leg of her journey.

When Lili emerged into the winter morning, announced by a yowl from the stable door, she was charmed momentarily into complacency. The sight called to mind the very first music she'd heard on a phonograph. It was some music by Mendelssohn her father had brought from Prague along with the phonograph itself. One record, one phonograph. David Bandel had said it was "A Midsummer Night's Dream" because it sounded like the woods and fields the composer had wandered through. What struck Lili that day, when she was no more than eight or nine, was that the notes sounded like the country they depicted, as free and as lively—she hadn't realized until then that there might have been different kinds of country meadow. And that was what it would sound like here, too, sweet and lovely, to anyone who heard it with the blue mountains standing over these fields covered in white linen, awaiting their silver and their summer supper.

Dr. Beck had once said that one could fall for a piece of music as deeply as one did for a lover. He said it after he'd played a recording of Schubert's songs without words. One piece in particular, which featured the cello, cried out at the listeners—seemed to fill them up—as they sat digesting their meagre dinner. When the music finished, Klari objected to what her husband had said about music and love, but then went about repeating it when he was not present as if it were wisdom newly distilled by her.

Lili heard the men's laughter and turned to see the truck the woman had told her about the day before. It sat parked across from a ramshackle house with a red porch. A forgotten blouse flapped from the porch railing like a flag. How could she have missed the house as she'd made her way to the stable? She heard another guffaw from the parked truck and then saw a man with a rifle standing beside it. He set down his rifle to urinate into the field, but as he began, he saw her, too, and there was a flicker in the flow of the urine before he resumed. He took a quick look at his rifle. Lili was conscious, now, that all that stood between her and the remainder of her days was the whim of this soldier.

The soldier buttoned himself up and picked up his weapon again. He called out to her in Hungarian. "Get over here. Hey, you, get over here."

A woman half-dressed in red and royal blue burst out of the back of the truck with a giggle and ran off toward the ramshackle house. Her hair was red, too, and half of its pins had fallen out so that she looked ruffled and plucked. The soldier who'd called to Lili turned and aimed his rifle at the woman's back as she ran, wriggling to adjust her clothing against the chill air. Lili gasped and paused in her tracks. The man continued to aim but then turned his rifle on Lili before pointing skyward and firing in the air. The report alarmed the horses again. Lili could hear them screaming and bucking.

She resolved to proceed toward the man. If she turned and ran like the woman, the next bullet would certainly be aimed at her back and, if it missed, the one after that. She had no choice but to advance. "Hey," the man shouted again, urging her toward him, the voice ringing around the mountains.

He aimed his rifle directly at her again, squinted one eye while locating her in his sights with the other. It might have been the forthrightness with which she now walked, the boldness of her stride, or maybe just the look of her, small, young, scrawny frame, maybe a look that reminded him of someone—his daughter, possibly, or a niece—but the man lowered his rifle again to his side and waited for her patiently.

When she got close, she saw he was a big man with a moustache and wore a Hungarian soldier's brown uniform. A Hungarian officer—he had a sergeant's three stripes on the arms of his coat. She remembered the Hungarians who'd rampaged through Tolgy, through her town and her house.

He said nothing to her but waited for her to speak. She heard a man's voice inside the truck, then another guffaw. The horses behind her were still kicking and complaining.

"Sergeant Erdo," someone called from inside. "You missed your turn with that red thing we had in here, and she was good and red all over." They hooted and howled as Erdo stared at Lili, not once averting his gaze. They listened to the men inside laughing, but she, too, kept her eyes on Erdo.

She'd heard his name before. It had appeared in Simon's letter. The nasty Erdo. A chill came over her. She felt for the satchel at her side, and he looked at it, too. "I would like to go to the labour camp where they make munitions," she said in a measured voice, as if speaking too quickly would jeopardize her chances of succeeding. "My husband is there. I'd like to see him and give him a few things to make him more comfortable."

"Your husband," he said, "and who might that be?"

"Simon Beck. He has black hair and brown eyes."

"An inmate. You don't need to describe him to me. I know who he is." Erdo stroked the barrel of his rifle. The steel must have been cold in the winter air. "Why don't you come into the truck? It's warmer inside." He said it like a wolf, his eyes narrowing, and he pointed to the rear of the vehicle with his weapon. The men inside had heard their voices and had stopped talking. One broke out laughing again.

Erdo stepped up to the back and opened the door. Lili could see three men sitting inside, two of them in some disarray, and the third, the one in the middle, the more composed one, holding a knife. They all sobered up instantly. Lili smiled. She didn't know she could have such a deadening effect on people and wondered how best, under the circumstances, to make use of the ability.

"Get in," Erdo said from behind, "we'll take you."

The one who'd laughed, the one to her left, who was the most dishevelled but looked the youngest, as young as she was, a year or two older at most, snickered again but looked away. Lili got a sick feeling in her gut as she climbed in quickly, unobtrusively, hoping only to sit on the floor on her bag. "Please," she said to no one in particular. She checked behind her suddenly, feeling Erdo might be smiling, but found him serious and earnest, almost gentlemanly looking.

As she stood uncomfortably in the back of the warm truck by the door, she could feel how musky it was and was grateful for the winter air pouring in behind her. She could smell the heat of sex, remembered the fresh scent of dung in the stable she'd crept out of.

Erdo had now climbed heavily into the truck behind her. She could sense his shadow on her back as big as a tree, could feel his breath on her. The soldier in the middle, directly in front of her, pulled a coiled sausage out of a bag beside him, a thick Romanian sausage big as an arm, and cut off a hunk and offered it to her with a greasy thumb and forefinger. She'd told herself never to refuse food but found lately she was doing so all the time. She shook her head. "Maybe later, thank you."

He smiled and passed the hunk of meat to the dishevelled man beside him. She tried to share his smile. He cut off another hunk and jammed it into his own mouth. He chewed with relish. Erdo slammed the door behind him, shutting out the light and the cold. Lili could still not see him without turning around entirely. The sausage cutter gave a third piece to the third soldier, and a fourth he offered to Erdo. Erdo didn't answer. She could hear him puffing, panting almost. The soldier held the piece up to her again. She felt she should accept it, but first she wanted to settle. The whole rear of the truck smelled of sausage now. It had overtaken the scents of sex and the winter air.

Lili made as if to sit down, setting her satchel carefully on the floor. The sloppy young man to her left shoved over, indicating she could sit with him, but then she felt a large hand on her side at her waist, then her hip. The man who'd offered his seat sobered up. His eyes widened as he saw what his sergeant intended.

Lili heard a belt buckle clang behind her and became light-headed, ready to faint away, but instead she picked up her bag and pressed it to her chest, as if lifting a bit of home with which to shield herself.

Erdo swung her around and tried to kiss her, but she turned her face and his clammy lips slid off to her ear. His pants were down around his ankles. The three other men didn't move or make a sound. They receded into the darkness of the walls of the truck.

"Please," she said.

Erdo advanced and she slipped and fell back onto her haunches. Nothing was there to cushion her fall and no one to catch her. Her coat was open, revealing her green serge dress. When had Erdo managed to undo the buttons? She tried to brace herself, to clench her teeth. She lay down, let her head drop back, because she could not bear to look. She gazed instead into the calm darkness of the ceiling. She decided at that moment that, if she survived, no one would ever know it had happened, not Simon, not Klari, not Robert, not Paul, not her family, if she ever saw them again.

She felt her dress being flipped up to her neck. She didn't want her dress torn. Then Simon would know right away. And how would she travel back? Would she even be seeing Simon now? Was this the price of admission into the camp? If not, would they let her go back? Could this be her last stop, this army truck?

Her underwear was torn from her body. She could feel the steamy draft between her legs. She'd be torn again, this time flesh. She struggled now to look up at her assailant. He was a bear, immense, with a dark battering ram ready to break open the gate. She managed against her slamming heart to squirm a hand into the pocket of her satchel beside her.

She remembered Mary. "Can I give you an egg instead?" She held it out to him in her palm.

He smiled broadly and snorted out a burst of laughter. "Yes, but not a chicken egg."

She felt the ram softening slightly against her inner thigh, like a mollified beast. He bent to his target again, determined to press on. She saw the whites of his eyes now, grey in the darkness, like the bucking Arab stallion's eyes, felt him between her legs, pressing against the opening, too immense by far for the opening, as big as the head of the baby, surely, that might pass out the other way. She must not imagine it. She must not think a single additional thought.

He wanted to tear open her dress at the neck, but she fought him, so he struck her hard across the face. She could taste the blood in her mouth, but she didn't cry, felt she shouldn't. The bear leaned forward to chew on her ragged lips.

She was plugged, felt she would be ripped in two. A fierce burning pain shot up from her loins, volcanic, and he was still not in her, not ready to proceed. Her innards tried to run from their assailant. He reared up below and slid over top. He grunted and huffed above her, his humid breath acrid and hungry with a bear's hunger.

And then she heard a slamming noise. It might have been a gun, but it wasn't, because light washed over the hulking mass above her and the cold fell over them again, fresh and alive. The back door was open. Behind her, upside down for her, were the three sausage eaters, boys now, she could see, no more, just boys who had left their fields and shed their ragged farm clothes to take up a proud uniform and bear arms more powerful than life itself, as powerful as heaven and Earth and the Lord and the devil.

"Get off her," she heard someone say. He'd found the way into her again and shoved at it, stopped his own breath as he prepared to buck. "Get off now!" the voice said again, this time more insistent. Erdo smiled like a madman—now I have you, his eyes were saying, now you're mine—and then his head took a crack and his face went silly, his own blood dripping into her hair, as he sank like a boulder on top of her. "Get him off her," she heard the voice say. The boys scrambled to their feet, all three of them.

Erdo was heaved off her to one side, and an officer, the voice's owner, a man with grey hair and stars on his epaulettes, flung the bear onto his back. "He needs an extra long rest," the officer said.

Lili got up on an elbow to gaze at her assailant. The ram still jutted out from his loins like a tree growing out of dense shrubbery with heavy thorn fruit hanging below it. This was not an instrument of love but an instrument of force. How would it have been possible to house such a tree in his pants? She swallowed more blood, felt Erdo's blood in her hair and on her cheek, looked between her outspread legs and saw none. She shut herself up quickly, dropped her dress, tried to sit up but took an extra moment. She should have felt humiliated. She did feel humiliated, but the beast had been vanquished, and she was alive to remember, even if not to tell. She took a wintry breath and let it out as quietly as she could. Her heart settled.

The officer ordered the men to button up their sergeant's protrusion. One snorted out a laugh but swallowed it quickly and leapt to carry out the task. The officer pointed to a wooden bucket in the corner. "Fill it with snow for the young woman. Let her pack some against her mouth and cheek."

Lili felt her cheek, could taste the swelling. She sat up and pulled herself toward the bench on the side opposite the officer. The soldier there shoved over. Erdo slept with a scowl on his face. Lili was more sore than she'd realized. She'd be unsteady if she stood.

"Thank you for stopping him," she said, feeling the flush on the cheek that was not sore. "If he'd succeeded, my life would never—I'd never—"

"Your life would have been over," the officer interrupted. "He'd have used you up, killed you with a single slug across the face and thrown you out the back."

For the first time Lili felt tears boiling up.

"Who are you?" the officer asked her, just as the men came back with the snow and set it beside her. They waited outside and whispered among themselves. Their colleague eagerly joined them. The snow in the bucket looked fresh and cool. She took some and packed it against her cheek, letting some of the crystals trickle into her mouth. She was so very dry. She took a bigger clump with the other hand and filled her mouth with it. It was an elixir. Then she took some for below. The officer turned his head.

After a moment, he cleared his throat to remind her of his question. She swallowed the cool snow. "I'm here to see Simon Beck, my husband. I've brought him some things."

"Do you think this is a tour bus?"

"No," she said. "Not any more than your camp is a proper place of business." She looked down now, amazed at herself.

"You are impudent," the officer said, and then added quietly, "and you are pretty, and brave." She looked at him, saw kindness in his eyes. If this was what she was, pretty to all, she wished she could soften the effect or heighten it at will, like a firefly, turn it off for Erdo, turn it on for the officer, down for the Germans, up for the Jews, reduce it for Mary on the train—the woman did not need competition—let it burn bright for Simon. The smile was a switch, she began to see, but could not gauge yet what other gesture would help. She hadn't been a woman very long.

The officer unbuttoned his breast pocket and fished out a handkerchief. He leaned across and offered it to her. It was monogrammed with an "F." He saw that she noticed. "Fekete, it stands for," he said gently. "Karoly Fekete. I am Commandant Karoly Fekete." He offered his hand now, too, and she shook it, feeling a little queasy again as she leaned forward. She glanced at her assailant and wished he could be covered over entirely or carried across the road to be left at the house where the woman lived. He could wake up in bed there and continue with his business.

"What have you brought for your Simon?"

"Something to keep him warm and a little something to eat."

"We don't allow visitors. Did you not know that?"

"I did, but I'd heard something."

"How could you have?"

She realized what path she'd stumbled onto and backed up. "Just a rumour, nothing more. I was hoping I could make it through. I wanted to appeal to someone."

"Young girl, where is your family?"

"My family?" She hesitated. "In Budapest."

"Aren't you sure?"

She paused again. "No," she said, and left it at that.

And so did he, softening his tone as he asked, "Are you indomitable?"

"I don't know. I don't know what it means."

"It means, not easily defeated."

"I don't know," she said.

"We don't allow visitors," the commandant said again and slapped the side of the truck. "Let's get a move on," he shouted. Two of the men clambered back into the rear of the vehicle, and the third, the one who'd sat on her right when she'd entered, jumped out and got into the front. She could hear the driver's door slam, heard the engine start.

She was expecting Commander Fekete to escort her off the truck, make her return to the train, maybe even send one of his men to help her board, and then she would have to walk to the labour camp after all with extra pain and wearing one garment fewer. But what, then, would be the point, if the commandant had already barred her? Who would be there to overrule him or persuade him?

She was surprised, as were the soldiers, it seemed, that Commandant Fekete hadn't taken a seat in the front with the driver. She tried to make sense of it. Surely it wasn't to look after her. Surely she was no more than a curiosity to the commandant. He didn't look at her across the darkness, or at anyone else. Maybe he just needed a moment to shut out the light and sit and think.

As for her, she was headed for Simon with the commandant of the camp to escort her in, albeit somewhat unwillingly. She felt bruised but hopeful. She was almost ready to ask for some sausage. She could have used a bite then, even if served by the greasy hands of the boy soldier sitting opposite her. She filled her mouth with snow again. It felt like a balm.

She would not tell Simon what had happened. He would take it upon himself to be gallant and react, and the commandant might not be there to intervene as Erdo slit their throats. As it was, she hoped she hadn't created unnecessary danger for Simon. But how could she have? Surely the impact she had could not be so significant.

Oh, dear Simon. Her *neshomeleh*, sweet soul. How she'd missed him. She was coming to make him a little warmer. The trip was worth it for that reason alone. She needed to come for her own sake as well as for his.

The truck grunted up the mountain, its gears shifting jaggedly and its engine protesting. She felt soothed by the vibration and the rumble, felt she needed the time to recover her balance and her spirit before seeing Simon. But it would not be a party, she knew that. She knew where she was headed and could only hope for the best.

"The Russians are coming," the commandant said across the darkness to no one in particular. "The Germans have taken over the reins now, and the Russians will come to try to drive them out. They will rampage over this land the way the Turks once did, and the Romans long before, and the Martians, for all we know. It's a land of rampaging tribes, and it always will be. They all are."

No one answered. "I don't know how long we can stay put," he went on, "especially with the Russians. They won't let us, not even if we made the munitions for them. They can't afford to let us. It's about saying who's boss more than anything, now."

And then the commandant stopped speaking. Everyone waited patiently for the next instalment of his thoughts, but he kept them to himself, and so the others went on with their own. Lili shrank back to considerations of Simon. She didn't want, just then, to think of anything else.

After two and a half hours the truck ground to a halt. Lili remembered what the woman in town had said. How could she have walked this distance up into the mountains in just five hours? Bad information, and it cost her. Erdo was still out cold, and the commandant ordered the guards at the gate to come and help lift him off the truck.

Lili didn't know what she'd been expecting of the camp. The kindness of the commandant had lulled her into believing that it might be tolerable if not comfortable, even with Erdo looming over it. The inmates were housed in four barracks that were more ramshackle than the horse stable Lili had spent the night in, and they were colder. Each building had a single small wood-burning stove at the far end but no wood left to fuel it. Whatever wood remained had to be used to fire the smelters for the making of dies for weaponry and for ammunition. There was a barracks for the soldiers attached to the kitchen, so it was a little warmer, and a smaller cabin for officers: Fekete, Erdo, a corporal and also official visitors. The factory, which the inmates walked to each day, was three kilometres away over rock and ice.

The inmates were off at the factory when Lili arrived. They wouldn't be back until dinner. They were fed once in the morning and once in the early evening, bread and coffee first thing and later a broth made of potato peels, carrot tops and turnips and hunks of stale bread. Once a week they were treated to an apple and another day to some cheese. Twice a week for breakfast, they ate salty porridge, which warmed their bellies for the walk ahead and the work.

Fekete told Lili when they arrived that, considering the hour, if she wanted to see Simon she could not get back to the train station until the next day. She of course had the option of leaving the package for Simon with a note and departing immediately. The commandant would see to it that Simon got the supplies. He looked upon her kindly—he was smiling—but he said, "If you decide to stay in the barracks tonight and cause a disturbance of any kind, I will have you both shot." The smile continued as the message hung in the air between them. "You'll spend the day working in the kitchen with Tildy, a local who works for us."

"Simon wrote that there was a man in the kitchen," Lili said, "an inmate—"

"He's gone," the commandant said as they walked. "He didn't make it. We need all the able-bodied men for the war effort."

Lili looked down.

"He didn't make it," Fekete said again without affect. She thought of Erdo, the cold.

Tildy didn't speak much to Lili as they got the food ready for the evening. Lili gazed into the cauldron of swill as it simmered on the biggest wood stove she had ever seen. Tildy didn't ask if Lili was hungry or what she was doing there, but she seemed to be wondering all the same. Maybe she was thinking Lili had been brought in to replace her. It was Lili herself who finally spoke. "I'm here just for a day. They've let me in to see my Simon."

"I don't know him," Tildy said coldly. "I don't know any of them. They're mangy." She looked straight at Lili with beady dark eyes, waiting to be challenged. Lili had a sister named Tildy. Nobody could have looked less like her sister than this woman. She was a big woman. Perhaps there was more to eat here in the kitchen than it appeared. She wore a tight hairnet to contain her short brown curls, giving her head the look of an animal caught in a trap. She had a scowl etched into her face, and she panted as she walked or spoke. "Set the tables," Tildy told her. "Then mop the kitchen floor and sweep the mess hall." Tildy pointed at each thing with her nose—the bowls, the dining room, the mop and the broom—and she snorted each time.

Lili rushed the work in the kitchen so she wouldn't have to spend more time than necessary with Tildy and drew out the work in the dining room, shining each spoon on the apron Tildy had provided. What kept her going was the thought of seeing Simon soon, in a matter of hours.

When the men came shuffling back, finally, she was not prepared for her second shock, a line of scrags entering through the gate. Simon's healthy, handsome face was drawn, his eyes were ringed with shadow, and his nose ran, a condition he shared with nearly everyone. He had lost all his youthful bulk, and he'd lost the lustre in his eyes. But then her eyes met his, and his face lit up. How was this miracle possible? his face seemed to be asking.

The other inmates looked even worse. They must have been here much longer than Simon. They were ragged. Some wore bandages unaccountably around their heads, one had a bandaged hand; some limped; many stared blankly, even at her, not even curious about who she might be.

As for the barracks, no one could care less that Lili was there. How could there be room for bawdiness in a place of such deprivation, so much dampening down of young men's spirits, turning them old and haggard in a few short months?

Lili kissed Simon in the dark barracks, and he held her as passionately as he was able. What was Lili doing here? Was she insane, risking her life this way? How could his parents have let her go? "It was my fault," he said, his eyes running now with his nose. "I should never have sent you the letter."

Lili showed him the fur sleeping bag, and his tears continued to pour. He put his head on her shoulder, and she told him it would not be long now before he would come home. It *could not* be long. She showed him the peppers and garlic and eggs and wafers, too, and his eyes and nose ran freely. Then she gave him the tobacco and he smiled.

It was only then that he noticed the swelling shine on one of her cheeks. "What happened to you?" he said. "Your cheek."

The other men were filtering out to the mess hall. As the last ones were leaving and Lili was about to answer, Erdo walked in. He, too, had a bandage around his head. The young lovers released each other and leapt to their feet.

"Go eat," Erdo said. Both Simon and Lili stepped forward. "Not *you*," he said to Lili. "What do you think this is—the Mercure Hotel?"

Simon looked at her and said, "I'll stay too." His voice shook with rage and fear.

Erdo stepped right up to Simon. He loomed over them both. "Go eat," Erdo said again and put the barrel of his revolver to the middle of Simon's forehead. "You're hungry."

"Go," Lili said, "*go*."

Simon left her, and she stood rooted in her spot, as did Erdo. Simon took as long as he could to get out the door and then waited outside, his chest boiling. A moment later Erdo followed. Simon walked quickly now, expecting a bullet in his back at any moment. At each step he told himself, now, or now, or now—but his hand was on the door of the mess hall, finally, and he was in.

Simon was the first one back to the barracks. He'd left his soup half finished, afraid he would find her gone when he got back. He'd never done that before.

He went straight to her. When he told her about the soup, she offered an egg again. "It will fill you the rest of the way," she said and cleaned the shell for him. "If only we had a little salt." They hadn't seen salt in months. She smiled and held out the egg in her palm, like a little white lamp in the dark room. Lili thought of Mary on the train, the wafers the previous morning at the church, the cabbage rolls, the horses, Erdo. Her mind raced.

Simon ate the egg with wolfish abandon, swallowing hard as she watched him. She thought she heard something and pulled her scarf up over her ears, covering her pretty Nordic features. "What a war," Simon said through a bulge in one of his cheeks. "Think of how different life would be if not for this war. I wouldn't have met you."

"We would have met somehow," she said. "What an awful way to bring about a fate, having to lose my family for you, much as I need you." She took his hand. "What a cruel trick."

They were sitting on his bed, the upper bunk, their legs dangling over the side. "Look how focused the war has made us—it's given us that—the power to focus all our attention." He swallowed the last of his egg with a good gulp. "Food, shelter, warmth, love, survival. Not parties, not ambling about the lake country, not cakes at Gerbeaud. Just survival. I've had so much time to think here, my God."

"I wish we could walk in the countryside," she said. "That's what I want."

He was happy to be speaking to her at all. He took both her hands in his.

"They brought new men today," Simon told her, "from another labour camp. They look worse than we do."

"Why did they come here?"

"Because theirs had been invaded by the Russians, and the Russians were brutal. They killed half the soldiers and half the inmates. The ones who made it here are the lucky ones."

"What a world," Lili said.

"And I know one of the men," Simon said. "I recognized him right away. It's Miklos Radnoti. He's a writer and an old friend of my cousin Istvan's."

"Did you speak to him?"

"Just for a minute. I don't know if he's staying. There's so much turmoil lately. Even the guards look worried."

"Were you able to ask him about Istvan?"

"Yes, he told me he warned Istvan when the Germans were entering Szeged, but he doesn't know what became of him. I'll try to talk to him again. Radnoti said he married a Catholic, but it didn't help him much."

"Who? Istvan?"

"No, Radnoti. Radnoti converted and then married a Catholic woman, named Fifi Gyarmati. We should look her up in Budapest."

"If only I could take you back with me right away."

He asked about his parents and about Rozsi and Paul.

What was to happen now? Lili wondered as they talked, as darkness fell in the drafty building. Would she spend the night with her Simon in a room full of men? Could they make love—their first time—when the barracks was quiet? Would it be right? Shouldn't they take whatever chances were handed to them—what if they could not again? Why should her true love not finish what the brute had begun back in the truck? She felt queasy again as Simon kissed her tenderly on the lips. His lips were cool and damp.

He looked at her close up. How was it possible she was sitting opposite him with her warm blue eyes looking back at him? "I began to tell you about Elemer," he said, wiping his nose on his sleeve, "in the letter." She dug out the handkerchief marked "F" for "Fekete." How would Simon ever have come by it, she thought, if not for the circuitous route by which he now held it? He was wiping his nose with the commandant's handkerchief.

"In the bunk below me. Elemer. He's very sick. He's going to cough his brains out tonight. I don't know how to help him. I found something out about him that nobody here knows." He was whispering. "No one, not any of the other inmates."

"Not the guards?"

"Especially not the guards. They don't know why he's here. They don't care. They just want to lord it over people—the more the better." They heard a sound, a knock, and he stopped talking. The men would be coming back from the mess hall soon. They waited but heard nothing more. The winter wind howled through the cracks in the walls. It was getting colder as darkness fell. "He's not even Jewish," Simon whispered. "Elemer's Catholic, but not like Radnoti. He started out Catholic. He's the one whose sister visited. I think someone did something awful to her here." He looked directly at the swelling on Lili's cheek. She thought he was going to ask again about it, but he didn't. "He spent time in Poland when the war broke. He's part Polish, from Warsaw. It was there—Warsaw—that the Germans erected a wall around a ghetto and sealed in the Jews. Some of his friends were sealed in, some people he worked with, maybe even a woman—he's a widower—when he's feverish at night he calls out the name of a woman named Delilah—that was not his wife's name—his wife was Dora—but it's *Delilah*, he moans. I asked him one afternoon at the factory when no one was in earshot who she was, and he turned red as an apple. You'd've thought I'd said I was sleeping with his daughter." Simon paused. That was not the example he'd wanted, but he pressed on. "Anyway, he acquired a great conscience in Warsaw, Elemer did. He's a physician. I didn't know that until I learned this story." He lowered his voice again. "No one knows that, either. He's a doctor, *was* a doctor, and he met someone in Warsaw, another physician by the name of Dr. Feliks Kanabus, who figured out a way to sew foreskins back on—skin grafts, they are, I guess. He figured out a way to graft skin onto the penis so that its owner could deny he was Jewish and prove it. Some had it done and got away." Lili could hardly hear Simon now, he was speaking so quietly. "Some went so far as to renounce their faith, start again, pretend they never were Jews. Dr. Kanabus was fearless. He performed the operation on hundreds of men. And apparently, when an old colleague from the university, another doctor, a Jew, got word to Dr. Kanabus that he—the Jewish doctor—and his wife were in the Warsaw ghetto and were doomed, Kanabus arranged to get some false papers issued for the Jewish fellow, marched into the ghetto himself under false pretences, and took the man and his wife out. He was like Wallenberg and Paul. So now they're living in Kanabus's house, for the remainder of the war, I guess, pretending to be a butler and a cook." Simon and Lili heard voices, footsteps outside. "Elemer did it, too, the operation, on quite a few Jews—he worked with Dr. Kanabus—but Elemer was caught and sent here because his citizenship is Hungarian. But his papers forwarded here merely said 'Resister,' nothing more. A document must have got lost in transit. Can you believe it?" Simon slapped his knee and chuckled, just as the men began coming back into the barracks. "What luck," he added quickly. "Fate—fate again."

The inmates looked at her, one after another, as they entered, and they stopped talking to one another. She tightened the scarf around her head and cinched it at the neck. She pulled her legs up onto the bunk. No one asked her or Simon anything, except Elemer.

He was the last to stumble in, coughing. He dragged himself toward the young couple. He was a man of fifty who looked seventy-five, an ill and feeble seventy-five at that. "Goodness," he said as he looked at her and coughed, doubled over, coughed again then pulled himself erect, as if it were an act of some kind. "You look a bit like my sister," he said, momentarily pleased, but then the coughing reminded him of his state. He fought to stay up, look a little healthier. He said hoarsely, "What happened to your lovely face?" He pressed a cold hand against her warm cheek, then pulled it away to cough into it some more.

Simon looked at her face again, too. "I fell on the ice near the train," she said. "There was a little patch of ice." Simon touched her cheek now, too, and kissed it.

"Can you *be* here?" Elemer asked. "Did the authorities let you in?" She nodded yes. "My sister came here—do you know that?" She nodded again and smiled.

And then he barked out a rapid sequence of coughs. He gasped and collapsed on his bed. He waved an apology at her. "You need a doctor," she said. "What can I do for you?"

He coughed out the word "nothing" and shook his head. "Nothing can be done," he said between bouts, and then he turned toward the wall and was asleep, coughing, spitting small coughs he could not swallow.

A corporal stepped into the barracks with a bang. He was the one officer Lili had not seen, and she felt caught in the act, worried her presence hadn't been explained. He looked directly at her, then down at Elemer, the only one fully recumbent already.

The corporal didn't say anything. People seemed to save their energy here or had nothing left to say. He didn't seem to care what he saw. In his gloved hand he held up a bright oil lantern, and the inmates all knew what that meant. They scurried into their bunks. No one in the room changed for bed. If anything, they bundled up with whatever warm layers they had for the cold night.

It was very dark with the lights out and very quiet, except for Elemer's cough, which hammered away at the dark and the silence like a lone protestor. Lili got down and laid out the fur sleeping bag for Simon, packed the few other things into the satchel and stuffed the bag under Elemer's bunk. She removed her coat to add to their bedding, then changed her mind. She covered Elemer with the coat, up to the chin, and he tapped her fingers in thanks. She took Simon's hand as she climbed back up to the upper bunk, stepping lightly on Elemer's bed to do so.

Simon whispered, "Let's get into the fur bag together—my mother's coat, goodness—you dears—what you cooked up for me." She felt his moist lips on her ears as he spoke and she trembled.

"We won't fit," she said. "How can we fit together?" She was afraid now and unsure.

"We wouldn't have a year ago, but now we will—for a single glorious night."

He removed his shirt and trousers, and she helped him slip her serge dress over her head, the chill bristling their young flesh. He breathed damp kisses into her mouth as he unsnapped her brassiere, and she pretended to remove underwear she no longer had on while he took off his.

They made love under cover of Elemer's coughs, Simon timing his movements to coincide with the poor man's bouts of hacking, all ears in the dark room alive to every errant squeak or grunt the lovers couldn't muffle. The inmates filled their final waking moments with thoughts of love and lust and, for the first time in some time, hope.

As the wind howled through the building's cracks, the whole place creaked and groaned. The lovers, the men, the coughing Elemer were sailing aboard an old galleon as it crossed a northern sea.

And then someone slammed into the darkness, a bright lantern preceding him. The dark figure was immense. Even though Lili didn't know who it was, she could guess it was Erdo. Lili closed like a flower, and Simon pulled away.

Erdo had come for them, she was sure, come for her, to settle a score. But Elemer stood in their way, Elemer's coughing, the wrenching of his battered frame, the beating of his chest and throat, an alarm that could not be quieted.

Erdo held up the lamp as he looked at the lovers in their fur bag, then down at the coughing lout, then up again at the lovers. He hooked the lantern to the post at the head of Simon and Lili's bed. Lili thought he was going to pounce. She felt Simon coil up, ready to spring at the man's throat. But it was Elemer that Erdo grabbed. He clutched the man's throat with his great, gloved hand, trying to choke off the convulsions, pulling the doctor to his rickety feet. All Elemer could do was rattle as he hung before the beast, rattle and cough, all the power of his being flying out through the cough. His eyes were closed as he dangled. He didn't have the energy left even to see.

Erdo left the lantern where it was on the bunk post, clamped the tiresome man's head under his arm and dragged him out into the blowing darkness. Everyone in the barracks could hear him cough, even after Erdo had stepped out and slammed the door shut behind him. The coughing continued, relentless, and then one shot sounded, and another, and the night fell quiet, except for the wind and the creak of the building.

Lili wept now, as did Simon. The lovers shone in the light, but no one dared look. Simon slid off the soft body that had held him, warm and perspiring—perspiring for the first time in two months. He turned away from Lili and cried, his body wrenching and choking, catching itself as they heard a sound outside, shuffling, the clomp of footsteps, a dragging sound. Soon, all fell quiet again, and the tears poured out, silently, cooling their faces in the cold room. Lili hugged

Simon from behind, and they waited in the halo of light for Erdo to return, but he didn't.

In the morning, before the others were up, Simon turned to Lili and whispered that he didn't know what was to become of their lives. "What if we never see each other again?" he asked. His eyes were red and tearful again.

"Please don't say that. Please rest some more. You'll need your energy." She hadn't slept a single moment in the lantern's cordon of light, but Simon had. His breathing had turned steady an hour after Erdo had left, and she'd felt the heaviness of his naked form. He flinched once or twice in the night but didn't wake up. It was the first time they'd spent a night in the same bed. She loved the smell of him, loved their smell together.

The corporal came into the room even before the winter light had peeped through the walls' cracks and ordered everyone awake. He had another lantern, but saw the one by Simon and Lili's head. It had just then sputtered out and was smoking menacingly. It drew the corporal to it to examine it, but he didn't say a thing about it to the couple. He was young and could have passed for Lili's elder brother. He was blond and had the same blue crystalline eyes, but they turned downward at the sides and were not as round or as big.

He looked only at Lili and said, "Commandant Fekete has asked me to inform you the truck is leaving in three-quarters of an hour to pick up a visiting official from the war office. He came in on the night train. He'd like you on the truck. There are no visitors allowed here."

"But I—"

"I urge you to meet the truck in half an hour."

Seeing the directness of his look, Lili said, "I will," and they watched him depart. Lili felt paralyzed inside the fur bag, naked and exposed. The prospect of another drive in the truck made her dizzy. But she'd already put herself at their mercy and got what she'd come for, considerably more than she'd come for. She'd known all along that the risks were great. She could walk. She'd rather walk, but she didn't want her fear to provoke Erdo the way Elemer's cough had. What little bravery she'd exhibited the day before had caused him to want to rape her, so anything was possible. He might assault a statue for standing unmoved by his presence.

"Poor Elemer," she said quietly, sniffling.

"You'd think he was coughing that way just to draw attention away from us," Simon said. "I'd never heard him cough as badly."

"He lost his life right before our eyes."

"He lost it years ago, I think, before he came here."

"Not if he had a sister he loved—not if he had Delilah to look forward to, possibly—*possibly*."

Simon didn't answer for a moment. And then he said, "The ghetto was wiped out. It's long gone. There was an uprising of the Jews in the Warsaw ghetto, and it was fierce, but it was squashed brutally. Elemer himself told me about it." Lili noticed that Simon's nose was not running for the first time since she'd arrived.

The men in the barracks filed out past the lovers in their bunk, some of them glancing at the spot where Elemer had lain, Lili's coat still spread out over top. Many paused just outside the door and gasped, put their hands to their mouths as they saw the blood on the rocks.

Simon hopped down from the bunk, retrieved his pants and his shirt and, shivering in the cold room, pulled them on quickly. He gave Lili her dress, which she slipped over her head and wriggled into inside the bag. Simon found Elemer's shoes, and inside one of them were his spectacles. He buried his face in his own bunk. Lili kissed his head and told him it would be all right. "I'll wait for you in Budapest. You'll come back soon, and it'll be all right."

Simon looked up at Lili's pretty face as she buttoned her dress dextrously in the back. He held onto Elemer's glasses. "I'm afraid here," he said. "I want to go home. I don't want to die."

The barracks had cleared out except for them. Lili took Simon's face tenderly in her hands. She'd never seen him this way before. She realized she didn't know him well. "We'll come through this," she said again and waited.

He had a stricken look, which reminded Lili of her brother Benjamin, who seemed just as upset once when they'd found a dead kingfisher on their stoop, like a bright blue blossom which had been crushed underfoot.

She wanted to say, "Be brave," but what would being brave mean? Standing up to Erdo when he next came in with his pistol and his lamp? Breaking out of this howling wind hole as they must have tried to do in Warsaw? What was bravery if not foolishness, and yet where was dignity without bravery?

Simon stood erect, hardened himself, smoothed himself down. "You should hurry now," he said, his voice quivering. "What a dear you were to come here. Unforgettable." She got to her feet before him, and he squeezed her hard. "Go," he said. "You've got to go quickly. You will not survive another day here. They won't let you stay. They won't let you live."

When they left the building, they looked only to the right, turning away from the reminder of Elemer, but then they saw someone else Simon knew. "Look," he whispered. Simon pointed with his head. "It's Miklos Radnoti standing in the yard there. They've brought him and some others from another camp."

"I know of him," Lili said, "the poet." Radnoti stood in a dingy trench coat. He looked very sad.

Simon gripped Lili's hand, and then she went one way and he another, as if they'd just concluded a business meeting.

Lili went to stand at the gate beside the roaring truck. Two of the three younger soldiers from the day before were aboard already. She dreaded the thought of getting in with them. Someone came to speak to the guard at the gate. Lili turned to watch the long line of inmates forming at the outhouse. She looked for Simon but couldn't spot him. He must have been inside the mess hall, now, having breakfast. It was porridge day, not to be missed.

But then Commandant Fekete blew a whistle and was coming straight at her. He had Erdo by his side. Two corporals opened the door to the dining hall and blew their whistles, too. "Everyone outside!" they commanded.

Fekete blew his whistle yet again, and then he was by Lili's side but with his back to her. Even Erdo looked preoccupied. The men hurried into the yard. Some were wiping their mouths, some stumbled, but all of them tried to arrange themselves in the orderly lines they'd become accustomed to.

There were several people bunched with Radnoti, the ones dressed variously, clearly the men from the other labour camp. When everyone was quiet, Fekete said, "The Russians are nearby. I've just had a scouting report. We have to leave here. If they find us, they'll treat us badly—of that you can be sure. You'll think of the camp as a tea party compared to the way the Russians will treat you, those of you they spare. I am taking the original men of the camp toward the Ukrainian frontier. We'll be safer there. Sergeant Erdo will lead the men from the other camp back to Budapest. Unfortunately, we haven't had time to arrange transport, so we'll all be on foot." He dropped his whistle into his other hand before saying, "If some of you would rather take your chances with Sergeant Erdo, you may."

Some of the three hundred assembled men muttered among themselves. Erdo shouted, "Fall in line now!"

Fekete turned to Lili. "Why don't you come with me?" he said. "I won't order you to do so, but I think you'll be safer."

Simon jumped to the front of the line before Fekete. The commandant walked down the line and hustled people along. Lili joined Simon. "Here's our chance," he whispered.

"What do you mean?" she asked.

He looked behind him and lowered his voice still further. "We'll say we're going with the other group but won't."

"But you heard what Commandant Fekete said."

"He's guessing, right? We talked about that. We're all taking our chances. We might not make it, and then we might. He might not make it, and then he might. We *won't* make it with Erdo."

They looked over at the other line. Simon nodded to Radnoti. He felt he was getting choked up. His nose began to run, and he found Fekete's handkerchief in his pocket and used it.

Now Fekete joined them at the front. Simon said quietly to him, "We'll go to Budapest."

Fekete looked at Lili. He said, "All right. The choice is yours, as I said."

Erdo's men—there were one hundred and twenty or so in his line—began their march. Then Fekete's men moved out. The commandant nodded at Lili and tipped his cap. He must have been assuming they would fall in at the rear.

Soon, everyone else was gone: the officers, the inmates and the camp staff, leaving Simon and Lili alone. They were expecting something to happen—hear the thundering hoofs and wheels of the Russians—but it was quiet. Simon ran to get his fur sleeping bag, and Lili helped him roll it up quickly and tie it together. He ran to the kitchen, took some celery, some carrots and an apple.

The walk to Vadas was long but happy. There was something easy about what they'd pulled off. It had been so simple. They kept expecting to run into one of the two lines of men on the way down, and once they heard someone up ahead shouting and another man laughing, so they held back, paused behind a tree. Lili gripped Simon's hand, and he kissed her. It took them the whole of the afternoon to make it to their destination.

They felt an electrical charge of some kind in the cold air, but nothing materialized. At the ticket counter in Vadas, only Lili stepped up to buy a ticket to Budapest, while Simon hid out back behind the small building. Lili showed her Swedish papers, which the old woman looked at closely with one eye, while closing the other. Lili saw the pepper and woollen mitt seller, but the woman turned away from her.

A man wearing a fez, followed by his three small children, entered the compartment Lili and Simon were sitting in, but he changed his mind and went elsewhere. Lili and Simon made it all the way back to Budapest without incident, as if they'd been tourists.

Twenty-Seven

MARTA FELT SHE COULD FLY like some mythic creature, like a feather-less raven with hooves, glancing off rocks and stubble. She flew until she dropped at last by a creek. She lay on her back looking up at the Northern sky, taking in its cooling blue scent. She felt warm enough but she was barefoot and couldn't take another step for now, just for a few minutes.

Or at least she thought it was a few minutes. She awoke to barking and then something licking her face. It was a vizsla, sharp and tough, and it barked again. A man's voice asked the dog to sit, and the dog took one more sniff and lick before obeying. The man was speaking Polish, but then he switched to German. "Please wake up," he said. "You'll freeze to death. I can't lift you."

Marta couldn't feel the ends of her fingers and toes. Had there been an early frost? She saw that the man was younger than she was by a few years. His hair was auburn, much like his dog's, but also rich and curly. He was neatly dressed in a suit and grey overcoat with a black lambswool collar. He sat in a wheelchair.

"Please," he kept saying, and now he offered Marta his gloved hand to help her up. "Can I give you my coat?" he asked. He seemed nicely groomed beneath his charcoal fedora. He had a purple birthmark at his left temple, but turned his head away when he saw that Marta had noticed it.

Marta shook her head. "I'll be fine."

"If you don't let me help you, you'll end up worse than I am, and I had polio."

The vizsla had had enough of sitting. It ran to Marta again, licked her and then circled her, urging her to sit up until she did. Marta rubbed the cold out of her upper arms, but then tried to pet the dog. She couldn't feel his bristly fur with her fingers.

"That's Frederic," the man said. "He's named after Chopin. I am Alfred Paderewski."

"Like the prime minister? Like *Jan* Paderewski?" she asked.

"Like the pianist. The same man." Alfred pulled at a lock of his red hair. "I have the great man's hair but very little of his talent for anything, politics or music."

"Are you related?"

"A distant cousin." She looked at him. "Very distant," he added.

She tried to get to her feet, and Frederic barked. He seemed to be getting set to take her on his back. "I live here, just outside of town," Alfred said, pointing to a car in the distance. "My man, Karel, can help you in—help us both, actually." He chuckled. "He can get us back to my house, where it's warm."

"Your house?"

"I have a nice warm home. I can give you something to eat."

He was still holding his hand out to her, offering to help her up, and now she took it. The hand was gentle.

"How did you find me?" Marta asked. She looked all around her. She bit down now, so her teeth would not chatter.

"Just by chance. We saw you from the road." He indicated his driver again.

"And you found me sexy in my Auschwitz ensemble?"

The man was quiet.

She didn't know why she'd lashed out at this man who was only trying to help. "I'm sorry," she said, then blurted out, "I'm not Jewish." She was surprised at herself and put her cold, red fingers up to her mouth.

"I imagine you've been through a lot," Alfred said. "Come on."

Alfred's driver came to help. He'd waited until now, as instructed by Alfred. When he saw how she was struggling, he picked her up in his arms, and Frederic yelped and leapt as Marta was carried to the road.

The car sat like some great black metal beast waiting to be fed human flesh—and dog for dessert. Marta managed to say, "That's quite a car."

Karel said, "It's English. It's an Austin Ascot Cabriolet. Fourteen horsepower."

"I wouldn't know about that," Marta said.

"Horsepower?" the driver asked.

"No, cars."

She couldn't believe she was being driven in a limousine by a chauffeur away from the gas chamber, from the goon, from Auschwitz. She sat by the far window and Alfred was helped in to sit on the near side. There was plenty of room in the back for Frederic, too. He leapt up between them, barked his approval, and made his warmth and affection available to both of them.

Marta felt warmer in the back seat of the Austin on the way to Alfred's house than she ever remembered feeling. She felt as if a down-filled quilt had been pulled over her. Frederic seemed to want to purr like a cat. She could faintly feel his warmth radiate from the thin-furred flesh of his stomach. She glanced at Alfred, and he tried to cover his purple birthmark with his gloved hand. Heavens—here she sat beside him, her head shorn, her body filthy, dressed in the tattered clothes of a camp inmate.

Alfred didn't ask her any questions, as if he sensed she needed to enjoy the warmth of the car without distraction.

Within ten minutes, Karel turned down a lane and drove through a wood until they were greeted by iron lions holding up a Gothic "P" crowning an elaborate wrought iron gate.

Beyond the gate stood an elegant white chateau in the French style with small turrets, mullioned windows and stepped gables. Marta might reasonably have concluded that she had died and come to the Promised Land. It was an impressive house, but more inviting than imposing. Its wings beckoned like embracing arms.

A housekeeper rushed out toward them. When she saw Marta in her tattered uniform, she gasped. Alfred said to her, "She's staying with us for a little while, Emilia, until she's strong enough to travel again. Please help her into a bath and give her some of mother's clothes." He looked at Marta. "I'm sure they're small enough for her."

Emilia hesitated until Karel appeared at the open door on Marta's side and without asking lifted her again and carried her to the house. Emilia, meanwhile, helped Alfred into his wheelchair.

Marta was hustled up a grand white staircase to a bedroom on the second floor. Emilia drew a hot bath for Marta in an adjoining bathroom and helped her into it. Marta felt she was being boiled up for dinner. The heat was like acid, penetrating her skin, dissolving her extremities. If she could have thrashed about like a lobster, she would have, if only to reassure her body that she got all the painful messages shooting to her brain.

Emilia's eyes were brimming with questions, but she had the decency not to ask any. As Emilia scrubbed down the unexpected visitor, they both stared at her arm: "181818." It was Marta who volunteered her name, and Emilia simply nodded.

After the bath, the first thing Emilia asked, in German, was, "May I take these?" She was holding up Marta's camp uniform.

"Please burn them. I'd rather leave here naked than in those."

Emilia nodded. "That won't be necessary," she said, and she went to the closet. She returned with soft, warm underclothing and a satin peach dress with mother-of-pearl buttons that travelled up to its white lace collar.

"Alfred's mother won't mind?" Marta asked.

"That wouldn't be possible, madam."

"And no one else will mind?"

"There is no one else to mind."

"Not even you?" Marta asked.

Emilia hesitated and looked at the young woman. "Of course not, madam. It's not my place to mind." She led Marta to a mirror and began helping her to dress. "But I thank you for asking."

"Look at me," Marta said. "I am red and bald."

"You will be black and pink again in no time, madam. And very pretty, I'm sure."

"Thank you, Emilia."

"It's not my fault I live in this town," Emilia said, "and it's not your fault you were brought to it. If we remember that, everyone will be fine."

Marta turned toward the older woman and embraced her. "I have to get home to Hungary."

"Of course you do," Emilia said. "But let my master have the pleasure of seeing you well again."

"I'm already much better."

Marta followed Emilia out into the hallway. It was lit at both ends by Gothic windows, and up and down the corridor, portraits of family members regarded one another from both sides. "This will be your room," Emilia said. "Mr. Paderewski is at the other end."

For whatever reason, Emilia led Marta down the servants' staircase. Halfway along the basement passage they came to the kitchen. The cook was killing fresh brown trout for supper. Marta watched as the cook, introduced as Teresa, took hold of the slippery live animals and thwacked their heads on a wooden block. The thud made Marta flinch, but she was surprised at how unmoved she was by what she saw.

They walked to the other side of the kitchen, and Marta's heart quickened when Teresa said, "Up these stairs is the dining room." Marta hesitated. "It's all right," Emilia said, "Mr. Paderewski is waiting for you. He hasn't had a guest in some time."

They climbed the stairs and stepped into the room, and Marta was taken aback by what she saw. Alfred sat in his wheelchair at the head of a long table, and a place had been set for her at his right hand. The room writhed with ornamentation unlike anything she'd ever seen. A great fireplace blazed behind him. On the stone mantel sat a life-sized jade mermaid embedded in black marble. Out of her head erupted carved onyx garlands and tumbling angels rising toward the ceiling, where they were met above the dining table by an immense chandelier of brass and crystal angels and elongated flowers.

The mermaid's tail pointed to an ironwork candelabra at one end of the mantel that snaked upward and branched into sinuous iron fingers, each of which held a glass tulip bulb within which a candle burned. On the mantel's opposite end sat a mysterious cobalt-blue figure in glass, suggesting ancient Greece, maybe Egypt, illuminated from within by another candle. Perched beside her was an extraordinary bronze. It captivated Marta. "It's called *Ariadne Abandoned*," Alfred said quietly so as not to disturb her gaze. The bronze body was folded over a rock in unbridled pain and grief.

On the wall to the right of the fireplace hung a great painting. "My mother favoured the Czechs over our own artists," Alfred said, quietly still. "This, my parents acquired on one of many trips to Prague. It is called *Finis*, by Maximillian Pirner." The painting, explained Alfred, depicted a tug-of-war between life and death. In it, a luminous and voluptuous Muse of Poetry holding a harp had encountered a Gorgon, out of whose back sprang a skull and the arm of a skeleton, extending toward Poetry's supple flesh.

Beneath the painting, seeming to swoop down upon the black marble pedestal on which it stood, was a bronze, which Alfred called *The Embrace of Love and Death*. He said, "It's by Bohumil Kafka, a Czech again." Kafka's sculpture, with its wide attenuated wings, embraced a deep shadow out of which people were emerging and into which others were disappearing, the contours devouring the light within their frightening embrace.

It all seemed too much at first glance, but the candlelight and fire-light together soothed the riot of detail in a calming glow. The warm light fell languidly over walnut tables and chairs, the white linen covering the dining table, set out as if for a little celebration, a small feast, the splendid tan carpet with its medallions of flowers and angels answering their brass and crystal relations in heaven, its warm spring beneath Marta's feet kinetic, suggesting a carpet ride somewhere far away, maybe the East, Marta's host the guide to strange new lands.

A tureen was brought in by Teresa and set down on the table. The tureen stood on goose feet. Marta realized how weak she felt and hungry. Emilia ladled out a steaming broth of potatoes and leeks for each of the diners. "Start," Alfred said. "You must be very hungry." But she was eating already. "You *are* hungry."

She swallowed hard, her mouth fighting off the heat. "I'm sorry," she said, after a few spoonfuls. It was the best soup she'd ever tasted.

"Just eat," he said.

She took another spoonful as he watched.

After a while he said, "Why did you tell me you weren't Jewish? Did you think it was necessary?"

"I didn't know." She set down her spoon, but he urged her to continue.

"Your uniform had a yellow star, like a Jew's star, rather than a red triangle to signify a political prisoner."

"I don't have papers to prove it, naturally, but that was not my uniform I was wearing. It was the uniform of someone who went to the ovens."

"The ovens," he said. He spoke as if this was news to him, how people were being disposed of.

She set down her spoon again. She felt full already. "You don't need to believe me."

"Please eat," he insisted. "I didn't ask you for identification papers when I picked you up, did I?"

"I have to go." She pushed back her chair. She felt preposterous sitting here. Istvan could be near death. She had to know, had to find him.

"You can't go now. First you have to eat dinner. Then you have to rest and recuperate." Marta glanced back at Emilia, who stood at the door. "You won't make it on your own. I can help you get back to your home. Do you have people waiting for you?"

Marta didn't know this man. She couldn't tell him whether anyone was waiting. Istvan might not even be waiting anymore. He might be gone, or he might be dead. Or she might say to Alfred Paderewski that he's there, and it could be Istvan's final undoing, after such a long, hard struggle. She couldn't even lie. She couldn't say a relative was waiting or a husband because surely he could check.

The trouble was evident on her face. "I can contact them for you," Alfred said. "I can reassure whomever. We can get word to them."

"No, there's no one. We were all deported."

"Who?"

"Everyone. I was the last one."

"You were all *political* deportees?"

"I don't know. I don't know where anyone is, but my home is there. I want to find people there. Maybe someone has come back, someone like me." Then she added, "I have a brother in America. Frank Foldi."

"If you went now, you might be overtaken by rampaging Germans."

"Why are they rampaging?"

"Because rampaging Russians are coming. *They* might not befriend a wandering girl either."

"How close are the Russians?" Marta thought of the poor souls still in the camp.

"Close," Alfred said. "You have to wait a little longer."

He was smiling, but there was a faint hunger in his eyes. As she gazed at him, Alfred brought a hand to his temple again to cover his birthmark.

"It hardly shows," she said. "Please relax."

He dropped his hand. "If you will, I will," he said.

And then a platter of warm trout on a bed of cabbage and onions was brought in and set before them. Emilia served Alfred first and then the visitor. Marta ate with relish. She sucked the supple, succulent flesh of the fish as delicately and politely as her satin dress would allow. She cleaned every bone of every morsel so that not a milligram of this animal's meat was wasted. She was done before Alfred had finished half of his, but he stopped, too, when she did, and he dabbed his mouth with his linen napkin.

Tea was brought in, along with caramelized bananas for dessert. How on Earth did bananas make it to Poland? Had a single bunch been flown in from the tropics through a war zone and delivered directly to this house marked with a "P"?

Marta was bursting, but she devoured the sweet treat until her stomach throbbed and she had to sit back to catch her breath.

Alfred said, quietly, "We can take our tea in the sitting room. I have a surprise for you."

"You have a *surprise?*" Marta couldn't help herself; she started laughing uncontrollably, a real belly laugh that threatened to disturb its contents. What could be next? Alfred smiled with her and waited patiently for her to settle down.

Then he led the way by wheeling himself toward the far door. He paused and turned to Emilia. "Has Judyta arrived with Tadeusz?"

"Yes, Mr. Paderewski. Karel went to get them."

Marta understood enough of the Polish to be alarmed. Her heart thumped against her satin dress. Emilia pushed her master into the room, but Marta hung back, wondering, now, how she would escape. She looked around at the door, then the door leading possibly to the front.

And then Karel came in to fetch her. "Madam?" He was indicating the door through which Alfred had gone. Karel didn't say more; he was not as confident in German. "The concert," he managed.

"The *concert?*" Marta asked. She put her hand on her beating heart. Was this a joke? A ruse? She was trapped. She couldn't run now.

The room she was led into was simpler than the dining room. It, too, had a blazing hearth, but the fireplace was fashioned out of basic black granite, and the whole was decorated with a rustic warmth. Colourful folk art and naïve art, like art done by children, adorned the walls. A great grand piano, cherry wood, possibly, or even walnut, sat opposite the hearth, and a single chair had been positioned to face the instrument. Beside it, Alfred was waiting in his wheelchair. Their tea was set out before them on a small walnut table. Extra caramelized bananas were heaped in an oval blue dish with duck's feet.

A young woman and man came out from behind a velvet burgundy curtain, evidently hung for this purpose, and Alfred clapped enthusiastically. "Judyta!" he called out. He looked at Marta, and she clapped, too, if weakly.

The young man, dressed formally in black tails, arranged himself and his music at the piano. Judyta was wearing a white evening gown and black shawl. She shrugged off the shawl, which Emilia rushed to take from her. The woman's shoulders were white and slender. She was slight—they both were. The woman gazed for a moment at Marta before she began. She announced in Polish that she was going to sing a Bach cantata, "Ich habe genug."

Tadeusz played the first notes. He closed his eyes. The music was plangent, doleful. At first, Judyta clasped her hands in front of her, but when she began to sing, she raised them like slender wings.

The music was transcendent. Marta felt unworthy to receive it, her ears still grimy with human ash. She was struck by the unreality of the scene, sitting here as she was, in someone's satin dress, her head shorn, her body tingling with nourishment, wanting to rise aboard the notes to enlightenment. It was too much. No soul could shuttle so quickly between these two poles.

But what was reality anymore? The tears flowed down Marta's face. Beautiful Johann. Beautiful. Of course, *Ich habe genug*. Of course you have enough. You have beauty. You have inspiration flowing in on beams of coloured light in your cold church in your cold time. And so you have enlightenment, floating on the voice of a human bird. You have your keyboard as the lovely Trieste first sings these notes in all their charm and sadness, the pure notes ringing out over the Thomaskirche's stone floor. You have enough, Johann. You have a pudding in your belly, and you have beauty, you have transcendence, and not up the chimney in smoke. You have the girl with the slender shoulders and that voice, all the sadness of her charming notes lifting you both toward the beams of light.

Du hast genug. You have life. But even that's not enough. You want it all, don't you, Johann? You want death, too. The ultimate beauty. The ultimate transcendence.

Marta wiped her wet cheeks with the palms of her hands. She stood up, and the singer stopped singing; the pianist stopped playing. "Please," Marta said. "I have to go to bed. I'm much too tired. But please don't stop on my account."

"Of course you're tired," Alfred said. "You need rest." He turned to the musicians. "Thank you for coming. Karel will take you home. Thank you."

"Please don't break up the lovely party," Marta said.

"It's not a party, just an entertainment, really," Alfred said. "Enough," he said to the musicians. "Thank you again."

If he could have, Alfred would have stood with Marta. He seemed to want to scramble in his wheelchair to see to things. They watched Karel lead the musicians out, and then Emilia led the way to a lift Marta hadn't noticed before. After Emelia had wheeled Alfred in, she told Marta to join them and they rode to the second floor. They escorted Marta to her room. "I have set out some flannel nightclothes for you," Emilia said. "I hope you'll find them comfortable."

"Please make yourself at home," Alfred added. "I'm glad you're here with us and safe."

"Thank you," Marta said. She waved weakly and waited for the two to turn down the hall.

As Emilia wheeled Alfred to his room, Marta opened her door and saw that a warm fire was burning, a lamp had been switched on beside her canopied bed, and as promised a flowered flannel nightdress was folded on the bed waiting for her.

It just then dawned on her. This was the next day after her death. It was November 8. Where had Libuse got to? Marta brought the flannel nightclothes to her face and breathed. Libuse had held Marta's hand as surely as she'd held onto life. Blind already and sick, she still spoke her mind, and she clutched Marta's hand until she had to release it and press herself into the others in the chamber—the woman with the cloche hat, the Transylvanian boy, the young man with the erect penis which he concealed before entering the chamber, the last speck of shame before inhaling the broth of death.

Libuse played piano. She would have known this Bach that Marta had heard Judyta sing on November 8.

Oh, Johann, what did you do following your afternoon at the Thomaskirche? Did you come in for dinner, the girl with the slender shoulders still fluttering behind your eyes? Did you come in to your children and make them be still so that the song could go on? Did Anna Magdalena, pregnant again, always pregnant with another Bach, greet you with a peck, the sweat of the day on her cheeks and neck? Did she ask you how your day was, and did you say you'd written a little ditty for her and the children, one they could remember and be proud of? Did you tell her you called it "Ich habe genug"? And did the children romp and scramble and slap and kick and run all around the table as the mutton stew was brought in, because they'd quite lost that little box of pride you'd wrapped for them that afternoon?

Marta was suddenly afraid to get out of her dress and into her nightgown. She didn't want to lose the dress and be trapped here in nightclothes. Maybe all the dresses and coats would be gone in the morning. She sat on the bed for a moment, then lay down on top of the duvet. She tried to smooth out the dress as she did so to preserve its freshness. She reached over and switched off the lamp, but the fire's embers still illuminated the wood-panelled walls. She rested her arms straight beside her, not across her chest, which could wrinkle the top. She closed her eyes, but then a strange foul smoke crept into the room. She groped for the nightdress still folded on the bed and brought it to her nose again to breathe through the flannel. And then she knew what it was and shot up in bed. She threw aside the nightdress and gulped. It was not wood smoke she was smelling at all. Her nose knew the difference between wood and bone. How far was she from the camp? How far could she have run? The smell was indescribable, repulsive, something between charred fat and ash.

She dashed to the window and looked out into the darkness. Not a light shone in Oswiecim, though she couldn't have said which way her window faced. A rain fell as lightly as snow and brushed against her window. She heard a faint creak. Could it be that he was coming to Marta? The sound stopped and she caught the distant clink of a latch being lifted or a key turned, so far away it could even have come from downstairs, deep within this big house.

Marta waited quite a while longer. Not another sound came. She heard the wind buffing her window, but nothing more. She didn't want to be heard, either, so she crept back to her bed and resumed her orderly repose on top of the duvet.

But it was Istvan, now, who came to visit her. Where was her Istvan? Where was her man, without his keeper, with just small Smetana to keep him company? How could they possibly have managed? Maybe she would find them dead, both of them likely, curled against one another in that pose of the transcendent. *Ich habe genug.* Surely, the two of you have had enough, without your hunter-gatherer, your jailer, your lover and mother. Surely, surely—how wonderful it must be, finally, not to need to eat or breathe or hide. The grave forgives all its occupants. The grave absorbs the passions—the protagonist's, the antagonist's, the artist's, the demagogue's, the servant's, the master's.

But Istvan stirred. Marta could sense it. What if he'd managed to cling to life for her? What if his passions had not been extinguished? She had to leave. She had to know.

Marta was up again. She stole to her door, turned the knob, was relieved to find it opened. She crept to the servants' staircase and, a step at a time, waiting to hear a reaction after each one, she made her way to the first floor and toward the front, she hoped. It was dark, but Marta had to be deft, had to plan her exit carefully. She realized that, by feeling her way along the walls, she eventually had to come upon a door.

She was as quiet and as careful as could be, holding her breath some of the time, using her hands and feet as eyes. When she found the door at last, a light came on. Emilia said, "Oh, Marta, Mr. Paderewski will be disappointed."

"I'm sorry," Marta said. "I know he will be. He's a dear man. And you're a dear woman. But I have to leave. Can you understand that?" Emilia stood in her nightgown with a brown cardigan pulled over her shoulders. She clasped her hands in front of her. "Won't you stay just a little longer?" she said. "You're weak—you're skin and bone."

"I'm strong enough. I'll manage, just as long as you don't mind my taking this dress. If I make it, I'll return it to you, cleaned and pressed and nicely packaged."

"Don't return it," Emilia said. "Just let us know you've arrived safely. I'll give you a coat and proper shoes and some food for the way." Emilia led Marta down the stairs to the kitchen. She set to wrapping bread in a linen tea cloth, as well as some cheese and sausage. "You'll have a struggle, my dear. You can't just hop on a train. I'll wake Karel. Mr. Paderewski won't mind if he takes you out of harm's way, at least."

"Don't wake him, please," Marta said. "I'll manage. I've managed worse."

"Maybe not."

"Maybe not," Marta repeated.

"Your fate is in other hands." Emilia crossed herself and waved at the heavens through the ceiling.

In the vestibule, Emilia dug out a trench coat lined with sheepskin and some clunky lined leather shoes. She hugged Marta, ran her hand along her brush cut and went back to the closet to find a fur hat. "It's sable. It was his mother's."

Marta felt a chill come over her again, as she had upstairs.

"Go with God," Emilia said, and she released Marta.

Twenty-Eight

BY THE TIME Lili and Simon arrived back at the Dutch insurance building, 243 people had taken up residence there. Lili could see Paul looming above the heads of people milling in the centre hall, and he saw Lili, too, and smiled. She smiled back, and Simon waved.

Rozsi and Klari spotted the newcomers and rushed at them. "You brought him back!" Klari said, squeezing her son hard.

Rozsi did the same to Lili. "I was worried to death about you. I didn't know if you'd come back to us." Her eyes were bloodshot. "There's been no word of Zoli."

Lili felt guilty to have left Rozsi behind. Since Paul had become so occupied with the deportations, Lili had been the one to sit with her, console her, reassure her.

"Mr. Wallenberg's here," Rozsi said. "I asked him myself about Zoli."

"Mr. *Wallenberg*'s here?"

Klari answered for her niece. "They all came at once. Yesterday. The embassy on Minerva Street has been blockaded by the Germans. They've moved here, now. Per Anger is in another building on the other side of Pest."

"Who are all these people?" Simon asked. "Where's Father?"

"These people came from a ghetto building that was bombed by the Germans. Half the people didn't make it. The other half are here.

There's nowhere else to put them. Mr. Wallenberg and Mr. Anger are already sheltering thousands of people—I heard someone say thirty thousand—in buildings around the city. And your father is tending to those who were injured in the blast. He's upstairs. He's glad to have been pressed into service, I think. Many of the people who've moved here are crowded into the upstairs offices. The nuns are helping, too, especially that young one, Beata."

Paul and Wallenberg walked by them now. "Mr. Wallenberg," Lili said right away. "I saw you at the railway station. I saw what you did."

"How did I do?"

"You did well, sir."

"Thank you," he said, looking up at Paul.

"And you, too, Paul," Lili added. Paul shrugged.

They headed to the back of the bank of offices, where the Becks and Lili used to sleep.

"Those are the new Swedish offices," Klari said apologetically. "We're relegated to sleeping on the floor, now, all of us. But it's not terrible. We're still here."

Simon held up the fur sleeping bag. "Well, I'm all set." He smiled, but he'd been hoping to share his bed with Lili that night. He could see it wouldn't be possible.

A bomb fell in the distance, and everyone ducked instinctively and looked all around.

Wallenberg had managed to transfer funds from his family's accounts in Sweden and had arranged with an old candy factory in Budapest to bring in a dozen pots of soup and pans of brown rice speckled with pieces of pork. He apologized to the Ulloi residents but said that it was all that was available. Some would eat only the soup, and Wallenberg, certainly, was not offended.

Another bomb fell, and everyone ducked again. "The Russians are here," Wallenberg told Simon and Lili. "They're pushing the Germans back. The Germans are blowing up the bridges as they retreat."

Still another bomb fell, this time shaking the building. Plaster fell from the ceiling. Everyone looked up again. A tank cranked through the street in front of the building, and they all stopped to listen, their heads turning toward the door.

THAT NIGHT, before going to bed, Lili sat with Rozsi, who still had a cot. She was the only Beck who did. "I missed you terribly, Lili." Rozsi took the younger woman's hand and kissed it, and then wouldn't let it go.

"The Russians are here in the city," Lili repeated to Rozsi. "It can't be long now. Then people will come back. We'll have people coming back."

"I don't know," Rozsi said. "I think I'm going to be a ghost bride of China."

Lili looked at Rozsi. "I don't know what that is, but it doesn't sound good."

A ghoulish look came over Rozsi's face as she lay back on her cot, still clutching Lili's hand. Lili was frightened. "When I was a young girl, my parents took me to China. Up in the northern provinces, in Shanxi and Shandong, there are 'ghost marriages.' Husbands and wives are buried together in a single plot, but if a man dies a bachelor—if he's killed in a coal mine, for instance, before he can be married—grave robbers are hired to get him a bride out of someone else's grave." Lili took her hand back and held it up to her mouth, but she stayed where she was. "Then a ghost marriage is held between the freshly dead miner and his dug-up bride. If she's freshly dead, she's still 'wet' and fetches a good fee. If she's long dead, they call her 'dry,' and she's worth no more than the price of a chicken. That's the kind of bride I'll be. A ghost. Maybe I'll be lucky and be a wet one."

Lili took Rozsi's hand back. "It's been very hard for you," she said. Lili moved the ruby to the front of Rozsi's finger. The ring had become quite loose. "But people *are* coming back. I have to believe people are coming back, and you do, too."

Rozsi smiled and said, "I'm tired." Then she turned away from Lili and fell asleep quickly.

Lili managed a minute alone with Simon, and they kissed. He was wearing fresh pyjamas the Red Cross had provided for everyone in the building, together with lined leather slippers. She told him what Rozsi had said. "Do you think people will come back?" she asked.

"We were on the deportation train. It wasn't an encouraging scene."

"Do you mean people were being taken to their deaths?" Tears were filling her eyes.

"I don't know. Who knows anything? Is it possible they could have killed all the people they took? It doesn't seem possible. Paul told me three and a half million people were taken from Poland, three million of them Jews."

She gave in to her sorrow, and he held her for another couple of minutes. Then she said, "Where are you sleeping?"

"I'm all the way over there, by the door, with some of the other young men, but my mother insists I keep the fur sleeping bag until I regain my strength. Can you sneak over later?"

"I don't think so," Lili said. "We have to be respectful of your parents." She was still wiping away tears. She remembered how the night before they'd made love, and then Elemer was taken out and shot. Poor soul. She thought of Elemer's sister and a shiver ran through her. Simon kissed her again, and she left him.

In the back, Paul sat up with Raoul Wallenberg. They were at Wallenberg's new desk. "I could use an espresso," Paul said.

"That would be a trick."

"It would."

"So we have to start thinking about reconstruction," Wallenberg said. "The war is finally grinding down. Eichmann is becoming more and more desperate."

"He has a job to do," Paul said. "He wants to finish."

"He'll finish us, or we'll finish him. He knows that it will all happen soon. And then there will be a city in shambles, buildings to rebuild, lives to restore. Look around this building at the faces. Look at your own life: the people you lost, the career you lost, the house you lost. What will you do, stand in the street and look cheerful? *Lie* in the street?"

Paul said, "But the Germans have confiscated all the properties."

"Whatever the Germans have confiscated, the Russians will confiscate from them. Then the question will become: Do you think they'll hand it all back to you?"

"And you'll stay here for all that?" Paul asked. "Assuming you're right and Eichmann flees, and we're still left standing, you'll stay to help rebuild?"

"What else can I do? I've got to finish what I started. At least that much."

A knock came at the door and Wallenberg opened it. It was Lili. She had two cups of espresso in teacups. "Oh, you blessed creature," the Swede said. He took her face in his hands even before she'd had a chance to set down the cups and kissed her cheeks.

"I'm sorry. I couldn't find the right sized cups."

"But you found espresso, Lili?" Paul asked.

"The candy factory sent a small packet of coffee," she said. "No one else can know."

The two men drank with relish. It was two more hours before they themselves retired to the pallets set out for them on the floor by the desk. Wallenberg had asked that the few cots be reserved for the old and the infirm.

SIMON WOKE to a cool stream of air flowing in from under the large front door. He could feel it on his face; inside his fur bag he was quite warm. He wanted to breathe the pre-dawn air, so he climbed carefully over the people sleeping nearby and crept to the front entrance. He opened the door quickly and stepped outside.

It was snowing. Blossoms of snow were falling straight down. The city was asleep. The warriors were resting. It never ceased to amaze him the way the world could be in upheaval and yet most people would silently agree that, at a certain time, they would all sleep, or try, or they'd all eat, or try, or they'd take turns doing these things, in order to replenish their bodies' resources. The whole building behind him was quiet, and the streets before him just as quiet, the gentle snow respecting their repose. He knew it was premature to take an accounting, but he couldn't help marvel that he stood here at all, that history had deposited him on these steps, and that, after all his family had been through in a few short months, they might now just make it, those of them who were left. He watched the snow clump on the pavement. He wondered how many layers of people below it future generations would count, whether the rubble of this building and its human contents could still be applied to the top to create a fresh layer, the way this snow was doing.

He wondered how the march to Budapest, led by Sergeant Erdo, was coming. He thought of Miklos Radnoti in his trench coat, wondered if it was lined. He wondered about Commandant Fekete and the group that went with him. Were they all holed up and sleeping somewhere now, too, before having to resume their winter march in the morning? Was there a barn somewhere for them, or a farmhouse?

A single gunshot rang out. Then another. A German soldier leapt out of the wet shadows at the side and grabbed Simon by the throat. He had a pistol aimed at his temple.

The German pushed Simon back in through the unlocked doors, startling the sleepers inside. Two young girls stumbled out of the bathroom and scurried up the stairs to their parents. A lamp came on in one of the offices. People sat up or stood. They saw Simon and the German, the pistol. They huddled up against the walls, clearing a path. Simon glanced toward the door to Wallenberg's office, but it remained closed. He couldn't spot Lili or his parents, but they were around the corner. It would take a minute for the message to get around the building. Someone, a teenager, saw that the German had a grenade strapped to his belt, and he called out. The German aimed his pistol at the boy.

A woman said, "We're Swedish. *Schwedische*."

The man turned his pistol back on Simon.

"Everybody, shut up!" the soldier shouted. "Quiet! *Sei still!*" The soldier couldn't have been more than twenty.

The building fell utterly quiet. The German dragged Simon to the stairs at the back of the building, then up the first flight, people clearing a path for them as if they were royalty. They worked their way to the next floor and then the next. Simon had to pull on the German's fist a couple of times or be choked to death. Surprisingly, the soldier eased up when he did. Simon could see the insignia of the Reich at his shoulder. The two of them were at the roof. They couldn't go farther, and then the soldier threw Simon aside and burst out on the roof itself, slamming the door behind him.

Simon listened at the door but heard nothing outside. Below him, he heard nothing. He could have been alone it was so quiet.

But the building's ears were open. Simon's ears were alive and wide open. And then a bomb went off outside. The building rocked. Simon fell to his stomach, covered his head. He heard debris raining down. The door had held. Had the building been bombed? Had the roof withstood the explosion? Simon had heard no plane overhead. Where was the German? Had he hurled his grenade at someone on another roof?

He waited patiently now, but full of apprehension, half expecting the soldier to come running back past him, down the stairs to the door below and the street. He would have to do something if the soldier did come back through. He'd have to surprise him, trip him up.

Simon waited a few more interminable minutes. No one came. Not another sound from below or above. He owed it to himself to give it another minute or two, owed it to his parents and Lili. But when the soldier didn't return, Simon felt confident it would be all right to seek him out, speak to him. He knew it was bold, but he'd been held in a labour camp during a bad winter and had survived Sergeant Erdo. Could anyone be worse than Erdo? The German at least hadn't shot him. He'd certainly had his chance.

Simon had to know what it was like to be a German, overrunning the planet, beating his chest and getting set to rule. He needed to look at a man of pure blood, just find out about him, not admiringly necessarily, but to satisfy his curiosity. He would stay calm, not threaten him, and he wouldn't be threatened in return. Surely that was the way these things worked, even with a lion or a snake.

Simon was at the door. He pressed his ear against it. No sudden moves. A sudden move would attract a bullet. He gingerly undid the latch and edged open the door. In came the winter air, and with it not a whiff of smoke or molten lead. He smelled only the air, damp with the Danube, heard nothing but the flapping of the Swedish flag, with its companions, the flags of Hungary, the Netherlands and the Dutch insurance company.

As Simon opened the door halfway, he felt suddenly exposed on the winter roof in his pyjamas. Dawn was breaking, and the snow had stopped falling.

He was ready to retreat, but he still had not seen what had become of the German. He got down low and pushed the door open the rest of the way, and then he saw. The chimney was splattered with blood, as was the gravel all around the roof. In the middle was a crater where the soldier had stood to blow himself up.

Simon stepped boldly out. There were bits of the man everywhere, bits of flesh, some seared by the blast, some fresh and scarlet. And there before Simon lay a hand, a whole hand, intact. At first Simon recoiled, thinking it alive. It was the same hand that had formed a fist and gripped him as the two men went up the stairs. The hand might even have twitched now. He got down on his knees to study it. There were no marks on the hand. It had been torn clean off at the wrist, sheared from the bundle of nerves that told it to go this way and that. It was a pale hand with long fingers and no ring. Had the other hand worn a ring? Simon held up his own hand to judge whether it was a left hand or right. It was left. Graceful. With long fingers that might have played piano, the lower notes, the rhythm passages, or held out a full fan of playing cards in a game of skat or bridge. Piano hands. Piano fingers. Every German family owed one of its members to music. Was it another to philosophy? Another to engineering? A last—if there were any left—to the priesthood? This was the hand that had held the grenade while, with the other, he'd pulled the pin.

Simon touched the hand, lay his own on top of it, measured his own against it. It was still warm, warmer than his own. But Simon's hand was dark against its pale friend, dark with black hairs and an olive tint. Simon squatted down on the red-stained roof with the hand in front of him, the tangle of red human wires pouring out of the wrist.

It was only then that he saw it, hanging bravely in the wind, flapping like the flags. The soldier's jacket was suspended from a nail on the outside of the door. It was imbued with a power all its own. Charcoal with starry epaulettes, and at its collar two bolts of lightning that had shaped themselves into *S*s. The man had hung the jacket up before his suicide, hung it there for Simon to see. One could blow up one's own flesh to escape defeat, one could fly like the Walkyries, but the jacket of the Reich must stand defiant, bolder than any flag, more powerful, more terrible. Even without its owner, the jacket made Simon shudder, its proud buttons and stars proclaiming that Germans had mounted their steeds to assume their place at the head of the world, to become the world. We are Empire. We are Earth. If we are not God Himself, we are the Ones minted in His name.

Simon approached the jacket as if he were creeping up on a Titan, a preoccupied Cyclops, Cerberus himself, guarding the portals of Hades. He took it from the nail on which it hung, on the very door Simon had come through. He held it out by its shoulders, ran his thumb over the Electric *S*-Sisters, then tried on the coat, just like that, pulled it on, then turned toward the blood and morning sun for just one second to gaze out at the roofs of his city, puffing himself out to fill the jacket. Just one moment, just one glorious moment in the arms of the great Father, when all of the delicious killing was free and possible. Imagine. Imagine, if you will. The power to take life equal to the power that made it. He closed his eyes for a moment, smelled the Danube, imagined the Rhine.

A crow cawed on the chimney, and Simon crumpled to the stones. He was wearing a Nazi jacket. If he'd been spotted by a Russian, he'd have been shot as an SS officer taking his last stand. How would *that* have looked? How would that have seemed to his family when they discovered him, shrouded in infamy, his impure blood flowing out to dye the Vestment of Empire? He could sacrifice himself now and become the subject of a story repeated for a hundred years—how Simon Beck had tried on the coat of the last dead Nazi and taken a fatal bullet for the brief pleasure. The picture of his face would be clipped for German school children straight out of Goebbels's textbook of the Hebrew face, with its sinister dark features and ample nose, and pasted into a new book: *Idiots of the Twentieth Century*.

He pulled the jacket off quickly, crawled on hands and knees toward the hand, and solemnly looked at it one last time. He said, "*Alova Shalom*. Rest in peace," over the hand and covered it with the jacket before scuttling back toward the door and into the darkness.

Twenty-Nine

Zebrzydowice, Poland – November 11, 1944

OUTSIDE OSWIECIM, Marta accepted a ride from a retired municipal worker who lived in Pszczyna and was going that far. She managed to make it by foot across the rest of the countryside southwest of Oswiecim for a day and a half at a good pace and with brief rests until the evening of the second day came and she encountered an exchange of gunfire in the open fields and on the roads. She imagined they were the rampaging Russians confronting the rampaging Germans that Alfred Paderewski had warned her about, but she couldn't be sure. What she could be fairly sure of, though, was that the Poles were not involved.

She hid in a shed outside the town of Zebrzydowice, not far from the Czech border. The little place held the discarded handles of saws, hammers and a wood plane. The steel must have been traded some time back for provisions, and then the tool shed, too, probably fell into disuse, except by small rodents and, by the looks of it, young couples looking for an hour or two to themselves. There was a little hay bed made up in the corner and even a greying pillow. Marta was happy to make use of the lovers' bower. It was best for her to stay put until morning. Other than fearing for her life, even she could see the irony of surviving the camp, being sheltered by a kind but lonely Polish nobleman and then dying of a wound from a stray bullet. She wanted to live to tell the tale.

She awoke to a warm and inviting fall day. She could hear the birds chirping, saw the sun beaming through the wooden boards of the shed and felt surprisingly rested and at peace. She saw a cobweb with its creator, a fat spider, in the centre presenting its work with a flourish like a magician with eight hands, the whole apparatus glistening in the light. She found a dingy blue hair ribbon beside her bed and wondered how long ago, in what circumstance and in what gust of passion it had tumbled from its owner's head. She felt more comfortable in this place than she had at the Polish nobleman's mansion. The shed brought her closer to home than she'd felt in some time. Certainly it more closely resembled her home in size and simplicity. Marta looked again at the ribbon. All the little place was missing was the lovers.

Then she heard a sound she couldn't identify. She couldn't say whether the sound was even a human one. She stayed still and waited. The noise came again, a dragging, whooshing sound, like the sound of a sail caught by wind. She didn't want to attract attention to herself, but neither did she want to sit by and wait for her end. She heard the noise again and had to know where it came from.

She got out of the hay bed as quietly as she could, edged toward one of the bigger cracks in the wall and peeked out. She thought she'd seen everything that was possible to see in these past few months, enough to fill a lifetime, but if she'd had to predict what today's experience would be, she wouldn't have guessed it would involve a balloonist in an open field, trying to fire up his rainbow-coloured balloon. He was wearing an aviator helmet, a leather bomber jacket and a royal-blue scarf that flapped in the sunny wind. He seemed frustrated, was looking around to see who might help him, but persevering nonetheless.

Marta found herself smiling. Was she in Oz at last? Were there sparkling ruby slippers hidden in the shed somewhere? If she waited long enough, would the shed be dislodged by a tornado and carried back home? "There's no place like home," she wanted to chant. "There's no place like home."

If this was indeed a balloonist, how many miracles was one woman permitted to experience in a lifetime, let alone a week? Or was it some kind of hoax? Where did it begin and where would it end? Was Marta shuttling to heaven still holding Libuse's hand, travelling together with her all along, sighted now equally, the two of them, breathing in the same glorious light?

If she was not hallucinating, then the man outside was going somewhere. Otherwise, he had gone to a great deal of trouble with his aviator outfit and his outrageous balloon just to squat in a field and make whooshing noises. Marta pulled on her trench coat, drew herself together and boldly exited the shed.

The balloon looked like a colourful but wilted musk melon. Marta said, "Hello," in cautious Polish.

The man responded in German. "Can you help me?" he seemed to be saying.

She said, "Where are you going?"

"I'm going across the frontier."

"That's where I want to go."

"If you want to get across the border," the man said, "you have to fly with me, but you have to help me first."

The man looked ridiculous. His leather helmet seemed far too tight and appeared to be compressing his skull. "I want to go across," she heard herself saying. She reasoned she would be better off in what used to be Czechoslovakia than she was in Poland, with the Germans being pushed back, and she would be closer to home. "I want to get over to Opava on the other side. I need to get to Prague, then to Hungary."

"The winds are favourable today," the man said. "But we have to get up high enough to go straight over the woods. The Germans on the frontier have not been very receptive to visitors." He paused to look at Marta. "Especially to you, possibly, most likely."

Marta put her hand on her scalp and nodded. "I'll go with you. I'll help you."

"It's not dangerous," he said. "Less dangerous than that." He pointed ahead to the border. "I'm experienced. But I need your help to get launched. I don't know what I was thinking."

"Is there no one else around here who can help us?"

She was putting her faith in a man with a hot air balloon and a child's aviator helmet, but sometimes putting your faith in someone else was as powerful as trusting science. She looked up at the sky, which was Prussian blue on this day, and took a deep breath.

The man told her his name was Hugo. He explained that they had to pull the balloon's envelope out full-length after setting the basket on its side. He grunted as he toppled the basket. She was at the envelope's crown, and he joined her, smoothing out the silk like a colourful great bedsheet. Hugo checked to see that the valve at the crown was sealed and then held the crown, pulling vigorously to stabilize the balloon. He rushed down to the balloon's mouth, leaving Marta at the crown, and then opened it up to catch the breeze. The balloon began to come to life. It threatened to stand upright.

"As soon as we're ready," Hugo said, "I'll ignite the burner and fill the balloon. But then we have to jump in here." He indicated the basket.

"How do you know the balloon will float to Opava?"

"I don't."

She let go of the crown and sent a ripple down, expelling air from the mouth. "Hold up your end," he shouted.

She took hold of it again. "Then how do we know we won't float back the other way into Poland?"

He licked his finger and held it up to the wind. "Because the wind isn't blowing into Poland," he said and smiled proudly. "It's blowing out."

"How do we know we won't be blown out of the basket by the wind?" she asked.

"Because we travel *with* the wind."

Just then a gust bucked the envelope, throwing her off her feet. "I'm sorry," she said. "I don't know if I can control this thing until you light the burner."

"I can help," someone said.

It was a young man, speaking Polish. He was rustic looking with scruffy red hair, a suede vest and old-fashioned breeches that looked soiled and dingy. He had a heavyset girl with him who stayed back by the bushes and put her hand to her mouth when Marta noticed her. Were these the young people of the shed? Was the ribbon hers?

Without waiting for an answer, the boy threw his considerable muscle into the enterprise. "Excuse me, ma'am," he said to Marta. Marta looked at the girl to get her permission, but she seemed content to cheer on her boyfriend. She was now looking at Marta's coat and dress. The boy heaved the envelope farther outward as Hugo held open the mouth, and immediately it caught more air.

Hugo said in Polish, "What a helpful lad you are. Maybe I'll take you up for a ride sometime."

"I'd be glad," the young man said, "if you take my woman, too."

"Of course," Hugo said. He lit the gas burner. "Hurry, into the basket," he called to Marta. "I don't have the balloon tethered to anything. The heat will soon make it rise."

Hugo set the basket upright again, and the young Polish man pulled the envelope's mouth toward the heat so that the balloon would catch the warm air.

The balloon filled in just a few minutes, more quickly than even Hugo had expected. He was in the basket already, but Marta was only half-in, still not fully believing in the contraption. The rustic saw her dilemma and rushed forward to help. He got her leg in just as the basket left the ground, but he held on too long and now he was clinging to the side of the basket and flying up with the other two.

"No," the heavyset girl screamed. She came rushing at the balloon. "No," she screamed again. She managed to grab her boyfriend's shoe but pulled it straight off his foot and fell back. The balloon was above the trees in a minute with the girl running after it, pleading with it to release her boyfriend.

The basket wobbled and tilted, like a boat about to capsize. "Get in here," Hugo yelled. He was trying to get hold of the boy's hands, but his grip on the side of the basket was too tight. Marta took hold of one of his elbows, but the basket tipped, the heat was misdirected, and the balloon threatened to plummet. They could hear her still in the distance, the rustic's girlfriend. "No. Oh, no." She was sobbing and then screaming some more.

The basket righted itself and the heat sent the balloon soaring, just as one of the boy's hands lost its grip and he cried out. They were too far up to do anything for the boy, and the wind was brisk, carrying the balloon southwest as it rode up into the air.

Hugo was fighting to steady the wobbly balloon while Marta nearly fell out herself as she attempted to get a hold of the boy's free hand. "Give it to me," she was trying to tell him in Polish. The hand flopped at his side, as if the boy were lame. She said it in German, in Czech, but the hand didn't understand or obey. The basket began to tip again, the balloon took a short, swift dive and whipped the boy loose. Marta watched as he landed with a thud in the field below and then bounced once before coming to rest against an old tree stump.

Marta called out to the boy. She couldn't see the girlfriend anymore. She pleaded with Hugo to take the balloon down, but he couldn't or wouldn't. She was sobbing, leaning too far out of the basket, straining to keep the motionless boy in her sight. Hugo pulled her back in. "Fate," he said. "Too bad. Fate."

"What do you mean?" Marta asked.

"I mean there's nothing to be done."

Marta looked back to see if she could spot the girl. The balloon soared ever higher into the blue air. Hugo didn't even turn to look.

"He got his ride sooner than he bargained for," Hugo said, and then tried to straighten his helmet, which wouldn't budge on his head.

Thirty

THE HORSE STOOD in the middle of Ulloi Street and nickered. He was harnessed to a cart on which there was a cannon, but had been left there by the retreating Germans. A passerby saw the animal and cart. The man ducked into a building, thinking at first the Germans couldn't be far away, but then came out again into the cold sun. Lili noticed the animal through the chink in the shutters of the Dutch insurance building. And then a second man, in a uniform, stopped to stare at the horse. The animal was a beauty, a shiny chestnut colour, and it stood tall. The man wore the uniform of an Arrow Cross guard. He detached the cart from the horse, giving the animal a couple of affectionate slaps on its haunches as he did so. Then the man removed the canvas satchel from his shoulder, took out a long knife, petted the horse's head, smoothed down its mane and plunged the knife straight up the horse's neck into its head. Lili's hand went to her own neck. The guard held the knife there, tried with all his might to twist it. The horse showed the whites of his eyes, then the eyes rolled back and he fell forward to his knees. The guard pulled the knife from the horse's neck, which seemed to take equal effort, walked to the far side of the animal and with his shoulder gave the horse a heave. He fell to his side, upending the cart altogether. People who had hidden themselves to avoid the Germans now emerged to watch the spectacle. The guard felt the flanks of the horse and the stomach, took out his long knife again and with some skill began to carve out chunks from the rump and place them in his satchel. He did so until the bloody satchel bulged and dripped. He picked up the bag, hung it from his shoulder once more and walked off. The first man advanced. He had a pocket knife at the ready and had acquired a good-sized pan from the building he'd stepped into. A woman and a man followed him from the same building. Each had a pan, and one carried a cleaver while the other had a carving knife. Lili was not far behind. She rushed out with a large stewing pot and knife. By the time she finished cutting out as much as the pot could hold, her arms were steaming and scarlet up to the shoulder. People around her were eyeing the pot—a woman looked ready to make off with it—so Lili thought she'd be better off stopping and letting someone else in. Three men shouted for everyone to stop and tried to turn the animal over to get at the meat on the other side, but they were too weak. Two women and a boy joined them, and they managed to flip the carcass. The frenzy began all over again. A woman with four girls stopped to look at the horse, but she hadn't brought a knife or a pot. As she lingered to see what might be left, her four girls surrounded a waiting boy and danced in a circle around him. He was pleased to be the centre of a carousel and raised his arms and spun as they danced. When it was all over, less than ninety minutes after the Germans had left the horse and cannon behind, the street was a bloody mess. Someone looking down from an upper storey window would have thought the horse had been dropped from the sky and splattered on the street below. Only the horse's head remained, some of it, and the small part of the rump that held the tail. A crow and a scrawny dog were now fighting over the head as if they were battling for their lives. The dog growled fiercely, but the crow continued to peck at the dog until it mewled and retreated to the horse's tail.

When Lili came in with her pot full of red horse flesh, Rozsi met her at the door. The nuns were huddled down the corridor in front of their room, and one was rubbing her hands together. They were surrounded by several residents who regarded the pot with interest.

Rozsi looked at Lili distractedly and said, "The Lord turned on the light and has now switched it off. Do you suppose He will be happy when the light comes on again?"

Lili shrugged her bloody shoulders.

"Do you think the light was a good idea, Lili?" Lili stood paralyzed with her pot. Still others had come into the hall and were watching Lili from a distance. Rozsi said, "Do you know about the ancient forbidden city of Hué in Viet Nam? Do you know the name of the river that flows through the city?"

"No," Lili said.

"It's called the Perfume River. Imagine that—imagine the rosy rain there, the pink clouds."

Lili said, "It must be lovely." She hesitated. "But I think you'll feel better once you eat something, dear Rozsi. We're going to have stew—look!" She held up the pot, and Rozsi stepped aside.

THE GERMANS were on the run from all parts of the city as the Russians moved in. Eichmann's troops had blown up two of the primary bridges over the Danube, linking Buda with Pest, the Erzsebet and the Chain bridges. There was no water or electricity in several parts of the city. The thousands of advancing Russian troops needed places to hole up, so they indiscriminately took over buildings themselves, took the residents' jewellery and watches and sent them into the winter streets. After the Swedish embassy staff were relieved of their watches, they, too, were cleared out of their makeshift offices on Ulloi Street.

Paul called together all the people in the building. When they were crowded into the front hall, just inside the entrance, he said that they all had to be very careful still—nothing was certain, nothing could be taken for granted—but the Germans were leaving Budapest. It would only be a matter of days.

A great cheer went up. People threw things into the air—caps, gloves, handkerchiefs—one boy threw a shoe. Klari kissed her nephew, and then the lineup formed. Rozsi kissed him; Lili kissed him; Simon shook his hand, but then kissed him, too; Robert only hugged him, but he did it hard. Most of the nuns came forward and bowed to Paul. Beata hugged him. And then she threw off her habit, and was dressed normally underneath. All the nuns then did the same and began hopping and dancing around.

"Beata, what are you all doing?" Klari asked. "Aren't you going to stay dressed in your habits?"

"No, we're not nuns," one of the older ones said. The woman hadn't spoken once. "We stole these habits from the Church of St. John the Divine. They'd just been laundered and nicely pressed and were piled on a cart just inside the entrance. Beata found them and brought them home to us in the ghetto. We're Jews like the rest of you, but our husbands were taken to a labour camp. We haven't seen a single one of them back yet. So we pretended to be nuns. We thought God wouldn't mind."

"No, God wouldn't mind," Klari said, as she looked over the bunch. "But why didn't you tell us?"

"We were scared, you see. We didn't know if it was wise to tell."

People wanted to thank Wallenberg, too, but he remained closeted in the back.

WALLENBERG AND PAUL and several of the staff soon left to take up residence at the offices of the Red Cross on Benczur Street at the invitation of George Wilhelm, the head of the organization in Budapest.

Two German soldiers still guarded the Red Cross building, an impressive villa near the City Park. The soldiers came courtesy of SS Colonel Weber because of his devotion to the charming Wilhelm. Wilhelm had studied at Cambridge, and had formed a natural bond with the other prominent English-speakers, Wallenberg and Paul. Wilhelm had not only attended Cambridge, like Paul, but had also been the son of a prominent Hungarian lawyer. He wore the black uniform of the SS commander, and, being more fluent in German than he was in English, he masqueraded as a senior officer about town, assisting in the Swedes' rescue operation whenever he could, intimidating even the Arrow Cross on occasion to get his way, or bribing them when he could not.

The few days Wallenberg and his small team spent at the Red Cross were like the still point in the eye of a storm. The one-time chef of the Astoria was housed there also and cooked as well as he could for them, under the circumstances. After a meal one evening with Paul and Wilhelm of duck a hunter had brought, together with beetroots and fennel, followed by English brandy that Wilhelm had saved for just such an occasion, Wallenberg told them that they were not at the end of their operation but the middle.

"How so?" Paul asked.

"As I began to say before, you can't just save lives, you have to restore dignity."

Later, in his room, Wallenberg told Paul, "I want you to meet the King of Sweden after the chaos subsides. I want to get his blessing as well as the support of the government to establish an institution here for restoration—the restoration of property, law, peace and dignity. Dignity comes last, but it is foremost."

Paul looked incredulously at his friend. He thought Raoul had finished what he'd come to do. The Swede said, "What did you expect? Did you expect me to go back into banking, or be an architect, or just a rich man about town, dropping coins into the cups of the poor? It's not enough for me."

"Of course not," Paul said. He sat on the corner of Wallenberg's desk so that he could look directly into the Swede's dark and determined eyes. Wallenberg's hair had thinned still more, it seemed, though he was only thirty-two, and he looked exhausted, though he steadfastly denied it.

Paul put his hands on the man's shoulders. It was difficult to look at him the same way now. It was like looking at history itself, like looking at Churchill. And yet here Wallenberg was: close, human and vulnerable, his hair thinning, his weary mind racing to the place of the next mission.

The next morning, Paul got to work again, trying to seek Zoli's release and restarting his search for Istvan. He couldn't spend another minute in his sister's company unless he had some kind of news. She had become inconsolable, distracted, and was turning darkly inward. She tore at his heart, got down on her knees, begged him. Not even Lili and Klari could calm her, not even Robert's sedatives. She'd even got Wallenberg involved, got him to agree, as a special favour to Paul, to petition his own government to press the Germans to release the Swedish nationals they'd taken away.

So Paul was at it again that morning. He'd sent two telegrams, one to Sweden's Ministry of External Affairs and another to the Wolf's Lair itself, Hitler's compound at Gierloz. Why not? What did Paul have to lose? Even in Hitler's insane scheme there was logic. Even the Fuhrer had allowed that Swedes were not Germans and not Jews. He also managed a call to the mayor's office in Szeged. The interim mayor could not be reached, Paul was told. "He's taken a holiday."

"He's gone into hiding, you mean?" The man was a fascist, a Nazi sympathizer.

"Yes," the man said. "A hidden holiday."

Now Paul waited. He drank his espresso and smoked. He was at Wallenberg's desk, and he looked across at the chair he himself usually sat in. Slung over it was the tie Wallenberg was going to put on that morning before he stepped out. The tie was baby blue and adorned with the golden crowns of Sweden. Paul spied a stain, coffee possibly, covering one of the crowns. He made a mental note to mention it to the Swede.

Wallenberg was in the front office, talking with some Russians who'd come that morning to ask him if he'd meet with General Malinovsky to discuss the complexities of the situation.

When Wallenberg returned to his inner sanctum, he described the proposed meeting with the Russian general as a debriefing.

Paul said, "Where? Here?"

"No, they have their base in the town of Debrecen."

"Debrecen?" Wallenberg nodded. "All right," Paul said. "I'll finish up later. It'll take me only a minute to get ready."

"Ready for what?"

"To go with you."

"No need," Wallenberg said. He took his tie from the chair. Paul wanted to mention the stain, but Wallenberg went on. "You just keep after the authorities, Paul. Work on getting people home again. Your sister is not doing well. You just keep after them."

"I will. I'll come straight back here and get back on it. But I think I should be with you. Your Russian is lousy."

"And what about yours?"

"It's lousy, too, but if we add the hundred words I know to your hundred, we'll have two hundred."

"I think they're the same hundred," Wallenberg said. "Vilmos will take me," he added. "I'll be back soon, and we'll continue the struggle. I won't be gone two days, three at the most. We'll take the Studebaker. I wouldn't want to deprive you of the Alfa Romeo. Besides, if I do, the Russians will probably pull it out from under me."

"*I'll* take you. It's no trouble."

"My driver will take me. Langfelder will take me. Trust me." Wallenberg touched Paul's cheek with his dry palm. The place burned. Paul watched the Swede as he took an apple from a wooden bowl on the stand by the door and left without looking back. His tie was slung over his shoulder.

Thirty-One

WHEN MARTA turned up the walk of her little house in Szeged, she could faintly hear music. She also saw, suspended from the door-knob, a white tag fluttering in the fall breeze. She feared the worst. She snuck up to the window and peeked in. The two floorboards stood leaning on the wall opposite the window. She saw Istvan with Smetana curled up in his lap. At first they seemed lifeless, but then she saw the hand move, petting the cat. Istvan looked reasonably fit, as did Smetana. He was reading a book, and they were listening to Dvorak's *Rusalka*.

She tapped lightly on the window, and Istvan leapt out of his chair. The book dropped to the floor and Smetana flew out of his lap like a crazed bird. Istvan turned and saw her, his mouth fell open, and then they smiled. He clearly still couldn't believe what he was seeing. He looked behind her, around her, but it was just Marta. His eyes filled with tears, as did hers.

He still hadn't reached for the doorknob. He brought his hands up to his cheeks, and she went on standing at the window. He was wearing her Alpine sweater, and she giggled. He saw what had amused her and laughed with her.

He let her in, and they embraced for a long moment before speaking. He kissed her forehead and then the top of her head. "You're still here," she said. Tears poured down her face.

He took her face in his hands. "What happened?" he whispered.

"Do you have a minute?" she asked, and then burst out laughing again.

He joined her, and then he took her hand and led her to the bedroom. "Don't leave out a detail," he said.

"Not today. Today, the news is that I'm back, and that you're still here—that's all."

"That's enough."

They sat down together on her small sofa. *Rusalka* continued to play. "The music's nice," she said. "Remember, no more news? I'm tired."

"You must be." He looked her over more carefully. "You came back to me."

"We have to sleep in the cellar."

"We can stay up here, now, in your room."

"No, we can't. I'll feel exposed. We're *both* in hiding now."

"We have a tag on our door. *Abandoned—Forgotten.*"

"It doesn't give us immunity," she said, and took his hand. "Let me wash up and get some things, and we'll go down."

"The end is near, I think."

"It must be," she said.

So he got up with her and followed her lead. She switched off the music, took some things from the bedroom and led him down into their dark cellar.

IT WAS NOT UNTIL CHRISTMAS that she told him she thought she was pregnant. He'd wondered about her morning sickness, and they'd both suspected. But he never asked her whose baby it was. He decided it didn't matter and he never would ask.

On New Year's Day, Anna Barta welcomed the Russians into Szeged as they rolled through the streets in tanks and in army trucks. She was so happy, she'd had a bit too much apricot *palinka* that afternoon and was close to toppling over as she spun and danced. She staggered toward a parked Russian truck, offered her *palinka* up to one of the soldiers, who took it and shot her dead.

Thirty-Two

Budapest – February 16, 1945

Dearest Rozsi,

I want to outwait this bad time, and then marry you, if you'll
have me. This ring was my mother's. May its ruby heart stand
up to your stout Beck heart. Please take it and accept it.

Zoltan
I love

Rozsi folded up the note for the hundredth time and asked Lili, for
the fiftieth time, about the people who'd returned. Could Lili go with
her to the Jozsefvaros station and wait for the trains to come in?

The Germans were gone from Hungary. The Soviets were in
charge. Wallenberg had never returned from his meeting in Debrecen,
and the Swede's whereabouts were unknown. Some suspected he'd
been taken to Siberia. Per Anger could not get an answer from Stalin's
government.

Robert and Klari had returned to their house on Jokai Street to
find that, in addition to Vera's family, another family, the Oszolis,
had moved in. Robert insisted on having his home back, but Vera's
uncle said they were not leaving. "We're willing to make room for
you, Dr. Beck."

"Willing to make *room*?"

Robert and Klari had no recourse. The provisional government was not discussing such trivial matters. Vera made the Becks a meal, and Robert calmed down.

Klari noticed her Turkish carpet with the great medallion pattern was gone, as was the tablecloth she'd bought outside the gates of ancient Ephesus. She was relieved to see her raspberry marble-topped table with the painting on it by Edvard Munch was still there. The silver griffins and eagle clock were gone, and so was the cabinet they had stood on. She had a blue-and-white platter, from the Ming dynasty, which she'd inherited from her mother, and it was gone. She noticed things missing every day. But they had one another, she kept telling herself. She had her Simon and her Robert, and Lili. And she had Paul and Rozsi.

Since Paul and Rozsi's home had been burned to the ground, Robert asked his nephew and niece to move in with them.

"We'll find another home," Paul said.

"I won't hear of it," Klari said. "It's roomier than Ulloi Street with all those people and the fake nuns."

"Please," Robert said to his nephew. "Don't insult us."

And now, sitting on the bed she shared with Rozsi, Lili swept the hair off Rozsi's forehead. "Of course we can go to the station, sweetie," she said. "I'll wash you up a bit. We'll see who has come back today."

Word was out that people were trickling back. Lili herself had heard from Maria at the Madar Café that Emil Gottlieb, the pharmacist from over on Kiraly Street, had reappeared one day. His wife, Izabella, and their unfortunate daughter, Nora, with the early onset of rheumatoid arthritis, hadn't returned with him. He had been hoping to find them at their old home on Rose Hill, but there was no sign of them. He described himself as the "first" one back. When he arrived at the house, he found five families living in it. He shoehorned himself in the way the Becks had, moving into a small sunroom at the back and saying it would be fine, but only until Izabella and Nora made it back. It was only a matter of time.

The florist, Monika Danzinger, had come back to find her husband, Oliver, sitting in their flat tending to their poodle, Arisztoteles, named after the Greek philosopher because the Danzingers could tell she was extra smart from the day she was born, and their parakeet, Mor, because he had so much to say, like the writer Mor Jokai.

Monika had stood, stunned, at the door when Oliver opened it. She'd hoped and prayed for his survival and begged the *kapo* at the camp to let her know about him, if not see him. But she eventually despaired that she would never lay eyes on her husband again.

"I was here the whole time," he said, meekly.

"I thought you'd been taken ahead of me. When I came home last April 11, you were gone. I thought you'd been taken."

"No, I was at the Fenix, having supper. When you didn't come back, I thought you might have been taken."

"So you went for supper?"

"Not right away. I looked everywhere for you and waited." He lowered his head. He was petting Arisztoteles, who was still not warming up to Monika. The talkative parakeet was quiet.

"Didn't you move to the ghetto?"

"No, I didn't want to."

"You didn't *want* to?"

"All Jews this way," the parakeet finally said. "All Jews out."

The humans looked at Mor in his cage. "It might have been mandatory," Oliver said, "but I didn't want to. I figured, if they wanted to take me, they'd take me. I'd wait. But no one came for me."

"So you've lived in our place all this time, since I was taken?"

"All Jews out," Mor said. "Curfew time. Let's close the curtain. Curfew."

She looked around the apartment before stepping in. They hadn't even hugged yet.

"I found provisions for us as best I could, Arisztoteles, Mor and me. I did the best I could."

"Well, weren't you clever?" she said. "Foolish, but clever."

"Yes, both."

She looked unspeakably skeletal. He looked better, but not much. The dog and parakeet looked best. Finally, the Danzingers embraced, painfully, her bones grinding against his. But she was home, now, and so was he, and they had to hope for the best from here on in. He gave her some tea and biscuits, for which he'd traded a watch some time before and was saving for just such a day, and the two had a little meal together.

Every story was extraordinary, every rumour, every anecdote. To the last possible minute—until three weeks before—Germans were still rounding up people. The Nyilas were still summarily executing Jews and dumping them into the Danube. Robert had heard, on one of his few forays out of the Dutch insurance building, that a colleague of his, Zsigmond Lengyel, a neurologist, was shot to death five minutes after he got off the train on which he had returned to Budapest. The news was mixed everywhere.

Robert was welcomed back to his clinic at Sacred Heart, though not to his old job as chief of surgery. He was happy to find the jacket he'd left behind hanging in the closet, still waiting for him—and his Swedish papers still in the pocket. His first order of business was to get his niece a bottle of sedatives.

But he was gone twenty-four hours. He narrowly averted capture by a squad of renegade Arrow Cross men out looking to spill some blood. He crossed through a park and ducked into the courtyard of a building where he believed an operating-room nurse of his, Lidia Szent Mihaly, worked. It turned out he was right. She was glad to put him up for the night, though her husband was nervous about it. Robert overheard him whispering to Lidia late that night, asking what time she would ask Robert to leave.

"Not before the doctor has had a little breakfast," she whispered back, "and is satisfied with us."

"*Satisfied?*" he asked.

"Quiet," she said, "and I *mean* it."

Robert left early, and by the time he stole back home Klari was frantic. She'd paced all night. She'd been imagining the fate that had befallen him after these long months, like his poor colleague, the neurologist. How could it have happened to her, to his decimated family? But then there he was, as before, relieved to be back. Klari had to excuse herself to go to the bathroom—she didn't want the young women to see—and cried the incident out of her system.

Rozsi asked Lili, the world traveller, "Who else is waiting for someone the way I am? Are there many others?"

"I'm waiting," Lili said.

"Of course you are," Rozsi said, and she took the blond girl's hands in hers. "I know you are. And how will they even find you? How will they know you're here, and how would they find you even if they *did* reason that you're here? I meant, are there many others?"

"Hundreds. Thousands. Tens of thousands."

Rozsi's eyes clouded over. She seemed to find comfort in this information. *Tens of thousands.* Surely that would mean that many, or even most, were coming back. Where could the Germans have closeted *tens of thousands* of people? What would they feed them? *Did* they feed them? They'd become a nuisance. Surely, they would feel that. They couldn't have turned as savage as all that, not *all* of them, surely.

"Lili," she said, still holding the younger woman's hands, "take me to Zoli's hideout, please. He had a perfect place nobody knew about. I know exactly where it is. I'm the only one, and I'd give anything to go there."

"I would take you if there was a point, Rozsikam," Lili said. "We'll go on another day. We'll go tomorrow."

"But I have to go. Even if you can't take me, I need to go."

"But why? You don't think that Zoli is there, do you? You can't be thinking that."

"What if he is?" Rozsi asked. She had an intense look in her eyes. She needed to feel that he might be there, could be, by some chance, but for whatever reason could not get back to her just now. There were so many reasons these days, you could take your pick. Maybe he was surrounded by the Nyilas and had to stay put. Maybe he was surrounded by *Russians*, for all they knew. Maybe he had broken a leg on his flight from someone and couldn't drag himself across town to her. Maybe he had set it himself with something, some planks or steel pipes in his boiler room, and had to administer to himself but might by now be needing some provisions only she could find for him, or she and Lili together. If they didn't check, he could die in his building of a broken leg with Rozsi foolishly waiting for him anxiously a few blocks away. How would she live with *that* realization?

That afternoon, Rozsi asked her Aunt Klari to give her the taxi fare so she could take a ride somewhere. "By yourself?" Klari asked.

"I can manage," Rozsi said, brushing back her hair.

"What about Lili?"

"I want to go on my own."

Klari was about to discourage Rozsi but saw the determination in her niece's eyes. Rozsi had the driver take her to the old building Zoli had stayed in, where he'd kept his darkroom. Some of the films were housed in the Swedish buildings and had been developed, but there might be pictures here that no one had seen.

When they arrived, the driver said the upper floors of the building had been bombed. She shouldn't go in. Rozsi didn't listen. She got out, and he asked if he should wait for her. She said she'd be a little while.

"I'll wait," he said.

Some of the furniture Zoli had scavenged was still there: the bed, the little table where they had drunk plum *palinka* together. She looked for hints of recent life, some food or water, the bed unmade, but saw nothing. He had tidied up nicely before he came to the building on Ulloi Street to see her on their last night.

She went straight to the door he'd told her contained his darkroom and found it was padlocked. Rozsi could have called the taxi driver to help her, but she didn't want to. She wanted to break into the room herself. In the boiler room around the corner, she found a chisel and a brick. Using the brick as a hammer, she banged at the lock until she got through. She rubbed her hands together and got her breath back before opening the door. Inside, she saw the jars of developing liquid. She hunted for rolls of film and was relieved to find a small box of canisters, but then she saw the newspapers. They were back issues of the *Csillag*, the paper Zoli used to work for. She leafed through one, and a photograph fell out. It was a picture of a father and his two young daughters being escorted to the river by the Nyilas. The smaller of the two girls trailed behind. She wore a kerchief, as well as sandals and socks, just like her sister's. Her legs were thin, and she was leaning forward in her rush to keep up with her father, sister and the soldier.

Rozsi searched the newspaper further and found another hidden photo. The same three figures, father and two daughters, were tied together, all of them facing outward, away from each other. The little girl had lost one of her sandals. If there were more photographs tucked into the paper, Rozsi didn't want to see them.

She picked up another issue, dreaded what she would see next. There was a photograph tucked in it, too. It was a picture of her, Rozsi, at their bench in the Strawberry Gardens. It was a later photo, she could tell, because the bench was stripped of its seat and because Rozsi was wearing her ruby ring. It was the moment before Zoli had arrived. In a moment the worry would subside—he'd be there—she'd feel at ease again. It had become her role to wait. And now she'd wait some more, but for how long could she bear it?

She couldn't look at anymore. She wanted to go, but had to see one last thing: the roof where the lovers had been shot. She worked her way up the stairs, past fallen brick, plaster and wooden beams. Three-quarters of the way up, she could smell the open air and thought she might get through. All she had to do was crawl over some rubble, which looked solid enough to support her. She made it all the way, had got her head out in the cool air, level with the gravel, when the crumbling stone beneath her feet gave out and sent her tumbling through to the floor below, plaster and wood coming down with her and covering much of her body.

It was the taxi driver who found her. When he dug her out, both of her legs were bleeding as well as her lower back. He rushed her out to the cab and laid her gently in the back seat. "You have to go back, please," she said to him.

"Where?"

"You have to go and bring out some photographs and a box of film."

That evening, her Uncle Robert looked Rozsi over and stitched the cut in her back. He gave her an extra tranquilizer to help settle her.

She wanted to know if there was any more news of people coming back. Robert said he saw people every day at the hospital. They were coming back with all kinds of ailments, but little that they couldn't cure.

Thirty-Three

AT FIRST, all they could say over the telephone was each other's name.

"Istvan?"

"Paul."

They'd made it.

"You're back?" Paul asked.

"I was here all along."

"I was hoping you were. We all were. And you're in your office."

"Yes, I'm back here in my dental office. Are you practising law?"

"No, not yet."

"Oh."

"I'm coming to see you," Paul said. "I'll get a car today. I'll be there later today."

"What about Rozsi?"

"Rozsi made it, too, but she might not come. She's been waiting for her fiancé."

"Oh, I didn't know."

"He was a photographer—*is*—he's—"

"I have a little place on Alma Street in Tower Town, Number 22," Istvan said. "Can you come for supper?"

"Of course I can."

They held on, not saying goodbye yet.

"I'm not Jewish anymore," Istvan said. "I gave it up. I've had it. The Russians don't like Jews either. It was the first thing they asked when I requested my dental licence back."

"What did you tell them?"

"I told them I wasn't Jewish. Who needs it?"

Then Paul said it again, "Istvan," not knowing what else to say.

"Come tonight, Paul."

Paul didn't want to drive the Alfa Romeo—it called too much attention to itself—but the Swedish embassy was glad to lend him the blue Buick that Raoul Wallenberg had sometimes used.

He first made a stop up near Rozsadomb, because he'd heard from a contact that Dr. Janos Felix, a man they'd saved from the transports, had an office there. Paul heard that Felix had treated a Russian man who might know where Raoul was.

Although Felix was not seeing a patient, Paul had some trouble getting in to speak to him. His secretary asked Paul to come back another time, but Paul knocked on the door to Felix's office until the man answered.

Felix stood blocking the way in, his hand remaining on the door handle. "Mr. Beck, how good it is to see you."

"Thank you," Paul said, giving the door a little push. Felix stepped back, but only a step, and Paul advanced. "Did you treat a Soviet man," he asked, "a Konstantin Zarodov?"

Felix merely looked at Paul, neither confirming nor denying what he was asking.

Paul said, "Zarodov might have information about Raoul Wallenberg's meeting with the Russians in Debrecen. Did he tell you anything?"

"I don't know what you're saying," Felix said.

"You don't know what I'm saying?" Paul could have strangled him. "Did you treat Zarodov?"

Felix broke into a sweat. From behind Paul, his secretary said, "Is everything all right?"

Paul said, "The man saved your life."

Felix continued merely to look at Paul and grip the door handle.

Paul turned and left. He had to sit in the car to catch his breath. His mind reeled. He thought of all the good people he hadn't managed to save. Was there a way of knowing in advance what they would be like?

Paul needed to move on. As he started the engine, he realized he was within a block of the place, years before, that his Uncle Bela had taken him and Istvan to see the Gypsy women. It was where he'd met Ruth.

He drove the block and parked again. The rickety old house was smaller than he'd remembered, but it was familiar to him. It was stubborn enough to have resisted the war and the weather. Paul stared at the building. He could not calm his heart.

He knocked lightly on the door but then stepped in. There was a woman there, sitting on a couch in the front parlour, smoking a cigarette. Could this have been the same red couch his uncle had sat in as he waited for his nephews to finish?

The woman said, "It's early, but I'm sure I can rustle up a little happiness for you, if that's what you're after."

Paul shrugged his shoulders. He felt awkward, embarrassed. "I'm looking for someone," he said. "Her name was—is—Ruth."

"We have no Ruth here." The woman stubbed out her cigarette.

"She was—*is*—a Gypsy. Very pretty."

"We have no Gypsies, never had them. We're all Hungarians here. Purebloods."

"Oh," Paul said, "lucky you."

"Do you want a cigarette?" she asked. He shook his head. She lit one for herself with her tarnished silver lighter.

"I've changed my mind," Paul said. "May I?" He took a cigarette and accepted the lighter from the woman. The letters were almost worn away with use, but they were unmistakable: "MM."

Paul took the Number 5 Road south toward Szeged. There was even a dusting of snow before noon, but shortly after the sky turned a chill blue. The air carried the promise of spring.

Paul asked himself what he was to do, now—renounce his Judaism, too, like Istvan—was that what one did? Was he to renounce his Hungarianism, renounce his manhood, his place in the species, his place among molecules?—or just the add-ons—the Judaism, the Hungarianism? He could be a man without a country, without a faith, without a woman. It was liberating—nothing limiting to hang on to, nothing to distinguish him. He could be Chameleon Man. Separation was the Fall, William Blake taught us. Starting up a universe was the Fall.

Yet he still felt affection for what he had, loyalty to his people, mixed with a little disdain. Why not? Could they follow him out of their differentness into the ocean of sameness? Could he lead anyone that way?

It was good to be Hungarian, good to be a Hungarian Jew. He did so miss Zsuzsi, the particularity of Zsuzsi, the way she spoke, the way she comported herself, the determined way in which she tightened her lips. And he missed Raoul, the grandness of his ambition, yet the humility special to him. Only he could be so humble, because only he could span a gap so wide between achievement and modesty. Paul would add to his complement his brother, his aunts Klari and Hermina, Lili, Rozsi. And he would add his father, because Paul could not have become what he'd become without his example.

He knew that even if he started a new planet, he'd be tempted the first night to lay down his weary head and say, This is mine. And that spot is for my wife, and those for my children. Over there, nearby, I need a spot for my friend Raoul—and just over there, a place for our café—and here a good school, because my children are very smart indeed—and there a house of worship—we'll keep it down somewhat this time—and then, here we are again, at Eden's exit—animals in a zoo, not in the wild—a Carnival of Animals.

Something stirred in him. He remembered the last time he'd seen Raoul, remembered the touch on the cheek. Paul's face burned again. He was glad he was alone, glad to be driving away from Budapest.

Where are you, Raoul, and *who* are you? Did you come from the spirit world to run among the devils, only to fly back to it with your Russian pilot?

And having been touched by the Spirit, who have I become? And what am I to do, now? Go back to defending people able to buy their freedom? Open a café with a monkey in it? Sell shoes? Start a new faith? Was this a religious need, after all, a need to worship at an altar of my own devising? It's a blessing to have served genius, but a curse to be one of the few wretches who recognized it for what it was.

Raoul, what have they done with you? Have they laid you out on some frozen Soviet slab to await resurrection? Shall I expect you by the eastern gates of Jerusalem?

How clever, Mr. Stalin, the cleverest of all—don't hate some people, hate everyone. Kill everyone in your path—German, Ukrainian, Swede, *Russian*—even if you have to glorify them in doing so, even if you have to martyr them. Raoul, how are you to outwit an all-hating man, a man who knows only fear and is its great monger? And what do I do? What do I do?

Who are these Stalins? The lids of their eyes are locked open to receive only the ice-blue light, the angels and martyrs indistinct, lost and floating in the blue vapour. I hope a small consolation awaits you, Raoul, in that blue gas, knowing you've done what you've done, saved the last of a generation.

Was it possible, Raoul, that we stood on trains, or *in front of them*, and blew whistles? Was it possible we met with the Devil's man, listened to his Beethoven, fully expected to be let go to resume our work, *were* let go?

If I can no longer follow, who am I to lead? Will you loom over the work of my remaining days, dear Raoul, blocking my view of all other life?

And there was the sun still, over the Number 5 Road, insistent, always aware of its place, its role.

Paul couldn't park the Buick on Alma Street, because no one else would be able to get by, so he left it a block and a half away.

Marta met him at the door. She was beautiful, pregnant.

"Istvan didn't mention me?"

He shook his head.

"I feel as if I know you. I've heard so much."

She asked him in, and he had to duck to get through the doorway. Istvan came out of the bedroom. He was wiping his hands on a towel. Again, they paused to look at each other before coming together in an embrace. "There's so much less of us," Istvan said.

"And fewer—less and fewer."

"This is Marta. She protected me."

Right away, Paul saw the number on her arm. "Thank you," he said. "It must have been very hard, terrible."

Marta kissed Paul softly on the cheek. "Welcome," she said, and went to get dinner ready while the two brothers caught up. They sat and went over the list, calling out the names, those missing, those who'd made it, relatives first, friends, public figures. They came back to the start, to their father, and both shook their heads and gazed at the floor.

Finally, Paul said, "You gave up your faith for a lovely Jewish woman?"

"She's Catholic."

"Barely," Marta said. She came out to them. "He gave it up for himself."

"I have little faith," Istvan said. "Except I do believe in one thing. Convenience."

Smetana jumped into Paul's lap, startling him. But the cat just as quickly calmed him down. He curled up instantly and went to sleep. Paul chuckled, petted him.

Over dinner, they talked about everyone again, guessing what other course of action each might have taken. "Why speculate?"

Marta asked them. "I know you're both thinking men, but if you second-guess yourselves, you could be at it for a long time—*decades*, if you let yourselves."

They knew she was right. Paul smiled and then went back to his meal. It was rabbit stew. "A patient brought the pot to me today," Istvan said, "along with this homemade wine. It's better than money."

Paul raised his glass. Istvan said, "Another lady made this same meal for me when Marta was taken. Let's drink to Anna Barta."

Later, though Marta and Istvan had asked Paul to stay, he said he wanted to get back to Budapest. He promised he would bring Rozsi and the others next time. The dark night sky was as calm as the afternoon blue had been, and the road and the air, the memory of the dinner, the cat, Marta and the little house, warmed his way home.

Thirty-Four

ONE OF THE STOUT SURVIVORS of the war was Lili's white dress, the one her mother had made for her for her sixteenth birthday back in Tolgy. While the dress would serve perfectly on this day as a wedding gown, it was far too big now for Lili and had to be taken in in a hurry.

Klari volunteered to help while Lili took Rozsi to the train station. Even on Lili's wedding day, the girls could not skip this morning excursion to the station to meet the returning Hungarians.

The train was delayed, but Lili didn't want to let her anxiety about getting back show. She held Rozsi's hand until the train pulled in and as Rozsi watched the faces of the people getting off. They didn't look very healthy, many of them, but they were alive and home. Robert said these stragglers might have been people who had to be hospitalized before they could go home. Word was out about where people had been sent. Pictures were being published all over the world about the ghostly survivors. But people returning had already spread the news. Marta had told the Becks what the situation was.

The station was not as crowded as it was the day before, but the waiting faces were just as eager, and then just as disappointed, once the cars had cleared and the whistle had blown. A few got lucky. One woman whooped and screamed and rolled around on the stone platform with her scrawny husband.

The young women returned from the train station empty-handed again, and late. Simon had asked Lili not to take Rozsi out this once, but Rozsi would not rest otherwise and could not be calmed down.

Simon met the women at the door and hardly waited for Rozsi to get out of earshot before saying, "It's *our* wedding day. How could she cut into our day like this?"

Lili was taken aback by Simon's temper. "You're not even supposed to see me today until we meet under the canopy."

"Don't be ridiculous," he said.

"Don't be *ridiculous*?" she repeated. "Think about it. Wouldn't it have been an extraordinary day if our wedding day had also turned into a homecoming?" She smoothed down the sides of the loose green dress she was wearing before asking, "What would you have done? Why don't you go tell Paul his sister is a nuisance?"

When Simon heard Paul's name spoken, he backed off. She was about to take him in her arms when he said, "Now, where *is* Paul this morning? Doesn't *anyone* respect this day?"

"I do," she said.

"I'm sorry," he said. "It's my wedding day."

"It's my wedding day, too," she said.

Simon was about to say something else, but his mother stopped him. She was holding Lili's white dress. "Is this the way to speak to your radiant bride?" Klari asked. "She'll stop radiating for you if you keep it up. You're not even married yet, and look how you're behaving." Klari put her arm around Lili's shoulder and moved her along to her room.

Cousins were missing and friends and acquaintances. Each day, the Becks would get word of people who had survived and those who hadn't, people who had come home and people who hadn't. Some kept visiting the cemetery as if to find news of loved ones there, but very few fresh graves had been dug since the war had come to Hungary. People died abroad or at the bottom of the blue Danube. Klari had news that a sister of hers, Hermina, and her husband, Ede, had both made it and turned up at the house they'd bought in Paris. Like so many others, they had a fantastic story to tell.

After the telegram to Robert and Klari, announcing their return, Hermina wrote a twelve-page letter describing their ordeal.

She and her husband, who was a prominent cardiologist, had been kidnapped in 1942 by German agents and taken to Munich to an officers' hospital. The head of an important unit, a Colonel Munsinger, lay dying of a bullet wound near his heart, and they wanted Dr. Izsak to operate on him to save him. "Ede refused," Hermina wrote in the letter. "You know how stubborn he can be, Klari. He said to the men that he could not, in good conscience, perform surgery on a killer. So they took me out to their courtyard. It was the dead of winter, January, colder than any on record in Munich. They made Ede watch, and they strung me out by my fingers on a steel cable, as if I were laundry, using steel clips for each of my fingers. They ran water along the line, so that my fingers stuck to the line and froze immediately. Ede begged them to let me back in—he would do the surgery—but they said they'd let me back only after he was done. It was a chance he would have to take.

"The clamps were so tight on my fingers, I was ready to faint from the pain of it. But the pain quickly and miraculously passed. The men tugged on the pulley. One of my bare feet clung to the platform while the other dangled above the stone yard. They tugged again. I said, 'Ede,' not loudly, but I could hear my voice careen around the courtyard. My clinging foot left the platform as they tugged again. Then, not looking at me, not even once, the soldiers heaved a last time. A strong pull. I was left hanging by my fingertips. I was frantic. I looked at the men who had turned away from me as I wriggled like a carp on a hook. I couldn't see Ede in the dark window, or anyone. I felt a dark heaviness as if I were being asked to lift a mountain. This was the weight of hanging by my fingertips, the weight of life, I guess, until quickly, surprisingly quickly, the dark heaviness of my body lifted, Klari, light as an angel, and I flitted upward, a pinned angel fluttering up above the courtyard. I remember falling into a heavy darkness again underneath the weight of the mountain. I was half-conscious. I remember feeling myself waiting for the lighting of the sun."

Klari's heart pounded. She turned to the next page of the letter. "And then they let me back in, if you can believe it. As soon as the surgery started. Ede succeeded, naturally, bless his heart, and we spent a year and a half in the place. In the months afterward, my Edward treated dozens and dozens of officers who filed through the place. They had any and every malady you can name. Ede was afraid of what they might do, mostly to me, if he didn't. 'Sick meat,' he used to call them in Hungarian to me. 'I am curing the sick meat, my girl, so it can carry on its ignoble task.'

"But the incredible part of my story, if you ask me, is that that Colonel Munsinger, after he recovered, treated us like a prince and princess. Princess Hermina of the Hebrews. We had plenty to eat and a nice flat and our own maid, for heaven's sake, and then finally they let us come home. They had someone take us by car all the way.

"But, Klarikam, my fingers are still bent. I can't straighten them. Can you believe it? I have partial use of them, but I'm not the same woman with the beautiful hands—remember? No one else had hands like mine, not Etel, not Anna, not Mathilde, and especially not you, dear. Remember? Now I have hands like a crow, like talons, always curled. Ede won't forgive himself. Give my love to everyone. Come see us in Paris, darlings."

The return of Hermina and the reappearance of Istvan, especially, continued to fuel Rozsi's hope. "*I love*," Zoli's note had said. She would often check that her note was still there, but no longer opened it. The paper was disintegrating. "I love," it had said, hanging the words out there, the open-armed words that held her now, too, waiting. Was her Zoli at a hospital somewhere recuperating? She would rush to his side, gladly, and bring him back to health if she could only find out. Had he been taken by his Russian liberators out to the Urals somewhere? The Russians had taken Wallenberg, too, and would not release him. Maybe they were together again, Wallenberg and his photographer. They'd look after each other if they could. The Swede would look after her Zoli the way he looked after everyone else. Save yourself, Mr. Wallenberg, as no one else can, and save my Zoli, too. "Physician, heal thyself"—isn't that what your Luke once said?

Lili and Simon's wedding was to take place at the temple on Rumbach Street, or at least in the courtyard behind the temple. The building itself had been bombed, and a couple of its walls had tumbled in on the others, its Eastern motifs, its arabesques, toppled. At one end, its stained-glass window depicting Joseph, looking himself like a sultan, complete with Arab headdress and magic multicoloured coat, which had drawn the sun into the building and scattered its light in a bouquet of gold, red, blue, purple and green all over the temple's walls, lay shattered and lightless on the floor and seats. The great temple on Dohany, around the corner, where the Becks had been members, Europe's largest and most imposing synagogue, with its Moorish minarets and onion domes, was all but destroyed, the towers toppled, the walls buckled. None of the temples could be used by the Jews that remained—over a half-million were still unaccounted for—but the Rumbach Street temple was holding services out back already, whether or not the season allowed for them, and Robert had known the rabbi for years. They'd often played cards together at Gerbeaud Café, and each was delighted to find the other still walking. The rabbi knew of another player who had survived, over on Sip Street, Imre Kerekes, but the man was recuperating from the flu, and his wife was serving up quite a soup to anyone who visited.

A law was passed that, each day, every family was to send a couple of its able-bodied young people—if the family still had any—to help in the reconstruction of the city, and the Beck household invariably sent Lili and Simon, while Paul and Rozsi stayed back. It was never much of a question. Rozsi didn't get out of bed in the morning, unless someone was going to take her to the train station, and Paul was occupied with the missing, especially Raoul. He didn't feel he could even start the reconstruction Wallenberg had described without him at the helm.

Paul travelled to Debrecen twice to inquire about Wallenberg's visit there. Very few people seemed to know much about it. One couple living on a potato farm just outside the city said the Swede's driver had been killed and his body dumped in a ditch just outside their place. "It was a mess," the woman said. She had leathery skin, but her face shone red in the light of a single naked light bulb that hung from the ceiling. They were sitting in the boot room. Paul had got no farther in.

"Did you see anyone else?"

The woman shook her head.

"How did you know it was the driver and not the diplomat?"

"It was the driver," her husband said. The man's face was a darker leather. "People said it was Vilmos Langfelder. They came in a Studebaker." The man rubbed the side of his nose.

"Are you sure there was just the one man?" Paul asked.

The two looked at each other. "We're sure," the man said. "We have his gold teeth."

"*Almos*," the woman yelled, and she smacked his shoulder good and hard.

"If you'd like to have them, you can have them," the man said.

"No," Paul said.

"The same night, a cart came with hay and stopped at the ditch by our place," the man said. "The next day, the body was gone, and no one talks about it. The Russians are not that nice. They call us Nazi traitors—in their own language, naturally—but I know a couple of words. *Predaatyel*—traitor, collaborator." He smiled, proud of his achievement.

Paul even took a trip, using the Swedish embassy's Alfa Romeo, to Tolgy, on behalf of Lili, to see if anyone had returned. He had found half the houses of the town occupied and the synagogue burned. Paul drew out almost all of the occupants merely by driving up and down the main street with his bright car, but no one had heard of any Jews living there. He told a friendly man who'd insisted on this fact that there was a synagogue on Fischer Street. "Really?" the man said. "I never go that far."

"I guess you don't get out much, then."

"I have a bad back," the man said, and rubbed a kidney to prove it. "I have a deed to our place, too," he said.

Paul lobbied the Hungarian and Swedish governments to press for the release of Wallenberg but was astonished to find that neither would help. The Russians had, after all, been on the side of the Allies and had been his country's liberators, even if they had now become its occupiers.

Paul had talked Per Anger and Lars Berg of the embassy into letting him travel with them to Moscow, but at the last minute Anger backed out unaccountably. Paul then got a letter from Anger, saying that it was hopeless. Anger and Berg had met the Swedish ambassador to Moscow, and he took them into his room to tell them to stop their efforts. He was shaking when he spoke to them. "They don't have Wallenberg," he told Anger. "The Gestapo blew up his car before he ever left Hungary."

Per Anger had heard the same report on the newsreel at the cinema, and Paul had heard this news over Hungarian radio. But the newsreels had to be approved by the Russians before they were released.

"Stay away," the ambassador said, "or they'll send *you* to Siberia, and *me*."

"So he's in Siberia," Anger said. The ambassador looked as if Anger had struck him. He left the room and would have nothing to do with Anger from then on.

Then Paul withdrew, to his uncle's study, mostly. He stared into space or put his head down on the desk. Where could Wallenberg have got to? How could this have happened to him, of all people? Could he not talk his way out of this one? Could he not pull whatever documentation he needed out of thin air? Why had Paul not insisted on going with him to Debrecen? They could have stood up to Malinovsky together, or they could have gone down together. Three men in a ditch, and gold watches to add to Langfelder's gold teeth. Or was Raoul's watch already gone by then? Did the Russians raiding the embassy take it, or did Malinovsky? Worker of miracles, could he not work a miracle now? If not for him, then for them. They had work to do, still, much work, as he himself had pointed out. Survival was not enough, survival without dignity. But how could he do it alone? How could any of them?

And where were his Hungarians? Where was *his* army? Where the Jews, pulled from the transports and ghettos, their babies born on his bed? They were free, now, free to be an army of the righteous. Where were they, his witnesses? Their saviour was at the gallows awaiting punishment for his good deed. What must he be thinking now? From here to there. Awaiting the testimony that would set him free. Where were you all? And where, he was surely thinking, was Paul?

As the days passed, Paul paid less and less attention to the wheeling of the sun and moon. He was becoming more like his sister. When he broke into a rant at the dinner table, he was thinking less of what to put in the way of evil, and less about how to get out of the way of evil, and more about what gave rise to it.

The trouble was the thinking itself. His thinking was crowding out experience, crowding out his life. Making sense of the world was no longer the point. What Paul tried to make sense of was hatred fuelled by feeling alone, by impulse, not thought, a hatred so pure and unblemished it banished thought. More importantly, it banished the countervailing signals of conscience, rose out of the natural plane to where the air was thin but pure and gave life to creatures who were untroubled by the world below. Plans, yes. These creatures hatched plans. Excellent, elaborate plans. A special kind of genius. How to round up the vermin, how to dehumanize them, how to develop Zyklon B and dispense it cheaply and efficiently for the eradication of all communists, homosexuals, Gypsies and Jews. But not if a Jew is Jesus? Not if a homosexual's wife bears a child? Not if a Gypsy violinist plays Wagner? Not if a communist turns nationalist-socialist? No. The plan does not allow for complications. The plan is not excellent; it is perfect. Complications admit thought, awaken conscience. Oh, how we complicate the world for you, we human pulp, you unthinking genius of evil; you cannot have second thoughts if you haven't had first ones. Just a plan. A good plan, carried out by loyal, thoughtless ministers.

Dare we feel it? Dare we utter the words? They become giddy with the weight of it, weightless, and the weightlessness buoys fearlessness. *They* are what have hurt us. *They* are what have hampered us. *They* are the ones who have stood in the way of our achievement. *They* are what we hate. He pounds his fist, and we pound ours. *Die Juden— ja, ja, ja—die Juden!* So pure. So simple. Beautiful as Bach. Pure as mathematics. The word clean as a bell. They. So simple and tidy. What a tidy little place to locate our hatred, roll it into a ball and fire it at them. They are the ones. Do you hear it? You.

Where, then, will the criminals' trials lead us, we nations united against you? Are you all to be found guilty? Were we all innocent? In the pure, untroubled air of certainty, yes. In the earthbound world languishing among the ruins of thought, no.

What would it have been like, this thoughtless, forbidden place? Paul asked himself. A place without consequences. And how must it feel to be dragged down now by your repressors into sullied consequence and thought? Imagine those unfettered days—off with his head, off with hers—anyone who offends you, anyone who might offend you, strangers from a group you've decided will certainly offend you. Off with their heads! How glorious! How free!—Headless Nation!

Only now, today, to be hauled back down into thought. God must be so weary. Dear God, if our Adolf stands before You, in that thin air, on that special plane, don't let him evade You. Seat him before his handiwork. Seat him at the gates of Auschwitz, his legs crossed, his soldier's back straight, his mouth stilled, and let him stare until the key to the vault of his conscience slips in through his eyes or his ears, slips in on the wings of a grey bird, or until the Polish winter buries him, scentless like a gas.

A LETTER CAME for Paul from Philadelphia. His former assistant, Viktor, had tracked him down and brought it to him. It was two days before he opened it. It was from Zsuzsi Rosenthal in Philadelphia, and it was dated April 19. Almost two months had passed since she'd mailed it.

> Suzanne Rosenthal Stein
> 22 Washington Boulevard
> Philadelphia, Pennsylvania
> April 19, 1945
>
> My dear Paul,
>   I'm writing on the chance that you have made it and will read this greeting. It has been too long. I thought of you often in the middle of the turmoil at home. I imagined you crusading in the way that you do. I had only a glimpse of that quality in you, but it stayed with me. The news reports that came to us here were quite incomplete. Only now are the stories and pictures appearing. I hope your family came through it all right.
>   I think about us in Komarom that day, how your aunts Klari and Hermina had arranged a lunch. I didn't think the lunch would turn out so memorable.
>   I have an eight-year-old son, but no husband any longer. Jonathan went over last June to fight in Normandy and, on July 6, I had word that he'd been killed in action. I guess there's no guarantee of safety wherever you go.

I have enclosed a photograph of my son and me, taken when he was six. His name is Sam. We're standing in front of the steps of the Philadelphia Museum of Art.

If it is ever possible, I hope you can visit.

Look after yourself, Paul.

Zsuzsi

Paul spent a long time studying the photograph. She looked exactly the same, slim and elegant—elegant as a calla lily—though this picture was taken at a little distance. The boy in the photo had curly hair, while hers was straighter. He stood quite upright and confident, in her care.

AS KLARI HELPED LILI get ready for her big day, Rozsi excused herself and fled to Robert's study to visit with her brother. Paul sat looking straight ahead in the half-light of the room. He had Zsuzsi's letter and photograph in front of him, and she asked if she might look.

He pushed the letter toward her, and she read it, examined the photo, and cried. She looked at her brother. His eyes were open and unblinking. He frightened her, until he said, "They're nice, aren't they?"

"Very," she said. Then she asked, "Are you going to the wedding?"

He didn't answer.

She approached him, placed a hand on the back of his head, grasped the auburn curls. "In the last days," he said, "Adolf was throwing choirboys at the Russians and Americans—did you know that? 'Rip them to pieces,' he must have been telling them. 'Throw off those robes, strap on these uniforms—off with their heads! Off! Off! Chew them up and spit them out. Chew them up with those same fangs and tongues and lips with which, after vespers, you daily sing 'Panis Angelicus' and dear Papa Bach's 'Schlafe, mein Liebster.'"

Rozsi stepped back from her brother. He smiled at her, looked contrite. "Palikam," she went on, "just tell me, please. You know everything, you and your Swede. Look into your crystal ball and tell me, is my Zoli coming back to me?" Paul looked up into her eyes but couldn't answer. She sat on one of his bony knees and hugged him. "Forgive me—please don't judge me," she said. "I'm in despair, that's all."

"That's plenty," he said.

"Why wouldn't you?" she said. "Of course you do." She kissed his cool cheek.

They sat quietly.

"I miss people," Rozsi said. "Even the ones who are still with us."

They sat for a minute. He heard her sniffle, and she said, "I miss you." He put his arm around her waist. "We're all here because of *you*. Zoli was not as smart as you. You knew how to get out there and order them around. That's what the Germans knew best—being ordered around."

He gave her his handkerchief and she blew her nose, tried to smile at her brother. "I know that you have the rest of Zoli's pictures. I can't even look at them. I saw a couple of them. The rest must be horrible. I'll look at them only when he gets back, and he can tell me what's in them." Paul nodded but didn't answer. "What if he doesn't come back to me?" she went on. She was looking down at her ruby ring, twirling it on her finger. It was far too big. Everything was too big. A heavy rain must have passed over them when they weren't looking, she was thinking, and shrunk them all.

"I sometimes think of our cousin, Alexander the Great," she said. "I want to ask him to remake the world for me like Hollywood. End it the way Hollywood does. Not Europe. Europe is no good at these things."

He tried to smile again, but couldn't find anything reassuring to say. "Listen to us," she said, getting to her feet. She looked unsteady. "You're talking about throwing choirs at people, and I'm talking about Tinseltown."

Hermina surprised the Becks by coming from Paris. The family had already been disappointed by Istvan. He had called to say Marta was not feeling up to the trip. They were very sorry. It was Marta's third trimester, and they wanted to be careful.

So Hermina's appearance brightened up the Becks' Budapest home. Klari was happiest to see her, and she laughed out loud. Hermina was got up in a splendid blue taffeta dress with a majestic black collar. "It's a *quinze-seize*," Klari said. Hermina wore a silk slip under it. "I asked one of the 'residents' living in my house—because we have had permanent visitors since we *abandoned* the place to go be kidnapped and hung off frozen cables in Munich—I asked one of them, a seamstress, to turn some curtains into a dress for me, clever thing. She agreed without a bribe, so I gave her a gift of a pearl bracelet my dear Ede had found for me in Munich, of all places, a bracelet I'm sure was confiscated from some soul in heaven by now. I didn't care for it much, to tell you the truth. But at least it's made it back to the right place, or close to it. Here's the matching necklace and earrings," she said, running her fingers over the pearls.

"Hermikem, only you could have conjured up such a thing," her sister said. "And your hair! Goodness. How did you manage the lovely black colour?"

"Klarikam, a girl doesn't give away all her secrets." Hermina patted a newly made curl at her temple. "But if I left it to Nature, she'd leave the job undone, save all her colour for the young. Heartless Nature. More snake than nightingale."

Then Hermina turned to Lili, and Klari introduced the young woman. "Like the gold stingy Nature has given to you. So this is the bride." She stepped back from the younger woman and took her hair in her warped fingers. "Nature has not lost her touch. We should be happy." But Hermina looked dramatically teary.

She said to Lili, "Look what I've brought for you for your wedding. The taxi driver carried it in for me." She closed the front door and, behind it, folded into a small silk Persian rug, was a grand portrait in oils of a young woman sitting in a chair. The woman was no older than twenty-seven or -eight. Soft eyes looked out from the picture; soft hands were folded in the woman's lap. One hand, adorned by a warm gold wedding band, rested on the other, which bore an amethyst ring.

Lili stared at the impressive painting and said, "She looks familiar, the eyes . . ." She turned toward Hermina.

"Yes, dear," Hermina said. "It's a portrait of me. Look at me then, and look at me now." She held up her hands to the light. The fingers were curled as if they were cradling something. "They're like talons."

Klari took her sister's hands in hers and kissed them, and then Lili stepped between the two and took the liberty of kissing them both. "What a lovely, thoughtful gift," Lili said. "I'll cherish it."

"And it was done by a fine artist, too—Ferenc Martyn. The man has strange ideas, but he's an immense talent, as you can see."

Simon turned up then, and Lili showed him the painting his aunt had brought, but Hermina held up her hands again. "I look like a crow," she said.

"No you don't," Simon said, and he hugged her, too. "A robin maybe, or today a bluebird," he was looking at her dress, "but certainly not a crow."

His mother swatted at him, but he got out of the way.

Lili burst into tears. Simon took her in his arms. "What happened, my sweetheart?"

"Nothing," she said, but her sobs intensified.

"It's your parents, isn't it?" Klari said. "Your family." Lili nodded. "It's her wedding day, and her family's not here."

Simon held her. "I wish I could meet them."

Just then Robert arrived home. "Tears?" he said. Robert was the most remarkably shrunken of them all. There were only so many times a suit could be taken in.

Klari explained, and Robert said, "Of course. Poor dear thing. It's an emotional day."

And then he saw his sister-in-law. "Hermina," he said, "what a wonderful surprise. Is Ede with you?"

"He couldn't come," Hermina said. She offered her cheek for Robert to kiss. "He's as busy as you are, I imagine."

"I'm sure he is. What an ordeal you went through," Robert said.

She held up the curled hands. "I'm a crow," she said.

He stood back from her and brought her fingers to his lips as he studied her. "Not a crow," he said. "A peacock."

Now his wife swatted at him. He almost tripped but caught himself in time. "Damn!" It was the suitcases. Klari had insisted on keeping a packed suitcase in the hall since the family had arrived home. She feared anything could still happen, and she wanted to be able to slip away at any time before they were dragged away. So the suitcase, containing a change of clothing for each of them, some flour, some sugar, some salt, yeast and lard, stood always in the vestibule just behind the door. Every second or third day, Robert stepped in, turned around and tripped over it. "Damn thing! Damn!" He glared at his wife. But Hermina's suitcase had been set down beside his wife's, so he didn't carry on.

He straightened himself up and said, "Look what I rustled up." He held out four corsages.

Klari said, "How on Earth did you manage these?" They were red and white carnations. "Gorgeous." She plunged her nose into one and inhaled its scent.

"Do you remember Dezso, over on Vaci Street? He's back. He made them. He looks like hell, but he's selling flowers again. He's determined. 'What should I do, apprentice to a blacksmith?' he asked me. 'It's all I know, and all my parents knew.' He was in Buchenwald. His parents and sister didn't make it back. Only him. And he's got his flowers going again. 'It's June,' he told me, 'and the land is full of flowers. They don't know any better, and neither do I.' Ha!"

"I need to get ready," Lili said, wiping her eyes with Simon's handkerchief.

She headed back to her room. Rozsi was still lying on the bed with her eyes wide open, but looking at nothing at all.

Lili said, "Uncle Robert brought us carnations—can you believe that? Some for you, too. They're sweet."

Rozsi sat up in the bed. "You've been crying," she said.

"Just the sniffles."

"I'm so tired, but I can hardly ever sleep," said Rozsi.

"Have a nap this afternoon, then, when we come back from the temple."

"Where will I sleep tonight?" Rozsi asked. Lili looked at her and realized what she was asking. "May I stay here in this room with you, just until Zoli gets back? I promise we'll find another place then."

"Of course you may," Lili answered.

"What about your husband?" Rozsi asked, like a child.

"My husband and I, if we make it that far today, will find our moments together, don't worry."

"It'll just be until Zoli gets back."

Robert checked for Paul in his study. When he saw the younger man, he smiled and told him about Dezso and the corsages. Paul said how nice it was that people were reappearing, a few of them, and Robert went quiet for a moment before saying, "Did you know that Manfred Weiss, the industrialist, met with Eichmann? *Adolf Eichmann.* The butcher who would not condescend to release a single Jew except to ship them off. He *met* with Weiss. He had to cut a deal with Weiss—that's how powerful the bastard was, powerful as Eichmann."

Paul didn't respond to his uncle. He'd behaved throughout the war like an agent for a secret service and had got out of the habit of talking about delicate matters. Robert never knew of Paul's own visit with Wallenberg to Eichmann's headquarters. Paul recalled the things he wanted to tell the little bastard, and he smiled now. Eichmann had still not been apprehended. He might have been in Germany still, somewhere, or he might have left the continent, for all anyone knew.

Fleeing Nazis were turning up in Argentina, living and working side by side with Jews who had fled earlier.

"Weiss arranged for transport out of the country," Robert went on, "a personal escort of Hungarian troops for him and his family in exchange for signing over his holdings to the Germans. They got out to Switzerland, and I heard today they might be heading to New York, those Weisses." Robert relit a small cigar he'd been carrying in his jacket pocket and shook his head. He took his stethoscope out of the same pocket and tossed it on the desk. "Imagine. He met with Eichmann. As determined as Hitler. He might as well have met with Hitler." Robert was still shaking his head as he blew smoke all around him. He was waiting for his nephew to react to the news, but Paul just continued to gaze at him, lacing his fingers together and blowing over them as if he, too, were smoking. "I wonder where Weiss is now, exactly, or if he'll come back to Hungary in the end. I wonder where bloody Eichmann is now."

Paul's silence bewildered Robert. "Are you ready for today?"

"I don't know," Paul said without affect, and the two men looked at each other.

Robert punched out his cigar in the lid of a jar he was using lately for that purpose. His crystal ashtray had gone missing, as had the porcelain Herend one in the living room.

Robert felt uncomfortable in his own study. "Excuse me," he said and departed.

Vera spoke to Klari in the kitchen about the wedding, because Klari had invited her and her family to attend. Vera said they'd feel too uncomfortable, but she offered Klari a braided egg bread she had baked and covered with a cloth. "For after the ceremony," Vera said.

Hermina's presence had emboldened Klari. She wanted everyone cheered and ready to go to the wedding of her son. So the sisters walked into Robert's study just as Robert left it. "Look at you, sitting here in the dark," Hermina said. Her presence caused Paul to smile again. Hermina went to open the curtains. "Look at you," she said again. You're like a bat." And then she held up the fingers again. "And I'm a crow. Fine pair we make."

Paul rose out of his chair. "You poor thing," he said. "I've heard about your ordeal."

"We've all been through a bad time," she said. "But now that time is over."

Paul hugged Hermina surprisingly hard. "Careful," she said, pulling away. "My hair."

"Paul, dear, you're not ready for the wedding," Klari said. "You were planning to come, I hope."

He didn't answer right away.

"He's your cousin. We're a badly reduced family as it is, and each one of us is important to this ceremony. Look, your aunt came all the way from Paris—dressed in curtains—can you imagine?"

Paul sat back down in a leather chair and covered his eyes with both hands. His aunts couldn't tell if he was crying. Klari wanted to tell her sister that Paul had heard from Zsuzsi—they'd introduced the young pair, after all—but she decided to wait until later. She wasn't even sure what Zsuzsi had said and wanted to find out first. Maybe Paul had left the letter in Robert's desk drawer.

"Come, my dear," Klari said more tenderly to her nephew. "The days of being locked up are over." Paul didn't budge.

"Why do you save people just to spook them with your moods?" Hermina asked. "We're *allowed* to go out, without an armband, without a cloth star on our chests, and we're allowed to head straight over to the site of a synagogue without being arrested. Time to get up." She was ready to hook her warped hands under Paul's arms and hoist the tall man to his feet.

Paul uncovered his damp face and said, "Of course, I'm coming." He got up again. "Who said I wasn't going to come?"

"And let's walk down Andrassy, not Kiraly," Hermina said. "Let's get noticed."

THE WEDDING PARTY that moved down Andrassy toward Rumbach was just a vestige of the original family, more like a band of itinerant actors playing the Becks, Izsaks and Bandels, the cast too small, the costumes too big. But the sun shone, the ladies sported carnations, and a new household was about to be established.

Paul strode ahead like a scout. The ladies refused to march. They walked calmly up the avenue and would not be perturbed by Paul's rush. "I don't know what to make of that boy," Hermina said. She stood out among the women in her bright gown—indeed stood out among all the people on the avenue—she was blue as the Danube once was, blue as the Danube of the waltz.

"I know what to make of him," Klari said. She wore her famous forest-green gown with the wide white collar, although the dress had needed to be pinned and taken in every which way. "I know exactly what to make of him."

"He needs to find someone," Hermina said. "That's all it is." Then she added, "Thinking is an illness, more harmful even than remembering. Paul started mourning people even before they were being led off to die."

"No," Klari said. "Paul's not like that. Some people were made for mourning. They mourn even before they have cause. They're in mourning-readiness. Not Paul. He wanted to stave off the day of mourning, prevent it from ever having to occur. There's a big difference. It's just that he couldn't win over followers. There were days, during the dark campaign, when Hungarians wouldn't heed his warnings. This couldn't happen to them, they believed, not here. They were Hungarian first and Jewish second—a distant second. Paul really is a Cassandra. He saw the future, but people didn't believe him."

And then they remembered they were walking with Rozsi, so Hermina said again, "He'll find someone, I'm sure. Why shouldn't he? *Everybody* will. And if not one person, then another. If not that nice Zsuzsi we once introduced him to, then someone. The world will remake itself. We're here. We're walking down the street, the sidewalks will refill and the coffee will pour again." She leaned closer to Rozsi and said, as if in confidence, "All I can say is, don't open a corset store in the near future," and then she hooted up a storm.

"Do you know what we should all do?" Hermina said. "The cinemas are starting to open again. We should take Paul and Rozsi out to see a Laurel and Hardy picture, like *Pack Up Your Troubles*. Do you remember that one, dear?"

"How could I forget?"

"I love them with a passion. They get into all kinds of danger but never come to harm." Then she said, "I wonder how our cousin, Sir Korda, is making out. Of course, only you would know, Klarikam. Has he written to you lately?"

"Not lately."

"Oh, I wonder . . ." Hermina said.

The wedding party had begun to spread out, with Paul up ahead, Robert and Simon in the middle and the ladies well behind. The streets had certainly changed. Some buildings were bombed-out shells, some shaded dark with flame. The Erzsebet and Chain bridges were still out between Buda and Pest, though their reconstruction had begun.

Lili felt thrilled to have Hermina with them. She smiled at the ladies while Rozsi gazed straight ahead, following her brother in spirit if not in pace. Lili took Rozsi's hand in hers. Rozsi tried a smile then.

"We need to find a candle," Rozsi said suddenly. "Another one of those *Jahrzeit* candles in a glass for tonight."

"We will, right after the wedding," Lili said.

Rozsi had been burning a candle in the window of their bedroom almost every night, a waiting candle, shining out to the street like a beacon. Lili had made a point of procuring the candles as often as she could during her lunch hour, hoping that lighting the flame would keep Rozsi's spirits up.

"And I need some more medicine," Rozsi said. "I'm almost out. I need more pills to calm me."

"I've already let the apothecary know, and they'll be ready by tomorrow."

Simon had a good look at each building as they passed, sizing up the damage, wondering whether he'd be involved in the repair. Robert was limping. His shoes were far too small, but they could find no other decent ones for the occasion. The pairs that had been in his closet at home were all gone when they returned to Jokai Street. His old friend Feher, the shoemaker, in Vorosmarty Square, had not returned from the war, and even Brun, from whom he'd bought fine handmade shoes in Vienna, had perished.

They passed a millinery, the old Lengyel family's shop. It had been looted, the windows broken. What a fancy shop it had been, Simon thought. There were four Lengyels altogether, a son and daughter younger than he was—Simon, the boy was called, and Edit. Simon didn't always remember, but this time he did. Not only were the hats all gone, the papier mâché heads they'd been displayed on had also been taken for good measure. Simon looked over his shoulder at the women, tried to get their attention, pointed to the store. He wondered where the Lengyels had ended up, where they were now lying.

Robert said, "The ghosts are all around us here. On every block. We're practically trampling on their skulls as we walk. It's a city with a brutal history, isn't it? A country with a brutal history."

The men had arrived at the intersection with Kaldy Gyula Street and had to turn left. They were gratified that a small café had opened here on the corner, the Lovas Café, a *new* café. They looked back at the women to make sure they knew they were turning. Paul up ahead was nowhere to be seen. He was surely at the Rumbach temple by now.

"I have to stop just a minute," Robert said. "My feet. But I'm afraid to take my shoes off, because I'll never get them back on. I wish I'd worn the other ones." He was leaning back against the brick wall of an office building.

"Take mine," Simon said. "They're bigger."

"But your feet are bigger, too. You'll never walk again if you cram your feet into these."

"Please, Father."

"It's your wedding day. If I switch with you now, you'll spend the next sixty-five years telling people how you wore tiny, torturous shoes on your wedding day. No, I'll suffer, and I'll tell the story, but not for as long."

They were nearly at the Rumbach temple, now, or the ruins of the temple, and looked back at the women. The streets were surprisingly quiet that morning. They had Budapest to themselves.

Paul had been looking at the temple, then at the battered Dohany Street temple around the corner. What had we been thinking when we built these piles? he asked himself. Was it the bigness of God we were trying to show off, or our own achievements? He saw the toppled temple more clearly now than when it had stood proud a year before. He'd hardly noticed it then.

The women caught up with the men, and the group was met at the temple by Lili's friend Maria and her fiancé, Patrik, as well as a small group of Robert's colleagues. The synagogue's yellow-and-white minarets, like the towers of a mosque, still stood in the blue June sunlight. The door was gone and the upper windows blown out from within their casements, and the walls behind the front wall were collapsed, so the front held on precariously.

The congregation, what was left of it, had done a nice job carting away the broken stone and sweeping up the brick dust.

Rabbi Langer greeted them as Paul stood straight and tall by the *chuppah*. Klari spoke to the rabbi first. "There is nothing to be solemn about, not today, if you don't mind."

Robert added, "This is a very good day for us, good days ahead."

The *chuppah*, under which the wedding party stood, must have come from quite a bed, because it sheltered all of them, including the rabbi and cantor. They were much diminished, Robert thought, but still—he looked up and was glad of the cool shelter from the sun.

At first the cantor sang as if he were performing a Kaddish, slow and doleful, a sound that came from somewhere deep in his chest. But he was just warming up.

The rabbi said to the small group, "I cannot talk today about ruling the planet or about being ruled, or about dying or surviving— listen to me, I sound like Ecclesiastes despite myself. To tell you the truth, I confess for the first time these are topics I can't even fathom anymore. This was not the great Flood, and I am not Noah. I was barely able to retain my own faith, let alone preach it to others." Lili glanced over her shoulder at Paul. "There is too much weight just behind us," the rabbi said, "and too much just ahead." Here, the rabbi paused.

He then gave the usual blessing as if they were standing in the usual place, on the blue-and-white mosaic floor, the congregation facing the glass Joseph in his colourful coat. Lili and Simon exchanged vows. And Simon slipped the ring, engraved with the name "*Ivan*" and the wrong date, "*13 Aprilis 1935*," the ring they had got from the deportation train, onto his wife's finger. He and Lili kissed.

Then Simon crunched the customary glass wrapped in cloth beneath his heel, except not a wine glass on this occasion—one couldn't be spared—but a burnt-out light bulb.

Rabbi Langer stepped up to his old card partner and asked, almost under his breath, if there was to be a reception afterward.

"Yes," Robert said, loudly enough for everyone to hear. "I have arranged a surprise for all of you at the Lovas Café. I've arranged a good lunch for us of herring followed by goose, courtesy of my colleagues at the hospital."

Just before they left, Hermina talked to Rabbi Langer about the synagogue. "I know you'll want to rebuild this place," she said. He nodded solemnly. "But if you're going to put Joseph back up in the window, I would drop the colourful coat," she said. She was whispering. "It does nothing for him, if you want to know the truth. Something in green would be lovely with the light coming through, or a blue with a dark lapel. Royal blue would work quite nicely."

The rabbi didn't know what to say. Hermina patted him on the cheek with her warped hand. "You know what?" she said, with a shrug. "We're here. Isn't that what counts?"

He shrugged, too, and said, "We are here, it's true. Here again."

The reception was better than anyone could have imagined. It featured a Gypsy quintet that played as if they'd been trained in a Berlin symphony hall. Robert recognized one of them right away from the days of the Japan Café. He was a favourite there, Kosmo Romani, and there was someone else from the Japan, Arista Barany. So nice to have them resurface. Four gentlemen and a lady, for how else could you describe them when they played Schubert's String Quintet in C Major the way it was intended. Their music transformed the room. Robert was whispering to his wife, but Lili approached her newly minted father-in-law and reminded him of what he'd once told her: "When you are in the presence of great music, it must occupy all your attention." The room was quiet throughout, as if the group were attending a concert, not a party.

At the end, the violist, the quintet's one woman, set down her instrument, stood and sang "Ombra mai fu" from Handel's *Xerxes*. She sang not like an opera singer, because she certainly wasn't one, but as if her heart were her instrument, sang like the naïve contralto she was, the amateur in love. Hermina sat with Paul and Rozsi at a round table in a corner of the small room, and she took Paul's hand in hers. Her eyes filled with tears, and Paul squeezed her hand. "Did you hear those notes?" she said, after the aria was over.

"Those notes were the most natural procession of sound imaginable," he said. "You'd never expect a lark to roar, so inevitable is its sound—obvious and inevitable. The art is to give those notes an inevitability, a forward tilt. It's true of everything, all the arts. The art of the humorist is to tell the joke as if it were spontaneous, rather than rehearsed a thousand times."

Robert approached Kosmo Romani and asked, "Where have you been?" Both were beaming. "I've missed seeing you."

"Well, I'm here," he answered. "The war kept us busy. *Now* what are we going to do?" He laughed heartily at his own joke, and Robert joined him.

As a single violinist played a Jewish hora, he was joined on the viola by the lady who'd sung Handel, and the revellers joined hands and danced. They swooped and kicked their feet and felt warm and happy. Simon and Lili were each placed on a chair and hoisted high above the other dancers. They were king and queen of the afternoon. And then they ate herring and challah and danced some more.

Lili could not consummate her marriage that night. She waited for Rozsi to fall asleep so she could sneak away, but Rozsi sat up over her candle in the window and waited until morning.

Thirty-Five

ISTVAN ASKED FATHER SEBESTYEN for two small favours: that he not be expected to renounce his original faith and that the conversion lessons be postponed until sometime after the ceremony. Going through with this wedding at the Church of Our Lady of the Snow, in King Mathias Square, was all his idea, not Marta's. In fact, she was against the silliness. She felt, for one thing, that there was plenty of time, and for another, she was the one who'd first offered to convert.

The church was one Istvan had always admired for its simplicity. It was all white, had a modest steeple and was more welcoming inside than intimidating.

Father Sebestyen was looking at some notes beside the pulpit when they arrived. While they waited, Istvan and Marta looked up at the impressive star-vaulted ceiling with its stone ribs, then turned their attention to the pulpit, which was carved with four alluring cherubs, embodying faith, hope, love and justice. The Virgin Mary stood on the high altar. As Istvan looked up at her, Father Sebestyen said, "Apparently, this lovely Virgin lay at the bottom of Lake Csoporke, beside our church, until a century and a half ago, when a Turkish soldier whose horse needed a drink spotted her at the bottom. The Turk arranged to have her brought back in."

"I wonder whether she was tossed into the lake in anger, or hidden there by worshippers," Istvan said.

Father Sebestyen agreed happily to Istvan's conditions for the wedding, just as long as the couple didn't insist on the pomp of a customary Sunday Catholic service. Everyone opted for simplicity and quiet.

The priest took out a standard form and began to fill it out: first, the mother's name, place of birth, date of birth. Marta said, "Marta Foldi, Szeged, June 16, 1917, and November 7, 1944."

Father Sebestyen looked at the couple over the top of his reading glasses. He said, "I can't put in your child's birthday." He coughed and added, barely audibly, "There's no place on a Roman Catholic wedding form for a child, you understand, except in the case of widows who are marrying again, after their loss."

"It's not my child's birthday," Marta said. "It's mine." The priest looked at Istvan. Marta said, "I have two birthdays now: the day of my birth here and the day I stepped out of a gas chamber."

Father Sebestyen looked at the resolve in Marta's eyes and without another word squeezed the second date into the box along with the first one.

After the ceremony, Istvan and Marta and their two witnesses walked all the way back to her house. Istvan's home, the one he'd shared with his father, had been taken over by the Russians as their headquarters for the city.

They had wanted to keep the ceremony quiet, even solemn, in deference to the memory of Anna Barta and Dr. Janos Benes. Marta had not even invited her brother, Frank, in Chicago, or Istvan his family in Budapest. They would explain later and apologize. Two guests did attend: Denes Cermak, who was back at his newsstand, selling news about the reconstruction of the world after the loss of fifty million souls, and Fifi Gyarmati, the widow of Miklos Radnoti.

The poet had taken his march back to Budapest from Bereck with a hundred other men, led by Sergeant Erdo, but only a handful had made it to the city. Fifi Gyarmati had hired an investigator and a lawyer to find out about her husband in his last days. They'd located one of the survivors, Denes Bekes, who told them that Erdo had become fed up with having to accommodate the men and drank a great deal along the way. "Mr. Radnoti was the most annoying to Erdo. He caught him scribbling in that notebook of his and beat him repeatedly. Finally, two nights before we got home, he shot the scribbler, along with a dozen other men, and we buried them in a shallow grave. I know where it is. Only sixteen of us made it all the way back."

Fifi said she wanted her husband's body found and exhumed; she wanted him buried at the Kerepesi Cemetery, as befitted an extraordinary artist; and she wanted Erdo prosecuted.

Commandant Fekete and his men, the ones who'd left Bereck and headed toward the Ukraine, had all perished.

MARTA HAD INVITED one other person to the wedding, Alfred Paderewski, the Polish nobleman who'd taken her in after her escape from Auschwitz. She wrote him a card, saying how much his help had meant to her and inviting him as an "honoured guest" to their wedding.

Paderewski answered that he couldn't attend, but he arranged to have a sumptuous feast sent to the little house on Alma Street. Marta and Istvan received goose and dumplings, trout, asparagus, sweet potatoes, cabbage, beets, rounded off with a chestnut torte. A dozen bottles of champagne came too. "Mr. Paderewski has clearly seen neither the size of this house," Istvan said, "nor the size of the wedding party."

Smetana had leapt on the table so often during the robust meal that Istvan was ready to put him outside, but Fifi said that the scrawny cat was the third guest, and a blessing, and loaded a plate for him with goodies from the wedding feast. She set the plate beside them at their feet.

It was warm in the small house, even though the cast-iron stove was quiet. Flotow's *Martha* played quietly on the phonograph. Denes

Cermak was describing the destruction he'd heard about over to the west in Germany. He said he had seen a photo of the once proud German city of Dresden, and it was bad. "It wasn't just destroyed," he said. "Other cities were destroyed, but Dresden was pounded down, hammered. The Allies' message to the German nation was, 'Enough of you, enough of your evil empire. Down with you, into the ground.'"

Fifi reminded Denes that this was a happy occasion and they didn't want to hear about destruction. She was holding up her champagne glass. "We have a new couple starting here this afternoon—a new trio, it looks like." She pointed to Marta's belly. She was showing now. Fifi smiled again and they all drank.

Later, Istvan got to his feet and raised his own glass. He studied the glass against the light. "Has there ever been a colour more reassuring than this golden wine?" He turned to his new wife. "Marta, my dear wife, you sacrificed yourself for me." He waited, closed his eyes for a moment. "We'll say, today, that we won't ever forget these things, and we'll instruct our children not to forget, but then . . . Today we step up to fill ourselves out the way we used to." Istvan took another gulp of his champagne and set down his glass. "We have made it out the other end of a hallucination. And guess what has lain in wait for us? The music has lain in wait for us. The poetry. Love. Maybe not youth, maybe not much of our youth. I think we might have lost that while we were still young." He took another drink. "But I drink, now, to you, my Marta—and I drink quite a bit, I might add." Everyone got to their feet. "I will stand firm as a sentinel in this place and raise a family in the middle of this history, to *defy* the history."

Istvan took his seat, and Fifi said, "What a speech," and immediately stood to spoon out some more food before anyone else started to talk. Denes took a good thick goose neck into his hands and sucked at the bits of flesh fenced in by the bone.

A MONTH LATER, Fifi Gyarmati succeeded in persuading the provisional government that a shallow grave outside Budapest contained the bodies of fallen heroes of the war. When her husband was exhumed, Istvan and Marta were present. Radnoti's body was easy to spot. He still had on his trench coat. Inside the pocket was his notebook containing his last lines, written in pencil. The poem, entitled "Picture Postcard," appeared on the penultimate page:

> The oxen drool saliva mixed with blood.
> Each one of us is urinating blood
> The squad stands about in knots, stinking, mad.
> Death, hideous death, is blowing overhead.
>
> I fall beside him and his body turns over,
> Taut already as a taut string.
> Shot in the neck. "And that's how you'll end too,"
> I whisper to myself. "Lie still—
> Now patience flowers into death." I hear,
> "Er springt noch auf," above, quite near.
> Blood mixed with mud is drying in my ear.

Erdo was never found. A cousin of his said he'd moved to South America. Radnoti was buried with honours in the Kerepesi Cemetery, as his widow had requested.

Thirty-Six

TWO SOVIET OFFICIALS showed up at Robert's clinic at Sacred Heart. He was performing surgery, so they waited in his office for two hours for him to finish. One of them wore a suit that was too big for him, a blue one, with sleeves too long. Maybe he'd taken it off a rack and walked out without trying it on. The one in the ill-fitting suit was the translator.

Robert hadn't even sat down when the other one, in a nicer tan suit, said, "Dr. Beck, do you know of the whereabouts and activities of your nephew Paul Beck?" The translator translated.

Robert was hoping these men could help get Paul to resume his old productive life. "My nephew?" he said. "If you're asking whether he's been on work detail, the answer is no. I know about that. My son and daughter-in-law go every single day, and now she's pregnant, so I'm quite concerned. I'm a physician, as you can see, so I'm concerned. Paul's probably out hunting for Raoul Wallenberg as usual, if I know him." And he smiled. "Why don't you go ask him yourself? He lives with us."

"We went by this morning. He wasn't home."

"Oh, you did?" Robert now realized he'd said too much. It was a childish thing to do, foolish even, possibly.

"Raoul Wallenberg has nothing to do with the Soviet regime," the official told him. "We met with him, but we're through with him. He had many enemies, and he was killed by one of them."

"Of course." Then he added, "Too bad."

"Yes, too bad." The man in the tan suit took out a card. "Would you please ask your nephew to come and see us tomorrow?"

"Yes, I will." Robert was anxious now. He didn't know what he'd done. Maybe nothing. Certainly nothing. The Russians wouldn't have come looking for Paul if they didn't have something on him already. Still, he should have kept Paul's activities to himself.

LILI AND ROZSI visited the apothecary that day to pick up another bottle of pills. The man behind the counter, dressed in a three-piece suit under a white lab coat with pens gleaming from the pocket, simply issued the medicine to Rozsi now without consultation with a doctor. Her Uncle Robert had refused to issue another prescription for the young woman. Rozsi stood in front of the pharmacist, unassuming, uncommunicative, and he counted out the hundred tranquilizers, the second batch since the beginning of February. Lili paid, and the young women left. They could easily have been foreigners, so few words had been exchanged.

Lili walked Rozsi home and headed back to the opera house, where she was helping to clean up still, assisting the plasterers and painters. Before that she'd been helping Simon and a crew of two hundred others on the damaged Liberty Bridge. Simon was working again as a tool and die maker and was now casting dies for iron rods required in the bridge's reconstruction. The aim was to restore the old bridge exactly as it had been, complete with the two majestic *turul* birds on either side at its peaks and the royal crests of the Austro-Hungarian Emperor Franz-Josef. From another time.

Simon and Lili didn't mind the requirement that they be part of the reconstruction effort. In fact, it was oddly reassuring to be made to do such things, to be called upon again, pulled out into the sunlight. But at the bridge there was too much lifting involved for Lili, and Robert had forbidden her to work there any longer and written a letter to the authorities to that effect.

After a good long second visit to Budapest in the autumn, Hermina had returned to her home in Paris, a property she and Ede had bought back in the mid-thirties, when he'd been a visiting professor of medicine at the Sorbonne. It was in the 16th Arrondissement, she'd said, off the Avenue de Versailles, "where Victor Hugo, Honoré de Balzac and Claude Debussy used to muck about." Her departure was hard on everyone, especially Klari and Lili, who found solace in her presence. Even Rozsi—who was saying less and less as a hard winter gripped Budapest with no regard for what it had just endured—could sometimes be coaxed into smiling when Hermina was present at their table. A friend of Hermina's, Erzsi Balaban, who'd owed the Izsaks a small fortune before the war, returned from Buchenwald alive but alone and had opened a bakery specializing in wedding and other party cakes. It was what she'd always wanted to do, what she'd dreamed about every day in the camp, what she promised herself. So in this time of shortage—but also of celebration and marrying and starting over—Erzsi opened her cake shop. Some people could pay; others couldn't. Hermina forgave the Balabans' debt to her, but thereafter Hermina often showed up at the Becks' place with great cakes, towering palaces of cream and marzipan, some of them reminiscent of classical architecture, complete with columns and caryatids and little triangular roofs. It was odd, having party cake so often, but Hermina was happy to share with her relatives because its cheer brightened their home. There was so much to go around, Klari shared some with Vera and her family, too, and with the Oszolis, the additional family.

After dropping Rozsi off, Lili calculated that if she rushed she could see Simon for a few minutes before they both had to get back to work. As Lili approached the Liberty Bridge, she began to feel dizzy and a little queasy. There was a bench within sight of the bridge, and she thought she would rest there just a minute. An older woman sat on the opposite end. She had a cast-iron sauce pot beside her.

The woman noticed Lili's distress and asked, "Is there something I can do for you, young woman?"

Lili wanted to say no but feared she might get worse. "Yes, please. My husband, Simon Beck, is working on the bridge just up ahead."

"I'll get him," the woman said. "Can you watch my pot?"

Lili nodded and the woman hurried off.

Soon Lili was lying down on the bench, trying not to moan, careful not to kick the woman's pot. Simon was by her side in a flash. "I'm taking you to the hospital," he said, as he put his arm around her shoulder.

The woman who'd helped out said she'd call for an ambulance.

"No," Lili said. "I'm better now. It was just a spell, nothing more."

"Let's be sure."

"I am sure," she said. "I wouldn't want anything to harm this baby." She was hardly showing, but she stroked her abdomen gently.

"It happens," the woman said to Simon. "Raging hormones," she added. "I've been through it, four times." She rubbed her own stomach.

Unexpectedly, there arose the worst odour Lili and Simon had ever smelled, like fumes rising from the underworld. It was so thick it was palpable. The woman retrieved her sauce pot. "Well, the Danube Fat is here," she said.

"What is it?" asked Simon.

"It's a boat," the woman said. "Really just a floating vat of fat from various animals."

"Fat?"

"Bacon fat, goose fat, *fat*. Lard. I have no oil or butter, so I use this fat. It's cheap, and if you heat it for a while, the stink cooks off it. Then you can throw in whatever you've got. I'm going to fill my pan right now. Can I get you some?"

"Not today," Simon said. He still had his hand to his nose.

Lili was using a handkerchief, but with her other hand she still held her stomach. She wondered if a stink this foul could affect her baby.

"She pulls in every Tuesday around this time."

"I'm amazed I missed her," said Simon. "Thanks for helping us out."

"It was nothing," the woman said and walked off with her pan toward the river.

WHEN ROBERT came home that night from the hospital, he almost fell again over the suitcase standing in the vestibule. He cursed once more, gave the leather case a good hoof. He'd had enough. It was over a year.

Simon and Lili lay on the big bed in his parents' bedroom. She hadn't gone back to the opera house, and his supervisor had given him the afternoon off, too. "It will happen soon," Simon said. "The federal government is going to release us from this duty, and I'll be able to open my own shop."

She smiled.

"Or we could try to get away," Simon said, excitedly. He was holding his wife's hand too tightly. "I told you, I know a man who can arrange exit visas for us to Canada or New York. Wouldn't that be something? *Toronto*—can you say that?"

"And we'd just go?" Lili said.

"Don't you think we'd be happier?"

"Yes, I do, but we can't leave your parents and cousins just like that. What would become of them?"

"I don't know," he said and let the matter drop.

Rozsi sat in the kitchen, pretending to watch her aunt prepare dinner, but her eyes weren't following Klari as she hustled about the room. Rozsi felt better here in the kitchen for two reasons. She was with her aunt, who reminded her of her own mother—Klari had the same auburn hair, the same caramel eyes as Mathilde, and there was the same warmth about her, maybe even more. The other reason was the room itself, the bright mosaic floor, the arabesques dancing across the walls, the crystal windows rising into exotic arches. This room took Rozsi out of the city, made her feel she had cast out beyond the horizon, possessed a telescope through which she could survey the continent in search of her Zoli, her wandering Odysseus, as he struggled back from the war, resisting the Sirens, eluding the Cyclops. Rozsi sometimes felt she was in another time, here, sat among the Moors, felt she could restart history, but this time govern its course.

Paul sat, as usual, in Robert's study, the curtains drawn, the lights switched off, a book in his lap. He had spent some of the afternoon with a group working with the Americans to implement the Marshall Plan. The plan, intended to help rebuild Europe, including Germany, was revolutionary, ingenious, the thinking being that, if you let the defeated languish and suffer, they'll rise up against you again.

When Lili heard her father-in-law fumbling at the door, she left her husband and rushed out to help her mother-in-law serve dinner and see whether Rozsi was coming to the table. Lili felt entirely recovered since the afternoon.

"You're both here," Lili said, smiling warmly. She liked being married. She had only to look ahead. "I'm so sorry, Mother," she said.

"Don't be silly," Klari said. "You've worked hard enough, and my grandchild is far more important than a little dinner. Besides, Vera was in here, too, earlier, making her own family's meal, so it would have been too crowded. Vera still loves this room."

"I do, too," Rozsi said. She watched as the two other women finished up, Lili running back and forth between the kitchen and the dining room.

Finally, Lili stopped by Rozsi, took her gently by the elbow and offered to help her freshen up.

Robert might have been the last one home, but he was the first at the dinner table, making himself comfortable at the head, asking Lili as she rushed about, "Where's everyone?"

"I'll get the others right away."

"Where's Paul?"

"He's in your study."

"Sitting in the dark?" Robert remembered the Russians. He wondered where it would all end.

Lili didn't respond. Robert was gripping his knife and fork like an impatient boy. "Why would he do that? Why would he sit in my study like that, in the dark?"

"I don't know, Father," she said.

He smiled, happy to be called that by Lili. "Where's everyone else?"

"Rozsi's getting herself cleaned up for dinner. She wanted to do it alone this evening."

"But *where's everyone else?* I mean why aren't they coming to dinner when dinner's ready? I'm starving."

"I'll get them right away, Father."

She saw him getting set to make a speech and didn't know whether she should run off just then to carry out his first request. "We shouldn't be asked to stay hungry one additional second after what we've been through," he said loudly. "Have we spent so much time in our Swedish-Dutch insurance offices that we've altogether got out of the habit of *eating?*" Now he was yelling.

Lili brought in Rozsi first and set her down in the chair to her uncle's left. Rozsi wore clunky heels she'd found somewhere. She didn't acknowledge her uncle. Robert patted her hand. The blush on her cheeks looked like red mistakes she'd tried vigorously to erase.

Simon came next and sat opposite Rozsi, to his father's right. "Hello, Father," he said, but then noticed his cousin's face, was stricken by how aged she seemed in the evening light.

"Go get her brother, please," Robert said, and Simon dashed off again. When he returned with Paul, everyone was present.

They'd managed goose again. A friend high up, as close to the prime minister as one could get, had brought Robert a whole goose the previous day after Robert had removed a cyst from the man's neck. Maria, Lili's friend from the Madar Café, had given her some fresh spinach and beets. It was all to be followed by cherry strudel, made with sour cherries Klari herself was able to procure from a stand around the corner. It was a feast, a rare feast.

Klari lit the silver candelabra, which had survived the looting. It held a dozen candles. She switched off the chandelier. The table was set with pink Herend china, a throwback to their pre-war splendour. The room looked festive in the evening light.

Robert said to Paul, "Thank you for gracing us with your company."

Simon looked at his father, surprised. Klari said, "Robert, please."

"I was reading," Paul said.

"What, in the dark?"

Lili helped her mother-in-law cut up and dish out the servings. Lili was especially adept at carving up the gleaming goose. Simon passed around the plates. On the wall behind Lili and Rozsi hung a photograph of the Becks, which Klari had brought out from her bedroom to help fill the space on the wall where Rippl-Ronai's *Summer Harvest* once hung. The photograph featured Heinrich, Robert, Klari, Mathilde, two other sisters, Anna and Etel, their husbands Imre and Bela, Hermina and Ede, Anna's son Janos, together with Simon, Paul, Istvan and Rozsi, all daughters, daughters- and sons-in-law and grandchildren of proud Maximillian and Juliana Korda, who sat stiffly in the drawing room of their country home, the black lacquered grand piano lurking behind them. Anna had returned to Debrecen, but her son had not. Her husband was still unaccounted for. Etel and her husband, Bela, the man who'd introduced Paul and Istvan to sex, had both perished. They were childless, like Hermina.

"I saw a nightingale outside the window this afternoon," Paul said. "*Heard* it, and then *saw* it in the elm when I stepped out on that grand balcony of yours."

"I'm delighted for you," his Uncle Robert said.

"Yes, the song was unmistakable. I was treated to a full concert before the little soprano flew off. It was a bird not made for our time and place, it seems—like something out of time. I remembered the poem by John Keats, his 'Ode to a Nightingale,' and I was thrilled to find it on your shelf, Uncle Robert. You didn't have the Hungarian edition, but I found the original English. Do you remember it, all of you?—any of you? Do you remember the stanza late in the poem?" Lili stopped what she was doing but stayed on her feet. Paul recited the lines:

Thou wast not born for death, immortal Bird!
No hungry generations tread thee down;
The voice I hear this passing night was heard
In ancient days by emperor and clown:
Perhaps the self-same song that found a path
Through the sad heart of Ruth, when, sick for home,
She stood in tears amid the alien corn;
The same that oft-times hath
Charmed magic casements, opening on the foam
Of perilous seas, in faery lands forlorn.

No one spoke at first. Paul said quietly, "The gramophone is gone. Poetry is the next best thing."

Robert said, "Do you think it appropriate to recite English poetry in this company at this moment?"

Simon was mortified. He found himself pausing even in his chewing. Lili sat down beside him. Klari said, "I think the words sounded lovely, like music—just as you said. The poem has the lilt of our own Petofi."

Robert began to say, "We've been through a bad time, but—"

"We're not through the bad time quite yet," Paul said. "The Soviets took Raoul Wallenberg and never returned him to us or to Sweden. *Raoul Wallenberg.*"

"I know they did," Robert said. "He was the greatest of men. I've met no one greater, and it's a terrible shame. But the rest of the world and you have not been able to ascertain what happened to him."

"No, I haven't, but his driver, Vilmos Langfelder, was found dead. What does that tell you about the Soviets?"

"It tells me we have lives to get back to. The Russians are not sending us off to gas chambers and camps."

"Not yet."

"What do you mean *not yet*? No, not yet, correct. And we're getting things back together again. We're starting."

"Uncle Robert, the Soviets liberated Hungary and never left. Hitler put in a puppet government here, and now that government is controlled by our liberators. Does that sit right with you?"

"They're not killing us, most of us."

"No, they're less systematic. They kill randomly—some Jewish Hungarians, some Catholic Hungarians, some Swedes, anyone who gets in the way. Stalin beat Hitler in the east as only Stalin could. He knew his type best. And Stalin's here now, in spirit. He's hovering, he's *looming*." Paul raised his hands in the air and wiggled his long fingers, as if he were describing a great monster.

Robert sighed. Several minutes passed before anyone was ready to resume the conversation. The Becks ate. Simon finally said, "We had a little incident today."

"Oh?" Klari asked.

"Yes, Lili felt unwell."

"In what way?" said Robert right away.

Lili said, "Oh, it was nothing. I felt a little light-headed, that was all—and just for a minute."

"You're pregnant," Robert said. "Every spell counts. You shouldn't be working anymore."

Then Robert set down his knife and fork, glanced at Rozsi, then aimed his gaze at Paul. He said, "I'd like you to go on work detail tomorrow. Our city lies in ruins, and my son and his bride go out every morning to help clean up the rubble, put everything back together, and Lili is pregnant."

Now Paul set down his cutlery and wiped his mouth with his linen napkin.

Robert said again, "I'd like you, Paul, and your sister to go out on work detail tomorrow."

Paul looked straight back into his uncle's eyes. He said, "What if we refuse?"

Robert answered, "Well, then, you should leave this house."

Klari stood straight up out of her chair. "Robert—"

"Stop," he said. He held up a flat hand.

Klari sat again. It was Paul who got to his feet next. "Thank you for dinner, Aunt Klari, Uncle Robert," he said, then withdrew to the study.

To everyone's surprise, Rozsi got to her feet, too. "Look, I found nylon stockings," she said, walking out to the centre of the room and spinning on a heel for all to see. "This nasty time without stockings has been a terrible deprivation." They all watched her intently. Rozsi had used an eyebrow pencil to draw a line down the back of her bare legs. In the dim light, they really did look like stockings.

Later, Lili helped Rozsi into her nightgown and got on her own. She then set out a glass of water for Rozsi, shook out a single pill from the bottle, out of which Rozsi invariably took a second and even sometimes a third, lay a wintergreen mint beside it, because Rozsi had said the pills were bitter, and lit her candle in the window.

As Rozsi brushed her hair, Lili told her things would be all right. "I *like* the work. I *like* rebuilding things," she said. Lili then said, "I'll be right back," and she slipped off to Simon's room to say good night to him.

She stayed in her husband's room longer than she expected and then fell asleep at his side. It was not the first time. She slept until she was woken by a thump, not a particularly loud one, but it gave her an uneasy feeling. She thought it might have been the front door.

She crept out to the corridor, into the sitting room, and then saw that the door to the study was ajar. She peered in, then entered the room.

A moment later, she was at Simon's side again. "Paul is gone," she said. "He's taken his things. He's *gone*."

Simon ran to the study while Lili went to check on Rozsi. When she entered her room, she was relieved to see Rozsi sleeping peacefully on the bed. The candle sputtered in the window. She turned to the little round night table. The water glass had been drained, the wintergreen mint was gone, and the pill bottle sat on a note.

"Rozsi," Lili said, but Rozsi didn't move. "Rozsi," she said more insistently, but then she turned to the night table again.

She lifted the small brown medicine bottle to the dim light and saw that it contained a single pill. She shook it to confirm her finding. She switched on the light, snatched up the note and read it.

Dearest Lili,

   Sorry about the mess. I couldn't go with Paul. I've left you a little something to help you sleep.

I love

Thirty-Seven

THE FACT that Paul didn't turn up at his sister's funeral could only have meant that he hadn't known her intentions the night before. Klari wouldn't let anyone tell Istvan and Marta. They had a small son. They'd suffered enough. They all had. She would find the appropriate time to tell them in person.

Within an hour of the service, she and Robert, Lili and Simon became a pack of hunters. They searched for Paul like the very oppressors they'd learned to evade. They telegraphed Hermina in Paris and Anna in Debrecen, only to alarm them. They did succeed, though, in enlisting their services in the search. Simon and Lili visited Paul's old law office, now defunct, to search for evidence of a visit from Paul, but they found none. The rabbi who'd married Simon and Lili and had just buried Rozsi helped spread the word, but no one had seen Paul. Robert contacted Andras Gaal, an official in the mayor's office, another man he'd treated in his clinic, to find out if Paul had been issued an exit visa, but the man found no record of one. Was he travelling as a Swedish diplomat? Was that it?

The first glimmer came from Istvan. His telegram read, "*Stop looking for Paul.*" Just four words, no more. Not even "*love.*" Even Rozsi had found a place for that in her note.

The very next morning, Robert and Klari travelled by train to
Szeged, almost without exchanging a word, but without shutting
their eyes either. A single weary tear rolled down Klari's cheek, and
Robert watched its progress intently, waiting for it to let go.

Stop looking for Paul.

Was it a command? A request? The bloodless piece of paper
contained no clue. Had Paul helped compose the message?

The spring windows beamed with promise. Though they'd
passed through a cold snap, the first fruit bulged with life. Horses
pranced in the fields as if they'd never known a rider. For a giddy
moment, Klari imagined that a nest of love awaited them in
Szeged, that a young woman, possibly Zsuzsi, would be there with
Paul, Marta and Istvan, that Zoli would be awaiting his Rozsi, and
that Rozsi herself would rise again. She pictured her cousin
Alexander, just arrived from his London Films, the only one who
could turn such a dream into reality, or his kind of reality, at least,
sometimes the only kind that counted.

She'd in fact contacted her cousin Sanyi—her Alexander—in
England to ask if any of their people had turned up magically in
England, and could he look up a family of Bandels from the
Carpathian region, and a Zoltan Mak, a fine photographer. Did the
agencies know of any of them, and could they locate them? Sanyi
answered right away that he was relieved to learn Hermina had
survived but was dismayed to hear of Etel, Bela, Janos and the many
others Klari had asked about.

A taxi dropped Klari and Robert in front of Marta and Istvan's
quaint little home in Tower Town. Though it sat in the shadow of
taller buildings, it was a bright and stalwart place.

Istvan met his uncle and aunt and tenderly hugged Klari, closing
his eyes, clutching her. Istvan still seemed gaunt and aged to her. She
could feel the bars of his ribs against her own. Istvan would merely
have shaken his uncle's hand normally, but circumstance compelled
the men to embrace.

Just behind Istvan, stepping out of the shadow of the little place and into the spring light, was Marta, holding a baby boy just as striking as herself, with black curls and brown eyes as warm as his mother's.

"How old is he?" Klari asked, running her fingers through the boy's hair. The boy watched the fingers as they withdrew.

"He's seven and a half months," Marta said, bless her heart, "almost eight."

"Heavens," Klari said. "And another one on the way?"

Marta smiled. Istvan stood with his hands on his hips, still commanding the door, commanding the little house. Then he said, "Come in, please."

As they entered, they continued to gaze at the infant. "Does he look like you?" Klari asked her nephew.

"If he does, then he's mine," Istvan said.

The visitors smiled. Could he be serious?

The boy's hair was not baby hair. It was prematurely thick and blue-black. How did such a young boy grow such locks? Even ravens started out covered in down.

"Did you name the boy Heinrich?" Klari asked, good-naturedly.

"No," Istvan said, but didn't explain. "We named the boy Janos, after someone we knew."

"Oh," Robert said, taking a seat. Istvan sat too.

They all sat, Marta on the floor with her son between her legs. The child bobbed drunkenly, then hunched over to try to take his mother's shoelace into his mouth.

"May I get you some tea and cake?" Marta asked. "I've made a cherry cake."

"Well," Robert said.

"Thank you," Klari said, "but we're not hungry yet."

Robert looked crossly at his wife. Her look urged him on: *You must tell them before we eat.*

"Your sister," Robert said, but then hesitated.

"Rozsi?"

"Rozsi couldn't bear to go on," Klari said.

Marta gasped. She looked at her husband to see whether she'd understood correctly.

"Foolish girl," Istvan said.

"She was in despair," Klari said. "In the end, we couldn't reach her."

Marta studied Klari's face, then rose to join her husband. She handed Istvan the baby, then kissed her husband on the head. He sorted out little Janos and bounced the boy on his knee.

Then Istvan burst into tears. Marta kissed him again on the head, took the child back, kissed Istvan's wet cheek, and moved aside so Istvan could have a moment with his aunt and uncle. When they separated, even Robert had a tear in his eye.

Marta said, "Let's have the tea and cake. It'll make us feel a little better at a time like this."

"Yes, the cake," Istvan said, distractedly. "My Marta makes the very best cherry cake." He was still crying.

The moment Marta left for the kitchen, the boy joined his father by crying, too, though she was still in plain view. They moved to the kitchen table, to follow Marta and to calm the boy, and soon they were drinking tea and eating cake, showing their approval and gratitude. Marta stood beside them, bouncing little Janos in her arms. When he grew still more restless, she turned away to give the child her breast. He took to it hungrily, and he hummed.

Robert set down his fork and asked, "What's become of Paul? Please tell me."

"I don't know," Istvan said.

"But he was here," Klari said.

"Yes, he was here."

Marta glanced over her shoulder to see what her husband would say.

Robert asked, "What did he say? Where did he go?"

"I'm not sure."

"Please, Istvankam," Klari said. "Please don't torture us; we're getting old. We came all this way to find him." He looked sharply at her. "And to see you again, of course. I didn't mean—I mean, we're so glad to see you and your little family. What a dear your wife is, and the lovely boy—"

"Paul didn't tell me," Istvan said. "He went to America—the Americas."

"The *Americas*?" Robert repeated.

Istvan nodded.

"North or South?" Robert asked.

"One or the other."

Robert jumped to his feet. "The Russians are looking for him. They came by my office."

"I know. They came by here, too. And Paul showed up an hour later. I told him they'd been here and hid him in the cellar, under those floorboards, but he didn't stay there long."

"What did you tell the Russians?"

"I told them Paul lived with you. I also said we were not the enemy. I told them my father was the first resister in this country, and he died for it. The records speak for themselves. He was on Russia's side, in fact, before Russia knew it and long before the Russians arrived."

"And then?"

"Then they left, and Paul left too, not long after."

"Please tell us something more," Klari said.

"He's out of the country already. He mentioned Philadelphia and Argentina."

"Did he mention Siberia?"

"Not to me."

"How can you treat us this way?" Robert said. "We're your family. And you and I have always been close."

It was true. Istvan had often felt more at ease with his uncle than with his father. He said gently, "I'm not treating you in any way. I told you, Paul didn't say. Maybe he himself didn't *know* what lay ahead. He

said it was time for him to make a move. But he didn't say where.
Maybe he foresaw this meeting."

They sat a long time in silence as if waiting for the baby to finish
his meal. He had drifted away to sleep, so Marta carried him to the
bedroom.

"May I look through the famous floorboards?" Klari asked. Istvan
rose to lift them. "Goodness," she said, as she joined him to look into
the hole. She was a little frightened.

Robert stayed sitting. Istvan and Klari soon rejoined Robert, and
Klari patted her husband's hand.

"What a place to have to hole up," she said. "How dingy." She was
wiping her hands together, though she hadn't touched anything.
"How could you stand it—and for all those months?"

Istvan couldn't answer. He no longer knew how it had been possible,
what had sustained him. He finally said, "It's difficult to keep out of the
way of someone trying to prevail so completely."

"Especially if he's trying to prevail over you," Klari said.

KLARI AND ROBERT STAYED in the Felix Mendelssohn Hotel, overlooking the square of that name, even though Marta had been willing
to give them her own bed. "It's not that big a sacrifice," she'd said. "It
would be a pleasure."

"You come to Budapest," Klari said. "Come stay with us. Come for
a long visit."

Before they entered the hotel, Klari and Robert turned to look at
the small square. They saw the pedestal on which the statue of the
composer once stood, and Robert looked at the trees around it and up
at the lampposts.

"Oh," was all Klari could say, and she put her hand over her
mouth.

"Let's go inside," Robert said.

In the lobby of the Mendelssohn, across the expanse of green
marble, Robert was sure he saw Paul. He rushed at the tall thin man

with curly red hair, almost skidding to a stop when he reached him. Then the man turned around. He was holding a violin and was getting set to play in the hotel's Felix Café.

The musical motif was apparent in the lobby, which featured white marble busts of the great composers, in the hallways, which contained ancient musical instruments housed in glass cases, and even in the rooms. Above Robert and Klari's bed hung a picture of restless music, its notes crossed out and reconceived.

The picture caused Robert to have a fitful night. In their big comfortable bed, Klari felt her husband shifting, pulling on the blankets, sighing and shaking his feet as if trying to jiggle himself to sleep.

They ate breakfast in the Midsummer Night's Dream Café, opposite the Felix, and Robert wanted to leave even before Klari had finished the last spoonful of her compote.

Outside, he would not wait for a proper cab but asked the concierge to fetch the horse-drawn carriage stopped across the cobblestone square. "Ask the driver, please, if he can take us to the train."

"Robikam," Klari said, "we have lots of time."

"I don't want to wait here, my dear. I need to go. I need to move."

And so the horse clopped along the boulevard in the direction of the station, but two blocks before the building the horse halted, and no one could understand why. There was nothing in his way. His master spoke gently to him, but he snorted and stood still. Cars whooshed by them, cabs by the dozens. The horse held his ground. The driver climbed down to talk to his horse. He spoke as though they were old mates in a campaign together, and the horse nodded as if he agreed, but then he turned his head away from the man to observe a vacant lot adjoining some townhouses.

"Mule," the driver said. "*Mule*."

Robert himself snorted and rolled his eyes. "Let's go," he said to his wife. "We can walk the rest of the way. I'll carry our bag."

"Darling, please calm down. Our train doesn't leave for hours yet."

He didn't answer, just reached into the back to pull out their bag.

The driver rushed to help, would not accept money, even when Robert insisted.

On the train back to Budapest, they sat alone in a compartment, but on the same side this time, rather than opposite each other. Again they were quiet. Klari held her husband's hand.

Finally, he said, "I do what I can."

"Of course you do."

"I did what I could."

"Yes, you did."

"I did something for Paul, too."

"Of course you did. You did things for each other."

He looked out the window, then his eyes met hers. "It was an evil thing I did."

"It was not evil," his wife said, "just a mistake."

"An evil mistake."

She patted his warm, dry hand, rubbed and patted it. Before long, they were in the spring country north of Szeged. Blond heaven looked in on them through the window. They saw a young couple lying under an oak in the field to the east.

"Maybe it *was* a mule," Robert said and smiled at his wife. She smiled back, just as he drifted off to sleep.

Acknowledgments

I could hardly call a book *Gratitude* without feeling a great deal of it. I'll start by thanking my sensitive and smart editor at Penguin, Barbara Berson, and my enthusiastic and skilful agent (of the HSW Literary Agency), Margaret Hart, both of whom loved this book as if it were their own. At Penguin, I thank David Davidar and Nicole Winstanley, who believed in the novel, as well as Karen Alliston, Debbie Gaudet, Chrystal Kocher, Don Robinson, Lisa Rundle and Mary Wong. I thank the extraordinary Alex Schultz, who did the line edit. I thank the Ontario Arts Council and the Toronto Arts Council for buying me valuable time to do some research.

I thank others who offered valuable advice on the manuscript: Kenneth Ballen, Craig Patterson and Antanas Sileika, foremost among them. But others, too: Nancy Burt, who praised the work, and Naomi Gordon, Mel Solman and Marianne Meyer-Krahmer, who inspired three of the episodes in the novel, as well as Mary Jo Morris, who repeatedly offered to help.

Many good friends and family have cheered me on: Linda and H.H. Au and their family, my Bandel cousins, Mark Breslin, Ernest Chambers, Robert Carr and Esther Lenkinski, Wayson Choy, Vassiliki Daskalaki, Jack David, Heidi Davis, Anthony De Sa, Sandy Fainer, Michael Helm, Lillian, Jesse and Andrea Kertes, Zoe and Talia Kertes, Ben Labovitch, John Lovatt, Kim Moritsugu, Athena Papageorge, Peter and Stan Papageorge and their families, Elizabeth Manson, the Nemets, Yolanda Perez, Dolly Reisman, Snaige and Antanas Sileika and their sons, Paul Quarrington, Grace and Henry

Sadowski, Eva Seidner and Michael Kedar, Eve Shea, Janet Somerville, Gunild Spiess, Jordan Sugar, the Ungars, especially Susie and Tom, Helen Walsh, Norma Weiner and Hubert Saint-Onge, and Dorothy Wahl.

And my loyal family at Humber College: John Bourgeois, Denny and Rose Christianson, Andrew Clark, John Davies, Charlotte Empey and Larry Grzebinski, David Flaherty and Jayne Eastwood, Lorne Frohman and Linda Chandler and the other Frohmans, Maria Gonsalves, Cynthia Good, Squee and Mary Gordon, Michael Hatton, Richard and Josette Hook, Madeleine Matte, Cathy Mitro, and Ian Smith.

I'm not sure why it's unusual to do so, but I thank the kind writers who took a chance and agreed to endorse this novel: Wayson Choy, Roddy Doyle, Bruce Jay Friedman, Ha Jin, Tim O'Brien and M.G. Vassanji.

And my loyalest of families: my wife Helen and daughters Angela and Natalie. They are always urging me on, always wanting to look over my shoulder as I write, always pushing my work on others. Dear, sweet girls, all three.

Gratitude

About the Book 500

An Interview with Joseph Kertes 501

Discussion Questions 505

A Penguin Readers Guide

ABOUT THE BOOK

Set in Budapest in 1944, *Gratitude* is the lovingly conjured portrait of the lives of a family of Jewish Hungarians as they find friends in unexpected quarters and scrape together the courage to outlast the devastating final months of World War II.

The novel opens in the tiny Jewish town of Tolgy, in rural Hungary. It's Lili Bandel's sixteenth birthday, and the day that her village is ruthlessly evacuated by German and Hungarian soldiers. Separated from her family, Lili spends two days and nights hiding behind her parents' wardrobe. When she resurfaces, her family is nowhere to be found—the entire town has been "relocated."

Disguised by her fair hair and blue eyes, Lili makes the long journey to Budapest. There, she is awed by the grandeur of the capital city but also chilled by how oblivious everyone seems to the events taking place mere hours away. Lili doesn't know anybody in Budapest—everyone she ever knew lived in Tolgy—but a sudden attack of appendicitis brings her to Dr. Robert Beck and his compassionate wife, Klari. The well-to-do Jewish family takes her in, and a romance builds between the sweet-tempered Lili and the Becks' brooding son, Simon.

Lili also encounters other members of Robert and Klari's family, including Paul Beck, a prominent lawyer who has been recently disbarred from practice. Forced from their homes, the Becks pose as Swedes, living in a Dutch insurance building that the Swedish diplomat Raoul Wallenberg has made into a safe house.

Throughout the harrowing months, as the horrific truth of what is happening to the people of their faith becomes clear, the Becks pool their strength to keep themselves alive and maintain their dignity. Lili finds she can tap in to an innate survival instinct to scavenge for food and necessities. Simon, the epitome of the European intellectual, must endure the extreme privations of a forced-labour camp near the border of Transylvania. Paul, ever a fighter, works tirelessly with Raoul Wallenberg to issue forged Swedish passports that will save thousands of Jews. Meanwhile, the fate of the rest of their friends and relatives remains unknown.

Seamlessly blending fact with fiction, *Gratitude* is a story of hope and faith, of love discovered and lost. It is a story that shows that compassion and kindness can be found even in the darkest moments of humanity. But it is also a story about real human beings; in *Gratitude*, victims aren't always right and perpetrators always wrong. ■

AN INTERVIEW WITH JOSEPH KERTES

Q: Your own family fled Hungary for Canada during the 1956 revolution. How many of the details in *Gratitude* are inspired by your family's experience, and how much of it is based on your own research and travels?

Many of the episodes in the novel were inspired by family stories, but the critical anecdote that inspired the writing of the novel was one that has haunted me my whole life and became a source of shame and wonder for me. It goes like this: imagine banishing the man who saved your life. How was it possible? My father's first cousin, Paul Hegedus, pretended to be a Swedish diplomat, stopped a deportation train bound for Auschwitz, and pulled my parents and grandparents from the train. He was so brash he even demanded that his family's jewellery be returned, and he waited until the family had a chance to go through the bag of confiscated valuables. (Until the end a few years ago, my mother wore a stranger's ring, with the person's name engraved on it.) Paul installed my parents and grandparents in the Swedish embassy in Budapest, where they lived in an office for eight months. Then when the war was over, Hungary passed an edict requiring two able-bodied people from each family to help rebuild the ruined city. Paul Hegedus and his sister Nadinka had by then moved into my grandparents' place because theirs had been destroyed. But it was my father and mother who went out each day on work detail.

One evening, after six months, my grandfather asked Paul and his sister to go out to work the following day in place of my parents. Paul wanted to know what would happen if they refused.

My grandfather said, "Then I'd ask you to leave my house."

Paul and Nadinka left in the middle of the night and were never seen again. My family learned that Nadinka had killed herself because her fiancé had not returned from the war. Paul and Nadinka's brother Istvan in Prague told my grandparents that Paul had fled "to the Americas" and did not want to be pursued.

These events occurred before my time. But what I have tried to do is create a novel around these people, turn them into characters and give them lives. What the story says to me—and what I hope sets it apart from others on the subject—is that all of us—victims, perpetrators, Christians, Jews, Muslims, saints, and criminals alike—are capable of making mistakes with tragic consequences. ■

Q: *Gratitude* boasts an army of complex characters. Did you have a favourite character?

I have a few favourite characters: Lili, of course, Paul, and Marta. Maybe Marta is my absolute favourite. She was brave though not superhuman, yet she triumphed over the overwhelming forces of history. The chapters in Auschwitz and just following loomed large in my own imagination. These chapters centred on Marta. ■

Q: Music plays a strong supporting role throughout the novel. Why is this? Do you have a personal interest in music, or did you educate yourself about it as part of the writing process?

I do love music. I think it is the supreme art, the universal language. As such, it plays a large role in the novel. A mayor dies protecting a statue of a beloved composer. A Jewish man is shot for playing Mahler, a forbidden composer (because of his Jewish roots). The most important chapter, though, is the one where a Polish nobleman takes Marta into his house just after she escapes from Auschwitz. He feeds her, gives her fresh clothes, and offers her a concert. A singer, accompanied by a pianist, performs the cantata of Bach called *Ich habe genug* (I have enough). It is too much for Marta. The distance between the beautiful music (the highest attainment of humankind) and the gas chambers (the lowest sinkhole of depravity) is too great for her to bridge, so she flees. ■

Q: What led you to choose "Gratitude" as the title? Was it your original title for the novel?

"Gratitude" has always been the title, and it stuck. It is, of course, inspired by the great act of salvation by Paul of the Becks, but it also calls upon readers to consider life's blessings even amid the depravity and loss. I am a Canadian and feel grateful for all we have here. It gave me great perspective on the time I was writing about. ▪

Q: *Gratitude* is a departure from your previous works, which were more light-hearted and humorous. Can you tell us how you came to write *Gratitude* and the difference between writing comic and tragic works of fiction?

The subject I chose for this novel could not be given the comic treatment. I do see the world as an absurd place, hence the comedy. But the time and tragedy covered here are too dark to be reached by comedy. Mark Twain also taught us that the "true source of humour is not joy but sorrow." So comedy and tragedy are two sides of the same coin. ▪

Q: Raoul Wallenberg, a historical figure, is a supporting character in the story. Raoul's interactions with Paul and other fictional characters are depicted in a realistic and believable manner. Can you tell us about the process of incorporating the real-life Wallenberg into your fictional storyline?

Of course, I did a great deal of research on Wallenberg. I read the biographies and heard from my parents and their friends what he meant to Hungarian Jews. He's a towering figure, a saviour, a saint. But I needed to make him real and human, to pull him into focus as he worked with Paul and others. He was human, albeit a very special human. So I had to bring him down to the level of the other characters, someone who ate breakfast and rode in cars. You cannot make him too mythic in his daily activities, though his accomplishments are indeed mythic. ▪

Q: While ultimately redemptive and hopeful, *Gratitude* covers much of the dark side of human experience. Actors have talked about how playing a very dark role can affect their state of mind. As a writer, did you find that immersing yourself in such a heart-wrenching story affected your psyche? Were you able to find ways to distance yourself from the tragedies you were writing about?

An excellent question. I could not distance myself from the characters and the tragedy occurring around them. I found myself becoming the characters and was caught up in their plight. They invaded my dreams, turned them into nightmares, but some survived, as did I psychologically. I'm actually an optimist, so I wanted to give my people as much hope as I felt and still feel. I believe in the resilience and kindness of most human beings. ■

Q: Despite surviving the war, Rozsi decides to take her own life. Why did you decide to make her character a survivor who couldn't face peacetime?

This question relates to the last one. Some people did not survive whole from the war. The cost for Rozsi was that she couldn't survive psychologically. Her fiancé, her one true love, was taken and never returned. She had invested all her hopes in Zoltan. I wanted to say that many people moved on, but some could not. She was one who could not. ■

Q: How do you hope readers will react to the issues you bring up in this story?

I hope people will remember that there are few saints among us and few demons, but there are some. Every generation produces its share. We can do much to avert a repetition of such tragedies, but we must be aware. Holocausts are occurring today, and we should act in however big or small a way we can. ■

Q: The city of Budapest figures prominently in the story. Can you talk a bit about why you chose Budapest, and your personal connection, if any, to it?

I chose Budapest because the family stories that inspired the novel actually took place in Budapest, and I'm from Budapest myself. Grand Budapest symbolized high culture, intelligence, education, and achievement, and the culture was bombarded, literally and figuratively, by the invaders, the Germans, and then the liberators, the Russians. ∎

DISCUSSION QUESTIONS

1. Why do you think Lili's mother tells her to stay in the house?
2. What do you think is represented by the stampede of wild horses that Lili witnesses? Do horses recur in the novel? Do other animals play a significant role in the novel? For example, how does Smetana the cat help Istvan to survive?
3. What is the role of music in this novel? How did the passages about music add to your reading experience? What is being implied by the music?
4. Istvan watches as his father, Heinrich Beck, dies defending a statue of the Jewish composer, Mendelssohn. Do you think Heinrich knew what kind of sacrifice he was making? Why do you think it was so important for Heinrich to take such a risk (pages 28–31)?
5. When Lili arrives in Budapest she is struck by how oblivious everyone is to the suffering that is going on. When Paul and Raoul Wallenberg issue Swedish passports to a group of Jews, one asks, "I'm wondering ... if my Swedish pass entitles me to admission at the opera" (page 283). Similarly, Anna Barta seems unaware of the risk she is taking by caring for Istvan. Why do you think Kertes included these examples of "selective reality" and denial in the story?
6. Simon Beck and Lili Bandel are clearly from different socio-economic backgrounds. Do you think their wartime experiences drew them together in a way that would have been much more difficult during peacetime?

7. Commandant Karoly Fekete mercifully saves Lili from Sergeant Erdo. In the concentration camp, a cruel guard spares Marta's life and helps her escape. Why do you think people capable of such cruelty are also depicted as capable of compassion?

8. Zoli becomes obsessed with photographing the events going on around him. Do you think he does so because of a sense of duty, or is it recklessness? Was Roszi right to try to stop him? Should she have tried to support him instead?

9. What character did you relate to best, and why? Which character did you most dislike? Does the story have a clear hero? A clear villain?

10. Was it reasonable for Robert to ask Paul and his sister to go on work detail? Did he intend for Paul to depart? Why do you think Paul decided to leave at the end of the novel without telling his family where he was going? Where do you think he goes?

11. Why is the novel called *Gratitude*?